KT-556-540

A CHILD AT THE DOOR

Maggie Bennett was born in Farnborough, Hampshire, in 1931. She worked as a nurse and midwife for many years before marrying and moving to Manchester where their two daughters were born. Having been an avid reader and scribbler all her life she took a correspondence course in creative writing after her husband's death in 1983, and won the Romantic Novelists' Association New Writers' Award in 1992. *A Child at the Door* is her second novel.

Also by Maggie Bennett

A Child's Voice Calling
A Carriage for the Midwife

A Child At The Door

MAGGIE BENNETT

arrow books

Published by Arrow in 2003

5 7 9 10 8 6

First published in the United Kingdom in 2002 by William Heinemann

The Random House Group Limited
20 Vauxhall Bridge Road, London SW1V 2SA

Random House Australia (Pty) Limited
20 Alfred Street, Milsons Point, Sydney, New South Wales 2061, Australia

Random House New Zealand Limited
18 Poland Road, Glenfield
Auckland 10, New Zealand

Random House (Pty) Limited
Endulini, 5a Jubilee Road, Parktown 2193, South Africa

The Random House Group Limited Reg. No. 954009

www.randomhouse.co.uk

A CIP catalogue record for this book is available from the British Library

The Random House Group Limited supports The Forest
Stewardship Council (FSC), the leading international forest certification
organisation. All our titles that are printed on Greenpeace approved FSC
certified paper carry the FSC logo. Our paper procurement policy
can be found at: www.rbooks.co.uk environment

Mixed Sources
Product group from well-managed
forests and other controlled sources
www.fsc.org Cert no. TT-COC-2139
© 1996 Forest Stewardship Council

ISBN 0 09 189972 9

Typeset by Palimpset Book Production Limited,
Polmont, Stirlingshire
Printed and bound in the United Kingdom by
Cox & Wyman Ltd, Reading, Berkshire

For Audrey Yvonne Smith,
SRN, SCM, QN, HV Cert, RNT

and

Joan (Paddy) Robinson, RSCN

With love and grateful thanks for all they taught me.

'. . . a stranger, and afraid,
In a world I never made.'

– A. E. Housman
Last Poems, XII, 1922

Prologue

Beneath a framed lithograph of Their Majesties King George V and Queen Mary, little Dickie wakes from his afternoon nap and discovers that he's feeling much better. He shakes the high sides of his cot and calls to the wax-pale girl asleep in the bed beside him, her arms outstretched on the counterpane.

'Wake up, Queenie, soon be teatime!'

Some of the women smile and wave to the undersized, snuffly-nosed five-year-old, but Queenie does not stir; the soft rise and fall of her chest is almost imperceptible.

'Shut yer gob, monkey-face,' snaps the sharp-faced older girl sitting opposite them in Women's I. 'Ye're not to disturb 'er, Sister said so, cos she's got manaemia.'

Dickie turns and stares at her.

'What're them things on yer legs?'

'Them're leg-irons, nosey, cos I got resistant rickets, if it's any business o' yours.'

'Will yer die?'

''Course not, don't be daft. An' stop rattlin' yer cage, it gets on people's nerves.'

He sticks out his tongue at her, but before she can retaliate Nurse Court comes hurrying down the ward to check on Queenie. Dickie and the girl with the calipers are all attention.

''E keeps 'ollerin' at 'er, Nurse Court – can't yer tell 'im to shut up?'

'An' *she* made a stink, blowin' orf!' he retorts, grinning and wrinkling his snub nose. 'Pooh!'

1

'Now, now, Dickie, yer mustn't be rude,' murmurs the young nurse, relieved to see him so much improved; last week he had been fighting for breath. She gently takes Queenie's hand and feels her pulse. The girl stirs and flutters her eyelids.

'Had a nice sleep, dear?' Nurse Court touches her forehead.

'Did yer dream anyfing?' asks Dickie.

Queenie smiles contentedly. The afternoon sunshine pours in through the opened window and bathes her in a pool of golden light. She has been halfway to heaven, carried upwards in warm and loving arms like a mother's, safe and happy. She clings to the last wispy vapour of her dream before it fades.

'She ain't got no blood, 'as she, Nurse Court? Can I feed 'er wiv 'er tea when it comes rahnd?' begs the older girl – but before the nurse can reply there is an urgent call from further up the ward and she has to leave the children.

'Be good, poppets, I'll be back soon's I can,' she promises.

'Can yer help me sit Mrs Graves up, Nurse Smith?'

'But I'm jus' fetchin' the pan for the ol' woman in the end bed – the one 'oo's 'ad the stroke.'

Nurse Court winces and rolls up her eyes. When will this girl learn to say old lady? *Young* woman is all right, but an *old* woman must always be a lady.

The two first-year probationers on Women's I are both aged twenty, though Nurse Court started her training six months earlier than Smith. They have been left in charge of thirty patients, including three children, with a ward maid to help with kitchen duties and act as messenger if an emergency requires a trained nurse, when they'd have to summon Sister on Women's II.

2

Women's I is a medical ward filled with mostly chronic, long-term conditions, the results of poverty and deprivation. The patients at Booth Street Poor Law Infirmary are of the older, poorer sort, who less than twenty years ago would have been workhouse inmates; but now the soot-blackened stone building has been elevated to the status of a hospital licensed to train nurses and midwives. Girls who can't afford the fees of the prestigious voluntary hospitals can train at a Poor Law infirmary with free bed and board and a small uniform allowance, that's if they can survive the long hours and harsh working conditions for three years. About a third of them drop out, giving rise to situations like the one on Women's I this hot July afternoon.

Apart from the children who are constantly on her mind, Nurse Court's attention is centred upon two patients: young Mrs Graves in bed 7 and the woman sinking deeper into diabetic coma behind wooden-framed screens next to Sister's desk. Her two daughters sit one on each side of her bed and Nurse Court peeps in from time to time to smile in silent sympathy at the sad-eyed women keeping vigil. There's nothing more to be done for their mother.

But Mrs Graves has a chance. She was admitted yesterday, having fallen, or been pushed after some kind of altercation, into the Thames. Fished out by a passing bargeman, her lungs have become infected by the contaminated water, but with a young child to support, she ignored the symptoms until she collapsed and was brought into Women's I with a high fever, gasping for breath and ominously blue around the nose and mouth. She now clutches at her right side, her eyes silently imploring Nurse Court to ease the needle-sharp pain that stabs her with every breath she takes.

'All right, Mrs Graves, we'll make yer comfortable,

3

don't worry,' soothes the young nurse when Smith at last comes to the other side of the bed. 'Put yer arm across her shoulder, Nurse Smith, and take hold o' mine at the elbow, so – and put yer other arm under her knees like I'm doin' – ready? One, two, three – and *up*! That's right – and again, a bit higher still – is that better, Mrs Graves? I'll make a nice warm poultice to put over yer bad side.'

The young woman moans faintly. The pleuritic pain in her right side is obviously worse, but she's not yet due for another dose of the opium tincture the house doctor has ordered. Nurse Court wonders if she could be given aspirin in the meanwhile.

While she prepares a kaolin poultice in the ward kitchen she ponders over the plight of Susan Graves who isn't a *Mrs* at all, but a disgraced maidservant reduced to soliciting to support herself and the baby girl for which she has lost her place and who's now in the dubious care of another young prostitute. The house doctor suspects a lung abscess, which could be fatal, and Nurse Court wonders what will then happen to her child – an overcrowded babies' home, most likely, and quite possibly death from lack of care.

A cumbersome metal trolley is trundled in by the ward maid, carrying a large teapot, milk jug, cups, plates and sliced bread and margarine. Nurse Court looks round the ward: some need help with feeding, like the strokes and the confused old lady in bed 13 who keeps shouting, 'Help! Help me, somebody, help, help!' in her cracked old voice that most of the women have learned to ignore, though one or two are driven to yell back, 'Shut up, Gran, for Gawd's sake,' not that she takes any notice.

Nurse Court asks the ward maid to see to the children's tea, saying she will come to them as soon as she can. 'And Nurse Smith, will yer feed number 13? Use a feeding cup and put a towel under her chin.'

At that moment a cheerfully wheezy woman with grey, begrimed skin gets out of bed 14 and offers her services.

''Ere, Nurse Court, I'll feed ol' Mrs Oo-jah for yer, an' Nurse Smiff can go an' see to them poor little kids. Give us the feedin' cup, dearie.'

'That's really good o' yer, Mrs Tollett, ye're a brick,' says Nurse Court, and the woman grins broadly and toothlessly.

'Got a nice young man, 'ave yer, nurse? Goin' aht wiv 'im tonight, are yer?' she asks with a knowing wink, and chuckles at seeing a blushing response. Approaching bed 13, she expertly tucks a towel round the old lady's scraggy neck.

''Ere, come on, Gran, stop 'ollerin' for 'alf a minute an' get this dahn yer – keep yer marf open, 'ere we go – whoops! Nice cuppa Rosie Lee, eh?'

Nurse Court pours out milky tea for Mrs Graves, and gently places the spout of the feeder on the gasping girl's lower lip.

'Come on, Susan, yer need to drink all yer can, so's to get better an' see yer little girl again.'

The faint gleam in Susan's sunken eyes shows that she's still fighting and Nurse Court longs for her to recover for the sake of her child. As the liquid slowly disappears she feels a tap on her shoulder and hears a sepulchral mutter in her ear.

'Don't want to interfere or nuffin', Nurse Court, but ye'd better go an' 'ave a look at 'er be'ind them screens. If yer was to ask me, I reckon she's jus' *gorn.*'

Mrs Tollett is right as usual. There is a sound of subdued weeping as Nurse Court hurries up the ward, and as soon as she sees the still, parchment-yellow face

5

on the pillow, she nods to the daughters and beckons them to follow her. The ward maid is despatched to fetch Sister on Women's II, and Nurse Court puts the kettle on in the kitchen to make tea for the bereaved. She's had scarcely a minute to spare for the children this afternoon.

And as always when she looks upon death, she experiences that lurch of the heart, seeing again her mother's drowned face on the mortuary slab.

And her father, felled like a tree in his own home.

For Nurse Court had encountered death long before she entered the Infirmary.

Part One

Girls in Love

Chapter One

The noticeboard outside the red-brick hall advertised times of meetings and offered an invitation to all. On this particular Sunday evening the meeting had been held outside in the Cut, now empty of the street traders that made it one of London's oldest and largest open markets. The strains of the last hymn carried all the way down to the Lower Marsh, the well-rehearsed brass band accompanying the hearty upraised voices:

> 'What a Friend we have in Jesus,
> All our sins and griefs to bear –'

Mabel stood a little way apart from the crowd, fanning herself with a hymn sheet, for the air was stifling and dust-laden. Her fair, wavy hair was once again escaping from its pins, and she put up a gloved hand to push back a stray lock under the wide-brimmed buckram hat that she had covered in navy-blue silk to match her skirt and jacket, beneath which her long-sleeved white blouse buttoned up to the neck. Harry must be sweltering, she thought, under his navy serge uniform jacket.

She nodded and smiled to familiar faces in the dispersing crowd, her widely spaced grey-blue eyes alight with easy friendliness. The Salvation Army attracted a very different mix of humanity from the congregations of the established church in which she had been brought up.

'Good meetin' tonight, wasn't it?' – 'Yes, praise the Lord' – 'Peace be with yer, sister.'

Mabel was prepared for a long wait, knowing that Captain Harry Drover might be required for some time. He had stayed behind in the hall to offer up prayers for those in special need, and Mabel could picture him kneeling down now with some troubled soul, placing his hands on a possibly verminous head and asking the Lord to send down his Spirit and the gift of grace to overcome a particular trial or temptation. All sorts of men and women who would never enter a church came to the mercy seat of the Salvation Army; the drunkards, the prostitutes, the victims of all kinds of social evils came to be consoled and perhaps transformed: all were welcomed. Mabel waited until Captain Drover's last penitent had been sent on his or her way with the Lord's blessing.

For Harry Drover was Mabel Court's young man. They were walking out together, an engaged couple, though marriage was still a long way off. Like thousands of others they had not the means to set up house for a year or two or three: he had just finished his training to become a fully-fledged Salvation Army officer, and she had nearly completed her first year at Booth Street Poor Law Infirmary. They both worked long hours, so their time together was all the more precious. She attended the Sunday meetings when she could and sometimes went back to his parents' home in Battersea; this evening there would only be time for him to walk her back to Booth Street. A church clock struck nine and she sighed: she had to be in by ten.

The crowd had broken up and Mabel's face relaxed into thoughtfulness. No longer obliged to smile, her mouth drooped a little and her eyes were shadowed. She had come on duty that morning to find Queenie's bed empty and the other two children sadly subdued. Her heart still ached for them, for she could never leave her work entirely behind her.

This was the picture that Captain Drover saw when he came out of the hall, locking the door behind him. He placed his crested cap squarely over his light-brown, rather floppy hair and held his trombone in its case under his right arm. For a long moment he stood unobserved by her, longing to hold her, cherish her and guard her from all the misfortunes of the world; but this he knew he could not do, for it was not in his power: he believed their lives to be in the Lord's hands.

She caught sight of him and made a quick movement.

'Harry! I didn't see yer come out.'

The smile that lit up her face made him catch his breath: the same smile that had won his heart four years ago when he'd worked on the railway depot with her brother Albert who'd taken him home one Friday evening. He had never forgotten his first sight of the pretty sixteen-year-old laying the table for a fish-and-chips supper and issuing orders to her younger brothers and sisters. Watching her push back a strand of silky hair from her forehead, he'd thought she was the sweetest thing he had ever seen; and when she shyly asked him to say grace for them as the packets were unwrapped and served on hot plates, his heart was hers from that moment on. He had never once looked at another girl.

He now linked arms with her and they walked down the Lower Marsh to Westminster Bridge Road and the river, where they lingered on the Albert Embankment.

Harry wanted to tell her how lovely she looked and how much he adored her, but straight after a Salvation

11

Army gathering the language of love did not come easily to him.

'Good meetin' tonight, Mabel. People are turnin' to the Lord, what with all this talk o' the ol' Kaiser stirrin' up trouble.'

'Yer don't really think he'd go to war with us, do yer, Harry? I'm shut up in that Infirmary, I only hear bits o' news. Is it that serious, d'ye reckon?'

She looked up at him anxiously. For her Harry Drover was the sort of young man that any girl would trust, with his open face and honest brown eyes that looked so earnestly into hers. Her brother Albert teased him unmercifully for his lack of humour, yet they were true friends, always pleased to see each other when Albert turned up on leave from the merchant service.

'I can't see the Kaiser darin' to take on the might o' the British Empire,' Harry replied slowly.

'But isn't he goin' to war against France and Russia?' asked Mabel.

'Yes, and we signed a treaty with France some years back to defend each other if need be – and we're both bound to defend the Belgians if he decided to march through their country. But no, Mabel, I reckon there's too much against him. From what I've heard there's more danger o' civil war breakin' out in Ireland 'cause o' this Home Rule, and we're more likely to have to send troops over there. I'd let 'em rule 'emselves if they want to, it's their country.'

Mabel did not know enough about the Irish question to agree or disagree, but she trusted his judgement and was willing to be reassured. Kaiser Wilhelm was after all King George's cousin, both being grandsons of Queen Victoria.

'And in any case, Mabel, I don't believe the Lord would allow such a war to break out in Europe, not

12

in this day an' age,' Harry added seriously, and Mabel was content to believe her wise young man.

They strolled along Bishop's Walk and stopped by Lambeth Pier.

'What about that day off ye're supposed to get at the end o' the month?' he asked as they looked down at the flowing water.

'We-ell, as a matter o' fact it's next Saturday,' she answered after a slight hesitation. 'And I've said I'll go down to Belhampton to see Daisy – oh, yer *must* understand,' she added quickly, seeing the disappointment in his eyes. 'I haven't seen my sisters for three months and I worry about my little Daisy, yer know I do.'

'Yeah, 'course I understand, Mabel. I was just hopin' that – oh, never mind, I couldn't get away Saturday anyway. Will yer stay down there overnight?'

'No, I'll get an early train and make it a day trip. Be back at Waterloo about eight, 'cause I'm on again Sunday mornin'.'

He considered for a moment. 'Tell yer what, Mabel, I'll meet yer off the train an' walk yer back to Booth Street.'

'Ah, would yer? Ye're so good to me!' She smiled up at him and as always his heart melted.

'I'd do anythin' for yer, Mabel.'

'I know.'

It was true and not for the first time Mabel was aware of a sense of unease. For him there was no conflict between his dedication to the Salvation Army and his love for her. Men were not pulled in opposing directions as women were, she thought. She needed to complete her training, knowing that he did not really like her working at the Infirmary. He worried about the long hours and the infections she might catch from the dregs of humanity admitted to the former workhouse.

13

His dearest wish was they would be a Salvation Army couple like his parents, like his sister Ruby and her husband, fellow soldiers together in the war against sin and social degradation. Mabel's dearest wish was to look after children in need of love and care, and she dreamed of a day when their aims would coincide, running a children's refuge on behalf of the Army. Harry always said that their future was in the Lord's hands, and that if it was His will that they should work with children, He would bring it about in His own good time.

And Harry did not want to wait another two years to be married. She knew that his parents thought her stubborn, and she suspected that they wished their son could find a more suitable young woman, more obedient to the Lord's will and ready to devote her life to the Army as Ruby had done.

But he had chosen Mabel Court and had stood by her like a rock through the tragedy of her parents' deaths and the break-up of her family. Dear Harry! Just as soon as she had her certificate from Booth Street Poor Law Infirmary, they would be married at a Salvation Army ceremony where she would vow to serve the Lord and her husband. And as she had already reminded him several times, she'd be so much more use to both as a trained nurse.

'Heard from Albert lately?' he asked as they turned away from the river and skirted the gardens of the Archbishop's Palace.

'Oh, yer know my brother, he's no writer! He sent me a birthday card in March, otherwise not a word. He'll turn up out o' the blue one day with his pockets full o' back pay – though he'll have to stay at that Sailors' Home down by the docks, poor boy.' Mabel sighed. 'I miss him, Harry, an' George too, just as I miss my

Daisy – and Alice o' course – but as long as they're happy where they are – yer know what I mean.'

He smiled and gave her arm a squeeze. Albert, a year younger than Mabel, was away at sea and fourteen-year-old George was working as a hand on a huge prairie farm in Alberta; he had been sent to Canada on a child emigration scheme following their father's death – and Harry knew better than to cause Mabel distress by bringing up that subject. Her sisters Alice and Daisy had been adopted by an aunt and her husband, and lived in the country.

It was time to return along Lambeth Road to Booth Street. The sun had gone down and the summer dusk had descended around them: it was the moment they had both been waiting for without saying so, the brief closeness when they said goodnight in a dingy brick recess near to the back entrance of the nurses' hostel.

'Dearest Mabel, I see so little o' yer – we're never alone, not for so much as a kiss,' he whispered, drawing her close to him. He had put down the trombone and she felt his arms around her body, the roughness of his uniform jacket against her cheek, his lips upon her forehead, his hand on her shoulder, her waist – and lightly on the soft curving beneath the layers of jacket, blouse, liberty bodice . . .

'Oh, Mabel, Mabel –'

A sudden sharp intake of breath, a quickening pulse: Mabel was conscious of her own physical reaction, the indescribable tingling of that secret place where a man becomes part of a woman's body. She and Harry had known each other for four years, they were closest friends, they would one day be married – but *that* was not allowed, was not even to be thought of.

'So give us a kiss instead, Harry.' Did she whisper the words to him, or were they uttered silently within

15

her head? She put her arms up round his neck, letting her hands clasp together, her fingers in his hair.

'Whoops, there's yer cap gone – oh, Harry!' She giggled nervously. 'Sorry!'

She would have stooped to pick up his cap with its red band and gold lettering, but he held her tightly and mumbled that it didn't matter. Her giggle was stifled by his lips pressed on hers and she felt the tremor that ran through his whole frame. Then he released her just enough to put his lips to her ear and speak in short, jerky breaths.

'Mabel, could yer – could yer think about – maybe we could be married sooner – then I – I'd be able to hold yer and love yer as yer lawful husband –' The words were almost incoherent, but she understood. And had to give him the answer she had given before.

'But we can't, Harry, not yet. We've got no money, and –'

'Yer could come an' live at Falcon Terrace, Mabel. Lots o' couples start that way, livin' with parents – and we'd get accommodation from the Army if we were both officers.'

He was practically pleading with her: she saw his eyes glittering in the faint light of the street lamp as he heard her refusing him what he wanted most in the world. But –

But she could not live with his parents in a Salvationist household run by his mother.

'Harry, I need to finish me trainin', yer know I must. We're young, we can wait, other couples have to –'

As if at the mention of other couples, they became aware of the whisperings of another young man and a girl near to them, also having a surreptitious cuddle in the grey shadow of the Infirmary – another nurse saying goodnight to her young man and canoodling like themselves.

Canoodling. In public, under cover of semi-darkness, after a Salvation Army meeting. The thought seemed to strike Harry at the same time, for he gave her a last despairing kiss on the cheek, replaced his cap, picked up his trombone and with a whispered 'God bless yer, me own dearest girl', he walked swiftly away.

So abruptly did he leave her that she almost called out to him, but checked herself because of the other couple. And also because she felt strangely ashamed, not of her feelings for him, but because their love was somehow tarnished by this furtive snatching of kisses and embraces: it did not seem right that his faithful love for her should be dragged down to the level of vulgar *canoodling*.

Suddenly sad at heart she hurried inside, ran up the stone stairway for two flights and opened the door of the room she shared with three other first-years. They were in and sitting on their beds, folding their caps for the next day. They looked up in surprise at her flushed face.

'Whoa! Steady on, Court!' said Nurse Tasker. 'Somebody after yer?'

'Thought yer was goin' to a Sally Army do,' said Nurse Davies with a wink at the others.

'Ah, now, don't be botherin' her, yer can see she's upset.' Nurse McLoughlin's soft accent reproved them. 'I'll get yer a nice cup o' tea, Mabel, so I will.'

She rose and went out to the little alcove along the corridor where there was a gas ring for boiling a kettle. Mabel followed her gratefully.

'Norah, ye're an angel. It's me young man, y'see, we're that fond of each other, but I can't marry him until we can get a place of our own,' she explained, blinking back tears.

'And aren't ye the lucky one, Mabel Court, for to be havin' a young man o' yer own? If I had a nice fella like your Harry, I'd wait for ever an' a day to be married.'

Mabel's only answer was to kiss her. Poor Norah was from a Cork orphanage and had not a relative in the world. The two girls had been drawn to each other from the very first day they had met, both being orphans, though Norah was never tired of hearing about Mabel's two brothers and two sisters, all younger than herself and now dispersed in different directions.

'Come on, Mabel, let's take the pot an' go back to the others.'

'Done yer cap for yer, Mabel,' said Nurse Tasker on their return.

'Thanks, Betty.' The probationers wore caps folded from lengths of finely woven cotton tied round the head and secured at the back with a double button like a collar-stud, so that the ends hung down in a 'tail'. Depending on how skilfully they were folded, they could look charming or unflattering, or even downright comical.

'Er – it's your turn for the bath tonight, Mabel,' said Nurse Davies, knowing that it was her own but wanting to show sympathy for her friend's trouble, whatever it was.

'No, it's all right, Ethel, thanks all the same. You have it.'

Mabel knew that she would have to tell them something about the evening, if only to stop them jumping to a wrong conclusion, like thinking that she and Harry had had a row.

'It was a good meetin', more people than ever turned up at the Cut,' she said lightly. 'Harry had to stay on for ages afterwards at the mercy seat.'

'Oh, ah.' The others murmured and nodded, eagerly

18

waiting for her to go on. They knew that Mabel's young man was a good chap and not bad-looking, but they couldn't believe that he'd be much fun to walk out with. No drinking, no smoking and you could bet your life not too much of the other . . .

'He just doesn't want to wait for another two years, that's all,' said Mabel in a sudden rush. 'And I couldn't give up me trainin' now that we've got this far, no more'n I could live with his parents at Battersea.'

'Ah!' The girls now understood and were in complete agreement with her.

'Oh, no, Mabel, 'course yer can't – an' we couldn't carry on here without yer,' said Ethel Davies. 'Told me mother only last week that I'd never've stuck it if it hadn't been for you, Court. Ye've kept me goin' when I was ready to give up.'

'Me, too – and yer couldn't live jam-packed in a little terraced house with his parents hearin' everythin',' added Betty Tasker with a significant look. 'Oh, Mabel, don't do it!'

'If ye love each other enough, ye'll wait an' be glad ye waited,' said Norah softly.

Mabel's eyes filled with gratefulness. How lucky she was to have such friends! They had started their training together in the previous September and had got on well from the start. Betty Tasker's father ran a fish-and-chip shop in Kennington and Ethel Davies's widowed mother made ends meet by dressmaking for the better-off families of Clapham, so neither girl was suitable material for the big voluntary hospitals where 'lady probationers' paid for their training. And Norah McLoughlin had been in service to an English-woman who had brought her over from Ireland and then decided that she no longer needed her, but had helped her to apply to a Poor Law infirmary for

19

free training. Sharing the day-to-day triumphs and disasters on the wards, and the added intimacy of a cramped bedroom, the four girls had learned the basic facts about each other's histories and knew that both Mabel's parents were dead and her family dispersed – something they accepted as unfortunate but no worse than some of the horrific backgrounds of their patients.

'Sure and isn't it grand to have friends like us!' Norah would exclaim from time to time and the others could only agree that it was a life saver.

'And now ye're goin' to see yer sisters and aunts in the country,' said Norah wistfully on the evening before Mabel's monthly day off. 'Little Daisy'll be longin' for a sight o' ye after so long.'

For Mabel had told her about Daisy, born when Mabel was ten, and now ten herself, the last of Annie Court's children.

'We were always extra close to each other, right from when she was born,' Mabel recalled fondly. 'I used to come home from school, and there she'd be, runnin' up to me with her arms open wide and callin' out, "Maby, Maby!" And then when she started school, I was workin' close by at the Babies' Mission, a sort o' nursery where the younger children could be left and looked after, 'cause – well, a lot o' the older girls used to miss school, kept at home to mind the babies and help out – washdays in the winter were a nightmare for my poor mum.' Mabel shook her head at the memory of wet sheets and clothes hung up indoors, and the number of schooldays she herself had missed.

'Mother o' God, what I'd give to have brothers an' sisters like yerself,' sighed Norah with innocent envy. She had never known any other home but St Joseph's

Orphanage in County Cork, run by the Sisters of Mercy. 'I haven't a single relative in all the world.'

Which was a timely reminder to Mabel to be thankful for having had a family life, for all its ups and downs and the double tragedy that had ended it.

'Mabel, Mabel!' Daisy came running to her with outstretched arms, just as she had done as a toddler, to be gathered in a loving embrace on the station platform. Alice, now an attractive girl of seventeen, stood back a little and rather awkwardly offered a cool cheek for Mabel to kiss. Both girls had the dark eyes and black hair inherited through their father from an unknown grandfather, while Mabel's fair colouring was her mother's, shared with George and little Walter who had died.

Aunts Kate and Nell greeted their eldest niece with smiles and kisses, and Uncle Thomas had his motor car outside to take them all to Pear Tree Cottage where the Somertons lived with their two nieces. Miss Chalcott, Aunt Kate, still lived at Pinehurst, the handsome house where the three Chalcott girls had grown up. Anna-Maria had been the youngest and prettiest, the darling of her widowed father – until the scandal of her elopement with Jack Court. Chalcott had suffered a stroke and died, it was said, from the shock; and only after their unfortunate sister's death had Kate and Nell emerged from the past and their long, bitter silence, to offer a home to the two younger girls.

All over now, but Mabel had mixed feelings about the Belhampton connection, the well-ordered lives of her aunts and sisters. She could never reconcile the two pictures of her mother, the lovely, wilful Anna-Maria Chalcott and the worn-out drudge Annie Court, dead at thirty-seven. Mabel had dearly loved her, defending her against the malice of her mother-in-law, comforting her when little Walter died and covering up for her on the occasions when she had given way to the oblivion of the gin bottle. Grateful as she was to her aunts and Thomas Somerton for their belated kindness, she had turned down Aunt Kate's invitation for her to live at Pinehurst as niece and companion; her heart was firmly fixed in London with Harry and her life at Booth Street.

Dinner at the Somertons' was at midday on that Saturday, with Aunt Kate over from Pinehurst to share it.

'Are you still happy at that Infirmary, Mabel?' she asked. 'It sounds a very hard sort of life.'

'Yes, but it's wonderful when yer patients thank yer for what ye've done,' answered Mabel eagerly. 'I know the big teachin' hospitals look down on the infirmaries, but Matron says we get just as good a trainin' – sick people need nursin' wherever they are, and besides, not havin' medical students means that the nurses get a chance to do more. We've got this poor young woman in at present, very ill with pneumonia and a lung abscess – the doctor thinks she got infected when she –'

'For goodness' sake, Mabel, do we have to listen to all this at the dinner table?' asked Alice with a pained expression.

'I'm sorry, but I can't stop thinkin' about her and her little girl,' muttered Mabel and said no more, though Daisy was loud in her indignant defence.

'I like listenin' to *everything* Mabel says – it's better than your rubbishy old dances and stuff!'

'Hush, Daisy,' reproved Aunt Nell, though Mabel smiled at her young sister. It was just as well that Alice had interrupted, for she had been about to say that Susan Graves had nearly drowned in the Thames – a painful subject in the present company.

'Do you have a room to yourself, Mabel?' asked Aunt Kate.

'And are your meals adequate?' asked Aunt Nell.

She assured them that she had as good a bed as any of the patients, and that the food was of the same standard as theirs. She did not add that the room she shared with three other girls was cramped and ill-ventilated, nor that all the food came from the same kitchen and had to be carried across an open courtyard in all weathers to the nurses' hostel.

'Do you have to nurse people with infectious diseases?' asked Aunt Kate with a look of distaste. 'Consumptives and – er – other horrible diseases?'

'Not very often, Aunt Kate. They get sent to isolation hospitals as soon as possible,' replied Mabel, not adding that the Infirmary held separate clinics for the Lock cases, the syphilitics who came up for their painful injections and applications; only those in the late second or third stage of the disease were kept in wards. Her mouth briefly tightened: her aunts had never known the real reason why their sister had drowned herself.

'And is there a children's ward?'

'No, we don't get that many children, only the very poorest, and they're put in the women's wards, poor little souls,' she explained, remembering Queenie. 'Miss Nightingale thought that sick children do better nursed at home if possible, otherwise they should go in women's wards, and older boys in men's.'

'And do you think that's a good idea, Mabel?'

'I'm really not sure, Aunt Kate. Quite a lot of ours are sent in from children's homes and they often die because they're so bad by the time they come in – but it's wonderful when they get better and they're the patients I most love lookin' after.'

23

It was time for a change of subject. Uncle Thomas asked if there was any news of George and Mabel had his last letter from the Alberta prairie farm where he worked with his good friend Davy. The farmer's wife had bought them new clothes from a catalogue.

'They're two hundred miles from any shops, but these catalogues come round an' people send away for what they want, an' pay the money when it arrives,' she explained.

There was a rather strained silence. The Somertons and Aunt Kate had never understood why George had been sent out to Canada at twelve, all by himself, so soon after the death of his father. However, they all agreed that Davy Hoek had been heaven-sent, and proved himself a true friend to George who looked upon him like another brother.

'Did they meet on the ship going over?' asked Somerton.

'No, it was at Waterloo Station. I just marched up to him and begged him to look after me brother. And so he has – even said he wouldn't go to McBane's farm unless George went too.'

'When will George come back?' asked Daisy and again there was a silence which Mabel felt obliged to fill.

'I don't know, dear. Perhaps he'll come and visit us again one day, and bring Davy,' she said gently, though she knew it was most unlikely that they would ever see George again; she only wished she could thank Davy for what he had done for her brother.

She had no news of Albert, and Thomas Somerton looked grave at the mention of the navy. Mabel realised that his views on the situation in Europe were far more alarming than Harry's.

'Do you mean to tell me, Mabel, that living in London as you do, you know nothing of the danger this country's facing? Good heavens, girl, are you shut up in an ivory tower?'

'No, Uncle, I'm shut up in the Booth Street Infirmary,' she retorted. 'I only hear what I pick up from what people say and I wish ye'd tell me about it!'

'It's been brewing for a very long time and ever since the Archduke Franz Ferdinand was shot dead last month, Germany's been mobilising men and artillery, ships –'

'Excuse me, Uncle Thomas, but *who* did yer say was killed? I never heard anything about it. Was it in London?'

'No, my dear, the Archduke was assassinated at a place called Sarajevo in the Balkans and it's caused repercussions all over Europe. It's a warning that no government should ignore.'

Mabel had to admit that she had never heard of the unfortunate nobleman who had been killed in a place she knew nothing about, nor could she see how this distant event might affect the destiny of Europe, especially of the British Isles, with or without Ireland. But it was not for her to question her uncle's superior knowledge on such matters.

There were tears, kisses and promises to write when Mabel boarded the London train on its way up from Southampton that evening. She found it unexpectedly crowded with men, mostly young though a few were older, some in the uniform of the Territorials or the Officers' Training Corps, others in plain clothes. The air was full of a strange excitement and Mabel heard enthusiastic talk of 'seeing some sport before it's all over'.

A bewhiskered old gentleman in military uniform ordered the young ones to make room for Mabel in a corner seat and she politely enquired of him where all these men were going.

'My dear young lady, we're reservists goin' to join our regiments and one or two fellahs are goin' to enlist with the Army Service Corps,' he told her importantly. 'We're gettin' ready to show the Kaiser that if he wants a fight, he's got Great Britain and her Empire to give him a run for his money. Huh! We'll show the bounder!'

Mabel was beginning to realise that something momentous was about to happen and when the train drew in at Waterloo her eyes darted among the crowds, looking for the familiar Salvation Army uniform.

But it was a man in a different uniform who hailed her.

'Miss Court! It *is* Miss Mabel Court, isn't it?'

Two smiling blue eyes met hers and a firm arm helped her to step down on to the crowded platform. She recognised Dr Stephen Knowles, the son of their old family doctor who had been such a friend to the Court family during that terrible summer of 1912 when Annie and Jack Court had met their deaths within six weeks of each other. And Stephen had treated Albert's injuries when he'd been involved in the railway strike the year before.

'Dr Stephen! Don't say *you*'re going to join yer regiment!'

'Not exactly. I've joined the RAMC in case they need extra medics. But how are *you*, Miss Court? My father heard you'd gone to train as a nurse and said you'd be ideal.'

Mabel glowed. 'That's right, Dr Stephen, I'm at Booth Street Infirmary. Are yer still at the London Hospital in Whitechapel Road?'

'No, no, I'm at the East London for Children at Shadwell – poor district but wonderful hospital. I always wanted to specialise in sick children.'

26

Mabel's eyes shone. 'It's what *I*'ve always wanted to do, care for children, only I couldn't afford the trainin', that's why I'm doin' me general at a Poor Law infirmary.'

'Jolly good experience, Miss Court – and once you're trained you might apply for a place on the staff at Shadwell. You'd be just right for it.'

'D'ye think there's goin' to be a war, Dr Stephen?' she asked him abruptly.

His face darkened. 'We all hope not, but it looks pretty bad now, worse by the day. And just as I've got engaged, too!'

'Oh, Stephen! Who is she?'

'A friend of my sister's, Miss Phyllis Rawlings, and I just can't believe my luck – she's the sweetest, most adorable girl. We're bringing the wedding forward because of all this war panic. Can't be too soon for me, Mabel!'

His eyes sparkled and he forgot to say Miss Court; his father had always referred to this pleasant girl as Mabel and had told him something of the family history.

'I'm happy for yer, Stephen, and I bet yer dad – I'm sure Dr Knowles must be ever so pleased. Remember me to him, will yer? He was so good to us all, I'll never forget what he –' She lowered her voice and looked away.

'I'll tell him, Mabel. And don't let them work you into the ground,' he added, looking sharply into her face. 'I know what these places are like, always short of staff and overflowing with hopeless cases –'

He broke off as Captain Drover came panting up to them and seized Mabel's arm, giving Knowles a questioning look.

'Sorry, Mabel, I got held up at the Citadel meeting –

there's so many troubled souls at a time like this,' he apologised breathlessly.

'Harry, yer remember Dr Knowles who looked after Albert when he was hurt in the Tower Hill riots?'

'What? Oh, yes, o' course – good evenin', Dr Knowles. I see ye're in the Royal Army Medical Corps.' Harry's face was flushed and he was still trying to get his breath back.

'That's right.' Knowles smiled and held out his hand. 'Though I'm still hoping I won't be called upon!'

'Stephen's getting married, Harry.'

'Gettin' married? Ah, congratulations, doctor.' There was a distinct warming of Harry's voice as he pumped Stephen's hand up and down.

'Thanks, Captain – er –'

'Drover.'

'Yes, of course, Drover. Well, I'd better be off. Remember what I said, Mabel, and take good care of yourself. I'll tell my father. Goodbye and good luck!'

As he disappeared into the surging crowds of uniformed and ununiformed men filling the station concourse, some with women hanging on to their arms, Mabel turned anxious eyes on her Salvation Army captain.

'*You* won't have to join up, will yer, Harry? Ye're in uniform already.'

'If I'm called on to fight for me country, Mabel, I'll have to go along o' the rest. But I hope it won't come to that. Please, Lord, let it not come to that,' he muttered half under his breath.

But it did. After Germany's declaration of war against France, *The Times* thundered that 'If we at this critical juncture refuse to help our friend France, we shall be guilty of the grossest treachery'.

And now the rumours of war were everywhere, inside

as well as outside the Infirmary. Prayers for peace were offered up from packed churches and Mabel's brow was furrowed with uncertainty as she bathed Susan Graves's hot, dry skin with cool water; the girl lay muttering in delirium, not expected to survive to set eyes on her child again.

But then on the following Tuesday, 4 August, Susan's temperature dramatically fell and she was pronounced to be past the crisis, 'over the worst' as Sister put it, and Mabel Court rejoiced to think of the little girl who would not after all be left like Norah McLoughlin, without a relative in the world.

But her thankfulness was immediately followed by the news that Germany had invaded Belgium, and Britain had therefore kept her word and declared war on Germany.

It was as if a bombshell had exploded. Outside in the streets at midnight the shouting of the exuberant crowds could be heard in the wards and the next day men flocked to enlist for military service.

England was at war and nobody could foretell the outcome.

Chapter Two

'It'll all be over by Christmas.'

This seemed to be the general opinion as war fever swept the country and queues formed outside recruiting offices. The minimum age for enlistment was eighteen, but boys as young as fourteen were trying to pass themselves off as old enough to join the adventure of 'Kitchener's Army', and enlisted men without uniforms marched, drilled and paraded in London's parks, cheered on by a populace fired by patriotic fervour.

Stories of German atrocities in Belgium led to an unpleasant upsurge of hate for all things German, and the homes and shops of law-abiding citizens were attacked and burned by angry Londoners. Harry Drover told Mabel of a brother Salvationist who had caught the lash of it.

'Poor Pieter Hummel, a bandsman of ours, got home from a meetin' to find his house full o' shoutin' rabble, an' Lili clutchin' their little boy in her arms and beggin' them –'

'But *why*?' asked Mabel in horror.

'His name – Hummel. Anythin' foreign-soundin' must be an enemy, they reckon, even though he's been a good neighbour an' local baker for years.'

'But what happened then? Did he manage to get rid of 'em?'

'When they saw the Salvation Army crest on his cap, they started to slink away, shamefaced, like – but it's shaken 'em up badly, Mabel. Pieter told me he'll never forget seein' the hate on the faces o' those people. That's not patriotism, that's downright wickedness.'

Mabel knew that Harry had his own inner conflicts, his doubts about where his duty lay.

'It's seein' that poster everywhere yer look,' he told her. 'Ol' Kitchener pointin' his finger straight at *me*. Oh, Mabel, if yer king an' country need yer, how can any chap *not* enlist?'

Mabel looked up into his troubled eyes and squeezed his hand. 'There's hundreds gone to enlist, Harry, and they say it'll all be over by next year, most likely. Just wait an' see how things go.'

'It's the thought o' killin' another human bein', Mabel, a brother man. Me own brother-in-law, Herbert Swayne, he don't hold with the takin' o' life, not even in wartime. In fact, he says he'll never join up, whatever happens.'

'But he won't have to, he's a married man an' they've got the two little boys!'

Harry shook his head and muttered, 'All I hope for Ruby an' the boys' sake is that Herbert'll have the sense to keep his mouth shut.' There were already murmurings against objections to military service, and because it was known that the Quakers were opposed to the idea of men fighting and killing each other, for whatever reason, they sometimes found their meetings disrupted by shouts and jeers.

After much heart-searching and self-questioning, Captain Drover decided to enlist, though to Mabel's infinite relief he was put on reserve and given a striped armband to wear.

'Ye're doing good work where you are, Captain Drover,' he was told. 'We've got you down as enlisted and ye'll be called on later if the need arises.'

Mabel prayed that his services would never be needed. The other army – 'God's Army' – was in greater need of men like her Harry, she believed. She knew that it helped him to be able to talk to her, though their meetings were briefer and fewer than ever. She seemed to be always hurrying to get back on duty or to beat the ten o'clock curfew when the hostel door was locked and latecomers had to go to the Infirmary's front entrance where their names were taken and reported to Matron. So far Mabel had always managed to get in by the skin of her teeth, to the envy and admiration of her room-mates.

It was mid-September and Mabel had an evening off. In the shared bedroom she was pulling off her cap and cuffs when Norah McLoughlin came panting up the stairs half a minute later.

'Isn't it grand to be away from work for the evenin', Mabel!' she exclaimed eagerly. Both girls had been on duty since seven, with a half-hour break for the midday dinner. 'Are ye comin' up to St James's Park to walk alongside the quality?'

'Er, no – Harry's callin' for me, and we're goin' to a meeting at the Elephant an' Castle, Norah, but ye're very welcome to come along,' answered Mabel, wriggling out of her uniform dress. Harry often asked if any of her friends would like to come to a Salvation Army gathering; a fair number of the probationers were regular churchgoers, and Norah said she had received 'a good Catholic education' from the Sisters of Mercy. She nearly always managed to attend Mass on Sundays at St George's Roman Catholic Cathedral, within easy walking distance.

'Sure, but ye'll want to be together, so ye will,' she said with a little sigh. 'I'll take meself up to town and maybe find a nice fella for meself, who knows?'

'Oh, be careful, Norah, there's some rum characters

32

around,' warned Mabel quickly. The Irish girl was such an innocent and liked nothing better than to wander around the West End goggling at its endless attractions. She could be an easy prey to some smooth-talking man on the lookout for a quick pick-up, thought Mabel; a few flattering words, a few drinks, and a girl could find herself in a very awkward situation.

'No, come along with Harry and me, Norah, ye'll stand a better chance o' meeting a decent chap than yer would wanderin' round Leicester Square.'

Norah did not need further persuading. She took off her shoes and stockings to give her feet a brisk rub; they were tender after pounding up and down Men's II all day. Mabel put on clean stockings and a pair of well-polished shoes with pointed toes she'd bought from a stall in the Cut. On went her high-buttoned blouse, navy skirt and jacket, and then the hat. There was only one small mirror on the wall, and the girls relied on each other to check that hair was securely pinned up and labels tucked away inside collars before carefully placing hats in position. Finally she pulled on her thin cotton gloves and smiled first at her reflection and then at her friend.

'Ready, Norah?'

Norah had to remain Nurse McLoughlin for the evening. She pulled her black stockings back on and tied up her shoelaces, then adjusting her cap and smoothing down her grey uniform dress, she pulled her grey flannel cloak around her shoulders and checked that the 'tail' of her cap was hanging outside it. She was ready.

Mabel smiled and said how nice she looked. Norah had a summer dress but no coat now that the evenings were getting shorter and chillier. Her cloak was warm, but was not to be worn with anything other than her uniform dress and cap. The only thing missing was the apron.

'Yer look better in yer uniform than I look in this old outfit,' Mabel assured her. 'Come on, Harry said he'd meet me outside at a quarter to six.'

Just as they were about to leave, an urgent hammering on the door made them both jump back in alarm.

'Mother o' God, who's that?' gasped Norah. Mabel opened the door, to be confronted by two flushed faces. One was the staff nurse on Women's I, the other was Nurse Smith.

'What's up?' Mabel asked sharply.

'Yer may well ask, Court!' replied the staff nurse grimly. 'Oh, my, ye're in trouble, and no mistake – ye're to come down straight away.'

Mabel's heart thumped as she thought back over the day on duty and wondered what she could have done, or failed to do, that had landed her in this sudden disfavour. She held her chin up as she looked the two messengers straight in the eye. 'What am I supposed to've done?'

'Don't hang about, Court, ye'd better come down now, this minute, an' explain yerself to Sister Mattock – she's out for yer blood!'

Did Nurse Smith give a sly little smile at seeing Nurse Court in trouble? Mabel thought she saw the girl's mouth twitch and her own expression hardened. 'Mattock? I haven't heard her name before – what ward's she on?'

'Never mind what she's on, Court, just get down an' face 'er, or she'll have yer guts for garters – in fact, she will anyway. I wouldn't be in your shoes for a fortune.'

'All right, staff nurse, ye've made yerself clear, I'll come down an' see what's troublin' the good woman,' said Mabel. 'Though if it's as bad as yer say, I wonder she hasn't gone straight to Matron. Where is she?'

'Downstairs in the dining-room – they're all agog, she's in such a temper.'

Mabel turned to Norah. 'Excuse me, Nurse McLoughlin, but if yer see Captain Drover, will yer tell him I got held up for a bit?'

'Sure I will, Mab— Nurse Court,' faltered Norah.

The two nurses clattered downstairs with Mabel following closely and Norah lagging further behind. If Mabel was sacked, what in God's name would *she* do? It didn't bear thinking about.

On reaching the ground-floor passage Mabel squared her shoulders and marched into the dining-room.

A semicircle of silently staring eyes faced her. And in the middle stood Sister Mattock, a tall, dark-complexioned woman whose eyes glared fiercely from below jet-black brows. Little tufts of wiry hair bristled from under her sister's veil, and her stout arms were folded across her chest. Her sleeves, like the rest of her uniform, fitted tightly and showed her red wrists; she looked every inch the dragon she had been made out to be.

Mabel stared at her in disbelief. One of the watching nurses gave a suppressed giggle and Nurse McLoughlin, coming slowly down the stairs, heard Mabel give a strangled cry as she leapt forward into Sister Mattock's arms.

'*Albert!* Oh, Albert, yer *blighter*, yer deserve to be –'

But her brother hugged her close and never heard what he deserved. Arriving at the Infirmary he had charmed his way into the staff dining-room and persuaded the off-duty nurses to fetch him a Sister's uniform from the soiled laundry.

'Hey, Mabel, don't start pipin' yer eye as soon as yer poor bruvver sets foot on dry land,' he protested as her

35

tears flowed. 'Get yer glad-rags on, gal, an' we'll go out for a pie an' mash!'

'These are the gladdest rags I got, Albert – we're just off to meet Harry Drover,' she told him, wiping the back of her hand across her cheeks.

Albert whooped. 'Wot, ol' 'oly 'Arry? Still blowin' his trombone, is 'e? That's better still, we'll all go aht togevver.'

'And er – and this is my friend Norah McLoughlin – she's comin' too.'

'Good, the more the merrier. Ah, an Irish rose, an' all!'

His dark eyes rested admiringly on Norah who blushed and lowered her lashes, utterly dumbfounded by this sudden transformation of the fire-breathing Sister Mattock into Mabel's brother, as swarthy as his sister was fair.

Hastily divesting himself of his borrowed plumes, he smiled at the nurses who had obtained them for him, and taking Mabel and Norah by the arm, one on each side, he led them out into Booth Street where Captain Drover's face lit up with delight at the sight of his old friend and workmate. Albert explained that he had been recalled from the Mediterranean for probable convoy duty in the Channel and North Sea, and the girls listened eagerly to every word as the four of them walked up St George's Road to the Elephant and Castle.

'I'd've fought it was a bad enough bottleneck already wivout *you* lot blockin' up the traffic an' all,' he remarked as they approached the open-air gathering and the banner aloft with the words emblazoned, *Enlist for Jesus*. Harry went to take his place in the band.

''Ere, come on, girls, let's go for a quick one while they're warmin' up.'

'*No*, Albert, we can't go into a pub right under Harry's

nose and besides, Norah's in uniform,' answered Mabel firmly. 'We'll wait for yer over there by the coffee stall.'

'All right, then – 'ere, get yerself an' the lovely Norah a couple o' hot pies. Get me one an' all, will yer?'

'Ooh, *ta*, Albert!' Mabel's eyes lit up at the handful of silver he pulled out of his pocket, half-crowns, florins and sixpenny bits. His free and easy way with money made her think of their father whom Albert now resembled more and more, though his speech was rougher and he never bothered about his appearance as Jack Court had done, yet both were dark-eyed charmers with an eye for a pretty girl and a willingness to spend freely while the money lasted.

'Ye never said he was that good-lookin', Mabel,' whispered Norah, completely bowled over.

'Yeah, he's the image of our dad when he'd had a good day on the horses.' Mabel smiled. 'He was a bookmaker and travelled around a lot, y'see. Only Albert and Dad never hit it off – he always sided with our mother. That was why he went to sea on the *Warspite* when he was only sixteen. Mum was ever so upset. Still, come on, let's go and spend his money!'

They bought cups of coffee and meat pies wrapped in greaseproof paper. Albert joined them on a corner where Harry stood with his back to them in the band, playing 'Bless His Name, He sets me free', to the tune of 'Champagne Charlie is my name'. Mabel looked swiftly at her brother, forbidding him to make any play on the words.

'The Salvation Army uses tunes that everybody knows, 'cause not all of 'em know the ones they sing in church,' she explained to Norah who saw Albert wink at her behind Mabel's back.

The skies had been clouding over and a stiff breeze from the west brought a flurry of raindrops. Mabel shivered and wished she'd brought an umbrella to protect her hat.

Albert noticed how pale the girls looked and, telling them to wait for a minute, he sidled up to Captain Drover between hymns. 'I say, 'Arry, them girls've been on their feet for ten hours, an' it looks as if this bleedin' rain's settin' in for the evenin',' he said. 'Tell yer what, I'll take 'em dahn the Souf London 'All for a bit, so's they can 'ave a sit down in the dry – all right, mate?'

Harry had little choice but to nod his assent and though he was disappointed to see them hurrying off, he knew that Mabel must be wanting to talk with her brother.

'C'mon, girls, we're goin' to the music 'all,' said Albert, steering them purposefully away from the meeting and down the London Road.

Their tiredness vanished as they began to speculate eagerly about what might be on at the South London Hall. It was a completely new experience for Norah and the last time Mabel had been to a music hall was at the Grand on St John's Hill, Battersea, back in those far-off days when she'd lived with her parents and brothers and sisters, before the tragedy that had changed their lives.

'It was you who treated us then, Albert, d'ye remember? Just after Christmas, it was, on yer first leave from Greenhithe.'

'Yeah, that's right, Mabel, so it was, Boxin' Day. Ol' 'Arry was there, an' yer friend Maudie an' 'er little bruvver. Little did we know it was the last Chris'muss before –' He glanced at Norah and checked himself. 'Come on, girls, we'll do it big tonight – get ourselves a box!'

Mabel felt a rush of affection for her brother, less than a year younger than herself, quick-tempered and impulsive, but always warm-hearted. He had been good to their mother and Mabel was the only person he had never answered back, even when she had given him a good telling-off as his elder sister.

Norah gasped as they entered the Victorian music hall, which seemed to her the very pinnacle of luxury and magnificence, with its plush seats and chandeliers. A heady fragrance of cigar smoke and perfume wafted up from the auditorium, and Albert got them a box for the enormous sum of a guinea, just as the show was about to begin.

'Sure, an 'tis the grandest place I ever did see,' murmured Norah as she took her place on an elegant, round-backed chair. Her nurse's cap was slightly askew on her dark hair and Albert leaned across to adjust the 'tail' over her cloak. He was touched by her childlike wonder at everything she saw and heard, and could not help contrasting her with the bold-faced women who waited down at the docks for sailors to come ashore with their pockets full of back pay.

'I'n't she a sweet little fing, Mabel?' he whispered, nodding towards the girl's shining eyes as the conductor lifted his baton and the curtain went up promptly at seven thirty.

The star of the evening was the popular Harry Champion, but first on were the girls of the chorus in daringly short dresses and waving coloured scarves to much clapping and cheering. Then a lady and gentleman sang a sentimental duet, and they were followed by a brawny man in a leopard-skin and sporting a huge moustache, who brandished a glittering sword and demonstrated its sharpness by slashing to ribbons a newspaper held up by a pretty girl. He then proceeded to throw back his head, point the sword into his mouth and swallow it, inch by inch, to gasps of incredulity. Then, having accomplished this amazing feat, he breathed out flames of fire which set light to another newspaper held up by the girl.

'Cor! It's given 'im the wind pretty bad,' said Albert and Norah's peal of laughter drew heads in their direction. Mabel was thoughtful. The girl assistant had a strangely familiar air and there was something about the saucy way she wiggled her hips. Could she be . . . ? Was it possible?

'Don't she remind yer o' somebody, Albert, that girl?' she whispered.

'Eh? Ooh, yeah, see what yer mean. She ain't Maudie Ling, is she?'

'I reckon she is, Albert – just watch the way she moves – it *is* her, I'm sure of it!' Turning to Norah, she explained that Maudie Ling had been a childhood friend.

'She used to beg in the streets with her baby brother in her arms, Norah. The parents were hopeless drinkers, and Maud and Teddy were the only survivors o' their children.'

'Sure 'tis a terrible curse, the drink,' murmured Norah.

'Got caught nickin' grub from some toff's kitchen up Belgravy way, di'n't she, Mabel?'

'Yes, that's when she an' Teddy got sent to the Waifs an' Strays at Dulwich. And then she went into service an' thought she was in 'eaven, but there was trouble there, too –'

Albert gave her a warning glance, for that had been another story and not one to share with Norah McLoughlin. 'Yer ain't kept in touch, then?'

'The last I heard she was in service with a family up St John's Wood and had got another young man. Harry and me saw 'em in Trafalgar Square last New Year. He was a proper toff, spoke very posh.'

''Im an' me'd've got on all right, then.' Albert grinned. 'Looks 's if she's fallen on 'er feet now, any'ow.' He winked at Norah who blushed and lowered her lashes.

A comedian came on next, with some hard-luck stories about his nagging wife and her fearsome mother. The war had brought him a chance to get away from them both, he said, and he was off to join the navy. Albert gave him a cheer, and the girls laughed when the comic looked up and said he would sing a little ditty just for the gentleman and ladies in the box above the stage. It was a song about a mermaid.

''Twas in the mid-Atlantic, in the equinoctial gales,
That a sailor-lad fell overboard, among the sharks
    and whales –'

The audience joined in with gusto at the end of each verse:

''Cause he's mar-ri-ed to a mer-ma-id at the
    bottom o' the deep blue sea!'

He got almost as many cheers and whistles as the great Harry Champion himself, who came on next to prolonged applause before he'd even opened his mouth. When the audience finally settled down he sang a medley of songs, ending with his famously speedy rendering of 'Any Old Iron'. Mabel and Albert who knew it well got even more pleasure out of Norah's merriment when she realised that the gold watch and chain proudly displayed across Mr Champion's chest was the subject of the song. Faster and faster he sang the derisive chorus, until the orchestra could hardly keep up with him. Norah leaned over the side of the box, almost helpless with mirth as she joined in the singing:

41

'I wouldn't give yer tuppence for yer old watch
    chain – Old iron! Old iron!'

Alas, the ten o'clock curfew meant that they had to
leave before the end of the show, but not before the
young lady assistant to the sword swallower returned
in a deceptively conventional gown and bonnet, to give
a very cheeky version of 'Who Were You With Last
Night?'.

'That's *Maudie*, Albert, no doubt about it, *look* at
her!' said Mabel excitedly as they reluctantly got up
to leave the box. All eyes were centred on the little
figure mincing up and down the stage, pointing her
parasol at various gentlemen in the audience.

    'Who was yer wiv last night?
    Aht in the pale moon light?
    It wasn't yer sister, it wasn't yer ma –'

A deafening chorus rose up in response: 'Ah! Ah! Ah!
Ah! Ah-ah! Ah-ah!'

'Wouldn't I just love to have a word with her, but
we'll have to step on it to get back in time,' panted
Mabel as they descended the stairs to the entrance where
they found Harry pacing up and down, waiting to escort
Mabel back to the Infirmary.

'It's ten to ten, we'll 'ave to hurry,' he urged her.

'Oh, Harry, I'm sorry – it hasn't been much of an
evenin' for yer, has it?' Mabel apologised guiltily, while
Norah sighed happily over 'the most wonderful time I
ever did have in me whole life, so!'.

'We had a good meetin', Mabel, considerin' the rain,
and there was a great sense o' the Lord's presence
among us,' said Harry seriously, tucking Mabel's arm

under his and hurrying her along the pavement. Albert took Norah's arm, and the four of them hurtled down Gaywood Street and into St George's Road.

'Guess who we saw on the stage, Harry, singin' her head off and lookin' as pretty as a picture? Maudie Ling! Yes, really, I'd know her anywhere. I wonder where she's livin'.'

'I'll go back an' see if I can find 'er at the end o' the show,' promised Albert behind them. 'Tell 'er yer was askin' for 'er.'

'Come on, Mabel, yer don't want to be locked out,' muttered Harry and when they reached the nurses' hostel at half a minute to ten, there was no time for farewells.

'Be round termorrer af'noon,' Albert told her as he pushed both girls in through the door, and over his shoulder Mabel caught a last glimpse of Harry's anxious eyes upon her as it closed.

'Mabel Court, as I live an' breave! 'Ow are yer, then, me ol' pal?'

'Maudie!' The two girls hugged each other while Albert stood by. They were at the entrance to the nurses' hostel and Mabel had just come off duty for the afternoon.

'Oh, Maudie, don't yer look gorgeous – like a fashion plate!'

Maud Ling, one-time child of the streets, was dressed in a pale-pink outfit with a matching hat, gloves and shoes, as charming as it was impractical.

'That grey uniform don't do yer justice, Mabel, 'specially the 'eadgear. Can't yer change into summat else an' come out for a chop or somefing? Albert says ye're free for a coupla hours.'

'Yes, till five.' Mabel hesitated, knowing that she had

43

not a penny in her purse, and Maudie looked as if she was used to going to decent eating places.

'Go on up and get changed, gal, and I'll take yer bofe aht to wherever Maud says,' Albert assured her, and she shot him a grateful look.

Half an hour later they were seated in Wilcox's Dining Rooms on the Kennington Road.

''Andy for the Canterbury, this place,' said Maud with satisfaction, picking up her knife and fork. 'Gonna be in the chorus o' the pantomime there at Chris'muss!' She chuckled. 'Cor, I was that pleased to see ol' Albert 'angin' rahnd last night! Ol' Nobby the stage manager fought 'e was one o' them stage door johnnies chancin' 'is luck and got a bit beefy – di'n't 'e, Albert? Very partic'lar abaht 'is gals, 'e is. But we soon got it sorted aht. So what did yer fink o' yer ol' pal on stage, Mabel?'

'Knew yer as soon as I saw yer – when yer came on with that sword swallower, I thought to meself, "That's Maudie Ling!" Funny thing, we'd just been talkin' about yer. Last time we met yer were at a place in St John's Wood.'

'Yeah, well, I got chucked aht, di'n't I? The missus found me an' Alex – 'er son – in what yer might call a compromisin' – er – well, she gave me the boot, but Alex is still me young man, an' 'elps aht wiv me lodgin's now that I've gorn on to better fings – an' gettin' better all the time, an' all.'

Mabel avoided Albert's eye. Did this mean that Maud was a kept woman?

'If only it wasn't for this bloody war! Alex has got the idea o' goin' into this flyin' lark – be one o' them special officers 'oo fly them machines dahn on Salisbury plain. They reckon they'll be able to fly over the Channel to France and see what the Jerries are up to. Don't like the sahnd of it meself — wouldn't stand a chance if one o' them bleedin' fings came crashin' to earf.'

Albert grimaced. 'They got 'em in the navy an' all. S'pose ye'd 'ave a better chance if it came dahn in the drink.' Seeing Maudie's genuine fear for her Alex and sensing the need for a change of subject, he asked Mabel, 'When's yer little Irish friend free again?'

'Saturday, I think – and she'd love to go out again.' Mabel smiled, knowing that Norah had lain awake half the night reliving her evening at the music hall.

'Might as well make the most o' me time – only got six days. Ask 'er if she'd like to come aht, will yer, Mabel? And yerself as well, o' course –'

'No, I'm on that evenin', an seein' Harry on Sunday,' said Mabel with a wink at Maud. 'Only ye'd better mind yer step with Norah, she's much too innocent for the likes o' you.'

'I'd treat 'er the same as I'd treat me favourite sister.'

'Sahnds like a dull evenin' to me.' Maud grinned. ''Ow's yer little bruvver Georgie over in Canada, Mabel?'

Mabel gave the latest news of him and asked about Maud's brother Teddy.

'Still wiv the Waifs an' Strays at Over'ill Road in Dulwich – 'e's twelve now, cheeky little blighter, reckon they'll frow 'im aht in anuvver year, an' Gawd knows what 'e'll do then.' She suddenly looked hard at Mabel. '*You* know what it's like, don't yer, gal, not 'avin' a proper 'ome, not bein' able to give yer own bruvver a bed when 'e's on leave, not 'avin' anywhere to go wiv ol' 'Arry for a bit o' slap an' a tickle – go on, no need to blush, yer know what I mean.' She leaned across the table and spoke slowly and clearly to her friend. 'I tell yer, Mabel Court, one o' these days I'm goin' to 'ave *money*, an' a nice 'ome o' me own, where

45

me friends can come an' 'ang their 'ats up in the 'all.'

'Oh, Maudie!' Both the brother and sister laughed, but Maudie was in earnest. 'Just you wait and see if I don't!'

Norah had her evening out with Albert and Mabel saw the tremulous happiness in her friend's soft blue eyes. When he said goodbye to them both at the end of his leave Mabel turned away tactfully to allow him to kiss the the pretty Irish girl and murmur something in her ear about being sweethearts and keeping in touch. Then he strode off towards the docks again with his rolled-up bag across his shoulder, singing as he went.

'Rule, Britannia! Britannia rules the waves –
    Britons never, never, never shall be – er –
Mar-ri-ed to a mer-ma-id at the bottom o' the deep
    blue sea!'

'Oh, Mabel, d'ye think he'll be safe?' whispered Norah as they watched him turn and wave once more before disappearing round the corner. 'Sure an' I'll never miss Mass agin, not if I have to get up at crack o' dawn.'

Mabel wordlessly put her arm around her friend. It seemed so unfair that as soon as Albert had found himself a girl as sweet as Norah, they should have to be parted.

The girls' contact with the outside world soon became even more curtailed when they were put on night duty, and Mabel thought she'd never been so tired in her life. She was one of three probationer nurses in charge of two thirty-bed wards, Women's I, medical, and Women's II, surgical. A Night Sister was in overall charge of six wards and made regular rounds during the night, but the actual nursing care was carried out by the probationers. On Women's II they had to deal with accident cases from the street or home, broken bones, burns and scalds. The operation cases included removal of cancers from various parts of the body, and other obstructions like gallstones and appendicitis; some had the dreaded 'women's trouble', and were in for removal of the womb. Most were in a weakened state by the time operation was decided upon as a last resort and many did not recover. The girls got used to 'laying-out' by the light of a flickering lamp to avoid putting on the overhead electric lights. On the medical wards there were the routine four-hourly toilet rounds for the bed-bound, helpless bodies to be turned, soiled sheets to be changed; and at any time there might be a sudden emergency admission to deal with, an operation to relieve a stoppage, to try to save an injured limb or eye. These usually had to be prepared for theatre and received back after success or failure – which might mean another laying-out.

Off duty at last, they stumbled to their room, drew the curtains, undressed, washed and collapsed into bed. Exhausted though they were, sleep did not come easily. Unless the windows were shut, rendering the room airless, the noise of traffic, trolleys and bins hammered at their ears all day. Inside the hostel voices called, doors banged and footsteps clattered up and down uncarpeted stairs; when one of them had to get up and pad down the corridor to the lavatory, she disturbed the others. They would take it in turns to creep out to the gas ring to make a pot of tea at around three or four o'clock, which was heaven for the wakeful but hard luck on the girl who had just dropped off to sleep.

'Holy Mother o' God, I don't know how I'm goin' to

get through the next twelve hours,' Nurse McLoughlin would groan as they went down to the dining-room at eight o'clock for bread, soup, cold meat or cheese before going to their wards at eight thirty. 'Me head feels as if it's turned to a block o' wood to carry around all night.'

And tomorrow night, thought Mabel, and the next and the next and the next until they lost count of the nights and the days, and discovered that it was a week later.

She had promised to meet Harry on her first night off, and was fast asleep when Nurse Tasker came and woke her at six that evening with a cup of tea.

'Come on, Court, wake up! Ye're meetin' yer young man at seven.'

Mabel yawned and opened one bleary eye. 'Oh, yes, so I am. Thanks, Betty, ye're a pal.' She gratefully took the cup and breathed in the steam to clear her head. 'Mm-mm! I just can't believe I haven't got to go on duty tonight.'

'No, yer got somethin' better on, yer lucky thing – and he ain't got to go to the Front,' replied Betty, her smile fading a little. The unexpected setbacks at Liège and Namur, and the retreat from Mons with its long casualty lists had dampened the first surge of war fever and a note of doubt had crept in, that this war might turn out to be longer and bloodier than at first thought.

'We're goin' to get a whole lot o' patients from the Stepney an' Poplar Infirmary, so's they can take in wounded soldiers,' said Betty. 'Coo, I don't half wish I was there, don't you?'

'Oh, *no*, I'd be so nervous o' hurtin' them,' shuddered Mabel, looking up over her teacup.

'Just give *me* the chance to look after some nice young fellas! Be a change from these poor, smelly ol' things we got here – an' they say we're gettin' more kids an' all. Anyway, enjoy yer evenin', Court – don't do anythin' I wouldn't!'

Chance would be a fine thing, thought Mabel, with nowhere to go but the Salvation Army Citadel. Her head ached and she felt as if she could sleep for a week.

Harry's eyes lit up when she emerged from the hostel, but he was shocked by her haggard appearance. 'Dearest Mabel, yer look whacked out! What've they been doin' to yer?'

She forced a smile. 'It's called night nurse's face, Harry. A little fresh air'll work wonders.'

He took her arm and they walked up to Lambeth Bridge. It was getting dark and she suddenly felt that she could not go another step.

'Harry, I'm so tired.' Her voice trembled and tears welled up in her reddened eyes. 'Let's find a seat and just be quiet for a bit.'

He was immediately all concern. 'Look, Mabel, shall we get on a bus and go to Falcon Terrace? It's warm there an' yer can rest. My mother'll get us somethin' –'

'No, Harry, no, I couldn't go anywhere – I just want to rest now.'

He led her slowly down to the Albert Embankment and found a seat overlooking the river. Mabel sank down on it and he sat beside her. Behind them the seven turreted blocks of St Thomas's Hospital cut them off from the noise of the streets, and straight across the water the Houses of Parliament rose up like a picture in the sunset.

Mabel laid her head on his shoulder. 'I'm sorry, Harry, but all I want is to be *quiet*. It sounds silly, I know, but let's just stay here and not say anything at all,' she begged, her voice shaky. 'Please, Harry.'

He put his arm round her shoulders. 'Tell me, Mabel,'

he said very gently. 'Are yer in need o' prayer? The Lord knows all our –'

'Oh, no, it's nothin' like that,' she said with a sigh. 'It's just that I haven't had a proper sleep for over a week, an' I'm worn out, that's all. I'm sorry, but –'

Her voice trailed off and she lay against his shoulder in silence. It was a clear evening and a light breeze blew in off the river, ruffling the ribbon on Mabel's hat and lifting the wide collar of her jacket. Her eyelids drooped and the tension of her mouth relaxed.

Within minutes she was fast asleep, encircled in his arm. A few passing strollers glanced at them in amusement or disapproval, for such public displays of intimacy had become more common since the declaration of war. Harry felt his arm turning numb, and his thighs and buttocks ached from staying in the same position on the hard seat, but he would not move a muscle in case he disturbed her. If she woke she might ask him to take her back to the hostel and he wanted to feel her warm body beside him for as long as possible.

And so they remained motionless on the seat until darkness fell and the air began to chill. When at last she stirred, he kissed her and she sleepily responded: he put both arms around her. Her face was very pale, her eyes dark hollows in the lamplight.

He gently disengaged himself, stood up, stretched and hauled her to her feet. 'Come on, Mabel, me love, ye're gettin' cold. It's time I took yer home – back to that place.'

Her sleep that night was deep and dreamless, but Harry Drover lay awake in his back bedroom at number 8 Falcon Terrace, staring up into the darkness and oppressed by fears and imaginings to which he could give no name. At some point in the night he suddenly started up in terror.

'Mabel! Mabel, arc yer there?'

Had he spoken the words aloud? There was no answer in the silence of the house, only a sense of inexplicable loss.

Chapter Three

Impossible as it might have seemed at first, the second-year probationers became adjusted to the upside-down world of nights and slept for longer periods during the day. As autumn advanced and the temperature cooled, the hostel became less stuffy. One of the Night Sisters gave Mabel a good piece of advice, which was to go for a walk and get some fresh air before going to bed in the mornings. At first she felt unable to make the effort, but Norah McLoughlin offered to come with her, and sure enough the walk up the Lambeth Road cleared their lungs of the smell of the wards and soothed their jangled nerves; they certainly slept better for it.

'Me head belongs to me agin, Mabel – we must get them others to come out wid us as well!'

And it was while walking out one morning with Ethel Davies that Mabel learned that Mrs Davies was dressmaker to two Mrs Knowles, a mother and daughter-in-law, both wives of doctors.

'Oh, I *know* them, Ethel!' cried Mabel. 'At least, I know their husbands. Old Dr Knowles was our panel doctor in Battersea and the best friend we ever had – and his son Stephen got married this year.'

'Yes, Mum worked on her weddin' dress, all white lace with real flowers sewn to the veil.'

'What's she like, did yer mother say?' asked Mabel curiously.

'Oh, she's a real lady, as delicate as a piece o' fine bone china, me mum says – and he worships the ground she walks on. They're livin' at Hillier Road with his parents for the time bein', 'cause he could be called up any day now, what with all these wounded.'

Mabel frowned. There was worsening news from the Front, as everybody was now calling the lines of battle drawn up against the advancing Germans.

'An' me mum reckons she's expectin',' added Ethel with a significant look. 'Wouldn't it be awful if he got called up an' went out there an' got killed, Mabel?'

Mabel's heart lurched. 'Don't say it, Ethel, don't even *think* o' such a thing!' she exclaimed in horror, for as always her thoughts flew to Harry. Suppose he had to go to the Front and risk *his* life? And Albert, somewhere at sea, though heaven only knew where, because there had been no word from him, and Norah McLoughlin asked her daily if she had heard any news. If he was doing convoy duty in home waters, carrying troops and horses, cargoes of equipment and foodstuffs, surely he would have let her know? Or was he transporting food across the vast Atlantic to Britain from the United States and Canada?

As always, Harry tried to reassure her.

'No news is good news, Mabel. If there was any – yer know – they'd've sent a telegram.'

Mabel shivered. Christmas was approaching and, far from being 'all over', the news from France got steadily worse. The mounting numbers of dead and wounded had turned the early euphoria into shocked disbelief and as injured men arrived home in huge numbers, stories began to circulate about the terrible conditions at the Front. The relentless rain in the marshy land around a place with the unpronounceable name of Ypres had caused a sea of mud to fill the trenches and shell-holes, where men stood with soaking, freezing feet and lice-ridden clothes, enduring the noise of shells exploding around them day and night. A man might see a friend killed in an instant, his body falling to the bottom of the trench to rot in filthy water.

And so *many* had died at the Front. Curtains were drawn in the houses along whole streets where sons, brothers and friends had all joined up together in 'pals' battalions' and gone out on the same wave of new arrivals at the Front, only to be mown down together; women were known to faint at the very sight of a telegraph boy coming up the path. So many pale women in black with stricken faces – mothers, sisters, young wives newly wed and newly widowed: so many men dead . . .

And it was at this time that Harry came to her with the news they had been dreading: he was to be sent to Aldershot for training in the New Year.

'Can't yer volunteer as a stretcher-bearer, Harry? Lots of other Salvation Army officers have,' pleaded Mabel, but he shook his head.

'No, Mabel, the Lord's made it clear to me that He wants me to go as a soldier, alongside o' me brothers out there.'

She clung to his arm as they walked beside the park railings. 'Ye've always said that it's against God's will to take another man's life, Harry.'

'Yes, Mabel, an' it's what burdens me most – bless yer for understandin'.'

She made herself say it. 'But ye'd have to do that very thing, Harry.'

'If the Lord wants me to go to the Front, Mabel, He'll show me what I must do.'

To this there seemed to be no answer, though she wondered whether any of the Germans would have the same scruples. She knew how deeply this dread of killing preyed upon his mind, in addition to the

54

natural fears of a young man for his own life and safety. And yet there was nothing she could say or do to reassure him.

Cards, letters and little gifts arrived from Belhampton, with the news that Alice was being courted by a young officer, Gerald Westhouse of the new Royal Flying Corps, which made Mabel think of Maudie's young man. She also got another letter from George, now fifteen and getting quite tall, he told her. Davy was talking of moving on to Vancouver and George was willing to go as long as they stayed together.

'Meeting him was the best bit of Luck I ever had and its a new Life for me here,' he had scrawled. 'I shall remember you Mabel but I wud not go back to England now. Thanks for all you did and Merry Christmas.'

She clutched at the short message, thankful that her younger brother seemed well settled but sad at the loss of him, for now she felt sure they would not meet again. In a strange way it felt like justice, knowing what they both knew. Had he told Davy? Yes, he must have done – and in so doing, had embraced his new life and left the past behind him for ever.

And Christmas brought something else, an unexpected but very welcome surprise: a postcard with a picture of Port Said. Albert was on a minesweeper.

'You ourt to see me now Mabel. We got the sun we got the sea we got the beer we got the lot. I dont need the girls I got two at home Mabel and my little Irish Nora. Love from Albert xxx.'

Laughing and crying, she lost no time in showing it to Norah and was astonished when with many blushes Norah shyly produced her own card from Albert. It showed two pink hearts pierced by an arrow, with a printed message about sweethearts being always in each other's thoughts.

'He's given me an address where the ship'll be callin',
in case I'd like to write a letter,' she confessed, her blue
eyes shining.

'Well, tell him to write more often, then, to save us
worryin'!' Mabel tried to speak lightly, but she felt
a little uneasy; Norah was so transparently innocent,
and having never known the love of family, she was
especially vulnerable to any attention paid to her of a
romantic nature. Albert would not knowingly cause her
any hurt, but he might not realise how intensely she had
responded to his sentimental card.

'Albert's a scamp, Norah, and ye'd better not take too
much notice of him!'

But Norah's fate was already sealed; she yearned
over the card, kissing it every night before she tucked
it under her pillow and prayed to the Sacred Heart for
Seaman Court's safe return.

'Thank ye, Blessed Lord Jesus, for hearin' me prayers
an' sendin' me a man to love – and his sister to be me
friend. If Ye'll send him back to me from the sea, I'll
never trouble Ye for another thing as long as I live, so.'
Crossing herself quickly, she would mutter, 'Father, Son
an' Holy Spirit, Amen.'

Harry's parents, sister and brother-in-law went to see
him off at Waterloo Station on a cold January morning.
Mabel could not get away from the Infirmary and they
said their farewells the evening before, embracing in the
shadows of Booth Street.

'Remember dancin' in Battersea Park the night o' the
Coronation, Harry? "Goodbye, Dolly Gray" – little did
we know then it was goin' to be true again –'

His arms gripped her so fiercely that she could
scarcely breathe and her words were stifled by his
long, fervent kiss. He paused only to whisper urgently

in her ear, 'God bless yer, my own dearest girl, an' take care o' yer. I'll need yer more than ever before.'

'I'll be waitin' to hear from yer, Harry.'

'God help me, I love yer, Mabel, since I first set eyes on yer. I'll always love yer.'

'I know, I know. And I love you, too.' The words sounded so inadequate, like something out of a cheap magazine, and snatched kisses were not enough to say all that was in their hearts – or the longing of their young bodies. Her arms tightened round his neck, but there was nothing left to say except goodbye.

Two days later Ethel Davies reported that Dr Stephen Knowles had been posted to a base hospital in France and that his young wife was absolutely devastated.

As always, work was Mabel's best remedy. As soon as she came off nights she was sent to work in the operating theatre where she quickly had to learn the principles of sterilisation, the boiling of instruments and the baking of dry dressings and towels. She soon became skilful at setting trolleys for operations, but assisting with the giving of anaesthetics could be harrowing. Open ether and chloroform were in use, and fire precautions had to be strict. The smell made Mabel's head ache and her eyes watered while she held the hands of patients with terror in their eyes as they faced 'going under' into unconsciousness.

On the wards the work grew harder then ever. As the stream of wounded men filled other hospitals and infirmaries, Booth Street was now taking double the number of civilian cases displaced from elsewhere, and patients were being discharged earlier, often before they were sufficiently recovered, to make room for the next lot of admissions. The number of child patients also grew, but not the staff to look after them, and the elderly suffered as a consequence. Yet who could deny a bed to a soldier injured in the service of his country?

Every day Mabel looked out for Harry's letters from Aldershot with their accounts of route-marching, 'square-bashing', cookhouse training and endless boot-polishing and whitening. Much more sinister was the time he had to spend learning to handle the horrible weapons of death. Rifle practice was bad enough, but bayonets were worse, and nothing in his Salvation Army training had prepared him for this obscenity. By contrast he was not bothered by coarse language and the lack of privacy in barrack life.

'All these boys are my brothers, Mabel, and their hearts are brave, it is not their manners I care about. But the thought of killing a fellow man troubles me far more. I think of you every night my own dear Girl and I see your sweet face in my dreams like a Guardian Angel.'

Which gave Mabel a sense of unease, knowing herself to be all too human.

She no longer had to wait for weeks on end to get news of Albert. Norah's reply to his Christmas card had begun a regular correspondence which reflected in Norah's eager steps towards the letter rack in the dining-room each day. Sometimes there would be nothing for a month or more, but then two or three scrawled, well-thumbed letters would arrive together, sending Nurse McLoughlin into a seventh heaven of delight. Mabel now learned more of her brother's whereabouts at sea, mostly around the Mediterranean. He was to spend the whole of 1915 away from home waters, but they always got news of him sooner or later, and Norah's letters were apparently as eagerly looked out for as his own. Mabel's feelings about this romance remained mixed, but she could not grudge her friend's newly found happiness.

It was wartime and didn't she know it! Nobody knew what the future might bring.

'What shall we do this afternoon, Norah – test each other on *Basic Surgical Nursing*?'

'Sure, an' won't me eyes close shut as soon as I lay me head down!' Nurse McLoughlin sighed wearily. Both probationers were off duty until five, and had been exchanging stories about what had happened in theatre that morning and on Men's I where chronic bronchitis was taking its winter toll. And inevitably their talk turned to Harry and Albert.

'Don't I think o' yer brother all the time, God love him, wonderin' what he's doin', ivery hour o' the day,' confessed the Irish girl.

'I know, Norah, I know. Same with me – him an' Harry both. Come on, we'd better test ourselves on reasons for gastric surgery. I'll ask yer the first question –'

There was a sudden brisk knock at the door and in sailed Maud Ling; she had come up the stairs from the side entrance.

'Maudie! Ye'd've copped it if Mrs Bullock'd seen yer!' cried Mabel, amazed at her friend's cheek.

'Nah! I'd talk me way rahnd any ol' 'ousekeeper! Listen, it's a lovely day, a real breff o' spring, so what're you two doin' layin' abaht in this 'ole? C'mon, let's go up over Lambeff Bridge for an airin'.'

'But Maudie, we're whacked out – an' we're on again at five,' protested Mabel.

'Then maybe we can find a nice little tearoom to 'ave a cuppa an' a bit o' cake, eh?' asked Maud and saw their eyes brighten. 'C'mon, I ain't takin' no for an answer – what you two need's a change o' scene – pooh, I can smell the pong o' the wards on yer!'

Within twenty minutes the three girls, two in their

nurses' uniforms, were standing on Lambeth Bridge, now so badly rusted that it was open only to pedestrians; they could look up and down the river where the keen February breeze carried a whiff of tar, timber and the indefinable tang of the docks and cargoes being unloaded in the Pool of London. Norah's misty blue eyes gazed downriver as if to follow her thoughts out to the open seas and wherever the SS *Christina* was ploughing her dangerous way. She felt Maud's touch on her arm.

'Time to move on, gal, an' go for that cuppa.'

Norah heard the understanding in the light remark. 'Sure an' it's a heart o' gold yer friend's got, takin' me on along o' yeself,' she murmured to Mabel as they followed Maud towards the north bank and up Horseferry Road, and Mabel realised that her childhood friendship with Maud Ling had become a trio with Norah McLoughlin; their three lives were to become more closely interwoven in the dark days to come.

In the up-market tea shop that Maud chose, her voice rose above the genteel tinkle of bone china, calling for toasted buttered muffins. She took charge of the teapot, and was about to pour out when her eye fell on the two women sitting at the next table; the younger one held a baby on her lap and they were accompanied by a bonny little boy of about two.

'Don't look now, Mabel,' said Maud holding up the teapot with its spout poised in mid-air. 'But ain't that yer pal Ada Clay?'

Mabel of course turned round at once. '*Ada*? Yes! That's her, Ada Hodges now, and that's her mother – and *that* must be little Arthur, named after his dad, an' another baby! Oh, it's been so long since we saw each other – I must speak to her!'

By this time they had been seen and recognised, and

Mabel leaned across to greet her old friend. There were smiles, introductions and mutual regrets at having lost touch.

'Yer know Maud Ling and this is my friend Norah McLoughlin who's trainin' with me at Booth Street Infirmary. Norah, this is my friend Ada and her mother Mrs Clay. Ada an' me worked together at the Hallam Road Babies' Mission after I left school, and Maud an' me went to her weddin' – an' now ye've got this dear little boy, Ada, and – is this a little girl?'

Young Mrs Hodges was only too pleased to show off her baby girl Jenny aged four months, and smiled fondly at her son and daughter. She had put on weight and had turned from a rather giddy girl into a complacent young matron who spoke with a more genteel accent than Mabel remembered from their days at Hallam Road.

'I heard you'd gone in for nursing, Mabel, but I didn't think it would be at a Poor Law infirmary – how awful! Are you still walking out with that young Salvation Army man? My poor Arthur has to work terribly long hours at Lipton's because so many of the young single men have been called up. He hardly ever sees the children, which is such a pity as he dotes on them so much.'

'Captain Drover – that's my Harry – he's at Aldershot, trainin' to be sent out overseas,' Mabel answered when she could get a word in. 'And my brother Albert's in the navy. And Maud's young man's in the flying corps, learnin' to drive those aeroplanes.'

'Oh, how simply *dreadful*, Mabel! Thank goodness my Arthur couldn't possibly be spared from his work, quite apart from his responsibilities as a family man, of course. My dad says it's all very well for the young, single men to go in for heroics, but –'

She suddenly caught sight of Maud's unsmiling stare

and looked a little confused. 'We try to do our bit for the war effort, make-do-and-mend and bring-and-buy sales – don't we, Mother? My friend Mrs Spearmann has started a Ladies' Committee to provide comforts for the soldiers serving in France, and that keeps us well occupied. Did you know we've moved to Rectory Grove in Clapham? Arthur thought we ought to have a larger house for the children.' She simpered and lowered her eyes. 'I don't suppose we shall stop at two! If only this wretched war was over! Anyway, you must come to Rectory Grove, Mabel, and bring your friend. Actually we'd better be getting along now, but it's been so nice to see you again – and Maud, of course.'

'Yeah, well, I reckon it's time we was gettin' along an' all, Mabel, seein' as you an' Norah are on at five an' I'm doin' me stuff at the Canterbury tonight,' said Maud drily. She rose and beckoned to the waitress for the bill, leaving Mabel to take leave of Ada while Norah, who had been quite overwhelmed by this charming, well-dressed young mother who was a friend of Mabel's, bent down to young Arthur and held out a hand to him.

'And aren't ye the fine little smilin' fella?' she said softly, at which he seized her hand in his chubby fists and shouted, 'You go home wiff *me*!' The ensuing laughter from his mother and grandmother trailed off as Maud swept out of the teashop with the two nurses in tow.

'Well! I'd say Ada's gorn up in the world and left 'er ol' friends be'ind,' she declared as they hurried back across the bridge. 'There she is wiv everyfing a woman can ask for, a nice 'ome, not short o' the ready, two little kids and an' 'usband comin' 'ome to 'er ev'ry night – an' all she can do is look dahn 'er nose an' moan.'

Putting on a would-be refined accent, she drawled, 'If only this wretched war was ovah! My poor Arfah has to work such frightfully long hours, yer know – but we try to do our bit, don't we, Mother, deah – knittin' comforts for the poor bleedin' soljahs!'

Mabel shrugged and said nothing. What was there to say? Her life and Ada's had taken different directions, in the same way that Alice's and Daisy's lives had changed. She glanced at Norah who smiled and said how much she'd enjoyed the treat.

And then all of a sudden at the beginning of March Harry appeared again and told his sweetheart that he had forty-eight hours' embarkation leave, and could she come to tea at Falcon Terrace on Sunday? An invitation from Mrs Drover could not possibly be refused, though Mabel had great difficulty in changing her Sunday shift, and was made to feel a thorough nuisance by the rest of the staff. She arrived at the Drovers' at four o'clock and found the whole family gathered for tea, including Ruby and Herbert Swayne and their boys. Harry was bound for Southampton the next morning and was being sent out to Egypt, of all places, for desert training at Alexandria.

Mabel felt tired and tense after trying to look after too many patients in an overcrowded ward; her head ached and her period had just begun. She did her best to behave in a polite and helpful way, offering to help Mrs Drover lay the table in the front parlour and set out the bread-and-butter to eat with tinned salmon, a special treat that had to be divided up into eight small portions. There were also home-made scones with jam and a currant cake. Harry said grace and they sat down to eat a meal for which none of them except the little boys had much appetite, though Mabel praised it all and forced herself to eat a little of everything. Ruth helped her mother wash up afterwards while Mabel and Harry sat awkwardly on the settee, unable to tell each other of the turmoil in their hearts – trying to hide their dread of the parting that lay ahead under a thin veneer of small-talk. It was a relief when they all walked off together to the Sunday meeting at the Clapham Citadel which began at half past seven and went on until nine. Mabel sat with the Drovers and joined in the prayers and hymn-singing without any real sense of the words; she found herself yawning in the middle of a new young brother's testimony – and felt Mrs Drover's eye upon her.

When Harry abruptly rose and said he had to leave before the end of the service it caused consternation to his family.

'But we're having special prayers said for yer, son – yer can't just get up and walk out!'

'I won't be late back, Mother, but I need to talk to Mabel. For God's sake, she's the woman I'm goin' to marry – if I come back!' And without further excuse or apology he took Mabel's arm and almost pulled her out of the Citadel, leaving John and Doris Drover open-mouthed.

Mabel clung to his arm as they walked quickly back to Booth Street. It was raining, but neither of them heeded the icy drops bombarding their faces like needles; Harry's outburst had expressed what they had both been feeling and Mabel was almost relieved. It was as if the truth had been spoken for the first time on this fraught Sunday evening, and when they stood together in the familiar dark alcove near to the door of the nurses' hostel, she asked him to tell her again what he knew about his destination and what was to happen there.

'They don't give us many details, but there's a big landin' o' troops goin' on in Turkey, and we're to follow on after the first wave,' he told her, adding in a rush of words, 'Mabel, my love, I'll never be ready to kill men. The thought o' shootin' a man and runnin' him through with a bayonet point – how can I ask the Lord to help me do that?'

She heard the note of desperation in his voice and wished with all her heart that she could give him a satisfactory answer. Instead, she put her hand in her pocket and brought out a little polished metal mirror.

'Look, I got this for yer, Harry, and on the other side it's got the Lord's Prayer engraved on it, d'ye see? Keep it in yer top pocket, over yer heart, an' I'll pray that the Lord'll show yer what to do when the time comes. Think o' me, my love.'

'Oh, I do, I do, dearest Mabel, all the time – every waking hour –'

He groaned and buried his face against her neck. She felt his breath warm on her skin and also felt his fear like something tangible between them. Was there anything, anything at all that she could do to help him?

And without him saying a word, she knew that there was: she knew what would send him off to the war with fresh courage in his heart. And that was to let him take her, to possess her body as a husband honours his wife.

But of course it was forbidden to them. Fornication was a serious sin – and moreover, a sin that might have dire consequences; and in any case, there was no time, no place. There was so little she could offer him as they stood in the shadow of the Infirmary – only perhaps an extra closeness, a brief moment of intimacy such as they had not had before . . .

Breathlessly she took off her gloves and unbuttoned her jacket. And then the front of her blouse. The cotton camisole beneath could be pushed off one shoulder and lowered.

'Harry . . . Harry, my love,' she whispered, taking his hand and guiding it inside to the curve of her right breast. She felt him cover it with his palm and gasped at the sensation, the hand of a man – the man she loved – cradling her soft warm flesh as they stood against the grey wall. She heard his long-drawn-out sigh and felt his mouth seeking hers while she put her arms around him to hide their secret contact from any onlookers; but they seemed to be alone in the dark and the rain, as if there were only the two of them left in the whole world. Their bodies pressed together and she felt the hardness that was his erection, the proof of his desire for her; on previous occasions when this had happened, he had moved a little away, or had turned to one side – out of respect, or so as not to alarm her – but now he let it thrust against her as if wanting to let her know of his agonising need. Offering her open mouth to his long, devouring kiss, she lowered her right hand to touch him through the layers of material that separated skin from skin, and felt him tremble from head to foot.

At length she had to take her mouth from his to draw breath, and it was he who spoke first.

'Thank yer, Mabel. Thank yer, dearest girl. I'll remember this all the time while I'm away.'

'Think o' me here, Harry, prayin' for yer every day,' she said shakily – 'an' thankin' God ye're not goin' to them dreadful trenches!'

She was right. It wasn't the trenches of France that awaited him, but the Gallipoli Peninsula overlooking the straits of the Dardanelles.

Chapter Four

There was a sudden stir at the bottom of Men's II. From behind the screen where she was changing a dressing, Mabel heard the patients' voices upraised in anger and indignation.

'Hey, they're shoutin' summat dahn in the street, summat abaht a big ship the Jerries've gorn an' sunk!'

'Shut yer marf, Grandad, an' listen!'

'Wot's 'e sayin'?'

'Bloody Jerries blew it up, whacking great liner wiv 'undreds aboard, lot of 'em Yanks – wivin' sight o' shore, they was.'

'Did yer say Yanks?'

'Broad daylight, 'e says.'

'Bastards.'

'D'j'ear that, nurse?'

Mabel had indeed heard and her heart missed a beat, thinking as always of Albert. The sinking of the Cunard liner *Lusitania* was a terrible reminder of the danger to all shipping, and as the details became known she shared in the general horror at its loss, along with twelve hundred passengers and crew members. Comparisons were inevitably made with the *Titanic* disaster three years earlier, but this was no tragic accident; this was a brutal act of aggression in home waters, just off the Irish coast on the last lap of a journey from New York to Liverpool.

The terror of the submarines, the German U-boats, had begun. All merchantmen would be under constant threat from the unseen enemy, to add to the fears of a nation already reeling from the loss of a hundred thousand men in France.

Mabel found herself suddenly waking in the night from dreams in which she was floundering in a sea of wreckage and Albert's drowned face was looking up through the water; or Harry was being run through by an enemy bayonet while throwing his own aside. She would wake gasping and choking from the toils of nightmare, and once she found Norah McLoughlin at her side, whispering soothing words.

'Ssh, ssh, Mabel, 'tis only a dream ye're havin' – don't worry, darlin', there's nothin' to be afraid of, ye're here in yer bed, an' it's meself beside ye.'

Mabel groaned and said she was sorry, though she almost wept with relief to find that it had only been a dream.

And there were other dreams of a very different kind. Before she fell asleep one night she lay repeating to herself the words of Harry's letter written from Cairo where he was training with men from Australia and New Zealand. They were housed in old cavalry barracks, and he tried to describe the awesome sense of the past as morning broke over the Pyramids: 'Dearest Mabel, you can't imagine the desert at dawn, so cool and quiet and still. And that's when your closest to me my own dear girl.'

In sleep she was back in his arms when he had kissed her goodbye and pressed his body against hers. And in her dream Mabel felt herself to be truly possessed by him, his weight on top of her, flesh straining against flesh, his hands upon her body, and more than his hands: that male part of him that she had never seen entered her in the union of man and woman, and she cried out in joy – and woke.

The room was silent except for the breathing of the other three girls; Davies was snoring lightly. Thank heaven none of them had heard – if there had been anything to hear. Mabel was a virgin and had been no closer to Harry than when he had kissed her and touched her with such longing, but she could well imagine the sexual union that preceded the conception of babies. This nocturnal fantasy had given her a sensation she had never known before, both pleasurable and disturbing: she lay on her back, panting softly as it subsided, her right hand between her legs. Only then did she realise what she had been doing in her sleep and she blushed for shame, remembering 'Family Doctor' booklets with dark warnings to young people about *dangerous habits* that they should avoid, usually directed at growing boys.

So then another thought came to her: did Harry do the same? Was that what he actually meant when he wrote, 'That's when your closest to me my own dear girl'?

She was certain that this was exactly what he meant. Yet she could hardly tell him in a letter that she had shared the experience. *Guardian angels* were not allowed *habits*, especially that kind.

Before that May was over, another shock was in store for Londoners. Out of the blue came the first Zeppelin raid on their city, causing widespread panic and rumours of destruction and many deaths. In fact, four deaths resulted from the bombs dropped by the airship which damaged a row of houses and some shops, but the fear of further raids at any time had a serious effect on civilians. For the first time in history the English no longer felt protected by the sea, and every night nervous ears listened for unfamiliar noises, the ominous grinding that warned of the approach of the sinister cigar-shaped raiders, long and silvery in the night sky. It added an extra dimension of fear to the dimly lit wards of the Infirmary at night, yet it also drew the nurses and their patients closer in a shared danger.

News of reorganisations at Stepney and Poplar Infirmary filtered through to Booth Street. Army doctors and nurses had complained about inadequate facilities and demanded more staff and better equipment for nursing wounded men. Eager but untrained young women from better-class homes came forward in large numbers to offer their services in the Voluntary Aid Detachment and First Aid Nursing Yeomanry.

'It just ain't fair, here's us sloggin' our guts for all we're worth while them posh girls who've never even seen a man's yer-know-what, they walk straight into nice new done-up wards to look after the boys,' grumbled Nurse Tasker.

But grim accounts of nursing the wounded men began to spread from hospitals taken over by the military: stories of foul-smelling, putrefying wounds that refused to heal, of burned and blinded faces, of limbs torn away. Nights that were seared by howls like animals in pain, of strong men weeping and calling for their mothers. Mabel could hardly bear to listen, and despised herself for not sharing Betty Tasker's eagerness to nurse these men. Every one of them, she knew, would be Harry to her, and the very thought was terrifying.

And then came the news of the Gallipoli landings and a long silence from Harry. No letters, no word came from any quarter as the weeks dragged by. The newspapers cautiously reported 'heavy losses' among the Australian and New Zealand men, but the full extent of the disastrous campaign did not become known until the end of the year. Wives, mothers, sisters and sweethearts waited endlessly, at one with the families of the men serving in France. The popular song of the day was 'Keep the home fires burning', meant to inspire the women left at home to be brave and do their duty by their menfolk.

 . . . though your hearts are yearning,
 Though the lads are far away, they dream of
   home . . .

It was sung everywhere, at concerts and music halls, at all kinds of social gatherings and was whistled in the streets. It began to get on Mabel's nerves.

'At least you haven't had a telegram, Court,' said her friends, but Mabel knew that she was not entitled to a telegram in the event of Harry being killed or missing; it would go to his parents in Falcon Terrace. To find out what they knew, if anything, Mabel attended a Sunday evening meeting at the Clapham Citadel, where she duly sought out the Drovers at the end of the hour of prayer and hymn-singing.

'We've heard nothin' since the landin's began,' said Harry's father bluntly. 'We pray that our boy's life'll be spared, just as other parents pray, but if it's the Lord's will that he – if he be promoted to glory, then we'll have to accept it and so must *you*, Miss Court.'

Mrs Drover looked pale and strained; her manner towards Mabel was cold.

'It was our Harry's dearest wish that ye'd answer the Lord's call straight away, Miss Court, an' it would've made a big difference if yer had. Are yer tellin' us ye've had a change o' heart?'

'I've *got* to get me nursin' trainin' done, Mrs Drover,' pleaded Mabel. 'But that doesn't stop me wanting to know about Har— Captain Drover.'

'Well, we've got no news. Ye're not the only one waitin' an' watchin' out for every post. We're 'is own flesh an' blood, remember.'

'Yes, Mrs Drover, I know, and I *do* have some idea o' what ye're going through,' Mabel answered with pity in her voice. 'Only will yer let me know if there's any news? Anythin' at all?'

Mrs Drover turned away, biting her lip and trying to hide her tears. Her husband answered briefly. 'If we hear anythin', we'll send word to yer at that Infirmary,' he conceded. 'And we'll pray that yer heart be opened to the Lord.'

They resented her intrusion on their desperate anxiety and Mabel could not blame them. She knew she could draw closer to them by joining the Salvation Army straight away, but first she simply had to complete her nursing training.

She found an unexpected source of understanding in Maudie Ling, who occasionally turned up at Booth Street and took Mabel out to a dark little tea shop in Brook Street, where she would listen endlessly to Mabel's fears about Harry. Like Norah, she urged her friend not to lose hope as long as there had been no news and she understood only too well about the coolness of the Drovers.

'Same wiv me, Mabel! Alex wants me to kiss an' make up wiv 'is ma an' pa, seein' as 'e's riskin' 'is neck on these Channel flights aht over the Jerry guns in France an' Belgium – an' yer never know if 'e's comin' back.' She touched Mabel's hand. 'So I'm ready an' willin' to be friends wiv Mr an' Mrs Redfern, I mean I'd do anyfing for Alex, kiss their arses if 'e wanted me to, but –' She paused and rolled up her eyes. 'It ain't that easy.'

'But why, Maudie? What's stoppin' yer?' asked Mabel.

'It's *'er*, she don't fink I'm good enough for 'im, she

finks I'm common, an' well, maybe I am, Mabel. 'E's an officer, y'see, a Flight Lieutenant already, an' 'obnobs wiv a rare bunch o' toffs dahn on Salisbury Plain. But we love each ovver, Mabel, I mean we really do, an' 'e wants to marry me when it's all over.'

'Me sister Alice is courtin' an officer in the Royal Flyin' Corps, Maudie, name o' Westhouse,' Mabel remarked. 'She's a proper little lady these days, ye'd never know her.'

Maud laughed. 'Always was a bit stuck-up, wa'n't she, Alice, though she wasn't no better 'n the rest o' yer – not 'alf as good as you an' Albert. But fancy 'er walkin' aht wiv an officer, eh?'

'Fancy *you*! But Maudie, yer really ought to try to get on with the Redferns. I mean, it's like the Drovers, they're just as worried sick over the boys as we are.'

'I know.' Maudie sighed and beckoned to the waitress. 'The ol' man 'ud be all right, it's just '*er*. Ever since she caught us 'avin' a bit o' – yer know, the ovver – oh, what the 'ell, let's go to the pictures an' see ol' Charlie Chaplin in *The Tramp*, ev'rybody says it's 'is best! C'mon!'

At midsummer Mabel was due for her week's annual holiday and there was only one place to spend it: she had hardly seen her sister Daisy for the past year, only on occasional snatched visits. Aunt Kate renewed her invitation for Mabel to stay at Pinehurst, saying that it would be quieter than with the Somertons, and reading the letter Mabel realised how tired she was, as much from worry as from work. A week in the country was inviting, though she had misgivings about being away from London if there was any news of Harry. She sent a note to his parents giving her aunt's address and told

Norah McLoughlin to save any letter that arrived for her at the Infirmary.

Both aunts and both sisters were there to meet her at Belhampton station, and could hardly conceal their shock at her worn appearance, the dowdy navy-blue jacket and skirt, the frayed silk ribbon wound round her hat. The aunts promptly decided to take her shopping for new clothes and shoes, and Daisy was awkwardly silent as Mabel embraced her.

'Oh, Daisy, dear, yer haven't forgot yer big sister, have yer? I know it's been a long, long time,' apologised poor Mabel, trying to hide her hurt. The truth was that for a split second Daisy had seen her dead mother in the thin, tired-looking woman who stepped down from the train and it had momentarily shaken her. Alice hung back, clearly dismayed at the sight of her elder sister: how on earth could Mabel go about looking such a frump!

'Alice! Oh, how beautiful ye've become!' cried Mabel, reaching out to her above Daisy's dark head. For Alice at eighteen had quite dramatically changed from a pretty girl to a truly lovely young woman. Her figure had filled out into soft curves beneath her simple white dress and every movement showed her young body off to advantage. With a plain straw hat tied over her shining black hair, she gave an impression of unaffected natural beauty. Which was exactly the picture she wanted to present.

'Mum would've been that proud o' yer both!' Mabel told them, putting an arm round the shoulder of each, at which they both stiffened, Alice with embarrassment and Daisy with shyness and something she did not quite understand. She had been counting the days to Mabel's arrival – dear Mabel, the sister she loved more than anybody else in the world – but now there was this horrible *war* and Mabel was part of it in some way:

she brought a touch of its fear and danger with her, just as she brought echoes of a past that Daisy was not encouraged to remember.

'Have yer heard from Harry yet, Mabel?' she asked, and Mabel's face fell.

'No, dear, not yet – but there's bound to be some news soon,' she said with a brightness that did not quite ring true.

That evening Mabel confided in her aunts about her fears for Harry and the total lack of information. Like her friends at the hospital they pointed out that no news was better than – well, a telegram with the worst news, but there was little they could say that was of any real comfort.

'You must have a good rest while you're here, Mabel, and eat plenty of nourishing country fare,' insisted Aunt Kate. 'And we must all put our trust in God and pray that your, er – Captain Drover will be spared.'

The next day was Sunday and Mabel walked to church with Aunt Kate between fields of ripening corn. The Somertons were waiting for them in the porch and, prompted by Aunt Nell, Daisy came forward to greet her sister with a kiss that warmed Mabel's heart. She noticed how young men's eyes strayed towards Alice who appeared oblivious of their glances, though Mabel detected a tell-tale sparkle in her sister's dark eyes and an upward curve to her rosy lips when a tall, well-dressed man in his late twenties approached their party on leaving the church. He would have overlooked Mabel if Aunt Nell had not drawn her forward to be introduced.

'Miss Alice's sister? I'm delighted to meet you, Miss Court,' he said, holding out his hand and giving a polite bow.

'This is Mr Westhouse, Mabel,' prompted Aunt Nell.

'Pleased to meet yer, Mr Westhouse,' replied Mabel, taking his hand in her cotton-gloved fingers and wondering if she should bow in return. Was there just the faintest touch of surprise in his handsome face? If so it was quickly hidden by a smile as he turned to Thomas Somerton, catching Alice's eye before she lowered her face beneath her wide straw hat.

'I shall be going over to Farnborough Common this afternoon, Mr Somerton,' he said, nodding in the direction of a new motor car in the lane. 'I was wondering if Miss Alice might be spared to accompany me to see some flying. The Army biplanes will be taking off and showing what they can do.'

'Will there be any other ladies present?' asked Uncle Thomas, aware of Alice's silently pleading eyes.

'Why certainly, Mr Somerton, Lady Savage and her daughters will be there to see Guy – he's in the Officers' Training Corps camped out on the Common. It should be quite a good show.'

The mere mention of the Savage family of Houghton Hall was enough to secure the Somertons' immediate consent and Mr Westhouse arranged to call for Alice at two o'clock.

'D'ye like him, Aunt Nell?' Mabel asked as they walked up the lane to Pear Tree Cottage for Sunday dinner, Daisy clinging to her arm.

'My dear, Gerald Westhouse is from a very good family on the other side of Belhampton, a junior partner in his father's law firm until he enlisted as an army officer,' answered Mrs Somerton, lowering her voice and giving a significant nod towards Alice's slender back as she walked ahead with Aunt Kate and Uncle Thomas. 'Only now he's in training at the Central Flying School at Upavon.'

'Isn't Alice a bit young to be courtin'? And he's much

older 'n her, and – and way above the Courts,' protested Mabel, frowning.

Aunt Nell raised a questioning eyebrow. 'Above the Courts, perhaps, Mabel, but the Chalcotts can hold their own in Belhampton circles just as well as the Westhouses,' she said with the faintest trace of a rebuke. 'Your poor mother married beneath her, it's true, but there's no reason why Alice should not do better if a gentleman makes her a proposal – and at eighteen she's certainly not too young. Many a girl is married by then.'

Mabel blushed scarlet. 'I'm so sorry, Aunt Nell, I didn't mean – I never thought –'

Nell smiled. 'It's early days yet, Mabel. Let's wait and see how things go.'

They did not have to wait long. When dinner was finished Mr Westhouse arrived to collect Alice, and the talk turned to the new army division, the Royal Flying Corps, and the fascination it held for men like himself and young Sir Guy Savage, just down from Oxford, who wanted to learn to fly the amazing machines that defied the laws of gravity and travelled at unheard-of speeds through the air. Since the outbreak of war there had been enormous strides in their development and manufacture, not to mention their use in warfare, especially on spying missions over the German lines and attacking their gun emplacements.

'Yer remember me friend Maudie Ling, Alice?' Mabel cut in, smiling. 'Well, *she's* walkin' out with an officer in the RFC, name o' Redfern.'

Alice coloured with embarrassment and Gerald stared in surprise.

'Alex Redfern? I know that name – he's making quite a name for himself as a flyer.'

'He's been out bombin' their guns an' all,' added Mabel. 'Maudie's ever so proud of him.'

'Come along, Gerald, we don't want to miss any of the flying,' Alice said quickly, taking his arm before Mabel could say any more about those awful Londoners.

'Would you like me to take you and Daisy over to Farnborough this afternoon, Mabel?' Uncle Thomas offered, but Mabel saw the alarm in Alice's eyes and firmly declined. Maudie had been only too right about her pretty sister: like Ada Hodges she had forgotten her humble origins and now considered herself far above them.

By the time Mabel returned to London, physically rested and carrying a suitcase of well-chosen new clothes and two serviceable pairs of shoes, Alice had become engaged to Gerald Westhouse. There was to be no official announcement until the war was over, but Aunts Kate and Nell were jubilant.

'You and Alice will draw closer together, Mabel, now that you both have young men serving in the defence of their country.' Mrs Somerton smiled, but Mabel was sadly aware that she and Alice now inhabited worlds so far apart that they had almost nothing to say to each other. It had been well and truly impressed upon her that Gerald Westhouse was an officer, while Harry Drover's captaincy in the Salvation Army meant nothing at all to her sister.

Boarding the London train, she hugged Daisy close and kissed her aunts and uncle.

'Goodbye, Alice,' she whispered as the girl held out a cool cheek for her to kiss. 'I'll pray for Gerald every day, same as I pray for my Harry.'

'Thank you, Mabel. Try not to work too hard,' Alice replied with conventional politeness but no real interest in her sister's life at Booth Street. On the contrary, she was revolted by it.

Seated in the compartment after waving goodbye to

them all, Mabel's eyes were blurred with tears, yet she felt a definite sense of relief at returning to her life at the Infirmary. It was where she now most truly belonged.

'There's a letter came for ye, Mabel, darlin', but that ol' crow Mrs Bullock wouldn't part wid it,' reported Norah McLoughlin. 'Ye'd better go an' get it off her.'

'Oh, my God – please let it be –' Mabel gasped as she ran to the housekeeper's room.

The note from the Drovers was brief.

We have word that our son is in hospital in Malta. He has been very ill. They will let us know when he is sent back to England.

Mabel swayed slightly and clasped her hands together in thankfulness. Harry was alive and safe and *coming home*! A great burden was instantly lifted and she went about her duties with an unaccustomed sense of lightness. Norah and all her friends shared in her rejoicing, and even the patients remarked on her improved looks.

'Got a nice young man, Nurse Court?'

'Yes, er – thank yer, yes, I have – an' he's comin' home!'

Another month was to pass before Harry returned, and September brought another and more terrifying Zeppelin raid on London. Bombs were dropped between Euston and Tower Bridge, narrowly missing the Bank of England and starting huge fires in warehouses near to the river. Almost forty people were killed and the effect on morale was devastating. Nobody knew where the next bomb would fall, so nowhere was safe. Ethel Davies was so nervous that she squeezed herself into Mabel's narrow bed, which prevented them both from sleeping.

Mabel was curiously fatalistic about the bombing; all she cared about was seeing Harry again, though she did not receive word of his arrival until a scribbled note was delivered to the Infirmary.

Come and see me as soon as you can Mabel. The sight of you is all I need to work wonders for me. Harry.

He was home and waiting for her.

It was a Thursday and she was off duty from one thirty until five. If she went without the midday dinner she could be on the Battersea bus and at Falcon Terrace by half past two or soon after. She trembled with anticipation, although she knew she was about to meet a sick and possibly changed man. Now into her third year of training, Mabel had learned to hide personal emotions, whether of shock, fear, pity or disgust, under a blank mask when confronted with harrowing sights and scenes. And she was prepared to suppress her true feelings on this first meeting with Harry.

Mrs Drover was not particularly welcoming as she opened the front door and led Mabel into the parlour. There was a murmur of 'Here's that Miss Court to see yer, son', and a gaunt, grey-faced man heaved himself up from a sofa.

Mabel's face at once lit up with a radiant smile: there was no need at all to suppress the upsurge of love that she felt, only to keep her voice calm and her tears under control.

'Don't get up, son,' cautioned his mother, but he was already standing and holding out his arms. Mabel stepped forward and he almost fell against her, enfolding her and saying her name – 'Mabel, Mabel' – followed by an incoherent string of words about missing her, needing her, living for the sight of her – as if he could not believe that she was real and present.

'Harry – oh, Harry, ye're home, ye're here, thank God!'

For this shadow of a man was her sweetheart, her young man, her dearest friend. The arms clasped around her were so thin that a remembered phrase came to her mind, 'a bag of bones'. His skin was cold and papery upon her cheek, and he shivered although there was a fire burning in the grate. He seemed to have physically shrunk and Mabel was aware of a stale, unwholesome smell that reminded her of the wards at Booth Street, the odour of sickness itself. Whatever had he been through?

'Sit down again, Harry, and I'll sit beside yer.' In spite of her efforts to stay calm, her voice shook. His mother stepped forward and the two of them assisted him to settle on the sofa. Mabel lifted his legs – so thin, so light – and his mother arranged the cushions behind his head.

Drawing up a footstool, Mabel sat down beside him, taking his wasted hands in hers and smiling as if nothing was amiss, though her heart ached for him. He gazed at her as if he could not get enough of her, as if she might disappear if he closed his eyes.

'He's been very bad with dysentery out there,' said his mother abruptly, and Mabel nodded.

'But ye're home now, Harry, and that's the main thing,' she said softly.

Doris Drover stood watching them as they held hands in silence. The parlour had been made into a cosy living-room for the returned soldier and every comfort was provided for him. Except for his greatest need and she was here beside him now.

'Kiss me, Mabel.'

She lifted her face and touched his cheek with her lips. She caught the sourness on his breath and, far from wanting to draw back, she put her arms round his neck and kissed him full on the mouth. Mrs Drover still stood watching them in silence.

'Again, kiss me, Mabel, kiss me, oh, kiss me!' he repeated, pulling her down towards him.

She heard the click of the door closing as his mother left the room.

For the next two months Mabel lived in a continuous whirl, forever dashing between her work on the wards and the snatched hours at Falcon Terrace. She learned how dysentery had brought Harry close to death but had also saved his life by removing him from the fighting and on to a hospital ship which took him to the military hospital on Malta.

And it was some time before he was able to talk about the landings or recall the fearful images that returned to his mind – like the eruption of bursting shrapnel that had split open the head of a boy who had trained with him at Aldershot and Cairo.

'One minute he was there beside me, Mabel, an' the next he was on the ground, his skull was broken an' his brains were oozin' through.'

And there was the unconscious man with blood spurting out of his neck – 'a big man 'e was, Mabel, and there wasn't a stretcher to carry 'im on. We just had to leave 'im to bleed to death.'

There were the swarms of flies that buzzed over their rations in the midday heat, the grim barrenness of the landscape, the confusion of changing orders from day to day – and the stench of diarrhoea, the dysentery that caused almost as many casualties as enemy action.

'Them poor New Zealanders an' Aussies were annihilated, Mabel, simply wiped out – they'd gone in first, and yer never met a finer lot o' men – it was worse 'n I ever dreamed of. There's nothin' glorious about it, Mabel, it's just a hideous, stupid, bloody waste o' good men.'

Never before had she heard him swear, it was a measure of how deeply he had been affected. And there was a question she felt she had to ask.

'Did yer have to do what yer so much dreaded, Harry? Did yer have to –?'

'No, Mabel, I didn't. The dysentery got me before I ever had to kill any o' them Turks. I was spared that much, thank God.'

He gradually began to regain weight and strength enough to resemble the man he had been before Gallipoli, but the constant pressure of her life began to tell on Mabel. In addition to an increasing turnover of patients, her afternoons and evenings off were taken up with an almost daily dash to catch buses to and from Battersea, and get back to Booth Street on time.

'I niver see anythin' o' ye, Mabel, ye're always in such a mighty hurry,' wailed Norah McLoughlin. 'Sure an' ye'll do yeself no good at all, missin' yer dinners.'

'I waited a long time for Harry, not knowin' whether he was dead or alive, an' now that he needs me, I must get over to see him all I can,' replied Mabel simply.

The Drovers began to unbend towards the girl who could bring a light to their son's eyes by her presence. As soon as she entered his room he made an effort to rouse himself and take an interest in his surroundings, to hear local news and stories of the continuing work of the Salvation Army in emergencies like the latest Zeppelin raid. Brother officers dropped in to visit and pray with him, but the only face he truly longed to see was Mabel's.

'Yer look tired, Mabel, properly whacked out. Here, lay down on the sofa,' he said as she rushed in one chilly late autumn afternoon. 'Come on, kick yer shoes off and have a rest.'

It was too good an opportunity to resist. Mabel took off her cap and sat down to untie her shoelaces, pulling off the stout black shoes and rubbing her feet. She loosened her belt and undid the top two buttons of her grey uniform dress, then with a thankful sigh stretched herself along the sofa beside him. She curled her body against his, her back towards him, and he locked his arms around her, clasping his hands beneath her breasts. She sighed and closed her eyes in the comfort of his embrace – and in less than a minute was fast asleep. Her head was nestled up beneath his chin and he kissed her hair; soon he too was asleep.

Neither of them heard the arrival of his sister with her two little boys.

Mrs Drover knocked softly on the parlour door. 'Ruby's here, Harry, with Matthew and Mark. Can they come in?'

There was no answer, so she opened the door and stared in disbelief at the young couple lying together on the sofa, Mabel curled in the curve of Harry's body, blissfully asleep in his arms. Her hair was unpinned and her stockinged feet were entwined with his; their discarded shoes lay untidily on the floor, and although they were fully clothed, they looked distinctly dishevelled, and the spectacle did not please Mrs Drover. Harry opened his eyes and put a finger to his lips.

'Ssh, Mother, she's asleep.'

'I can see that, son, and a fine sight for yer sister to see, I must say! Ruby, take those dear children out o' the way,' ordered his mother, tight-lipped. 'Get up at once, Miss Court, what d'ye think ye're doin'?'

Mabel stirred, opened her eyes, sat up and looked in horror at the clock on the mantelpiece.

'Heavens, look at the time, and I'm on at five! Yer should've woke me, Harry, I'll be late!' She sprang to her feet and put on her shoes, lacing them up under Doris Drover's disapproving eye. She grabbed her hat and coat, nodding apologetically to Ruby.

'I'm sorry, Mrs Drover – Mrs Swayne – I'll have to run for the bus, I'm sorry – goodbye, Harry – I'll try to get over tomorrow evenin' –'

And with a quick kiss on his cheek, she picked up her handbag and rushed from the house, doing up her coat buttons as she went. As she turned into Lavender Hill she saw a bus going down towards the Wandsworth Road and ran to catch it, waving her arms to the driver.

But before she reached it the sky tipped over and the ground shifted to meet it: shops, traffic and pedestrians whirled round her head and disappeared into blackness. Silence.

From a long way off came the sound of footsteps and voices getting nearer. Somewhere she heard the word *doctor*, the light of day returned, and she opened her eyes to find herself lying on the pavement and looking up into the face of her old family doctor, full of concern.

'Mabel Court! Mabel, you poor child, you've fainted.'

'Dr Knowles,' she whispered.

'Come, my dear, let me help you up. Here, lean on me, I've got Stephen's car over there – can you walk a few steps? Good girl.'

A woman bystander helped him to get her into the passenger seat, where she drooped and closed her eyes, trying to remember where she was and why she was in a hurry to be somewhere else. She suddenly sat up.

'I must go straight away, Dr Knowles, or I'll be late back on duty!' she said urgently.

'You're coming home with me, Mabel, to rest and recover – no, don't argue, you're not fit to work and I shall make a telephone call to your Matron. Now don't worry, just sit back and take some deep breaths. When did you last eat?'

Chapter Five

The Knowleses' home in Hillier Road seemed deserted as he led her into the consulting-room, familiar to her since childhood.

'I'll see if there's anybody to make us some tea,' he said, disappearing down a passageway and calling to a maid in the kitchen. Mabel looked around at the chairs, desk and couch. Not a sound could be heard except for the old long-case clock ticking in the hall: an air of melancholy had descended on a once busy household.

She heard the doctor speaking into the telephone, giving his name and number. 'Hello, operator. Please connect me with the Booth Street Poor Law Infirmary . . .'

When he joined her he was smiling. 'I knew Sarah Brewer when she was a probationer at the London – an admirable woman, self-educated but strong and determined. She's got a thankless job now, but she's doing it creditably, I'm sure.'

Mabel realised that he was talking about Matron and remembered how he had written a highly commendatory letter when she had applied to train at the Infirmary.

'Oh, what did she say, Dr Knowles?'

'You're to be back at the hostel this evening – I'll drive you over. And she'll see you tomorrow in her office. Don't worry, I've put in a very good word!'

Mabel still felt weak and dizzy, and when a maid

appeared with tea and buttered toast on a tray, she realised how hungry she was.

'I'm glad we've met again, Mabel, even though it's happened this way. I've thought about you very often. Stephen told me that he'd met you, and I get news from my wife's dressmaker, a Mrs Davies – her daughter's a probationer at Booth Street.'

'Oh, yes, Ethel started when I did,' said Mabel Between mouthfuls. 'She told me that Stephen's at the Front –' She checked herself quickly, dreading that there might be bad news.

'Yes, he's at a base hospital in Boulogne, doing what he can for the injured, but oh, it's terrible out there, Mabel –' It was his turn to check himself, thinking of Mabel's own situation. 'I heard via Mrs Davies that your friend Captain Drover is in the Gallipoli campaign,' he continued. 'May I ask –'

Mabel told him of the circumstances of Harry's home-coming and he heaved a sigh of relief. 'Ah, so that explains this rushing to and fro in your off-duty periods when you should be resting. But I'm thankful he's safe, Mabel. I believe as many have died from dysentery as in the fighting. Young Rupert Brooke is dead of it.'

'Is he – was he a friend of Stephen's?'

'No, my dear, he was a brilliant young poet with everything to live for.' The doctor sighed. 'How this war has changed all our lives, Mabel! I should be enjoying a leisurely retirement now, but I'm still in practice because of the shortage of doctors. I've actually learned to drive Stephen's car at sixty-seven!'

Mabel smiled, remembering his visiting rounds in Battersea on a bicycle.

'And – young Mrs Knowles, how is she?'

'Ah, poor Phyllis. When Stephen was posted to France she suffered a miscarriage. It was her second.'

Mabel gave a gasp of sympathy. 'Oh, dear, I'm sorry, Dr Knowles. And is she recovered?'

'Very sad and moping, my dear,' he said heavily. 'And my poor wife simply couldn't cope with her, not being in the best of health herself and worried to death over Stephen, so Phyllis has gone back to live with her parents in Northampton until better times. But enough of our troubles, Mabel, what about *you*? Tell me, do you hear from George?'

Mabel told him of George's scrappy letters and her gratitude to his friend Davy Hoek.

'I'm so glad to hear that, Mabel. I had many a sleepless night over that poor boy and whether we did the right thing in shunting him off across the Atlantic in the way we did.'

'I'm sure we were right, Dr Knowles,' said Mabel with conviction. 'He wanted to go, didn't he? He needed to be *away*, right away from – what had happened.'

Or he might have landed us all in a very awkward situation. The words were unspoken, but Henry Knowles and Mabel Court knew each other's thoughts.

'I sometimes wonder how much these emigrant children are followed up, Mabel. There have been some very questionable reports –'

'Yes, George said that the distribution centre at Calgary was like an army barracks and the man in charge was a brute,' said Mabel with a shudder. 'But the Lord sent Davy to look after George and I'll never be able to thank him enough.'

'Ah, so you share Captain Drover's faith in God's guiding hand in all this, Mabel. I only wish I could. If I thought I could change anything by praying, I'd spend all day on my knees.' He sighed. 'How's that young rapscallion Albert? Still in the navy?'

'In the merchant service and we – I haven't seen him

for a year. But he writes regularly now because he's courtin' a friend o' mine, Norah – a lovely Irish girl. We never know when he's goin' to turn up out o' the blue.' She managed a smile and the doctor thought, *poor children*.

Aloud he said, 'Thank heaven Captain Drover's been sent back to you, my dear.'

Refreshed by the food and relaxed by their talk, Mabel exchanged a specially understanding smile with the old doctor she had known all her life and who shared the secret of her parents' deaths. They had been fellow conspirators, and successful ones at that, for George's sake.

'Tell me, Mabel, what happened to that grandmother of yours, Mrs Court, the midwife who lived at Tooting? Didn't you live with her for a while after the – er –'

Mabel lowered her eyes before replying. 'Yes, I did, Dr Knowles. She left Tooting in 1913 and nobody seems to know where she went. There are strangers livin' at her old home.'

'Forgive me asking, Mabel, but wasn't there some sort of a scandal? Something about a – a society woman dying after a – an abortion? It was in the papers at the time, about two years ago, but then we heard no more.'

Mabel continued to stare at her hands in her lap, remembering the beautiful Lady Cecilia Stanley who had been so kind to her personal maidservant, Maudie Ling. And who had died at the hands of Mabel's grandmother.

'Yes, Dr Knowles, there was a police inquiry and my grandmother disappeared. I was taken in for questioning and spent a night in a police cell at Amen Corner.'

'*Mabel!* Good God, if only I'd known, I'd have come over and demanded your release!'

'Harry Drover came and rescued me,' she said quietly. 'As soon as Maudie Ling told him where I was. And then Sir Percy Stanley dropped the case to protect his wife's name and my grandmother came home. She wanted me to stay with her and help with the maternity cases – I never had anythin' to do with the others, o' course – but I couldn't bear to live in that house any longer and went to start me training at Booth Street. She must've left Tooting soon after, 'cause I never heard any more.'

'She was a very devious woman, Mabel.' He could hardly call her paternal grandmother an evil old hag. 'And didn't she have a sister – a gentle soul who gave piano lessons?'

'Yes, my dear great-aunt Ruth. She went into the Tooting Home and died last year.'

'The Tooting Home for Aged Poor, you mean? But my dear, haven't you heard? It's been turned into a military hospital.'

'Oh, my goodness! But what about the poor old people?'

'It's been a tragedy for them, and thank heaven that your aunt died before it happened. They were all despatched to the Mitcham workhouse and many of them have died there. One poor old chap drowned himself. They have to wear a badge to show they're from the Tooting Home, but they're just treated like the other paupers, so I hear.'

'Oh, Dr Knowles, how *awful* – and what a blessing that Aunt Ruth never lived to see it!'

He was silent for a while, then asked another question. 'Mabel, you mentioned Maud Ling. Wasn't she the poor girl who got sent to the Waifs and Strays home at Dulwich?'

'Yes, with her brother Teddy. But yer needn't feel

sorry for Maudie any more, Dr Knowles,' she added with a smile, ''cause she's gone on the stage! Me an' Albert saw her at the South London Music Hall, and she was really good – and now she's got a part in a pantomime at the Canterbury at Christmas. Trust Maudie to find her feet! *And* she's walkin' out with an officer in the Royal Flyin' Corps!'

'Never!' He laughed and shook his head. 'You know, Mabel, this war has changed the world we knew and things will never be the same again when it's over. But I'll never forget your courage, my dear, the way you brought your brothers and sisters through that ordeal.'

'I shan't forget what you did, either, Dr Knowles,' she said very quietly.

He rose. 'Come on, I'd better take you back to the Infirmary, or Matron Brewer will be on my track!'

Looking back, Mabel always thought it had been well worthwhile to faint in the street and renew her acquaintance with Dr Knowles. But there was still Matron to be faced the next day.

'Well, Nurse Court, what's all this about rushing around Battersea and falling down in the street from hunger? Do you realise that I had to bring a nurse back on duty yesterday evening to take your place on Men's II?'

Matron looked sternly across her desk at the girl who had been a favourite of hers from the day she'd come for her interview and Mabel hung her head.

'Dr Knowles told me that you had eaten nothing since breakfast. Why didn't you have dinner in the dining-room before gallivanting off to Battersea?'

'I'm sorry, Matron. I've got a soldier friend who's been very ill, and –'

'No excuses, nurse. Your duties to the sick patients

here must always come first. And besides, what use will you be to this young soldier if you make yourself ill? Dr Knowles says he's been out in Gallipoli, so thank heaven he's safely home and has his mother to look after him. Tell me something, Nurse Court: how am I supposed to replace nurses who fall sick through not looking after themselves? Whom do I put in their place on the wards?'

Mabel looked up into a pair of searching and not unkindly eyes. Matron herself looked weary, not surprisingly, constantly struggling to maintain standards of care under increasingly difficult conditions. A girl like Nurse Court was an answer to prayer, but now it seemed that she too was chasing after a soldier and so might be lost to the profession.

'Are you planning to marry this young man, Nurse Court?' she asked point-blank.

Mabel was taken aback by the question, but answered clearly and directly. 'Yes, Matron, just as soon as we can afford to. He's a captain in the Salvation Army,' she added with a touch of pride.

'So you've given up the idea of nursing sick children, then?'

'Er – no, Matron. I'm hoping to work in one o' the children's refuges in the Salvation Army when I'm – when we're married.'

'I see. Now listen to me very carefully, Nurse Court. You're one of my best third-years and you'll make an excellent nurse when you're trained, but if you neglect your health and your studies, you'll throw it all away, d'you hear me? If you marry before you complete your training, or fail to pass your final examination, you will not be able to call yourself a nurse.'

'Er – yes, er – no, Matron,' stammered Mabel uncomfortably.

'Right. Now then. Heaven forbid that you'll ever need to support a husband in poor health, but it seems especially important in your case that you gain your certificate, whether you nurse children or take up district or private work. Such options are not open to the unqualified, not any longer. Do I make myself clear, nurse?'

'Yes, Matron.'

'Good. Now I have a suggestion to make to you. I have a problem on the Maternity Ward here. The consultant obstetrician, Mr Poole, delivers a large number of women by Caesarean operation because they have deformed pelves due to rickets and can't deliver normally. These operations are performed in the general theatre and the poor women often have to wait a long time until it's available. Babies have been lost because of the delay. Now Mr Poole wants to do these operations on the maternity ward, in a small theatre next to the delivery room, which he has equipped at his own expense. It sounds an excellent idea, but needless to say the midwives are objecting. They don't see the need to have theatre experience, nor do they see themselves as handmaids to the doctor, and especially not to Mr Poole, it seems. I have often found that midwives tend to be a law unto themselves and I could wish for – er –'

She checked herself from making any personal criticisms to a probationer. 'Now, Nurse Court, *you* did very well in theatre and *you* could assist Mr Poole, as well as gaining your midwifery training, so as to qualify for the Central Midwives' Board in addition to general nursing. You've done some informal midwifery at a mother and baby home before you came here, and I believe you assisted your grandmother with her district practice, so now's your opportunity to become registered. It would be extremely useful to you. What have you to say?'

'It sounds – er, all right, Matron. Thank yer,' said Mabel, pleased at the thought of working with mothers and babies again.

'Good. You'll start on maternity next week, then. Very well, you may return to your ward.'

'Thank yer, Matron. I – I'm very grateful.' Mabel smiled as she rose and left the office, for she felt she could now see her way more clearly. Once qualified as a nurse and midwife in the summer of 1916 – less than a year to go – she would always be able to support her husband – and children when they came along – if Harry's health should fail and prevent him from working. She would be an independent working woman in her own right, and when this horrible war was over she and Harry could at last begin their life together in the Salvation Army!

Poor girl, thought Sarah Brewer with a sigh. If her captain gets sent back to the fighting, he may never return and she'll need her nursing skills to make a decent living. In which case she won't be alone: there were going to be a great many lonely spinsters when this war was over.

Chapter Six

'Oh, Norah, what a dump, what a *hole*! I'll never be able to stand it!'

Mabel was close to tears when she told her friend of the shock she had received. Any eagerness she had felt at the prospect of working with mothers and babies again had been dispelled in the first hour on the maternity ward at Booth Street.

'That *horrible* woman Mrs Higgs, she's been there for donkey's years, back when it was a workhouse – and as far as *that* ward's concerned, I reckon nothin's changed. Matron ought to get rid of her!'

Norah listened in sympathy, knowing that Mabel had previous experience of maternity work and would not criticise without good reason.

'At least the Rescue home was clean and me grandmother treated her mothers like human bein's, Norah. These poor women are so downtrodden and ill-lookin', some've got no teeth, one's nearly blind and they all look as if they've never had a square meal in their lives – an' that awful Higgs treats 'em like scum, shouts at 'em, tells 'em to stop makin' that stupid noise when they're cryin' out in pain – she's so *cruel*! And the smell o' the place, Norah, I can't describe it, it's partly that horrid green soap they use for enemas, an' a sort o' sickly, sour pong as if they'd never had a wash. I can even smell it on my uniform – ugh!'

Mabel soon came to understand that the kind of women who were delivered in a Poor Law infirmary were either homeless or came from the sort of homes that doctors and midwives did not care to visit. The majority of them were below average intelligence and had been unlawfully used, sometimes by men who were close relatives: it was all horrifying to Mabel.

The maternity ward had ten iron beds with horsehair mattresses, five down each side of its dark-brown walls. In the middle stood a coal-fed stove with a pipe going up through the ceiling and next to the main ward was a smaller one reserved for infectious cases, mothers with puerperal fever, babies with sticky eyes and diarrhoea, patients infested with fleas, head-lice or scabies. There was a kitchen with a flagstoned floor and a kind of office-cum-sitting-room where Mrs Higgs glowered over her knitting with a kettle always on the boil. Mabel had yet to understand Matron's problem with the likes of Higgs: the difficulty of dislodging unsatisfactory staff from well-entrenched positions held for as long as anybody could remember.

'So is this Mrs Higgs a Sister?' asked Nurse McLoughlin.

'They're not called Sister or nurse on that ward, they're all Mrs Somebody or other, an' the only half decent one's a Mrs Hayes who's havin' a week's trainin' on general theatre, so as to be able to assist Mr Poole with these Caesars. Otherwise there's only me, which means I can't ever get away to visit Harry –'

Mabel broke off, unwilling to tell her friend about the embarrassing scene with Mrs Drover and Mrs Swayne. She had mentioned the faint on Lavender Hill and being rescued by Dr Knowles, but not what had preceded it.

'So I'm stuck here, Norah, an' can't ever get away. Even when I get time off I have to stay around to be on call for Caesars. Whatever can I *do*?'

Mabel's transfer to Maternity coincided with a cold

97

wind of disapproval directed against her from the Drovers, for of course they blamed her rather than the son they had so nearly lost. She was no longer welcome at Falcon Terrace, even if she could have got away, but the effects of this were not all bad. Harry was roused to bestir himself, to get dressed and get out of the house in spite of his mother's protests that he would catch his death of cold. Within two days of Mabel's hasty departure he had got on a bus and turned up at Booth Street, to Mabel's joyful surprise.

But where could they go to talk and be together? The nurses' hostel was absolutely out of bounds to all males of any age and the Infirmary had no private waiting-rooms; the days were growing shorter and chillier, and soon there would be fogs which could be lethal to a convalescent, however well wrapped up against the cold. With Mabel on round-the-clock 'Caesar-call', there seemed to be nowhere for them to be together.

Love, it has been said, will find a way. The Infirmary was constructed around a small square courtyard from which all its buildings could be accessed: the men's and women's wards, the maternity ward, the nurses' hostel, the kichens and storerooms – and the boiler-room with its adjoining coalshed. A covered walkway ran round two sides of the square, meeting in the corner where the boiler-room stood, forming a sheltered angle. There were a couple of wooden bench seats where staff could sit out in warm weather and Mabel found that one of these just fitted in the doorway of the boiler-room. It gave them a reasonably comfortable seat, warmed from behind by the boiler and protected from the weather. With a blanket brought from Mabel's bed to tuck around Harry's legs, and with her hooded cloak over her shoulders, they could be reasonably comfortable in this makeshift nook. It was not private:

they could be seen by anybody crossing the courtyard, so Mabel could be called at any time for a Caesar. There was no question of cuddling close, but they could hold hands under the blanket and talk in low voices without being overheard.

The midwives' comments were predictable.

'It's a scandal, that's what it is, a disgrace, the way that hussy sits there of an afternoon, canoodlin' with 'er fancy man!' declared Mrs Higgs, even redder in the face than usual.

'I blame Matron for allowin' it,' sniffed an untrained assistant who kept her job by always agreeing with Mrs Higgs.

'Huh! That one's always bin able to twist Matron round 'er little finger, same as she gets round that Poole man – all these Caesars, it ain't natural, an' I don't 'old with it. If it ain't meant to be born the proper way, it shouldn't be interfered with, that's what I say.'

Mabel was happily oblivious to this combination of ignorance and spite; and no longer having to rush between Lambeth and Battersea and miss meals, she found the arrangement more relaxing in some ways than the Drovers' front parlour. She now heard more about Harry's experiences of Gallipoli.

And he told her a very strange story of something that happened while he was in Malta.

'I've never said a word o' this to anybody else, Mabel, not me parents or brother officers – but I want to tell *you*, my love, because it makes a difference to the way I look at life now.' He paused, turning something over in his mind. 'Though yer may find it hard to believe.'

'Go on, Harry, yer know yer can tell me anythin', an' o' course I'll always believe yer.'

'It was in that hospital on Malta. They'd been standin' round me bed, and I heard one o' the doctors say there was nothin' more to be done and he thought I'd be gone by mornin'.'

'*Harry!*' Mabel clutched at his hand beneath the concealing blanket.

'They walked away, an' soon after that I felt meself floatin' up in the air, Mabel, out o' me body – I could see it lyin' there on the bed, as white an' still as wax, along o' the other men in their beds. Some o' them were talkin', but I looked – dead.'

'Oh, Harry, did yer *really*? Are yer *sure*?' Mabel's first thought was that this must have been a dream.

'And then I was outside an' up in the night sky, the stars were all around me and I was goin' up an' up – it was like a tunnel, and I was travellin' at a tremendous rate, up an' up an' up.'

'Weren't yer scared, Harry?' Mabel's eyes were wide.

'No, that was just it, I wasn't in the least bit afraid, I was as light as air, an' there was no pain. I felt – oh, it's hard to say, Mabel, but I know I was happy. An' *peaceful*. I knew that everythin' was all right, there was nothin' to worry about. An' then, I don't know how long it was, I saw that there was a light at the end o' the tunnel, an' it was gettin' nearer an' nearer until I found meself right up close to it an' lookin' up into a – a – oh, it was light an' bright an' shinin' like the sun, I can't put it into words, Mabel, it was like nothin' in this world.' His features softened into a dreamy smile of recollection, while Mabel had an extraordinary sensation of losing him: of not being able to follow where he led.

'What was it like, Harry? Try to tell me, *please!*'

'There was happiness an' peace, Mabel, and above all there was love. The air was full o' love, and I saw a man standin' there – and his face, Mabel, it was so kind an' lovin', and I knew him from somewhere long, long ago, more familiar than any face on earth. I just wanted to gaze an' gaze on him. An' 'e called me Harry an' asked if I knew his name.'

'D'ye mean – are yer sayin' that this was the Lord, Harry?' asked Mabel in a low, awestruck voice, wanting to know but aware that her words were clumsy and inappropriate for such a solemn confidence.

'I think he was, Mabel – he was like the dearest an' closest o' friends, and so *kind*. He smiled as if he understood everythin' I was feelin', and then he said, "Well, Harry, here's somebody yer know!" An' there was me dear old grandfather Drover, standin' there as large as life, just as when he used to take me to meetin's as a boy – an' play football an' fly a kite up on the heath. I saw him an' heard him, but I couldn't get really close to him – he was inside an' I was outside.'

Harry's voice faded to silence and he paused again. Mabel waited, not speaking, hardly daring to breathe. She tightened her hold on his hand.

'He said I couldn't stay there, Mabel, not yet. He said I had to go back, there was work for me to do, duties to be done. It wasn't time, he said, and I had to go back.'

Harry swallowed and his voice shook as he said, 'And so we had to say goodbye.'

There was a very long pause, till at last Mabel broke the silence. 'So then – yer came back.'

'Yes, Mabel, it was a fallin' back, fallin' down an' down. I saw the stars again, whirlin' in the night sky, an' I think I saw the earth, a great big ball hangin' in space, beautiful it was, gettin' nearer an' nearer – and then I fell and landed in that bed in that ward, same as I'd left it, back in the pain an' the weakness. An' I cried. I remember I cried, Mabel.'

'Yer *cried*, Harry? 'Cause ye'd come back?'

'Yes, my love, 'cause I'd come back.' He spoke very softly, almost inaudibly.

'But didn't yer *want* to come back? Didn't yer want to live an' see me again? An' yer parents an' Ruby an' all yer friends in the Salvation Army?' Mabel almost pleaded, bewildered both by the strange story and his absolute belief in it.

'It's very hard for me to say, Mabel. When I first realised I'd come back, o' course I thought o' you, an' that I'd see yer again, an' I was glad about that, 'course I was. Only it changed me, Mabel, and I shan't be afraid again. Not now that I've seen – and know.'

In the fading light of that November afternoon, Mabel had no reply. For him it had been no dream but reality – a true vision, as far as he could describe it. Mabel sensed that this had been something beyond human experience, and what he had shared with her was only a faint echo, a fragment of what he had seen and heard.

She glanced up into his face, which had become very pale.

'Come on, Harry, ye're tired, yer must get yerself home to rest,' she said, rising quickly. 'Do yer buttons right up to the top. Got yer scarf?'

She took his arm, and they walked out of the yard and down a passage that led to the battered wooden doors where ambulances drew up in Booth Street and stretcher cases were carried in. Her down-to-earth fussing seemed to restore their relationship to normality and she had an odd reluctance to mention the subject again, knowing it to be beyond her understanding.

Matron Brewer knew, of course, about the young couple's meetings on the seat by the boiler-room. She knew of the complaints, the gossip about Mabel's behaviour and the criticism of herself for tolerating it. But Captain Drover was an officer in the Salvation Army and a survivor of Gallipoli, and as she pointed out to a disapproving assistant matron, Nurse Court was far too valuable a member of staff to risk losing over a few innocent and very public meetings. Why, Mr Poole would go mad!

'Come on, come on, girl, I haven't got all day,' barked Poole as Mabel fished the steel instruments out of the bubbling steriliser and laid them on the trolley. He was a stocky, balding man who did not waste words, and as a surgeon was neat and quick at his work. Where deficiency diseases like rickets had bowed the mothers' legs and flattened their pelves, he had no choice but to deliver by Caesarean, and having the small maternity theatre made this much more convenient. After his skirmishes with Mrs Higgs and her obstructive attitude, this probationer Court was a godsend, and he nodded in silent approval as she handed him the knife, the clamps, the dissectors and retractors in correct sequence, mopping out the pelvic cavity with a gauze swab while he pushed his gloved hands into the opened womb, grasping the baby and hauling it up and out into the air. She watched its tiny face contort, its limbs jerk: she waited for its chest to expand, drawing in air, to be exhaled as a gasp – a grunt – a cry. Her eyes closed in relief and opened at once: Poole severed the cord and handed her the new human creature, and she saw that it was a boy: another child born into poverty.

'Good! This is going to halve the mortality rate for Booth Street,' said Poole in satisfaction and Nurse Court knew better than to point out that the child would very likely die in his first year, which would not affect the Infirmary's statistics. She only spoke to the surgeon when spoken to and had not made up her mind about him. He was kind enough to the mothers in his way, though he could be sharply impatient at their slowness to answer his questions, which annoyed Mabel, though she later realised that it was his way of hiding his pity for them, not being a sentimental man. Any communication between him and Mrs Higgs was carried on in an atmosphere of mutual contempt, not to say loathing, and he had little time for the rest of the midwives. But this one was different and he gradually unbent to her.

'So, Court, I hear you're a Salvationist, then!' he remarked one day while stitching up the layers of muscle and skin after another Caesar.

'I hope to be a Salvation Army wife, sir,' she answered, handing him a curved needle threaded with catgut.

'Ah, yes, your young man. I believe he's survived Gallipoli, is that right?'

'Yes, he's home again, sir.'

'Good! Are they sending him back to the Front when he's fit enough?'

She winced. 'I hope not, sir. I'm hoping that the war'll be over first.'

'H'm.' He shook his head gloomily. 'Y'know, you ought to go in for midwifery, my girl, and get work with a private practice such as I have. That's where the money is.'

Mabel looked up in blank astonishment. '*You*, Mr Poole? But yer work's here, ye're the only consultant –'

'My dear girl, how do you think I turned this glorified cupboard into a maternity theatre? How did I purchase the table and all the equipment, and pay this anaesthetist to come in?' He nodded towards the tired-looking doctor who sat holding a gauze Schimmel-Busch mask over the patient's nose and mouth. 'My private patients paid for all this, Court, and in return they get the benefit of my expertise, the experience I've gained by practising on these poor wretches here. This is where we learn our trade, Court!'

Mabel stared in disbelief. 'But that's not right!' she

exclaimed, holding a needle-holder in mid-air and forgetting to say 'sir'.

He gave a short laugh. 'Isn't it, young woman? Don't I do *anything* for the women who come in here to be delivered? Would they be better off if I stayed away and left them to the tender mercies of the charming Mrs Higgs and company?' He glanced towards the new baby, crying in its cot close by. 'I'll tell you what, Court, that child would never have got through the mother's pelvis. At least it's now got a chance – it's alive!'

To which there seemed to be no reply, and Nurse Court was left to ponder over the moral compromises contained in Mr Poole's argument.

To Mabel's relief Mrs Hayes returned to maternity after her theatre course, so now there were two trained theatre nurses to stand by for Caesar-call; they usually took it in turns, so Mabel was no longer confined to the building, though the afternoon meetings beside the boiler-room had to finish. December came in with bitter winds and lashing rain, and in any case Captain Drover had resumed some of his Salvation Army duties, particularly as bandsman; his trombome was taken out of its case and polished, and Mabel attended the indoor meetings when she could. Neither of them mentioned the possibility of his return to active service, though the thought was never far from their minds, like Norah's anxiety which showed in her shadowed blue eyes. There had been no word from Albert for over two months.

Mabel's cautious overtures of friendship towards Doris Drover met with a polite but cool response and there were no invitations to Falcon Terrace. It was clear that the Drovers thought her an undesirable influence on their son and this was upsetting, though before the year was out she found an unexpected ally.

Quietly getting up to leave before the end of a Citadel meeting, she felt a hand lightly laid upon her arm, and turning round she looked into the flushed face of Mrs Swayne, embarrassed but determined to speak.

'I must have a word with yer, Miss Court. Excuse me, but I've got to thank yer for what ye've done for me brother – the difference in him since he's been back.'

Harry's elder sister was a capable woman who held herself erect and had a strong, sensible face; Mabel remembered Harry saying that she had worked with prostitutes and was 'used to dealing with all sorts'. She hardly knew how to reply, and Mrs Swayne continued speaking.

'I'm sorry I haven't said anythin' before, Miss Court, but there hasn't been much chance o' seein' yer. If we're going to be sisters one day, and I hope we will, then we ought to be friends as well. That's what I think, anyway,' she ended with a tentative smile.

Mabel's heart seemed to melt with gratefulness. 'Oh, Mrs Swayne –'

'Call me Ruby.'

'An' call me Mabel! – there's nothin' I'd like more than for us to – to get to know each other, Ruby. An' Matthew an' Mark are such lovely little boys.'

'Then yer must come and visit us at number 3 Deacon's Walk, off the Kennington Road. Come over to tea one afternoon, get Harry to bring yer – ah, here he is!' She smiled up at her brother who had just joined them, having left his place in the band to escort Mabel back to Booth Street.

'That'd be really nice, Ruby,' said Mabel hastily. 'I must go now, 'cause I've got to be in by ten, but I'd love to come. Goodnight, Ruby, an' thank yer.'

Harry was pleased at this gesture from his sister, but he looked grave, and Mabel soon found out why as they walked arm-in-arm along the unlit streets.

'I'd like yer to be friends, Mabel, and poor Ruby's goin' to need all the friends she can get if Herbert's called up.'

'But he can't be, he's a married man with children!'

'He could still be called, Mabel, in the New Year. There's goin' to be a change in the regulations an' some married men'll have to go.'

'But can he be *forced* to fight at the Front?' asked Mabel, frowning.

'That's just it, Mabel, he says he won't fight, he won't take the life of a brother man in any circumstances. That means he'll be hauled up before a tribunal and asked to give his reasons. And if he still won't agree, he could be sent to prison.'

'*Harry!* Whatever will Ruby do – and the boys?'

'The Salvation Army'll look after their needs as far as possible, but it wouldn't be easy to face the mockers. We can only pray that it'll soon be over.'

But from the set of his mouth she could see that he had no early expectations of an end to the conflict that was tearing Europe apart. She took a deep breath: it had to be said.

'An' you, Harry – will *you* have to go back in the New Year as well?'

'It looks like it, my love.'

'Oh, no, Harry, *no*!' she cried out in anguish, unable to contain herself. 'Please, please, Harry, go as a stretcher-bearer this time, an ambulance driver, anythin' – only not to the trenches!'

Her cry echoed down the near-deserted street and he put his arms round her as they stood on the pavement.

'Dearest Mabel, I can't even drive. We have to leave

107

it in the Lord's hands. Hush, dear, hush, let's wait to see what happens. No sense in jumpin' the gun, is there?'

The figure of speech had an unintended sinister ring. And all of a sudden she thought of Ada Hodges and her indispensable Arthur . . . just suppose *he* were called up?

Maud Ling's eyes were sparkling when she turned up at the nurses' hostel on the Thursday before Christmas.

'What a lark, Mabel, guess what's come up! Y'know we got *Cinderella* on at the ol' Canterbury Featre after Chris'muss – well, the Principal Boy's gorn orf wiv summat in 'er stomach – an' I got a fair idea o' what it is, an' all, poor fing – so guess 'oo's takin' over!'

'Yer don't mean *you*, Maudie?' asked Mabel, smiling at her friend's excitement.

'Yeah, *me* – aht o' the chorus an' into the lead – Prince Charmin' in person! Startin' on the twenty-sevenf, seein' as Boxin' Day's a Sunday. Oh, wait till my Alex 'ears this, 'e'll be that prahd o' me! 'Ere, you an' 'Arry'll 'ave to come an' see me doin' me stuff, bring little Norah wiv yer – oh, Mabel, talk abaht bad luck for one an' good luck for anuvver!'

They hugged each other, and as always Maudie's exuberance was a tonic at a time of difficulty on the ward and anxiety about Harry and Albert.

'Are yer gettin' on any better with Alex's mother, Maudie?' she asked, thinking of her own situation with the Drovers.

Maudie's face fell briefly. 'Nah, the Redferns don't like 'im spendin' 'alf 'is leave wiv me. It's 'ard on 'em, I can see that, but if they'd only meet me again, they could see 'im all they liked. Cuttin' orf their nose to spite their face, that's what they're doin'.' She gave a little sigh.

Mabel turned down the corners of her mouth in sympathy, but did not think she should encourage her friend to hope for a change of heart from the Redferns. What privately worried her more was the possibility of young Alex eventually tiring of Maud. She had caused a rift between him and his family – and perhaps more significantly, she might show him up before his friends among the officers and their young ladies. She remembered Alice's expression when she had mentioned Maud and Alex to young Mr Westhouse – how her sister's lip had curled in surprise and annoyance when Gerald had praised Alex's achievements as a flyer. Could Maud ever hope to be one of their circle? It was all very well during these exciting, dangerous times, but would Alex still feel the same when the adventure of war was over and life returned to normal? Mabel was not happy about her friend's romance.

Chapter Seven

Christmas Day dawned over a grey city of uncertain hope and Matron Brewer shivered as she dressed, contemplating the long day ahead, the overcrowded wards and disgruntled sisters, the nurses complaining of chilblains and chapped hands. Yesterday there had been three deaths in the Infirmary and today could bring another three or more.

She had fought the Board for extra beef and pork to be supplied for the Christmas dinners which would be taken on the wards by everyone, staff and patients alike; and she had personally supervised the mixing of the puddings which today would be boiled and served with custard. She would be in and out of the kitchen to see that it was done properly – and to check that no strong drink was being passed around. In the afternoon she would visit all the wards and make a point of speaking to everybody. There would be no shifts: all staff were to report on duty from 7.30 a.m. until 8.30 p.m., so that the work would be evenly shared and the nurses would have time to visit other wards during the afternoon, handing round the sweets and biscuits that she had been saving in a locked cupboard. She had little gifts for the children in the women's wards, and baby clothes, not new but clean and ready to wear, for the babies in maternity. Nurse Court could be relied upon to make a fuss of them and of any older children who came to visit their mothers, no matter how much that Higgs woman might grumble. Sarah Brewer smiled to herself: she had told Nurse Court that her soldier friend could visit on the men's wards during the afternoon, provided that he wore his Salvation Army uniform, to speak a word of comfort to patients as seemed appropriate. The poor young man still looked pale and wan, she thought, three months after his return from the Dardanelles.

Dressed in full uniform with starched white collar and cuffs in place, her iron-grey hair pinned up and crowned with a stiff white cap edged with a narrow frill, she was ready to face whatever this Christmas Day might send . . .

Harry Drover accompanied his parents, sister, brother-in-law and nephews to the Clapham Citadel for morning praise and worship, and afterwards took his place in the band at an open-air meeting in Battersea Park. They played and sang carols for whoever cared to listen, but the atmosphere was far from festive and there were few to brave the bitter east wind which knifed though Harry's greatcoat. His feet felt like two blocks of ice.

Christmas dinner at 8 Falcon Terrace was shared by the Swaynes, after which Mrs Drover suggested that they should sit round the fire and 'Grandad' would read *A Christmas Carol* aloud to them all. The boys' faces brightened, but Harry stood up and said he had to go out.

'I'm sorry, Mother, but I'm due to call in at Booth Street this afternoon for an hour or two,' he explained, putting on his greatcoat again.

'Oh, no, son, not on Christmas Day, surely!' protested Mrs Drover.

'Father'll be at the Blackfriars' Shelter tonight, Christmas or not, Mother – the need's just as great, perhaps greater,' he said gently. 'The Matron's asked me to take the Lord's word to patients on the men's wards, so pray that one or two hearts'll be touched.'

Doris Drover pursed her lips; in fact, she pressed them together hard to stop herself saying that she knew perfectly well why he was going to that Infirmary; but she had no wish to fall out with her boy.

Ruby Swayne caught the tension in the air, and when he had left for Lambeth she pointed out that he would only be visiting men's wards and Mabel Court worked on maternity.

'He certainly won't be allowed in *there*,' she said with a smile, but her mother sniffed. That Court girl had ways and means, and Mrs Drover had heard about the boiler-room at Booth Street.

Alex Redfern had sat through Divine Worship at fashionable St Mark's Church with his parents, his two sisters and brother James, sister-in-law Lilian and their lively toddler Jamie whose constant fidgeting had annoyed him less than the fond mamma's ineffectual shushing. Back at Elmgrove, the Redferns' handsome villa in Hamilton Terrace, he was required to feast on roast goose with sage and onion stuffing, followed by rich plum pudding with brandy sauce, served by two maids who swept in and out of the dining-room with steaming silver dishes and tureens. Well-polished mahogany surfaces reflected the gleam of the candlelit tableware and Mrs Redfern's centrepiece of Christmas roses and holly, but Alex was in the wrong mood. His giggling sister-in-law got on his nerves, and all he longed for was the rambling lodging house in South Lambeth Road where on the second floor Miss Maud Ling entertained her raffish theatrical friends and always kept a place for him. Oh, Maudie, Maudie! He had never realised how necessary she would become to him, and all because of this war.

Alexander at twenty-four was the younger and cleverer of the Redfern brothers, the darling of his mother who had always spoiled him, though his father had begun to look for some return on his expensive public school education – but not any more. Not now that Alex had become a hero. He had never been booky and an early interest in motoring took him into Vickers' prestigious engineering works; the rapidly expanding car industry was migrating out of London into the suburbs in search of more space, and with the new craze for flying, many of the big names were abandoning cars for aero-engines. When enlistment fever swept the country in 1914 Alex bypassed Sandhurst and chose the new flying corps of the army, and now he had passed out as a flyer and could pilot a de Havilland biplane.

In an open cockpit, cruising above the earth in blue summer skies, into vaporous clouds and out again into the sunshine, he thought it the most exhilarating sensation he had ever known. For centuries man had dreamed of flying like a bird and here he was, Alex Redfern, one of the early chosen few to fulfil that dream. And if by daylight it was exciting, by moonlight it had an unbelievable magic, and he thanked whatever deity there might be that he was young and living at a time such as this.

And when the glorious new invention was put to far more daring uses, and the danger increased tenfold, Redfern boldly rose to the challenge. Taking off into a night sky full of cloud, his fur-lined leather helmet and goggles his only protection against buffeting winds and rain, he patrolled the south coast on home defence against the German Zeppelins. Then came the posting to France when he crossed the grey Channel to a makeshift base at Le Cateau, from where his squadron went out on sorties over enemy lines, above the infantry slogging it out amidst constant shelling. This was like nothing he had ever imagined. Danger too could be intoxicating, but it also brought fear, and he discovered that there was only one remedy for it.

At the Central Flying School at Upavon Redfern had made friends with other young men from similarly privileged backgrounds, and there had been no shortage of pretty girls to escort to parties, tennis clubs, picnics and drives through the green Wiltshire and Hampshire countryside. He had walked with a girl hanging on to his arm along sandy tracks beside tall, fragrant pines; there had been kisses under the stars and his blood had coursed faster, though so far there had been no girl he had desired above the rest.

Until he'd begun to feel fear. That was when he'd needed to know that Maud Ling was waiting for him, to hold him in her arms and envelop him in her warm softness. He could talk to her and not pretend: he could even tell her about the fear, the sudden shiver of dread when the de Havilland took off into the empty sky. Maud had seen life: he didn't have to try to explain things to this child of the streets who had begged with her baby brother in her arms on cold winter nights.

'Chris'muss was when me muvver reckoned it was 'er turn to get as drunk as the ol' man. Teddy an' me was that farnished – an' I got nabbed for pinchin' from some toff's kitchen up Belgravy way, an' we was sent to the Waifs an' Strays 'ome at Dulwich. 'E's still there, young Teddy, cheeky little blighter – Gawd knows what I'm goin' to do wiv 'im when 'e comes aht!'

Yes, Alex could be himself with his darling, common little Maudie. He could let himself go.

Their relationship had begun light-heartedly enough. Mrs Redfern had taken on the cheeky cockney house-maid who had no references other than that her last

114

job had been as a kitchen assistant in a women's shelter run by the Salvation Army, and that she had spent several years of her childhood in the Dulwich home. Girls were leaving domestic service in droves to work in the munitions factories now springing up everywhere to keep the army and navy supplied with ammunition, and one could not afford to look too closely at the backgrounds of employees these days. However, the new maid quickly set about sweeping, dusting, polishing and scrubbing, carrying hot-water jugs up and down stairs, and emptying chamber-pots with unfailing good humour. Then one day Mrs Redfern had entered Alex's room and found him lying on the bed with the maidservant: she was minus her cap and apron, her buttons were undone, her shoes were off and her black skirt was up above her knees. She had stared back at Mrs Redfern's shocked face, and made a sound halfway between a gasp of horror and a stifled burst of laughter. It had meant instant dismissal for Ling, and an embarrassing interview between Alex and his father.

'It was my fault entirely, Pa. I'd been talking to her, teasing her while she put out the clean linen, and one thing led to another. She tried to ignore my nonsense, but then I started tickling her, so of course she had to laugh, couldn't stop herself. *She* didn't behave improperly in any way, it was just a bit of foolery on my part and I deeply regret it.'

It was no good. Maud had to pack her small case and leave Elmgrove forthwith. Alex had managed to slip her a note asking her to meet him at a coffee house on Edgware Road, where he had given her money to find lodgings and promised to keep in touch with her, and not only from a sense of obligation: it was the beginning of a real commitment.

But she had surprised him by her independence and initiative: she quickly set out to find a foothold in the world of entertainment which had always fascinated her. From the chorus line in whatever ramshackle vaudeville show would take her on, she progressed to solo spots where her personality and special brand of cockney humour appealed to wider audiences in the better-known music halls and variety theatres. And now she was a star in a Christmas pantomime – and Alex Redfern yearned for the sight and the touch of her, far more than for any of the girls his parents would have welcomed as a daughter-in-law.

Christmas dinner over, Mr Redfern brought out the port and cigars, inviting James and Alex to share an hour of men's talk about the progress of the war while the women sat round the fire in the drawing-room, cooing over little Jamie. And somewhere between dining- and drawing-room Alex made his escape with a quick apology to his father, saying he had a hospital visit to make to a wounded friend of a friend and wasn't sure how long it would take. By the time Mrs Redfern gave a wail of dismay he was out of Hamilton Terrace and literally running down the Edgware Road, heading for Lambeth.

Christmas Day was going fairly well. On the maternity ward Mr Poole made an informal afternoon visit accompanied by his wife, two rather gawky daughters and another lady who seemed very interested in everything she saw. The girls self-consciously followed their father round the ward as he nodded to the mothers and asked them how they did, ignoring the furious looks from Mrs Higgs.

'Bad enough havin' all the visitors bargin' in without *'im* bringin' 'is women as well,' she grumbled, nettled at the sight of him talking to that probationer Court and Mrs Hayes.

'My wife says you've improved me, Court! She says I'm in a better temper when I get back from Booth Street these days,' he told Mabel. 'And *this* lady is Mrs Spearmann who wanted to come and see the mothers and babies, so perhaps you could show her the nursery and our little broom cupboard.' This was his name for the operating theatre. 'Mrs Spearmann is one of my *private* patients who helped to equip it,' he added with a meaning look, amused that the lady was clearly shocked at everything she saw.

'Good heavens, what poor, unfortunate women you have here, Mr Poole!' she said. 'So sickly looking – and such dreadfully bad teeth! When I think of my own dear children, and the comforts I take for granted, I feel quite ashamed. What will happen to the poor babies of these – er – patients?'

'Half of them will probably die in their first year, ma'am, and half of the rest will end up in somewhere like the Midway Babies' Home, I dare say. They'll get the bare necessities there, but precious little care and attention.'

'Merciful heaven, how dreadful to think of it, in this day and age!' exclaimed the lady who was about twenty-six or -seven, on the plump side and well-dressed. 'Would I be able to visit this, er, Midway Home?'

'I don't see why not, ma'am, it's run by the same local government board as this Infirmary.' He turned back to Mabel. 'You ought to go and see the Midway, too, Court, seeing that you're so keen on nursing children with disadvantages.'

Mrs Spearmann heard this, as he had intended her to. 'Very well,' she said, 'I'll arrange for your Nurse

117

Court to accompany me. Would you like that?' she asked Mabel who nodded politely.

'Thank yer, Mrs Spearmann.' She remembered an occasion back in the warmer weather, seeing a dozen or so very young children all dressed alike, being pushed out in a handcart by a couple of youngish women who said they were from the Midway. And where had she heard the name Spearmann mentioned before?

At this point Matron arrived at maternity on her afternoon Christmas round of the Infirmary. Having spoken to the Poole ladies and Mrs Spearmann, she beckoned discreetly to Mabel.

'I believe you're wanted on Men's I, Nurse Court, if you can leave your duties here for half an hour. A young Salvation Army officer has arrived to visit the patients, and he'll need somebody to introduce him and then show him up to Men's II in due course.'

Her eyes twinkled and Mabel could have kissed her. 'Oh, thank yer, Matron, I'll get over there straightaway – oh, thank yer!'

Mrs Higgs glowered afresh at this display of favouritism and muttered that it was a good job that *some* folks were on hand to look after the patients. Mrs Hayes assured Mabel that she would take over her duties for the next half-hour and Mabel joyfully slipped away, hurrying along the main corridor. Men's I was filling with visitors and Harry was waiting at the door.

'Mabel, dearest!'

'Ssh, I'm Nurse Court and you're Captain Drover!' she warned him, though her radiant smile left him in no doubt of his welcome. 'Matron's sent me over to introduce yer, and then show yer up to Men's II, that's surgical. Come on, let's find Sister.'

The Ward Sister, a down-to-earth Londoner, told

Harry that he might go round the ward from bed to bed, exchanging a word with each patient, especially those who had no visitors.

'Have yer got any music with yer?' she asked.

'Er – no, I've just come to speak the Lord's word,' he replied, and Mabel secretly wished that he'd brought his trombone.

'All right, Captain, I'm sure some o' them'll be glad to see a Salvation Army uniform. Yer could start with that poor man in the last bed on the right. He's lost his son at the Front.'

Harry set off on his round. Mabel stayed at the door and watched as he stopped at the bed of a grey-faced man who cared not whether he lived or died.

Then she heard Nurse Davies call to her softly from the sluice-room, and joined her beside the big enamel sink and row of battered enamelled urinals.

'Talk about a Christmas party on maternity, Ethel!' she grinned. 'We've got Matron, Mr Poole an' his wife an' daughters, an' a Mrs Spearmann who's asked me to go an' visit a babies' home with her!'

'Spearmann, did yer say? Is she one o' them dressed-up-to-the-nines women who makes out she wants to help the poor? Me mother's done some alterations for a woman called –'

Nurse Davies broke off in mid-sentence as she caught sight of an extremely smart young woman stopping at the entrance to the ward. She was accompanied by a tall young officer.

'Mabel! I fought yer was on maternity – what yer doin' 'ere, then?'

Mabel spun round, her eyes wide with surprise. 'Maudie! What're *you* doin', I could ask! And where did yer get that hat?'

For Maud looked every inch a star. She wore a red

velvet jacket trimmed with fur at the edges, beneath which a boldly printed skirt swirled, daringly short at calf-length, showing her slender ankles and red high-heeled shoes. Her wavy light-brown hair was crowned with a very stylish hat in matching red velvet, its fur-trimmed brim turned straight up at the back and dipping at the front. She was as pretty as a picture, and all eyes turned to look at her.

'Cor, I see the Duchess o' Lambeff's arrived, then,' muttered a woman to her male companion as they passed through into the ward. He did not reply, but his eyes gleamed.

'Alex 'as come over for the af'noon, so I said let's go up Booth Street an' pretend to be visitin', so's we can see ol' Mabel an' Norah!' Maud explained. 'C'mon, Alex, say 'allo to me very best friend.'

Redfern held out his hand. 'I'm very pleased to meet you at last, er, Mabel.'

Mabel looked up into a handsome face that matched his well-bred tones and easy manner; she had no idea that he was making a real effort to conceal his horror at everything he saw, heard and smelt in this ghastly Infirmary.

'H-how d'ye do, er –' Should she say Mr Redfern or Lieutenant?

He smiled. 'Maud says you work with mothers and babies.' He glanced down the ward at the two rows of mostly old and ill-looking men. 'This can't be your patch, then. Oh, I say, the Sally Army's in! Don't they ever take time off from saving souls?'

''Ere, you watch yer step, Alex, that's Mabel's Captain 'Arry, as good a bloke as ever was. Is Norah around anywhere, Mabel?'

'She's up on Men's II. Harry'll be goin' up there when he's finished here, an' –' Mabel saw that Matron had appeared beside them, and assumed a very respectful expression. 'Good afternoon, Matron.'

Matron smiled, with a side glance at Maud. 'We meet again, Nurse Court. I see that Captain Drover is at his good work. And is this young lady another friend of yours?'

Mabel was momentarily at a loss, but Maud graciously inclined her head, showing off the hat to perfection.

'I 'ave that honour, Matron,' she said, sounding the 'h' clearly. 'And this is Flight Lieutenant Redfern o' the Royal Flying Corps – on leave from France,' she added proudly. ''E's been flyin' out over the German lines –'

Mabel felt that she should make some excuse for Maud's presence. 'Er – my friend Miss Maud Ling is the Principal Boy in *Cinderella* at the Royal Canterbury Theatre, Matron,' she said quickly, glancing up to see how this information was received. To her amazement, Matron actually laughed.

'Oh, Miss Ling, how wonderful! I've always loved pantomimes and now here I am meeting a real, live Principal Boy! I'll certainly look forward to visiting the show and seeing you perform.'

'Why, fank yer, Matron.' Miss Ling bowed again, and Sarah Brewer's thoughts went back to an occasion when she'd seen Marie Lloyd at the peak of her career. This girl's looks and accent made her think of the great music hall star, and an idea suddenly came to her; she had done what she could to make Christmas more cheerful for the patients and staff of the Infirmary, but here perhaps was something more . . .

'Miss Ling, I suppose I couldn't ask you – I wonder if you might consider – er, seeing that it's Christmas –'

Maud foresaw her request and her hazel eyes danced

with merriment. This was a splendid chance to show off in the nicest possible way – and impress Alex!

'Yer mean ye'd like me to do a bit o' patter an' give 'em a song from the show?' she prompted. 'Somefing to cheer the poor ol' chaps up, like? 'Course I will, no trouble at all. C'mon, Alex, ye'll 'ave to be Prince Charmin' for this, an' I'll be Cinderella!'

'For heaven's sake, Maud, I can't sing!' he protested, laughing self-consciously.

'Nobody's askin' yer to, all yer got to do is stand there an' look soppy. I'll do the singin'.'

Matron warmed to this irrepressible girl who had appeared from nowhere like an answer to a prayer.

'Thank you so much, Miss Ling. Shall I go in first and introduce you to the staff and visitors? Ah, here comes Captain Drover, I think he's finished his round. Good timing!'

Harry came towards them, wearing his serious look.

'I think a few hearts've been touched, Mabel,' he said earnestly, 'but it's a sad Christmas for a lot of 'em this year, an' bein' in a place like this doesn't help.'

'*Ssh!*' hissed Mabel. 'This is the *Matron*, Harry, and here's Maud, er, Miss Ling and Mr Redfern. They're goin' to sing a song for us all – the patients, I mean.'

Harry coloured and bit his lip, but Matron regarded him kindly. 'I'm sure you've done a great deal of good today, Captain Drover, and now Nurse Court will take you to the other men's ward. Right, Miss Ling, come along!'

The mutterings of patients and visitors fell silent as she strode into the middle of the ward and held up a hand for silence.

'Ladies and gentlemen, I'm happy to bring you a special Christmas treat. Miss Maud Ling who is appearing in *Cinderella* at the Canterbury Theatre will now entertain us with a song from that delightful show. Miss Ling!'

There was complete silence. Tired and listless faces turned towards the figure of Matron as she stepped aside, to be replaced by a pretty girl who tripped lightly forward in her eye-catching outfit. Alex Redfern stood back, looking distinctly embarrassed.

Maudie began by speaking the lines of the first verse, adapting them as she went along.

'I been worried all day long,' she said in clear, carrying tones. 'Don't know if I'm right or wrong!' She spun round, twirling her skirt. 'I can't 'elp just what I say –' She sighed deeply and then looked towards Alex. 'Yer love makes me speak this way.'

She took hold of his hand and drew him towards her as she began to sing.

'You made me love yer – I didn't want to do it, I
    didn't want to do it!
'You made me want yer – an' all the time yer knew
    it, I guess yer always knew it!'

Smiles of recognition began to dawn on faces at hearing the popular song.

'You made me happy sometimes, you made me
    glad,
'But there were times, dear, you made me feel
    so bad!'

Maudie's voice took on a plaintive note, and Alex looked round the ward, shrugging his shoulders and causing a ripple of laughter to spread.

'You made me sigh for – I didn't want to tell yer,
    I didn't want to tell yer –
'I want some love that's true – yes, I *do*, 'deed I
    do, yer *know* I do!'

Maudie was now shaking her forefinger vigorously at
Alex. Then she held out her arms to him.

'Give me, give me, what I cry for –
'Yer know yer got the kind o' kisses that I'd *die* for!'

He opened his arms and gathered her close to him,
joining in with her on the last line.

'*You* know you *made* me love *you*!'

There was a round of enthusiastic applause and a few
feeble cheers.

'Sing it again, little gal!' called out one old man and
this was followed by requests for 'More!'.

Maud needed no second bidding, but this time she
made Alex sing it with her. He was much bolder by
now and sang the first part of each line, while she sang
the 'didn't-want-to-do-it' and 'didn't want-to-tell-yer'
bits, pirouetting around him as she belted out, '*Yes* I
do, '*deed* I do, yer *know* I do!' with much saucy gesturing
and winks at the now attentive audience.

It's a success, thought Matron Brewer thankfully. And
she must do it on all the wards.

Mabel had obediently taken Harry up to Men's II, and
they had heard the sounds of singing and appreciation
drifting up from below.

'Ah, will ye listen to that!' sighed Nurse McLoughlin.
'D'ye think Sister up here'll let Maudie come an' sing
to 'em?'

'Yes, if Matron says so, an' I've got a feelin' she will,' Mabel said hopefully. Her half-hour was up and she feared she would have to return to maternity without saying goodbye to Harry who was still doing his round. She had not even wished him a happy Christmas, let alone exchanged a kiss. 'Oh, Norah, I'd better get back to face the ol' battleaxe. It'd be just wonderful if Maudie could come over an' sing to our poor mothers – they deserve a Christmas treat!'

'Ask Matron if she can, then, and maybe on Women's I and II as well – sure and she can't leave any of 'em out!'

And Matron did not intend to leave any of them out.

A death had just occurred on Women's II and the Ward Sister said she wanted no singing during a laying-out.

'Of course not, Sister, but perhaps Captain Drover of the Salvation Army could visit the ward instead, to speak to patients and their visitors,' Matron replied. It was an order rather than a suggestion, but the Sister was shocked.

'What? A young *man*, Matron, comin' round my ward an' speakin' to these women in their *beds*? It'd be most improper!'

'Not if I personally accompany the Captain on his round, Sister. You won't be put to any inconvenience, and he'll do your patients nothing but good.'

After her success on the general wards, Matron escorted Miss Ling to the maternity ward and Alex took the opportunity to go out for a smoke in the dingy central courtyard. *God, what a dump*, he thought, shivering in the chill, damp air. And yet . . . how well his little Maudie had gone down with the poor old bastards! He had learned a lot about the world since he had known her and realised that he no longer fitted within the confines of life at Elmgrove. He also knew that he would not be returning there this evening and didn't care that his parents would be upset: they had refused to see Maud, so they had only themselves to blame.

I must have you, darling Maudie, or I can't go back to face it. There might be no next year, no next month, no tomorrow: he only had today – *tonight*! He would hold her in his arms, he would love her, lose himself in her . . . he longed to forget everything. Everything.

Mrs Higgs raised every conceivable objection to more visitors to the maternity ward.

'Bad enough 'avin' Poole comin' in with 'is women lookin' as if they owned the place and upsettin' the routine,' she told Matron defiantly. 'An' that probationer Court's been orf the ward 'alf the afternoon with 'er fancy man. I 'aven't stopped all day, and now me ward's goin' to be turned into a music 'all.'

'I can understand you feeling aggrieved, Mrs Higgs, which is why I'm sending *you* off the ward for two hours,' replied Sarah Brewer briskly. 'Hand me the keys, please.'

'But 'oo's goin' to see to –'

'*I* shall take charge of the ward, Mrs Higgs. Off you go now and have a good rest. Be back here at seven.'

'But I don't want –'

'You may go, Mrs Higgs. Give me the keys, please. Thank you.'

There was no denying the note of finality and Mrs Higgs waddled off with rage in her heart. She had been counting on spending the rest of the day in her cosy little office-cum-sitting-room – and she was far from happy at the thought of Matron nosing around in it, opening cupboards and looking behind the medicine bottles . . .

The mothers' eyes brightened as Miss Maud Ling was introduced, waving and curtseying, and for the next half-hour they were treated to a deliciously personal entertainment as Maudie Ling used every trick in the book to raise their spirits, to make them feel that they were not only part of her act, but necessary to it. She led them into a colourful world of romance, far away from the impoverished grey backgrounds most of them knew.

'Use yer imaginations, girls, an' picture me wiv me Prince Charmin', lots o' gold braid on 'is shoulders an' a great big wavin' fevver in 'is 'at – come on, sing along o' me!'

'Give me, give me what I cry for –
Yer know yer got the kind o' kisses that I'd *die* for!
You know you – *made* me – love *you*!'

From the nursery where she was attending to the babies, Mabel heard the singing and clapping, and she smiled in spite of her sadness at not having said goodbye to Harry.

Suddenly Matron appeared at the door. 'We'd better let Miss Ling go now, Nurse Court, because Lieutenant Redfern is waiting for her. He's been very patient, poor man! Oh, and by the way, will you put the kettle on in the kitchen and make tea for Captain Drover? After the sterling service he has given us today, he deserves some refreshment, don't you think? The babies aren't due to be fed until six, so I'll take over from you here. The Captain's in the kitchen, and Mrs Higgs will be back at any time, so –' She left the sentence tactfully unfinished.

'Oh, Matron, that's so good o' yer.' Mabel was truly overwhelmed, and sitting with Harry at the kitchen table, they shared ten uninterrupted minutes of each other's company.

'I'll always thank the Lord for this day, Mabel. I've been blessed far above anythin' I hoped for.'

'Dearest Harry, ye've taken the words right out o' me mouth, cos that's just how I feel! And Matron's grateful for all the good ye've done today – she said so.'

'It's the Lord's doin', Mabel. He led me to them who was in the greatest need, an' gave me the right words to say to each one.'

He raised her hand to his lips and reverently kissed the palm, roughened by work and constant contact with water.

'I know I shouldn't wish for anythin' more, Mabel – God knows I can't help longin' for yer, me own precious angel – but I'll be content with this.' His voice shook, and Mabel saw that he had turned very pale, with shadows around his eyes; the afternoon on the wards had tired him.

'One day, Harry, *one* day I'll be yer wife an' wear one o' them bonnets with a great big bow on,' she teased lovingly. 'And we'll look back to today an' say, "D'ye remember that Christmas o' 1915 when Matron let us have time on our own in the maternity kitchen?"'

They were chuckling over this when Matron came to call Mabel for the six o'clock feeds; the Captain took his leave with Matron's repeated thanks, and in the nursery she took Mabel aside.

'I thought Nurse McLoughlin seemed a little upset when Miss Ling was singing. D'you think she's homesick for Ireland, or is there something troubling her that you know about?'

'Oh, Matron! It must've been the song.' Mabel's eyes filled with sadness. 'It's me brother, y'see. They're – er – courtin', and we haven't had word o' him for ever so long. He's in the merchant navy and they've got him on convoy duty now, back an' forth across the Atlantic.'

'My dear Nurse Court, I'm so sorry. Poor Nurse McLoughlin. We must follow Captain Drover's example and pray for – for them all.'

'Good God, Maud, I thought you were never coming. I've been going out of my mind.'

'What was yer worryin' abaht? Yer knew where I was,' she panted as they hurried along the South Lambeth Road.

'It wasn't *worry*, Maud, it was the sheer waste of time I could've been spending with you. There I was hanging about, smoking one fag after another –'

'I wasn't wastin' *my* time, Alex. Yer should've seen them poor gals in that maternity ward, and them little tiny babies. Made me fink o' when I used to carry me little bruvver Teddy aht to market stalls to see what we could beg or pinch. Some o' them'll be doin' the same, I reckon.'

He was silent and she tightened her hold on the crook of his arm.

'Fanks for comin' this af'noon, Alex. I know it must've been 'ard leavin' yer family an' all that on Chris'muss Day, an' then waitin' arahnd all this time. But I done a good job there, an' it meant a lot to that Matron an' them poor sods stuck in that place. An' what abaht ol' 'Arry Drover? Finks the world o' Mabel, 'e does, an yer don't 'ear '*im* complainin', even though they 'ave to do their courtin' in a bleedin' coalshed.'

He stopped and put both arms round her. 'I'm sorry, Maudie. It's only that I need you more than anything and I want you all to myself.'

She smiled up at him, a hint of a promise in her bright

129

hazel eyes. 'C'mon, let's get goin', then. No more 'angin' arahnd!'

At the lodging house, Maud led Alex straight up to her room on the second floor, ignoring the sounds of voices from other rooms. She unlocked her door and closed it quietly behind her.

'Maud!' His arms were round her, but she wriggled free. ''Old on, I need to 'ave a pee, light the fire an' 'ave a cup o' tea.'

'Oh, come on, Maudie, do!' Alex sighed while she put a match to the newspaper and kindling sticks laid in the tiny grate. The room struck cold, but he had no doubt that they would soon be warm enough in bed, and he had no wish to delay further.

'There's a WC dahn the passage, but I don't want to run into nobody, so I'll use the po,' she said, pulling the pot out from under the bed, squatting on it and shoving it back again without replacing her drawers.

'Make yerself at 'ome!' she told him cheerily, disappearing behind a curtain in a corner, for there was something else she had to do. Taking a piece of bath sponge out of a small jar of vinegar, she tied a length of white tape around it, knotting it firmly so that about six inches of tape hung from it like a tail. She hoisted her skirt and pushed the sponge up as far as it would go into what she called her alleyway. Either it'll work or it won't, she thought: whichever way, it was about to be put to the test.

The fire was now burning well and Maud put three pieces of coal on. The kettle had boiled, and she brewed a pot of tea and poured out two steaming cups.

With the curtains drawn and the gaslight turned down, only the flames lit the room, casting huge, leaping shadows on the wallpaper. Maud held out her arms to him.

'Ain't yer goin' to undress me, then?'

Ah, the fumbling of fingers at buttons, hooks and eyes, suspenders, elastic – the warm flesh revealed, the gleam of shoulders, breasts and thighs in the firelight: what desires about to be fulfilled, what dreams waiting to come true! Redfern trembled.

'Maud! Oh, my own darling Maudie, how beautiful you are . . .'

He unbuttoned his own jacket and threw it aside; then there were shirt buttons, cuff-links, braces, fly-buttons. Trying to pull off his trousers, he found he still had his boots on and cursed.

Maud giggled, though her own heart was racing nineteen to the dozen. He knelt beside her in his singlet and underpants.

'Let me take 'em off.' She smiled, a naked nymph in all her glory.

'Let's go to bed.'

And then the cold sheets, the blankets and eiderdown covering them.

'Ugh, yer feet ain't 'alf cold, Alex!'

'But I'm not cold here, am I?' He took her hand and led it to his hard erection. She gave a happy little 'mm-mm' as she took it in her hand, encircling it with her fingers and gently sliding them up and down the shaft. This was too much for him to bear, and he writhed and groaned.

'For God's sake, Maud, my love, my darling, help me, I need you – oh, *God*!'

'All right, Alex, here I am, here, like this –' She eased herself over so that she was lying above him, their loins touching. She separated her legs and lowered herself on to him.

'Help me, Maud, I'm afraid. Help me! Only you can help me,' he repeated wildly, and her heart seemed

131

to melt as she heard the words that she understood only too well; he had told her of what he had seen at first hand of the war, and she knew about his fear of injury and pain, a young man's unpreparedness for death. *Death*. And this was the only way that she could help him to overcome that fear – or rather to forget it for a few hours. So Maud did not hesitate; at whatever risk to herself, she had to give him what he needed.

'Alex, Alex, come to me, come on, forget everyfing. Everyfing.'

There was no time for any more preliminaries; in fact, there was only just enough time for him to enter her as she pressed down upon him. There was a shudder, a brief muffled cry from her and then a huge explosion of pleasure. His arms gripped her body round the middle, her arms were up around his neck. Time stood still while love flowed, there were wordless sounds as they both experienced climax at the same moment. Forgetting everything.

And then the downward slide, the descent to earth out of a night sky filled with shooting stars. Forgetting everything. Everything.

'Everything,' he was saying as he stirred beneath her. 'Everything, my darling. I'll remember everything.'

They fell asleep almost at once as they lay, for what might have been minutes or an hour, until she woke and raised her head.

'Alex.'

'What?'

'Yer parents'll be aht o' their minds, yer clearin' orf like this on Chris'muss Day.'

'That's their funeral.'

But this did not satisfy her: she was troubled.

'Alex, this is only cos o' the war, innit? Chaps like you don't go wiv girls like me.'

'I do.'

'But I can understand yer muvver, Alex. She finks I'm common, an' so I am. I mean yer wouldn't take me to meet yer friends in the Flyin' Corps club, nah, would yer?'

'I would if you wanted me to. I'd never be –'

He stopped, not wanting to say *ashamed of you*.

'Ashamed o' me.' She said it for him.

He reared up in the bed and took her face between his hands.

'Maud! Get it into your head, can't you? I *love* you, I need you, nobody else will do, can't you understand that? I've been with other girls, of course I have, and might have married one of them – but the war happened, and the Flying Corps, and you came to me, my darling Maudie.'

He rolled her over on to her back and pushed her thighs apart. He put his first and second fingers inside her and circled them with a roughness that matched his words as his desire rekindled.

'My common little Maudie, my naughty cockney girl, my vulgar little sweetheart who pulls down her drawers and pees into a chamber-pot in front of me – no shame, no modesty, no so-called bloody manners – Christ, Maudie! Again, Maudie, again!'

This time he was in control, riding her, thrusting into her again and again until the bed rocked and the brass headrail thumped rhythmically against the wall, causing shouts from whoever lodged beyond it, though whether of protest or ribald encouragement Alex Redfern neither knew nor cared. To Maud it seemed to go on for an eternity, and when at last he collapsed sweating and sobbing on top of her, she was bruised and sore, and her breasts were tender from his teeth marks. Yet when the storm had passed and he wept uncontrollably in her arms, she soothed him as tenderly as a mother comforting her child.

In the fireplace a coal shifted, sending up a last, leaping flame from the dying embers. Again the shadows flickered eerily up and down the wall. Maud shivered.

It had been a long day and Sarah Brewer was very tired, but her prayers of the morning had been answered beyond her best hopes. Her much criticised indulgence of that excellent Nurse Court had brought rich rewards for the whole Infirmary – comfort and counsel from a Salvation Army officer and sheer enchantment from a pantomime star.

Getting down on her knees beside the bed, Sarah wondered what 1916 would bring for Nurse Court's brother, Miss Ling's dashing lieutenant and that serious young Captain Drover. Would the longed-for victory be accomplished before another Christmas came round? Or would the fighting continue, and the lists of killed and wounded grow ever longer? She could only pray for them.

At Southampton just before midnight a handful of hollow-eyed, bearded survivors of a torpedoed merchant vessel, pulled out of the water more dead than alive six days ago, finally stumbled ashore.

Against all odds, they were home.

Chapter Eight

Cinderella opened on the twenty-seventh of December and Maud made the most of the lucky chance that had put her into a leading role. She gave out half a dozen complimentary matinée tickets at the Infirmary, but for Mabel, Harry and Norah she had seats reserved in the back row of the circle for the evening performance on New Year's Day.

'Don't tell me yer can't swop shifts an' get yerselves aht o' that place on Sat'day evenin',' she said airily. 'Tell 'em ye'll work every other perishin' night this week, only yer want *that* one orf, or else!'

In spite of Mrs Higgs's grudging objections, Mrs Hayes agreed to be on Caesar-call for Mabel, and the Sister on Men's II showed her appreciation of Nurse McLoughlin by giving her the evening off. Harry also said he could come, though his family were sorry to see him prefer that type of entertainment to the evening meeting at the Citadel. For him the prospect of sitting for three blissful hours beside the sweetest girl in the world was too great to resist. Any day might bring the summons to report for a medical examination and, although seldom mentioned, it was never far from Harry's mind or Mabel's. Alex Redfern had already returned to France, flying from Eastchurch on the Isle of Sheppey to the makeshift air base at Fienvillers, from where the RFC squadrons flew out over the lines to engage in skirmishes with the German fighter biplanes now appearing in larger numbers; Maud made a point of mispronouncing Fokkers.

Then came the message to Nurse Court on maternity, just after ten o'clock on the Tuesday morning following Christmas.

'Ye're to go up to Matron's office right away, Court.'

Mabel was trying to persuade a puny baby to latch on to its mother's flat nipple.

'D'ye mean now, this minute?' she asked, straightening herself up.

''Course I mean this minute, what d'ye think? Leave that an' go an' see what's up.'

Mabel smoothed her apron and tucked a few stray wisps of fair hair under her cap. Whatever could Matron want? Was there some reason why she or Norah weren't able to go to the pantomime on Saturday? Mystified, she hurried off to obey the summons.

'Come in, Nurse Court.' Matron's face was grave. 'Please sit down.'

Sit down? You didn't sit down in Matron's office, you stood to attention throughout the interview. Mabel's eyes went straight towards the open copy of *The Times* spread out on the wide desk, and her heart lurched at the sight of column after column of names stretching across the page, listing the names of men who had been killed, wounded or reported missing. Including those missing at sea.

And she knew before another word was said.

'*Albert*,' she whispered, her hand on her throat.

Matron looked up. 'Yes, Nurse Court, I'm afraid it's sad news about your brother, Albert Edward Court. He's listed here as missing.' She indicated the chair. 'Do sit down, my dear.'

But Mabel remained standing, though she gripped

the edge of the desk. 'Missing,' she mouthed. 'Not . . . killed.'

The Matron sighed. Breaking bad news to relatives never became easier.

'I'm afraid there appears to be very little cause for hope, Nurse Court. The merchant ship *Christina* was torpedoed by a German submarine in mid-Atlantic on the night of December the twenty-first, with the loss of all crew members, and your brother's name is among them. I am so very sorry to have to tell you this.'

White-faced but outwardly calm, Mabel shook her head slightly as if in disbelief.

'He could've been picked up. He was in a convoy, an' there were escort ships o' the Royal Navy there. They might've picked him up,' she repeated in a dull, flat, curiously stubborn tone.

'I don't think you should allow yourself to hope, Nurse Court,' answered the Matron heavily, thinking that if any of the crew had managed to throw themselves clear before the vessel went down, they would not have survived for long in the icy water with the darkness all around them.

Mabel was still standing in front of the desk. To sit down would be like accepting the dreadful finality of her brother's fate. 'What about Norah, Matron – I mean Nurse McLoughlin – will yer tell her as well?'

'Perhaps you had better tell her, Nurse Court, as you are friends. My duty is to inform the next of kin, which is yourself. Nurse McLoughlin isn't a relation.'

'No, but she – oh, how can I tell her this?' Mabel clasped her hands together pleadingly.

'Shall I sent for her now, so that you can speak to her here in my office?'

'N-no, thank yer, Matron. We're both off from two to five. I – I'll have to take her to our room and break

137

it to her. Let her get her dinner first, otherwise she'll miss it.'

'Very well, Nurse Court. You can spend the afternoon with Nurse McLoughlin, but you'll both have to report on duty as usual for the evening shifts.'

'Yes, Matron.'

'A nurse's chief consolation comes from serving her patients, that's been my own experience, my dear,' said Sarah Brewer, moved by the girl's stoic attitude and her concern for her friend. 'All over the country today women are hearing news of losses like this and carrying on with their duties – the mothers, the sisters, the young women like Nurse McLoughlin who –' She hesitated, and then went round the desk to lay a hand on Mabel's shoulder. 'We must put our trust in God, my dear. That's what Captain Drover would say, isn't it?'

'Yes. Thank yer, Matron.'

'Are there any relatives you need to inform?'

'I'll write to me brother in Canada and me sisters at Belhampton – oh, they'll see it in *The Times*, an' so will Captain Drover. It's poor Norah who hasn't got any relatives at all.'

'Mother o' God, Mabel, yer face! Somethin' wrong, is it? Has Harry been sent for to –'

'No, Norah, it's not Harry. Listen, dear, ye've got to be very brave. It's Albert. His ship was torpedoed, an' he's missin' at sea.' Mabel brought out the dire news in a rush, rather as the Matron had done; there seemed no point in trying to soften such an irredeemably bitter blow.

'Aah. Well, now, then.' Norah automatically crossed herself and her body was strangely unresponsive as Mabel's arms encircled her. 'But didn't I dream about him last night, an' didn't he look me straight in the eye an' say he was on his way home to me? As plain as I'm seein' ye now, Mabel, that's what he said.'

'Oh, Norah, dear, I'm sorry, but it's been a week and Matron thinks he must be drowned, else we'd've heard by now. She says we shouldn't let ourselves hope, 'cause we'll only be disappointed when – when we don't hear anythin'.'

Norah rose from the bed where she had been sitting in their shared room and went to the window that overlooked the roofs across to the river. 'I'm goin' straight over to St George's to pray for him, whether he be livin' or dead.' She replaced her cap and picked up her cloak.

'D'ye want me to come with yer, Norah?'

'If ye want to, Mabel, darlin' – only I must go now, before me two knees give way under me.'

Both girls remained dry-eyed throughout that day and neither actually admitted that Albert Court was almost certainly dead. 'Missing at sea' was not the same as 'killed in action' and their talk was about the living, breathing young man they knew. When Norah returned from St George's Cathedral she went straight to the little Oxo tin where she kept his treasured letters and cards, scrawled and creased as they were, and set them out on her bed.

''Tis the first time in me life I've had somebody o' me own, y'see,' she murmured, touching each one in turn. 'The Sisters o' Mercy at St Joseph's were kind to us – Mother Patrick was a darlin' – but it wasn't a family like yours, Mabel, though they gave me a convent education such as other girls had to pay for. When Miss Greene came an' took me to be her maid, she brought me over to live in London wid her – but as soon as she met this fella wantin' to marry her, she didn't need me any more, an' sent me here to train.' The blue eyes gleamed. 'An' didn't

139

I straightway meet yerself, Mabel – an' shall I ever forget me first sight o' yer dear brother, all dressed up like a wumman, d'ye remember? The grandest, handsomest man I ever did see!'

Both girls smiled sadly and shook their heads at the memory of Sister Mattock, then held each other for a long moment.

'I shan't give up hope, Mabel, not yet. Only I don't want to go to *Cinderella* now, 'cause that song'd break me heart for sure. Come on, now, let's have a cup o' tea before we go on duty again. There's enough poor souls needin' us to see to 'em, God knows.'

Harry Drover was deeply affected by the loss of his old friend and workmate on the railways and was not sure how to console the two white-faced girls. He dared not encourage them to hope for Albert's survival, yet his attempt to pray with them and exhort them to accept the Lord's will sounded empty and comfortless, even in his own ears. His parents sent Mabel a message of sympathy, hoping that her brother had entrusted his life into the Lord's hands, but she was more touched by Ruby Swayne's hand-delivered letter which expressed her real grief for Mabel on the loss of a beloved brother.

'I feel for you as for a sister, that's how I think of you, Mabel,' she wrote. 'And for your friend Norah, what you must both be going through, not knowing for sure.'

One thing Harry said which surprised, even shocked Mabel, was that he thought they should still go to the pantomime on New Year's Day.

'It's what Albert would've wanted, Mabel,' he said. 'Think about it, ye've got to go on workin', seein' to yer patients an' doin' all yer usual jobs as if nothin' 'ud happened – and I reckon he'd've wanted us to go to the pantomime, too, seein' as Maud's got us tickets for it.'

'Oh, Harry, we *couldn't*, it wouldn't be right. Norah's already given her ticket to Ethel Davies and I thought we'd give ours back to Maudie for somebody else. Me own brother lost at sea – no, we couldn't.'

'And I say we *should*,' he argued with unusual persistence. 'Can't yer just hear him – "Why the 'ell are yer sittin' arahnd on yer backsides mopin', when poor ol' Maudie wants yer to go an' see 'er doin' 'er stuff? Go on, get aht an' 'ave a good laugh, the pair o' yer!"'

This sounded so exactly like Albert that Mabel smiled in spite of herself. 'Oh, *Harry*! That could just've been him talkin'. All right, I'll come with yer on Saturday – and we'll think about him while we're there,' she added, though her voice broke as she spoke.

Harry breathed a sigh of relief. If he was recalled to active service, there might never be another opportunity to sit beside Mabel in the cosy darkness of the Canterbury. And it was because she was aware of this that Mabel had capitulated, hoping that Norah wouldn't mind. It was a strange world where mourners went to pantomimes to laugh and cry for the sake of those who were lost . . .

Norah uttered no reproach. 'Sure an' Harry's right, Albert would've wanted ye to go an' see Maudie, poor darlin', wid her Alex away to France, an' not knowin' if he'll be back.' She sighed. 'Don't worry about me, Mabel, go an' give Harry a happy evenin' while ye can.'

So Mabel allowed herself to look forward to Saturday evening, though her grief for her brother was always present; she tried not to think about those moments following the torpedo's impact.

*   *   *

On the very next day, Wednesday, Mr Poole had a message for Nurse Court from Mrs Spearmann.

'She wants to visit the Midway Babies' Home one afternoon this week, Court, and asked me when you'd be free to go with her – if you feel up to it, of course,' he added, noting her pallor and shadowed eyes.

'We-ell, I'm off this afternoon, sir,' she replied without enthusiasm. 'An' I've got to be back on at five.'

'Oh, you nurses, always rushing to be *on* at such a time and *in* at such a time!' he teased. 'I'll tell her to be here at two and you can arrange with her when you've got to be back.'

'All right – I mean thank yer, sir,' she answered wearily, and Poole felt slightly guilty. The girl looked all in and visiting the Midway would give her no pleasure, he knew.

Over the mutton hash and cabbage served to the staff at the midday dinner, Nurse Davies encouraged Mabel to swallow a few mouthfuls.

'Ye've got to keep yer strength up, Mabel. What're yer doin' this afternoon – spendin' it with Norah?'

Mabel shook her head. 'No, she's had a mornin' off, and spent it on her knees in the cathedral, poor lamb. I've got to go out this afternoon, though I don't feel the least bit like it. It's this Mrs Spearmann I told yer about, the one who visited on Christmas Day. She's comin' to take me to visit the Midway Babies' Home with her. And Mr Poole wants me to go, 'cause it's where a lot of our babies end up, so he says.'

'Ah! I been askin' me mum about this Mrs Spearmann,' said Ethel Davies. 'She comes from ever such a posh family – only they lost all their money when the war broke out, 'cause it was invested in some German company that went bust an' took all their shares with it. They hadn't got a penny – until this daughter, Olive, went out an' hooked Amos Spearmann whose people had made their money out o' furs. Jews, they are, came over last century with nothin' in their pockets, worked all the hours God sent, an' made a packet. So Olive saved her mother an' sisters from goin' bankrupt, an' *she*'s yer Mrs Spearmann! Ye'd better keep on the right side of her, Mabel, she's a walkin' gold mine!'

Mabel sighed. 'Let's hope she'll find somethin' useful to do with it, then.'

At two o'clock promptly a horse-drawn carriage drew up at the Booth Street entrance and Mrs Spearmann waved to Mabel who was standing on the steps.

'Ah, there you are, Nurse – er, Coates, is it? Do get in. I use this to save petrol, though my husband says it's antiquated. Do you mind facing backwards? Good. Wilson, let's go.'

'Very good, madam.' The driver jerked the reins, and they proceeded towards the Elephant and Castle and into the New Kent Road, under a railway bridge and then took a left turn into a maze of narrow streets, manufactories and warehouses. Mrs Spearmann questioned Mabel about her work in a pleasant but slightly patronising way and Mabel answered briefly, adding, 'The name's Court, Mrs Spearmann.' *Blowed if I'm going to call her madam*, she thought.

The carriage stopped in a narrow street beside a dismal passageway.

'This is it, madam.'

'What, *this*? But there's no children's home here, Wilson,' replied the lady, looking up and down the thoroughfare.

'Beg pardon, madam, but there's the notice.' He pointed with his whip to a board above the passage.

MIDWAY BABIES' HOME, it said, with an arrow pointing downwards.

'Good heavens, we'd better get down, Wilson, and you must take the carriage on to some more convenient place to wait for us. Call back here in half an hour. Come on, Nurse Court, I'm quite glad to have you with me in a place like this. Most unpromising!'

Mabel's heart sank as the two of them proceeded down the passage and came to a small open yard with a bare tree in the middle, a rusty swing and a see-saw. Ahead was a heavy wooden door with a notice, *Children and Visitors*. Mrs Spearmann went and lifted the tarnished knocker, bringing it down three times with a reverberating bang.

The door was opened by a young, untidy-looking girl in a checked dress, cap and apron. Somewhere behind her a child was crying.

'Yes?' She held the door ajar as if half inclined to shut it in their faces.

'I beg your pardon, miss!' said Mrs Spearmann indignantly. 'I am Mrs Spearmann of Maybury Place and this is Nurse Court. We are expected this afternoon, so take us at once to the Matron or whoever's in charge of this establishment.'

The girl opened the door to let them enter. 'Beg pardon, marm, I'm sure, only I got to shut the door again quick, 'case any of 'em get out. Shoo, get back to yer playroom, nosey!' she snapped at a runny-nosed boy of about two who stood staring round-eyed at them. Mabel caught an all-pervasive smell hanging in the air, compounded of vegetable stew, carbolic and another odour she remembered from schooldays: sassafras oil. There was an atmosphere of *lack* in this place, she sensed, a want of both love and of money.

'That's Mrs Lovell's room, there,' said the girl, pointing to the first door on the left of a long, bare corridor. At Mrs Spearmann's imperious knock, a harassed-looking middle-aged woman emerged, peering at them through round spectacles. She wore a dark dress with some kind of a badge pinned to the front, and a crumpled cap.

'Mrs Spearmann, is it? Oh, Lord, I though yer wasn't comin' till three. They distinctly said three o'clock, I'm sure they did.'

'Good afternoon,' said Mrs Spearmann coldly. 'Am I addressing the Matron?'

The woman gave an awkward half-curtsey. 'In a manner o' speakin'. I'm Mrs Lovell.'

'Very well, Mrs Lovell, I've come to visit this Home and the children staying here, and this is Nurse Court from the Booth Street Poor Law Infirmary. Kindly show us round the Home and introduce us to the staff on duty. How many children have you in at present?'

'Er – yes, madam. Nearly thirty-five we got now. We take 'em up to five years. Would yer like to start with the playroom, they're mostly two or three an' upwards. This way, if yer please.'

And so began their tour of the Midway Babies' Home. Mrs Lovell first showed them into a fairly large room where there were about fifteen children, some crawling, some toddling, while others sprawled on blankets put down on the bare wooden floor. A little girl smiled at Mabel who longed to pick her up. Instead she mouthed a 'Hello', smiling in return and waving her fingers.

'Now I'll show yer the nursery,' said Mrs Lovell, leading them to another door on the opposite side of the corridor. Nine babies lay in three rows of canvas cots, some crying, some sleeping, none being attended to. 'It's not time,' said Mrs Lovell. 'They've just had their two o'clocks an' been put down.'

A third room contained ten larger cots crowded together, in which children of up to a year old lay or sat up, their little faces looking at the visitors through the bars. Most of them stared in silence, though a few shouted out such words or sounds as they knew or remembered.

'Ma-ma!' – 'Ba-ba!' – 'Po-po-po-po-po!' – 'Wee-wee, wee-wee!'

Mrs Spearmann stood and stared in undisguised horror. 'Good heavens, what a wretched place for children to be in!' she exclaimed, glancing at Mabel who shook her head. She had seen too many of these unloved children in the women's wards at Booth Street.

'They know it's potty time,' said Mrs Lovell. 'No tea without potties first, it's the only way to train 'em in clean habits.'

'I don't see many staff around,' observed Mrs Spearmann, frowning. 'Who cares for these poor infants?'

'That's just it, we can't get the staff, nobody wants to do it – the war's put everythin' back,' replied Mrs Lovell wearily. 'No sooner do we get new girls than they give notice an' clear orf again. We has to do the best with what we got.'

'But surely there are girls who are interested in nursing children?' protested Mrs Spearmann. 'Why, Nurse Court here can't wait to –'

She turned to find that Mabel was no longer at her side; she had gone back to the toddlers' playroom where she was talking with the girl who had let them in.

'Haven't they got any toys?' she was demanding. 'Don't their families bring anythin' in for them to play with?'

'Sometimes they get dolls an' things, but they soon get 'em filthy dirty, suckin' at 'em and tearin' 'em to bits,' answered the girl with a shrug. 'Some women

146

brought in a load o' teddy bears at Christmas, an' yer should've seen 'em by Boxin' Day – we 'ad to put some away before they ruined the lot. I'll tell yer what, miss, I'll be glad to be out o' this place, I will.'

'But don't yer *enjoy* lookin' after children?' asked Mabel, unable to comprehend that any girl or woman might not do so.

'Not *this* sort, I don't! I thought I wanted to be a children's nurse, an' they sent me 'ere to start trainin' – I'm sixteen this year and not as green as I was! They come in 'ere full o' lice and fleas an' worms, and I've caught the lot – 'ad to 'ave me 'air cut off same as the kids. I've 'ad nothin' but colds an' coughs an' sore throats off 'em, an' me mouth's full of ulcers. I ask yer, look at them snotty noses – did yer ever see anythin' like it?'

As a school-leaver of fourteen Mabel had worked at a pre-school nursery in Battersea, where she had met Ada Clay and discovered her vocation for caring for young children. Some of the children there had shown signs of poverty, but she had seldom encountered such deprivation as this, and for a moment her pity and indignation overcame her grief for Albert.

'Don't yer ever pick up yer poor little mites an' cuddle 'em?' she asked, looking round at the motley collection of over-large clothes the children wore. Most of them had nothing on their feet.

'What, an' pick up another lot o' lice an' stuff? No fear! 'Sides, they'll scream blue murder, as likely as not – they holler for their mothers.'

'So where *are* their mothers, then?'

'Beggin' – thievin' – street-walkin' – prison – why d'ye think the kids've been dumped in 'ere? I tell yer, I've 'ad enough of it – can't wait to get a job in one o' them munitions factories, an' see a bit o' life.'

147

She clapped her hands. ''Ere, come on, it's potty time an' we don't want no accidents. Go an' get yer potties an' sit on 'em, else there'll be no tea.'

There was an uncertain surge in the direction of two rows of tin pots hanging along one wall, and within a few minutes the girls were each seated on one, while the boys stood two or three to a pot, to perform their hourly duty. Mabel caught sight of the little girl who had smiled at her earlier, pulling at her drawers. The tight elastic had left a red mark all round her body and before she could get them down she had wet them. Standing in a puddle, her little face crumpled and she began to cry. The young assistant began to scold her.

'Ye've wet yerself again, Mary, yer dirty pest! I've a good mind to smack yer –'

'*No!* Let me see to her,' Mabel cut in quickly and, getting down on one knee, she removed the wet drawers.

'It's all right, Mary, dear, Mabel's here and we'll soon have yer nice an' dry again. Oh, just *look* where that elastic's cut into her, yer poor little duck. If only I could take yer home with me!'

The unhappiness on the child's face turned like magic to a trustful smile, which seared Mabel's heart even more, for she had no home to offer Mary. Two thin, soft little arms went round her neck and a flushed cheek was pressed to hers: it was almost too much to bear, and Mabel had to close her eyes to blink away the tears that threatened to well up for all unwanted and abandoned children. And also for her brother Albert, lost at sea: it was the first time she had actually shed a tear for him.

'Why, Nurse Court, what's the matter? Do you know this little girl?'

Mrs Spearmann had appeared at the door of the play-room and was surprised by the sight of this rather surly probationer tearfully hugging a bare-bottomed child.

'I feel as if I do, Mrs Spearmann,' Mabel replied tremulously. 'Did yer ever see anythin' like these poor mites all sittin' on pots?'

'No, Nurse Court, I don't think I have,' the lady replied, conscious of Mrs Lovell just behind her. She too had been shocked and oddly shamed by this introduction to the Midway, and as she looked helplessly at Mabel and Mary, the conviction came to her that she would have to do something for these children – though how best to set about it Olive Spearmann had not as yet the slightest idea.

'We'll have to go now, Nurse Court, Wilson's waiting. Say goodbye to this little girl, and – er – we shall come again. Yes, Mrs Lovell, we shall most certainly come again and I shall speak with the Board of Guardians about the staff situation here.'

Somehow or other Mabel disentangled herself from Mary's clinging arms. All her early longing to care for underprivileged children had been fired with fresh determination this afternoon, and on the return journey she forgot her former irritation with Mrs Spearmann and listened to what she had to say.

'We mustn't be too hard on Mrs Lovell, Nurse Court. She's trying to cope in the face of impossible odds, and I think she means well in her way. She'd probably be quite adequate in a subordinate role under a good Matron.'

She paused, turning over the ideas that were forming in her mind.

'I've been working with a Ladies' Committee in Clapham to raise funds for sending comforts to the men at the Front, Nurse Court, but now I see that I must leave that work to others and turn my attention to these poor children. They've been overlooked because of the war effort and forgotten about. I think I'll ask Mrs Hodges to take over the committee and just hope she'll understand that I've found something in more urgent need of – er, whatever I can do.'

'What was that name yer just said, Mrs Spearmann?' asked Mabel. 'Mrs Hodges?' For now she remembered where she had heard the name Spearmann before – and the Ladies' Committee which sent comforts to the fighting men. 'Is she the Mrs Hodges who used to be Ada Clay?'

'Why, yes – do you know her?' asked the lady in surprise.

'We worked together at the Hallam Road Babies' Mission in Battersea and were really good friends. I knew her when she first walked out with Arthur Hodges and I was at her weddin'.'

'Good gracious!' Olive Spearmann was astonished. 'And have you seen Mrs Hodges lately, Nurse Court?'

'Only when we met by chance in a tearoom. Ada's gone up in the world since she moved to Clapham. But yer can tell her that ye've met her old friend Mabel Court.'

'Yes, I *will* tell her and I'll say how impressed I've been by you, Nurse Court. And I'd very much like to stay in touch. You're just the sort of girl I think I'll be looking for!'

Olive Spearmann spoke with feeling, for she thought she had found her mission in life.

Friday morning had been busy on maternity, and while Mabel was clearing away after the second Caesar, Mr Poole questioned her about Mrs Spearmann's reaction to the Midway.

'She was as shocked as I was, I think, sir – an' says she's goin' to see what she can do for them poor children,' answered Mabel, who had been wondering about her own next move after completing her training at Booth Street in September. With Harry's situation so uncertain, she was wondering if the Midway was calling her to do something dear to her heart, something which would give her valuable experience for that distant future life as a Salvation Army wife, caring for children in need.

'That good lady needs an outlet for her time and money, and I thought I'd show her where to find one,' said Poole with a sharp look. 'I shall help her to get on the Board of Guardians and learn something about management. It's no good just pouring money into a leaking bucket, that place needs root and branch reform; in fact, it needs pulling down altogether and replacing. But for now, with all the pressure on beds and caring for the military, we can only do a patch-up job, and I've got plans for our Mrs Spearmann!' He grinned knowingly at Mabel, but getting no response, he peered into her face.

'You're not looking very jolly these days, Court. Is something bothering you – other than old Higgs, I mean?'

Mabel hesitated. Should she tell him about Albert? No, better not. She might start crying and that would never do.

'What's the matter, girl?' he asked with brisk concern. 'Has your young Salvationist been recalled for service?'

'No, it's my –'

'I say, Nurse Court, ye're to go to Matron's office – message just come down!' said Mrs Hayes, looking round the door.

'You'd better go straight away, then,' said Mr Poole. 'I'll lay a pound to a penny that it'll be to do with Mrs S. She was greatly taken with you!'

He smiled to himself as she went off to change out of the shapeless theatre gown and put on her uniform. *I may have done that girl a bit of good*, he thought with satisfaction.

The tall man standing beside Matron looked much older than when Mabel had seen him last, but his eyes lit up at the sight of her.

'Ah, come in, Nurse Court.' Matron was smiling. 'As you see, I have a visitor, Captain –'

'Dr Stephen! Oh, Dr Stephen, d'ye know that me brother Albert's lost at sea?' The words broke spontaneously from Mabel's lips before she realised it, and she lowered her eyes and muttered, 'I'm sorry, Matron.'

'All right, Nurse Court, but you must allow Captain Knowles to speak.' Matron glanced at the doctor whose shadowed blue eyes were fixed on Mabel. 'As a matter of fact, he's brought very important news this morning. You may sit down.'

'Yes, I have, Miss Court,' said the doctor. 'I'm working at the Stepney and Poplar Infirmary for the time being, while I'm getting over a – an injury. Shellfire.'

'Oh, I didn't know – I'm sorry. Yer father –'

'Hush, Nurse Court! Just listen to the Captain.'

Mabel sat with downcast eyes and Stephen Knowles saw the strain she was under. She wanted to ask him about his wife, and where he had been wounded, but Matron's stern look kept her silent.

'We're full up and overflowing with wounded men at Stepney, Miss Court, and – well, yesterday a train arrived from Portsmouth with yet more. Two of them had been in hospital there, suffering from cold and exposure –'

Mabel leapt up from her chair with an involuntary shout. '*Albert!* Oh, Stephen, are yer tellin' me that

Albert – oh, tell me, tell me, for God's sake – is he alive?'

'Nurse! Control yourself and let Captain Knowles speak,' cut in the Matron, but Mabel had controlled herself for long enough and could not keep silent. 'Just tell me if he's alive, that's all, only tell me, *please*!' she cried wildly.

'All right, Mabel. Yes, your brother survived the wreck, but he's been very ill with pneumonia, and –'

'I knew it, I *said* he'd be picked up, didn't I? Didn't I?' And Mabel began to cry. Her whole frame shook with hard, dry, convulsive sobs as she stood holding on to the edge of the desk.

'Nurse Court, get a grip on yourself!' ordered Matron, surprised that this girl who had been so brave in the face of bad news seemed unable to cope with good.

'All right, Mabel my dear, all right.' Stephen came round the desk and put an arm across the girl's shoulder, gently lowering her into the chair. 'Just take some deep breaths and keep your mouth closed – good girl! Otherwise you won't be able to hear what I've got to tell you about Albert, will you?' He stood beside her chair and kept his hand on her shoulder as he continued, 'I didn't recognise him at first, but I learned that he'd been taken from the sea by an escort vessel, and lucky to be alive out of a small handful of survivors. Your brother's been returned to you and you can see him – so no more tears!'

She clung to his arm as he stood beside the chair and Matron Brewer looked on in some bewilderment at the obvious degree of intimacy between them, though she remembered that his father had been the Courts' family doctor and had written a letter of recommendation when this girl had applied for training.

'Miss Court and I were involved on another occasion

concerning her brother, Matron,' he said pleasantly, as if by way of explanation. 'It was in the rail strike of 1911 and Albert nearly got his head broken. It was thanks to Mabel and Captain Drover that he – er – got out of trouble.'

'I see. Perhaps Nurse Court should return to her ward now, Captain. It was very good of you to come over with this wonderful news and I'm sure we're all most grateful.'

'Ah, but I have a favour to ask you, Matron, before I go,' he said quickly. 'We're extremely short of space at Stepney since the last batch of admissions, and Able Seaman Court and his fellow survivor are not wounded, nor are they strictly military personnel. I've been asked to request a transfer to a medical ward here if it can possibly be arranged.'

That afternoon as the early winter dusk was falling, Matron Brewer took two third-year probationers with her to Men's I where two beds were screened off at the end of the ward. Raising a hand to push the screen aside and putting her left forefinger to her lips for silence, she beckoned them forward to the first bed.

'Only a few minutes, remember, nurses. These men are still very weak and there is to be no noise, no upset of any kind.'

Mabel stepped to the left side of the bed where her brother lay, gaunt and grey-faced, his black beard obscuring the lower half of his face. His eyes were closed and sunken, and she might have thought him dead but for the air that rasped in and out of his chest. He was twenty-one and looked like a man of forty.

'Albert!' she whispered, and repeated his name a little louder. 'Albert!'

He opened one filmy eye and stared unseeing into space.

'Albert, it's yer sister, Mabel. And here's Norah to see yer, too.'

The Irish girl stood quietly on the right side of the bed. She made the sign of the cross, then put her hands together and bowed her head.

'Thanks be to the Sacred Heart o' Jesus, for ever an' ever,' she mouthed silently and put out a hand to touch Albert's as it lay on the counterpane.

He opened both eyes and slowly brought them to focus on the two girls, his sister and his sweetheart. He drew a sharp, painful breath, coughed and took hold of Norah's hand. A tear oozed from the outer corner of each eye and trickled down to the pillow beneath his head.

'I fought I was a goner,' he muttered hoarsely. 'An' now I know I am – 'cause I've landed up in 'eaven.'

Chapter Nine

The brilliantly lit stage of the Royal Canterbury Theatre might have been miles away from the young man and woman sitting together in the back row of the circle, cocooned in a world of their own. They had watched at the beginning when Prince Charming came on to cheers and applause, scanning the horizon and slapping his shapely thigh as he told of his lonely search for the girl of his dreams; but while he was off stage, their whole attention was centred on each other. In the semi-darkness, thick with the smell of oranges, cigars and sweating humanity, Mabel heard the gusts of laughter as from a distance, while Harry's whisper of 'dearest Mabel' was close to her ear. She sighed with sheer contentment, made perfect by Albert's restoration from the sea.

Her hat lay in her lap and she had unbuttoned her coat. He breathed in the fragrance of her skin, the clean scent of soap. He slowly raised his left arm and let it encircle her shoulders; she responded by laying her head upon his shoulder and closing her eyes, thankful that they were in the back row. Had Maudie thought of that when she'd got the tickets? Nestling against his brown serge jacket, for he was not in uniform tonight, Mabel let herself imagine that they were truly alone, somewhere quiet and private, far away from the Canterbury, from the Infirmary, from the horrible war. Yet she was grateful for these few brief hours' respite.

'I'm so happy,' she whispered and felt a tremor run through his frame.

For Harry Drover's desire for her was like a physical ache – a fire within him, that must be kept under control. He had to quieten his breathing, slowing it down to something like normal rhythm, and make an effort not to tremble. He swallowed and silently prayed that the girl beside him, so dearly, desperately loved, might never be affronted by the carnal lust that warred against his better nature. But oh, how he yearned over her, his precious girl without an impure thought in her head!

Ethel Davies, seated on Mabel's left, was chuckling at the two Ugly Sisters, one in a blonde wig, the other dark, who were trying on gowns for the ball and talking in raucous voices.

'I got this feelin' that we're bein' watched, know what I mean?' leered the blonde, pulling an elaborate blue gown over her head, with much wriggling of her hips.

'Ooh, d'ye think there's a peepin' Tom around 'ere somewhere?' asked the other. 'Tryin' to get a look at two young maidens in their next-to-nothin's, the dirty beast!'

''Ere, come to think of it, it could be that Prince Charmin' takin' a stroll round the back –'

'Ah, well, I don't mind givin' *'im* a bit of a treat – y'know, show a bit o' leg!'

The resulting contortions and generous glimpses of hairy calves and knobbly knees had the theatre howling. When they clumped off the stage to loud applause, the curtain descended for an interval. Ethel leaned across to ask how they were enjoying the show. Harry hastily lifted his arm from Mabel's shoulders.

'Pity Norah and yer brother can't see it, eh?' said Ethel.

'I bet she's as happy as a lark, waitin' on him hand,

foot and finger!' Mabel laughed affectionately. Norah spent every moment she could spare at Albert's side. There had been no need to declare their love, for their eyes had said it all to each other and to the world; Mabel saw that she must now accept second place in her brother's affections and had told herself very firmly not to be silly. Albert was still her brother and theirs had always been a special relationship, a different kind of love. She had her beloved Harry, so how could she possibly grudge such a dear girl as Norah the devotion that now filled Albert's dark eyes?

The lights went down and the curtain rose on the next part of the pantomime. Poor Cinderella sat weeping in her ragged gown, not allowed to go to the ball – until with a sudden bang and a flash the Fairy Godmother appeared in a cloud of thick blue smoke that trailed out over the orchestra pit. Mabel suddenly thought of Mrs Spearmann: would she turn out to be a fairy godmother to little Mary and the other pathetic inmates of that loveless babies' home? And would *she* have a part to play in their lives? She could not get them out of her mind.

Harry sensed her preoccupation and took her hand lightly in his. From now on they must watch the show and applaud Maud's triumph as Prince Charming; he was seated beside his dearest girl in the cosy darkness and ought not to wish for anything more.

All three of them joined in the prolonged applause at the end, when the Prince and Cinderella took their curtain calls and led the whole house in the final chorus of 'You Made Me Love You'.

But jostling down the uncarpeted backstairs with the departing crowds, Harry Drover felt that he was leaving a place of warmth and comfort, to be tipped out into the chilly darkness of the Westminster Bridge Road.

Mabel and Ethel took an arm on each side of him as they hurried back to Booth Street.

'D'ye think Norah and Albert'll get to see it before it finishes?' asked Ethel. 'Isn't it wonderful to see them two together – the way he looks at her!'

The girls chatted on, but Harry Drover's thoughts were of Mabel and himself, the evening they had just spent together and what it had meant to him. There might not ever be another like it, so he would have to remember every moment. And another voice within him insisted that his physical longing for this dear girl was not shameful at all, but natural and God-given. And that it was no sin to want to show his love for her in the most intimate way before he was torn from her again, to face danger and the threat of death. He shuddered at the thought of losing his life – his young life now restored to health and vigour.

Lord, how can I bear to leave her again?

To be so much in love and to be loved in return must be the greatest joy on earth. So thought Norah McLoughlin in those early weeks of 1916, the happiest girl in London, though all around her she saw distress and anxiety. Booth Street Infirmary was bursting at the seams with civilian patients forced out of other hospitals to make room for the never-ending stream of war wounded who poured in from the Front. The shortage of doctors and nurses was daily becoming more acute, and the quality of care more difficult to maintain.

But Norah's man had been snatched from the jaws of death and was improving with every day that passed. She spent every available minute at his side, bringing him drinks, shaking his two pillows and indulging in the sweet, whispered exchanges of lovers.

'Me little Irish rose,' he would murmur reverently.

'It was the fought o' yer waitin' for me that got me frough.'

'An' didn't I know ye'd come back to me – I saw ye in a dream, so I did.'

Hearing that she had given up her free ticket for *Cinderella*, he was determined to be well enough to take her to see it before it finished in February.

'An' I'll get yer the tickets,' promised Maudie Ling, tripping gaily into Men's I with a Lyons cake in a cardboard box and a tin of Mackintoshes' toffee. 'Cor, it's good to see yer again, Albert, lookin' better 'n I expected – must be Norah's doin'. And ain't she just gorgeous? I mean she was always a sweet little fing, but blimey, all of a sudden she's turned into a ravin' beauty!'

It was true. The Irish girl seemed to have undergone a transformation, so that heads turned whenever she walked down the ward. Staff who had known her since her arrival at Booth Street now wondered why they had not noticed the large cornflower-blue eyes fringed with black lashes, the creamy skin, the softly waving dark hair beneath her white cap and the pretty little rosebud mouth that was always curving up in a smile these days. She gave an impression of glowing from within, visibly radiating happiness.

And Albert Court worshipped her. As he gained strength, Mabel expected him to revert to his familiar uncouth manners, cocking a snook at any kind of authority and resorting to ill temper and profanity if he did not get his way – and then what would his Irish rose think of him? Mabel had always been a little worried about Norah's infatuation with a man she did not know as Mabel did and feared that closer acquaintance might disillusion her.

But in this she was entirely mistaken. His brush with

160

death at sea had had a profound effect on young Seaman Court, in fact it had been a turning point in a life which now included a girl who clearly adored him. With her wide eyes fixed on his face and her lips softly parted, Norah hung on his every word and thought him the wisest as well as the bravest of his sex. Never having known family life or a mother's love, her heart was now given unreservedly into Albert's keeping.

And it changed him. Here was a reformed Albert Court who actually wanted to show his better side to the world instead of hiding it under a surly exterior. He was gentler, softer of speech, more ready to listen than to answer back as had been his habit from early boyhood. And yet when he and his sister were alone, she found that the old Albert had not quite vanished.

'Hey, Mabel, guess 'oo come to see me 'saft'noon? Ol' Dr Knowles. Said 'e'd 'eard from Stephen that I was in 'ere, an' fought 'e'd come an' see for 'imself.'

'Oh, bless him! How was he lookin'?'

'Whacked aht, poor ol' chap. Says 'e'd like to retire but can't, 'cause there ain't enough doctors to go rahnd. 'E asked after yer, Mabel, wanted to know what yer was thinkin' o' doin' when yer finish 'ere.'

'Oh, I wish I'd seen him, Albert, I'd've asked his advice,' she replied, thinking about the Midway Babies' Home. 'What did yer talk about?'

'This an' that. Well, 'im an' us go back a long way, don't we?' The brother and sister exchanged a meaningful look. ''E asked abaht George. I said yer 'adn't 'eard nothin' lately. I reckon there won't be much news from over there while the war's on.'

They were silent, both thinking about the U-boats. Mail was the least important of cargoes.

'He'll be sixteen now,' said Mabel. 'I don't even know

if he's still at McBane's. Davy was talkin' o' goin' west to work on the Canadian Pacific Railway.'

''E's well aht of it if yer ask me,' muttered Albert. 'I dare say 'im an' Davy'll do all right.'

'Did Dr Knowles say anythin' about Stephen?' asked Mabel after a pause.

'Oh, yeah, poor ol' Stephen – caught it in the bum.'

'What? Ye'd better not talk like that in front o' Norah! What d'ye mean?'

'The buttocks, then. Lacerated to ribbons by a shell splinter while 'e was pickin' up wounded at a clearin' station up front. Muscle torn right away from the –'

'Ugh, stop, stop, don't say it, Albert!' Mabel shuddered and closed her eyes tightly. 'I can't *bear* to think of it – those horrible injuries – how can God let it happen?'

'Hey, don't upset yerself, gal, it's healed up pretty well, so the ol' man said. Only trouble is, 'e can't sit dahn, an' 'as to sleep on 'is belly, poor bloke.'

'That's right, he didn't sit down in Matron's office that day when he brought the news about yer bein' rescued,' Mabel recalled. 'Matron and me was sittin' at the desk, and he came an' stood beside me. Oh, poor Stephen, whatever does he do at mealtimes?'

'Eats standin' up, I s'pose.' Albert gave a grimace and looked hard at his sister who sat with her hands clasped rigidly together.

'Y'all right, ol' gal?'

She shook her head. 'This horrible, hideous war, Albert.'

He nodded gloomily. 'Yeah. They're callin' up a whole lot more single men – conscription, that means they got to go – an' askin' the married ones to fink abaht it. Give 'em a chance to get away from the wife an' muvver-in-law!'

But Mabel was in no mood to joke. She thought of Stephen Knowles whose marriage had been disastrously interrupted so soon after it had begun. *Two* miscarriages, Dr Knowles had said. She found herself wondering about Phyllis Knowles, what sort of a woman Stephen had chosen to be his wife.

February brought the dreaded summons. Harry was recalled for a medical examination and on the strength of it was told to report to Wandsworth barracks for home duties with the intake of new recruits. He was made a Corporal with the 10th London Rifles and once again exchanged his Salvation Army uniform for khaki, a soldier in the service of his country.

'It's a relief in a way, Mabel. At least I know where I stand, an' it gives me a chance to get to know these boys before we go over there,' he said with all the maturity of twenty-five years.

They had met hurriedly on a cold, drizzly evening and, rather than walk in the rain or shelter in a doorway, they had slipped through the door of the nearby Prince of Wales where they hid themselves in a corner. For Corporal Drover it was a necessary compromise; Captain Drover's uniform would have debarred him from entering a public house except with a collecting tin, and Mabel in her grey coat and untrimmed hat also hoped not to be recognised. They drank ginger ale and felt the warmth of the place gradually getting through to their chilled hands and feet. The pub was crowded with soldiers and their women companions, some of whom were smoking; Mabel wondered what her aunts at Belhampton would say if they could see their eldest niece in the fume-filled atmosphere of a public bar.

Harry took a gulp and stared down at his glass. 'I'm afraid there's more unwelcome news, Mabel,' he said in the sombre manner that had become almost habitual with him, and her heart lurched. 'Somethin' I've seen comin' for a long time.'

'Oh, my God.' She instinctively seized his arm. 'Ye're bein' sent to the Front.'

'No, Mabel, dear, not yet, though that'll come sooner or later. No, it's Herbert, me brother-in-law. He's to go before a tribunal on the second o' March for questionin' under the Military Service Act.'

'But he's married – he's got a family –'

'Yeah, but he's been on reserve an' his views are known, that's the trouble. He reckons he'll be made an example, of, an' he's told us that he won't give way. He's prayed about it and says he's not puttin' on khaki at any price.'

'But would he *have* to, if he went as a stretcher-bearer or ambulance driver?'

'Yeah, *and* hold a rank, even if it's only a private, like an orderly in the RAMC. A non-combatant is still in the army.'

'So what'll happen, then?'

'I don't know, Mabel. I've heard these tribunals can be pretty hard. Men who won't fight get called cowards an' shirkers, even traitors – an' if he still won't change his ideas an' go as a non-combatant, he could be sent to prison.'

'Oh, poor Ruby! And little Matthew an' Mark! He *can't* refuse to go, Harry, surely! Can't yer speak to him, tell him how it'll affect yer sister an' the boys?'

'I've said me piece, Mabel,' he replied wearily. 'The fact is, y'see, I agree with him in principle, but I reckon he'd be better off doin' useful work as a non-combatant than coolin' his heels in a cell. But it's up to him. He's a responsible family man, five years older 'n me, an' it's his life, not mine.'

*   *   *

To Mr Poole's dismay Nurse Court was taken from the maternity ward and put on night duty on Women's II where she was also on call for emergency theatre cases. Overcrowding and an acute shortage of medical and nursing staff meant a lowering of standards of care for patients, especially the elderly who developed pressure sores; Sarah Brewer considered this a disgrace to her hospital.

'Do what you can, Nurse Court, to encourage all the nurses to treat pressure areas during the night,' she urged. 'Wake the bed-patients up if necessary, to turn them four-hourly at least.'

But in spite of the toilet rounds, the rubbing of bony backs with surgical spirit and dusting with boracic powder, the bedsores appeared and quickly became foul-smelling craters over the base of the spine and on the hips and heels, that had to be dressed with lint soaked in fish oil or friar's balsam. Lack of assistance with feeding the helpless led to malnutrition and the death rate rose, to Matron's deep distress. Staff continued to leave to look after war victims elsewhere and civilians were neglected. Everything had to be sacrificed to the war effort.

Seaman Court suddenly found himself discharged from Men's I and sent to the Tooting Home for Aged Poor, now commandeered as a military hospital; its former residents had been summarily despatched to the Mitcham Workhouse where they languished miserably. Albert was put in a temporary building erected in the grounds and used for other ranks in various stages of recovery. Here he played cards, argued over the running of the war, turned up his nose at the soft drinks bar, coughed, wheezed and moped for his Irish rose. Norah had to get the electric tram from Westminster Bridge to Tooting in order to see him during her brief off-duty periods, just as Mabel had done when Harry was first home from Gallipoli. Mabel found that her own best time for visiting was in the morning after night duty. She wore her uniform and spent half an hour with her brother, sitting in one of the wicker armchairs that had been supplied. The convalescents sat round a central stove with a pipe going up to the ceiling and Albert stretched out on a chaise longue with a blanket spread over his knees. He regarded his sister intently, his jet-black eyebrows drawn together.

'Yer get time to fink, stuck in 'ere, Mabel. Take that poor blighter over there 'oo's lorst an arm an' a leg. It upsets 'im when 'is poor ol' muvver an' farver comes to see 'im, tryin' to put a good face on it. It's easier wiv you, Mabel, we've never 'ad to pretend abaht anyfing, 'ave we?'

'I know what yer mean, Albert, we've always said what we think to each other!' She smiled.

'But it's different wiv little Norah, i'n't it?' He shifted his position, crossed one leg over the other and uncrossed them again. 'Er – Mabel, ol' gal, I want yer to do somefing for me.'

'Depends what it is. Here, put these slippers on, Albert, yer feet'll get cold.'

He stuck his feet into a pair of stained carpet slippers left behind by some departing inmate. 'It's abaht Norah.'

'What, d'ye want me to propose to her for yer?' she teased.

'Nah! No need for that, she knows I'd marry 'er tomorrer if she 'adn't got to finish 'er trainin'. An' I'll be back at sea by the time she's got 'er certificate. Nobody knoes 'ow long this show's goin' to go on.'

Mabel nodded. 'I know, Albert. It's the same with me and Harry.'

She waited for him to continue, but he hesitated, chewing his lower lip and showing the two strong white incisors that always reminded Mabel of their father. A thought came to her.

'Yer do realise ye'd have to marry in a Catholic church, don't yer?'

He grinned. 'That's no sweat. I've told 'er I'll turn 'oly Roman for 'er sake, so's we can 'ave it done proper wiv all the trimmin's.'

'Albert! Would yer really?' she asked in surprise.

'Listen, I'd turn into a bleedin' 'Indoo wiv a striped tea-cloth rahnd me 'ead if that's what she wanted – the little darlin'.'

Mabel gave a yelp of laughter, instantly suppressed. 'Ha! An' ye'd look the part an' all, with *your* colourin'!' In that moment they caught each other's eye and both thought the same thing. After an awkward pause, Albert spoke again.

'Which brings me to what I was goin' to ask yer, Mabel, gal. The fam'ly 'istory. It ain't such a pretty story, is it? D'ye fink Norah ought to be told abaht it?'

'Oh, so *that*'s what botherin' yer – oh, Albert, dear.' Mabel was all concern at the sight of his worried eyes, still shadowed and sunken after his ordeal. 'No! I don't see why she needs to be upset by a lot of ancient history from the past. Ye know what they say – let sleepin' dogs lie!'

'But these fings 'ave a way o' comin' aht. Yer know, like skeletons in the cupboard. One day some chump says somefin' wivaht finkin', the sort o' fing I might say meself – an' aht they all come rattlin'. If yer was jus' to tell 'er the bare facts, Mabel, it'd be better comin' from

167

you – then there wouldn't be the risk of a shock later on, if yer see what I mean.'

'No, Albert, I'm not sure that I do,' she replied thoughtfully. 'I've told Norah an' me other friends at Booth Street that we lost our parents in 1912, an' that both were tragic accidents – she drowned an' he fell downstairs – and the family broke up, which is what happened, isn't it? You were in the merchant navy, the girls went to live with their aunts in the country, George went to Canada –'

'Yeah, that's the bit that worries me, Mabel, the way poor little George was shunted orf aht o' the way all on 'is own, an' 'im only twelve. If Norah ever asks me abaht that, what am I s'posed to say? Tell 'er 'e bashed the ol' man over the 'ead an' did for 'im? An' that our poor muvver drahned 'erself 'cause she'd got the pox orf our farver? An' that our grandmuvver Court got 'im off a wanderin' Lascar sailor an' made a livin' doin' 'igh-class abortions for the gentry?'

'Ssh, ssh, Albert, that'll do,' Mabel cut in quickly, catching her breath anew at the roll-call of human frailty which she and her brother shared but never had cause to mention. She glanced round at the men reading or dozing in armchairs.

''Arry knows, don't 'e?' he persisted. 'And never fought any the less o' yer for it.'

'His family don't,' she said. 'He reckons that if the Lord knows, there's no need for the rest o' the world to be told, an' I agree. Where's the sense in upsettin' Norah with all that stuff? None of it was *your* doin', Albert, it isn't like a crime that *you* committed, somethin' on yer conscience. After all, Alice an' Daisy don't know, nor do the aunts, so why should Norah?'

'I ain't plannin' to marry any o' them others.' He yawned and suppressed a gentle belch. 'I still fink she ought to be told abaht George, though – why 'e was sent all that way from 'ome.'

Mabel saw that he was genuinely troubled, and guessed that his intended marriage to Norah McLoughlin had brought old family secrets to the surface of his mind. As if reading her thoughts he began to rhapsodise on his favourite subject, like lovers the world over.

'She's such an innocent little soul, ain't she, Mabel? I've never met a gal 'oo was anyfing like 'er, an' to fink she's fallen for me – I'm scared I'll wake up one mornin' an' find it's all a dream!'

Mabel smiled. 'Yer needn't worry, Albert, she worships the ground yer walk on.'

'That's what worries, me, y'see, if she was to find aht –'

'Oh, don't be silly, Albert, it's *you* she loves, not yer family. And besides, we're not doin' so badly these days; in fact, the girls are bein' brought up like little ladies. Which reminds me, Aunt Kate's lettin' Pinehurst be used as a convalescent home for wounded men and Alice wants to help with the nursin', she says. Yer never know, Albert, yer might find yerself sent down there!'

'No, fanks – too far away from Norah. When I fink abaht 'er, Mabel, brought up by nuns an' goin' to that convent school – look at the way she reads an' writes, better 'n any of us – an' so neat and clean, wiv 'er white cap pinned rahnd 'er 'ead an' 'angin' dahn 'er back, she's like a little nun 'erself, i'n't she?'

Mabel smiled. 'I can't see a real nun workin' in a place like Booth Street, Albert! We get all sorts – drunks, down-and-outs, yer wouldn't believe the state some of 'em are in. *And* the way they swear an' curse! Norah gets her share of 'em, the same as the rest of us.'

'Yeah, but it ain't *touched* 'er, 'as it? She's just as sweet an' – an' – sort o' *fresh* as she must've been as a little girl at St Joseph's in Cork. There she was on 'er knees in that church, prayin' for me to be sent back safe – I don't feel worvy of 'er, know what I mean?'

Albert's voice faltered and Mabel's blue-grey eyes softened at the sight of her rapscallion brother struggling to express feelings that were quite new to him. She rose.

'Ye're just as dear to her as she is to you, an' that's what counts, Albert. Look, I'll have to go now – and when I think the time's right, I'll drop a hint to her about what happened to George. But as for all the rest, I don't see how any good can come o' rakin' it up.'

She bent down to kiss his cheek and he looked up at her gratefully. 'Franks, Mabel, ye're a good 'un. I'll leave it up to you what yer tell 'er, then.'

Meanwhile the constant rushing between Lambeth and Tooting during limited off-duty periods was beginning to tell on Norah. There were purplish smudges beneath the blue eyes and worry lines between them, and she was always tired. Mabel became concerned.

'Yer know, Norah, ye're goin' to have to cut down on these visits to Tooting.'

'But ye know I have to see the dear fella as often as I can, Mabel – he looks out for me.'

'Yer know what'll happen, ye'll fall down faintin' in the street like I did, an' ye won't get much sympathy from Matron,' Mabel told her severely. 'Don't encourage him to be selfish.'

'Ah, Mabel, he's not selfish at all! I don't want him to be gettin' up an' comin' over here before he's fit. It's a terrible cough he's still got, so!'

'But ye'll be no use to him or anybody else if yer crock up. He's doin' fine layin' around playin' cards an' tellin' tall stories –'

170

'An' waitin' on the poor fella that's lost an arm an' leg – talkin' to him, keepin' his spirits up.'

'Oh, Norah.' That was the worst part about visiting the Tooting Home, the sight of young men crippled for life. 'I'd never be able to nurse the wounded,' she declared once again. 'Every one of 'em would be Harry.'

Albert was able to keep his promise to take Norah to see *Cinderella* on the last night, to their mutual joy and satisfaction. While she waited for his taxicab to arrive at the hostel entrance, Norah put on the new hat she had bought at the Cut.

'Yer look a picture,' Mabel said admiringly. 'He'll be bowled over by the sight o' yer.'

'An' there was me thinkin' I was gettin' another stye on me eye, but it's gone away, thanks be to God. Ah, there he is now, I can hear a bangin' at the street door. 'Bye, Mabel, darlin'.'

Sitting enthralled in the semi-darkness, holding hands and joining in the laughter at the antics of the Ugly Sisters and the applause for Prince Charming and his Cinderella, every moment of the performance was engraved on Norah's memory, right to the end when Maud Ling led the whole house in the final chorus of 'You Made Me Love You'.

'Give me, give me, what I sigh for,
Yer know yer got the kind o' kisses that I'd *die* for –'

'Ah, 'tis a grand voice ye've got, Albert – ye should be up there on the stage with Maudie, so!'

Tired as he was, this was music in Albert's ears, and he warbled through the chorus again, ending on a bout of coughing.

'Sure an' I could listen to ye all night!' Norah said rapturously as they were clattering down the stairs, which made Albert grin at the innocent implication, though his dark eyes softened.

'What abaht that ovver song, the one abaht the sailor lad 'oo was – 'ow did it go?

'Mar-ri-ed to a mer-ma-id at the bottom o' the deep blue sea!'

'Jesus, Mary an' chaste St Joseph, Albert, never sing that one again – *never*, d'ye hear me?'

And he realised his mistake.

Herbert Swayne proved to be immovable as a 'conscientious objector', as men like him were called, among many less complimentary names. Harry reported to Mabel that Herbert had squarely faced a contemptuous major at the tribunal and, when offered non-combatant service in the RAMC with immediate rank as sergeant and pay and separation allowance for his wife and children, he had risen from his chair and boldly declared, 'I can't accept it.' Asked why not, he had replied, 'Because it means taking part in war and killing my fellow men.'

The major then asked him angrily what he would do if his country were to be invaded by a foreign power: suppose he had to watch his wife raped before his eyes, would he then be so squeamish about killing a man? Herbert replied that this circumstance had not arisen, and that he had no personal quarrel with young German soldiers who were in the same situation as the British men. He repeated that all forms of killing fellow human beings was against God's commandment.

He was then taunted as a coward, a man who would

let other men fight to defend his own freedom while keeping out of harm's way himself, and when he opened his mouth again, he was ordered to shut up. Hauled off to the guardroom at the same barracks where Harry was stationed, he appeared a few days later at a court martial where he was found guilty of contravening the Military Service Act and sentenced to 112 days' solitary confinement in the military prison at Wandsworth. His widowed mother broke down and sobbed when she heard the news, but Ruby Swayne held up her head and vowed she would stand by her husband. The Salvation Army would take care of her and the boys, she said, and refused to accept a penny from her parents; it was not their fault that her husband held the views he did.

Mabel sent a note of sympathy to Ruby which Harry passed on, but there was little else that she could do. Deep down in her heart she had mixed feelings about Captain Swayne's brand of heroism. Knowing of Harry's fears and her own on his behalf, of Albert at the mercy of the U-boats, Stephen Knowles's experience at the clearing station that had been shelled and Maudie's Alex flying his fragile craft over the scenes of battle – and the tens of thousands of killed and wounded, the endless 'In Memoriam' columns in the newspapers . . . she could not be wholly sympathetic towards the pacifist objector.

'What'll Herbert do in prison?' she asked.

'Sew mailbags, same as the rest, I s'pose,' Harry replied gloomily. 'He's not to have any visitors for the first month an' his letters to Ruby'll have to be read by the military. I doubt he'll be allowed any exercise out o' doors, an' the food'll be bread an' water. Poor Herbert.'

'And when the sentence is finished, what'll happen then?'

'Another conscription board, an' then it'll be up to him, Mabel.' Harry turned down the corners of his mouth. 'It's his life – his decision. Poor Ruby.'

'Norah, I been wantin' to talk to yer for ages an' there's never enough time. Put yer cloak round yer an' walk down to Lambeth Pier with me.'

It was one of those blowy March days with spring in the air but winter still evident in the leafless trees around Lambeth Palace and the pinched faces of Londoners hurrying with heads down against the wind. The two young women reached the embankment and paused, looking down at the uninviting grey surface of the water.

Mabel swallowed. How to begin? And how much to say? She linked an arm through Norah's. 'There's somethin' Albert wants yer to know, an' I said I'd have a word with yer.'

'Albert?' The Irish girl was immediately alert. 'Good or bad, is it?'

'I wouldn't call it good, Norah. It's about our family. About the Courts.'

'Ah – d'ye mean yer poor mother an' father?'

'Well – er, yes. Yer know they both died in 1912 within weeks of each other, an' that broke the family up. And – an' me brother George went to Canada on a child emigration scheme with boys from Dr Barnardo's.'

'Ah, yes, the poor little fella. Ye took him to Waterloo Station, an' by the grace o' God ye met Davy Hoek to look after him. It must've broken yer heart, Mabel.'

'But Norah, I've never told yer *why*, have I?'

'Why he went away, yer mean? Didn't he say he *wanted* to go after yer parents had died so sudden and the home was given up? And didn't them kind aunts o' yours offer to take him wid Alice an' Daisy, but he said he'd rather go to Canada? Wasn't that it?' asked Norah, who had clearly taken everything she had been told at face value. And what she had just said was true, of course, only . . .

'I've never told yer how me father died.' Mabel heard her voice falter as she spoke and Norah heard it too, for she smiled and took her friend's hand.

'Didn't he fall downstairs and hit his head awkward, like? Maybe ye're tryin' to tell me he was drunk – is that it?'

The river flowed on silently below them as Mabel hesitated. 'Yes, Norah, he was, and poor George, y' see, he – he saw his dad fall downstairs an' realised he was dead. He was in a shocking state, poor boy.'

'Sure 'twas a terrible thing, a man full o' drink, his own father an' all,' said Norah softly. ''Twas no wonder he was so keen to get right away from everythin' that reminded him of it. But why should dear Albert worry about what I think?'

'It's always bothered Albert an' me that George was sent all that way so soon after the trouble, and him only twelve,' answered Mabel. 'But it was for the best, Norah, an' George's own idea – even Dr Knowles said it'd be better to let him go with the Barnardo boys.' Or land in court on a murder charge, she thought, trembling as she remembered the scene that had met her eyes on returning home on that fatal June afternoon: her father's body falling to the floor of the living-room, and George with his face full of horror and his arm still upraised after delivering the fatal blow.

Norah put an arm around her waist. 'Oh, Mabel, I'd never blame yer, nor Albert, sure I wouldn't. Ye had to do what ye thought was best for the boy and so it's turned out, wid him meetin' Davy and them bein' such good friends an' all. Don't let it trouble ye any more.'

The girls stood together by the pier, the 'tails' of their white caps flapping in the wind. Mabel wiped her eyes with the back of her hand. Eventually Norah spoke quietly.

'And yer poor mother, Mabel, she'd already gone when this happened, hadn't she?'

'Yes, Norah, she drowned. Don't ask me to talk about her – she'd been troubled an' unhappy for a long time, an' –'

'Ssh, Mabel, not another word. Yer father was a drinker, that's for sure, an' she must've had a hard life, God rest her soul.' Norah crossed herself and Mabel knew that there would never be any need to divulge poor Annie Court's shameful secret.

'Me father was a weak man rather than a bad one, Norah. His mother was never married an' she passed him off as the son of an Indian official or some such, but it's more likely his father was a sailor from the East Indies. That's why Albert's so dark, an' Alice an' Daisy both got the same black hair. I'm fair like me mother and so's George – and so was poor little Walter who died. Me own sisters don't know what I've just told yer, Norah. Only Albert an' Harry know – an' Maudie's got a pretty good idea, too – she's always been a good friend, like yerself.'

'And did Albert want ye to tell me this old unhappy story, Mabel?'

'Yes, he thought yer should know, seein' that ye're goin' to be married,' said Mabel with guilty relief that this partial revelation had been so willingly accepted.

'Oh, God love him! As if he could help what happened all them years ago, before I ever knew yer,' said Norah, unconsciously echoing Mabel's own words to Albert. 'Look, Mabel, ye're gettin' cold, we both are. Let's take ourselves back an' have a nice hot cup o' tea!'

176

Stepping briskly back along the familiar street, Norah tightened her hold on her friend's arm.

'Y'know, Mabel, there's somethin' I've been wantin' to say to *you* and I might as well say it now if ye don't mind listenin',' she began. 'I been thinkin' about a lot o' things since Albert's come back, an' the way me life's changed 'cause of meetin' yeself an' him. Bein' in love, Mabel, ye know it makes ye look at everythin' in a new way –'

''Course I do, Norah,' Mabel answered, though unable to guess at what was coming next.

'Ye know I've always been so sorry for meself, brought up wid no family o' me own.'

'Oh, Norah, dear, I know – and I've always felt for yer, not havin' a mother – or anybody.'

'Once upon a time I had a mother, Mabel, and I know now that she must've suffered for it. She couldn't keep me, and maybe she held me an' kissed me for the last time when I went to the Sisters o' Mercy.'

'Oh, Norah –' As always, Mabel's heart was touched at the thought of a motherless child and she set aside her own dark memories.

'But I was much better off than some. We were well cared for at St Joseph's, Mother Patrick saw to that, and when she saw I was quick to learn, she let me go to the convent school. The other children in the orphanage had to go to the school in the town, but I got a free convent education that other girls had to pay a lot for, an' it's only now I see how favoured I was. And Sister Dymphna, her that was always smilin', she gave me a beautiful doll that she'd had as a little girl, and showed me how to make clothes and hats for her. And the old lay sister in the kitchen used to let me help her to bake bread – ooh, I can smell it now!'

'Why, Norah, ye've never said anythin' about this before! I always thought yer were lonely there.'

'I was sorry for meself, Mabel, that was the trouble – and I let Mother Patrick down, after all she did for me.'

'How d'ye mean, let her down?'

'Well, Sister Dominic said I'd make a good teacher one day, so I was prepared for the Irish entrance examination – an' I failed it. Mother Patrick was that disappointed – and then Miss Greene came lookin' for a lady's maid to take wid her to England – and so I left in disgrace.'

'Oh, Norah, don't blame yerself just for failin' an exam! An' if ye'd gone in for teachin', ye'd still be over in Ireland an' we'd never have met. And me brother wouldn't've known yer – just think about *that*! Harry would say that it was all the Lord's doin'.'

They had reached the entrance to the nurses' hostel and were climbing the stairs.

'Sure ye're right, Mabel, but I'll *never* again say that I was a poor orphan – not like those little children ye've told me about at that babies' home. Meetin' yerself an' Albert has made me see the *good* things o' me childhood, an' I'm grateful to the Sisters o' Mercy. I'll write to Mother Patrick an' say so.'

Mabel had no words left. She simply clung to Norah McLoughlin and thought of George and little Mary at the Midway and all the lonely, forsaken children in the world.

Chapter Ten

Spring had come again and a glimmering green haze covered London's parks; in suburban streets the humble privet hedges put out new shoots and even in the bleakest slum the sunlight penetrated down to sooty courtyards, drawing pale children out into the warmer air.

The Midway Babies' Home felt the benefit of the change of season, along with the other improvements brought about by the new benefactress on the Board of Guardians. With Mr Poole's support and her husband's generous allowances, Olive Spearmann had had walls repainted and brightly coloured prints put up; rugs had appeared on bare wooden floors, and there were hard-wearing toys to play with, like building bricks, bouncy rubber balls, tin drums and steel triangles to make satisfying sounds. Best of all were the various lady helpers who put on overalls and spent an afternoon each week playing with the children. Mrs Spearmann's latest idea was to advertise for local families to invite a child from the Midway – or two or three – to tea in their homes, as a special treat.

'It's uphill work, but it's a start,' she told Sarah Brewer after a joint meeting of the Board. 'The great need is for good quality staff and I'll be after your newly qualified nurses, Matron!'

'But I shan't have any to spare, Mrs Spearmann,' answered Miss Brewer sharply, knowing that the lady had her eye on Nurse Court. 'My staff are working under tremendous pressure as it is and if I lose just *one* of this year's finalists, I'll be stretched beyond the limit.'

Olive Spearmann sighed. She was already unpopular for resigning the chairmanship of the Clapham Ladies' Committee and now Mrs Hodges had also withdrawn from it, and not only because she was expecting a third child. Arthur Hodges had been summoned to attend a conscription board where he had been put on reserve for military service, and Ada was distraught, railing against the inhumanity of removing husbands and fathers from their families, to go and fight in a war they had never asked for. When she met her old friend Mabel Court taking her usual morning walk after night duty, she subjected her to a bitter tirade.

'It's making me ill, the worry of it all, Mabel. I wasn't half as bad when I was expecting the other two. If my Arthur has to go abroad, what will become of us? He sees little enough of us, now that half the staff have left Lipton's. Dad couldn't possibly manage without him. I'd give anything – *anything* – to have the whole hateful business over!'

'It's the same with Harry, Ada, he could be sent for any day,' Mabel pointed out gently. 'And Maudie's Alex is out in France with the –'

'For heaven's sake, Mabel, it's all very well for you and your single friends with no ties or responsibilities. I don't expect you to understand what it's like when there are children to feed and care for – how much a family needs the husband and father to take care o' the home!'

Her eyes filled with tears and she hiccuped painfully.

'It's my nerves, y'see, Mabel. I get morning sickness all day long.'

'Ada, dear, yer must try to think about the little one on

the way,' Mabel urged her. 'Gettin' into a state won't do you or the children any good. Try to be brave for them – and for Arthur.'

In spite of Ada's self-centred attitude, she could count on her friend's understanding, for Mabel still saw the high-spirited, giddy girl she had known in the days when they'd both worked at the Hallam Road Babies' Mission. Now she could imagine Ada's helpless terror as the Military Service Act spread its net ever wider, snaring married men as well as adventure-seeking youths. Not that there was much left of the early enthusiasm to join up and fight for king and country: the horrendous lists of dead and wounded had brought the gruesome reality of the war home to the nation.

'D'ye see much o' Mrs Spearmann these days, Ada?' she asked in an attempt to divert her friend's thoughts.

'No, no, she's completely taken up with this children's home and doesn't bother with the Clapham Committee any more,' replied Ada crossly. 'She's tried to interest some o' the ladies in visiting the place and taking children home to tea, but of course *I* can't do anything like that, not as I am at present and with my own poor children to look after. Old Amos Spearmann has gone into uniform production, so they'll be making a pile,' she added bitterly. 'Anyway, I can't stand here talking all the morning, Mabel, I've got far too much to do at home. You're free for the rest o' the day now, I suppose?'

Mabel did not bother to point out that after being on duty all night she needed to sleep before facing another night. Poor Ada! What on earth would she do if Arthur was called up?

When Seaman Court was pronounced fit to leave the Tooting Home his Aunt Kate wrote from Belhampton to invite him to stay at Pinehurst, now filled with convalescent men. As one of the family Albert would be a special house guest.

'No fanks,' he said at once when Mabel showed him the letter saying how much they all wanted to see the young hero. 'The ovvers'll be officers, most like, an' I'd be a fish aht o' water. Besides, my Norah couldn't travel forty miles to see me. No, I'll go an' bunk dahn at the Sailors' 'Ome by the docks. 'Tain't a bad place, I been there before.'

'But it's a long way out and a rough area for Norah to visit alone,' objected Mabel, wishing for the hundredth time that she could offer her brother somewhere local to stay.

But a solution was at hand. Matron Brewer's sharp eyes did not miss much that concerned her nurses, especially the best ones. She had taken note of Nurse McLoughlin's pale looks and tired eyes, and had heard on the hospital grapevine that Seaman Court was leaving the Tooting Home. She sent for Nurse McLoughlin and informed her that she was due for a week's holiday and could take it at the beginning of April.

'I think you should get right away from London, nurse. A breath of country air would do you a world of good. I believe your friend Nurse Court has got relatives at Belhampton down in Hampshire, so why not ask if you can go there for a few days?'

Norah duly reported this to Mabel who stared in blank amazement until light dawned – and then she gave a whoop of delight.

'Hooray! Hooray, Norah, that's wonderful!' she cried, jumping up and down in the main corridor like an excited child. 'Good old Matron! Don't yer *see*? You an' Albert can go together, and he can introduce yer to the aunts and Daisy and Alice! Oh, Norah, Norah, just *wait* till me brother hears about this – he'll be turnin' cartwheels!'

Sure enough, Albert changed his mind forthwith and Mabel wrote on his behalf to the aunts, accepting Kate's offer of hospitality and telling them of his engagement to a close friend of hers who had got a week's holiday and was looking forward to meeting them. A cordial invitation was extended to Miss McLoughlin from the Somertons by return of post, and so it was arranged that Albert would spend two weeks at Pinehurst, getting reacquainted with his aunts and sisters and with Pinehurst itself, his mother's home that he had visited only once before; and then Norah would join him for the second week as his intended bride, staying at Pear Tree Cottage with the Somertons. The pair would be able to meet every day and take local walks unchaperoned as an engaged couple. Norah was in raptures.

'Ah, now, Mabel, this is above me wildest dreams, to meet yer family and stay in a real house in the country – and see the dear boy every day! I just hope yer aunts'll like me an' think me good enough for Albert, that's all.'

Mabel smiled affectionately. ''Course they will – it'll more likely be the other way round!'

Daisy wrote to say that she was counting the days to seeing her sailor brother again and meeting Norah, about whom she had heard so much. The only regret was that Mabel was not coming too. However, this was perhaps all for the best, Mabel felt; Albert should be the one to introduce his Irish rose to his relations, rather than leaving this to his sister if she were there, while he lurked in the background. And there was another reason why Mabel wanted to stay in London: as spring advanced, so did the dreaded order that would send

Harry with his platoon of men across the Channel to the battlefields, and Mabel wanted to spend every available minute with the man who loved and needed her, while he was still at hand.

There were growing rumours circulating about a huge new assault on the German lines, a 'big push' that would thrust the enemy back and let the allies take possession of their trenches: it would bring the war on the Western Front to an end and release troops to go to the aid of their comrades fighting in Italy, Greece and Turkey. New conscripts streamed into the army, older men, family men who had heeded the new recruitment drive and the posters showing wives and children urging Daddy to go to the War. Actresses and music hall stars addressed them from the stages of theatres or at open-air meetings: Come to your country's aid in her hour of need! Finish off the war and come home safely to your womenfolk!

When Nurse McLoughlin went on her holiday at the beginning of April, Nurse Court was taken off night duty and sent to Men's II, where a porter gave her a knowing wink and passed her a note from Corporal Drover asking her to meet him at Battersea Bridge on her first afternoon off from the ward, which was the following day.

Harry was already waiting for her when she arrived and had the look of a man who had made up his mind about something.

'Bless yer, Mabel, I haven't got long – let's go into the park.' He took her arm and held it tightly as he led her along paths familiar to her from childhood. A few other strollers were enjoying the sunshine dappling through the burgeoning trees and the daffodils were coming into their full glory, but Harry seemed scarcely to notice his surroundings; she felt the tension in every step he took, every movement he made.

Unable to bear the suspense, she asked him to tell her straight away why they were there.

'Harry, dear, if ye've got somethin' to tell me, ye'd better say it. Have they sent for yer?'

'No, Mabel, not yet, but it'll be any day now. I don't how long I've got – it could be next week.'

He quickly drew her aside, off the path and towards a clump of laurels where he put his hands on her shoulders. He spoke urgently, breathlessly.

'I don't know how long I've got before they send me over there, dearest Mabel,' he repeated. 'And I want – I *need* – to hold yer, to look upon yer before I go. Somewhere we can be alone, somewhere we can lay down together and not be overlooked – to hold yer, to touch yer, Mabel. I'm askin' yer from the heart. I could go out there with courage if –'

His hands cupped her face as he pleaded with her; intense longing gave him boldness, while respect for her made him hesitate – hoping and despairing, yearning yet fearing.

'I could face whatever's out there if I could take the memory with me, Mabel, the memory of you – of us – together. D'ye know what I mean? D'ye understand me, Mabel?'

'Oh, yes. Yes, I do.'

'Oh, my dearest, dearest girl –' The peak of his uniform cap bumped against her forehead as he bent his face over hers. 'If only yer knew how I've fought against what I feel – about –'

'I've known for a long time, Harry,' she told him softly. 'And I've felt the same, only – only it'd be a risk, wouldn't it?'

'What d'ye mean, Mabel? I'd never take any *risk*, yer

185

know that. I'd never disgrace yer, Mabel. I'm not talkin' about – fornication.' Even saying the word cost him an effort. 'No, just to hold yer – to look at yer, to touch yer – yer lovely body. That's all I'm askin'.'

'But –' Mabel paused on the obvious question. 'But where could we –'

'Listen, Ruby's goin' to visit Herbert in Wandsworth next week, Tuesday probably, an' my father an' mother are goin' to spend the day at Deacon's Walk so's to be there for the boys when they come in from school. And Ruby'll need a lot o' support when she gets back. So there won't be anybody at Falcon Terrace, Mabel. Could yer get the afternoon off an' come there? I'll get a couple of hours by hook or by crook – trust me, Mabel, I wouldn't take advantage. I only want –'

'Not in yer parents' home, Harry, I couldn't. I'd be on tenterhooks all the time in case they came back. Just think, suppose we heard the key turnin' in the lock! Remember that time when yer mother came in with Ruby an' the boys, an' found us asleep on the sofa? Oh, no, Harry, we couldn't risk that again.'

'But Mabel, my love, where else? Now ye've said ye'll agree, I *must* have this to take to the Front with me! There's nowhere safe I can think of –'

His voice rose in his agitation and she put a finger over his lips.

'All right, my love, I think I can arrange it for us. I'm pretty sure I can find us the sort o' place we want – just for a couple of hours.'

'Where d'ye mean, dear?'

'Maudie's lodgin's.'

'Aah! I'd thought o' there, but never could've asked her, 'cause of what she'd think.'

'I know, but *I'll* ask her,' said Mabel, now quite determined.

186

'It'd have to be soon, Mabel, I could be posted within a week. But thank yer. Thank yer, an' bless yer for understandin'!'

'Good Gawd, Mabel, yer look all in. They're killin' yer at that place. D'ye want a cup o' tea or somethin' stronger? Gin?'

Maud Ling was also showing signs of strain. Eight weeks of pantomime at the Canterbury, doing eight shows a week, making time for Alex Redfern on his brief appearances and yielding unreservedly to his demands upon her, parting with him and worrying about him until he appeared again – all this had taxed her to the limit, and now she was filling in at various music halls doing chorus work and the occasional solo spot. And she was attending auditions for the West End.

'There's some whackin' great musical shows comin' up, Mabel, *Peg o' My Heart* at the Globe an' a real bull's-eye at His Majesty's, sort o' like Ali Baba an' the forty fieves, ever such lovely songs and fabulous costumes, romance, drama, the lot. I'm goin' for a part in it – it's called *Chu Chin Chow*. Anyway, what can I do for yer?'

'I – I don't know how to say this, Maudie, an' I hope yer won't think the less o' me for it, but – it's to ask a favour. A big one.'

'Yeah? Anyfing for you, Mabel. Go on.'

Mabel's whisper was so quiet that Maud had to ask her to repeat what she'd said.

'If Harry an' me could come here one afternoon to be on our own, Maudie, before he gets sent to the Front. And that'll be any day now.'

Maud drew a deep breath and her pale features softened into a half-smile, though her eyes held a strange expression. It might have been pity, Mabel thought, recognition of a common human need. Was there surprise, too?

'This bloody war,' she said, shaking her head. 'It brings aht the same in all of us, don't it, gal? 'Course yer can. When? Sat'day'd be fine, 'cause I'll be on stage. I'll give yer Alex's key.'

She asked no questions and when Mabel tried to assure her that the meeting was for nothing other than privacy, Maud waved her hands in a dismissive gesture.

'Don't want to know. Just mind yer take care, gal.'

'Thank yer, Maudie. I shan't forget this. He might not ever come back again, y'see.' It was the first time she had ever voiced this possibility.

'Yeah, an' 'e must be scared stiff, poor bloke, just like Alex. An' we 'ave tŏ do what we can for 'em, don't we, Mabel? Nah then, that's enough said. What abaht that bruvver o' yours? Still 'ead over 'eels wiv little Norah?'

When she heard that Albert and Norah were staying at Belhampton as an officially engaged couple, she clapped her hands.

'Go on! I'm that 'appy for 'em, Mabel, it does me 'eart good just to fink of 'em! Can't yer just see 'im, struttin' arahnd, prahd as a peacock, an' 'er all smilin' an' shy? Yer aunts'll take to 'er straight away, an' Daisy'll be chatterin' 'er little 'ead orf.' She grinned as a thought struck her. 'Oho, the Lady Alice'll be in for a big surprise, seein' what a beauty 'er bruvver's fahnd for 'imself, eh?' Suddenly Maudie was grave; without her powder and rouge she looked older than her twenty-four years. 'Gawd 'elp 'em, Mabel. Gawd 'elp all our boys an' bring 'em back to us.'

Mabel said softly, 'Yer know, Maudie, Albert wanted me to tell Norah about our family history, 'specially

188

about George – but I couldn't. It just wouldn't come out. I told her about our grandmother, but that's as far as I got, 'cause it just didn't seem necessary for her to know. But it brought it all back to me, Maudie, and what a good friend yer were all through that awful time.'

'Don't seem to matter so much nah, does it, Mabel? Not wiv all these poor devils gettin' blown to bits ev'ry day.' Maud blinked away tears and reached for the bottle. 'Don't know abaht you, gal, but I'm 'avin' anuvver drink.'

Mabel declined, and watched with some misgiving as Maud poured herself a generous glass and raised it to her lips. 'Cheers, Mabel. It's good to 'ave a friend yer can rely on. Yer meet some pretty dodgy characters in the featre, an' I'm not in the business o' tradin' me favours, if yer see what I mean. Not now I got Alex.'

Mabel sensed that Maud's life was lonely with Alex away for most of the time.

'D'ye see much o' Teddy these days?' she asked. 'Is he still at Dulwich?'

'Comin' up for the day on Sunday,' answered Maud, brightening a little. 'We'll go up on 'Ampstead 'Eaf an' see the sights. 'E'll be touchin' me for a bob or two, the cheeky little bugger,' she added affectionately.

Maud's picture of Albert and his Irish rose at Belhampton was not far from the reality. On her arrival Norah exclaimed at the beauty of the Hampshire countryside in spring – 'Sure it's as good as County Cork!' – while the comforts of Pear Tree Cottage quite took her breath away. She had feared that she would be shy when meeting Albert's relations, but with her darkly handsome young man at her side, now looking fit and well, she rose to the occasion and made an immediate impression on the Somertons and Miss Chalcott. If she lacked some of the social graces, she more than made up for it with her soft speech and pleasing manners.

'There's something very straightforward about her,' remarked Aunt Nell to her sister.

'And she's had a very good influence on *him*,' replied Aunt Kate approvingly. 'He's a changed boy – or I suppose I should say man.'

It was true. Anxious to smooth the way for Norah's visit, Albert had behaved in an exemplary fashion during his first week at Pinehurst. The handsome family residence had changed into a nursing home with the unmistakable smell of sickness, and paradoxically Albert Court felt more at ease in it. He shared a room with two other men and cheerfully fetched and carried for them, while generally making himself useful in the house, helping to serve meals and clear away, taking men to the lavatory without fuss, listening to the stories, some of them horrific, of how they'd come by their injuries. He did not object to being treated as a batman by some of the officers who were somewhat disconcerted when they found out that he was Miss Chalcott's nephew; it was she who told them, not Albert, who merely grinned. They heard a brief account of how he'd been torpedoed while in convoy, and it raised their awareness of the part being played by the merchant navy in wartime.

If he clashed with anyone, it was with his sister Alice. Her role at Pinehurst had been to put on a crisp white apron and look decorative. She gave out the mail and newspapers, arranged flowers and accepted compliments from the men. Practical care was given by a rota of local women who came in daily to help with washing and dressing, cooking the meals, taking away the bedlinen to wash and iron. Miss Chalcott was quite enjoying the challenge of running a convalescent

190

home, and found that Albert was always ready to run errands, open and close windows, replenish the fire and push wheelchairs when Alice was nowhere to be seen. And he began to make a definite effort to improve the way he spoke.

As soon as he brought in Norah McLoughlin to meet the men, she stole all hearts, and Albert positively swelled with pride in her. A natural nurse, she at once saw what need doing, unlike Alice who had to be asked to plump up pillows, refill water jugs or hot-water bottles, put crutches and walking sticks within reach – the little details that made for the patients' well-being.

'Bit of a busman's 'oliday for yer, Norah,' remarked Albert, but she assured him that there was nothing she would rather do. Alice found herself outshone and was in any case losing her early enthusiasm for comforting the wounded. Gerald Westhouse was serving in France with the Royal Flying Corps and young Sir Guy Savage, who was still completing his training, had invited her out for a drive and to take tea with his mother and sisters at the Hall. She had not actually mentioned this to Aunt Nell who had views about what was allowable and what was not for an engaged girl, and Alice was beginning to be bored with the war. She was also tired of the fuss being made over the Irish girl, and could not understand why her uncle and aunt should entertain a native of that rebellious province which was causing England so much trouble, demanding independence right in the middle of a ghastly war.

However, there was one good thing about the girl: she took Albert with her to Belhampton on Sunday to attend a poky little Roman Catholic chapel, which spared Alice the embarrassment of Albert in his ill-fitting suit and

191

hobnailed boots, clumping into the parish church and sitting with them in the family pew.

Mabel was already there when Harry arrived straight from Wandsworth in the uniform he detested but which gave him anonymity. London was full of New Army men, enlisted in the last three months and waiting to be sent to take part in the massive onslaught on the German line. There was new hope in the air, new expectation of an earlier end to the war.

She let him in at the front door into a dim passage where a stale smell of cooking lingered, and up two flights of stairs. They neither spoke nor touched until they reached the second landing and she turned the key in Maud's door. He followed her in and she relocked it. Then she turned to face him.

'Here we are, then, Harry. It's just gone two o'clock. I've got till four.'

'Mabel –!' He held out his arms to her. 'Yeah – yes, I can stay till then.'

Mabel did not move. 'Maud says there's tea an' milk in –'

'No, no, we've only got two hours, Mabel. I – I only want you.'

They were speaking in whispers and Mabel was rigid with nerves. The room was not large and much of the space was taken up by the three-quarter-size bed with its blue woven counterpane: it had a brass-topped rail at the head and foot. A sash window gave a nonde-script view of the back of Old South Lambeth Road, all drainpipes and blank windows, and Mabel wondered whether she should draw the curtains. There were two small cane-bottomed chairs and a curtained alcove with a wooden stand on which a water jug and washing bowl stood. There was also a gas ring with a box of matches beside it. The fire grate was empty, and the air struck chill and unwelcoming: they felt like intruders without Maud's cheerful presence, though a faint whiff of her scent hung on the air. *Bed's made up wiv clean sheets, gal.* They were alone. And yet Mabel stood rooted to the spot, unable to move.

Harry came and folded her in his arms. 'Oh, Mabel, Mabel, my dear,' he said, no longer whispering. 'Don't let's waste precious time. Take off yer hat an' coat.'

He removed his peaked cap and uniform jacket, hanging them on one of the chairs. She put her hat, bag and gloves on the other chair, and they sat down on the edge of the bed. Harry pulled her towards him.

'Kiss me, Mabel.' His arms went round her and she tried not to stiffen. Her lips felt dry.

'Kiss me, Mabel, my love. My own dear girl.'

She obediently raised her face and put her arms round his neck. They kissed gently and he stroked her cheek.

'Mabel, Mabel – I feel as if I can't ever let yer go.' His lips were on her forehead and he slowly kissed her eyes, her nose, her cheeks, her chin; she raised her head and he kissed her throat, nuzzling into the warmth of her neck, half covered by the frilled collar of her blouse.

'Sweet – oh, ye're so sweet, my love.'

She gave a long sigh and felt her body gradually softening in his arms. There was not a sound to be heard in the house. Down in the street there was the clop-clop of a horse drawing a cart and a man's voice briefly shouting an order. A dog barked, people passed by, far away from this room which now began to fill up with their presence, becoming less strange as they breathed the air and made it their own. Mabel tried not to think of anything but the present moment, here and now.

'Take off yer shoes, Mabel.'

With shaking fingers she untied the laces of her stout

black walking shoes and eased them off her feet. He removed his boots and then his socks, tucking each into a boot. Mabel's stockings were held up by the suspenders attached to her corset and she felt unable to draw her navy skirt up that high. She rubbed her feet together and he lifted them up on to the bed.

'Here, my love, lay down here with me.'

She let herself lie full-length on top of the bed, encircled by his left arm. With his right hand he stroked her hair and drew her face towards his again. Their kiss was longer and deeper this time, and she could feel the thud-thud-thud of his heartbeat beneath his shirt, the tremor that ran through his whole frame. When at last they had to draw apart to take a breath she was conscious of her own heart racing, and she gasped as his hand covered the curve of her breasts beneath the buttoned blouse. He spoke in a whisper again, but an urgent whisper, imploring, almost demanding to be obeyed.

'Open yer collar for me, Mabel – let me kiss yer shoulder – yer lovely warm skin.'

She fumbled with the top button of her blouse, and then the one below it. His hand was over hers as she undid each button down to the waist, revealing a cotton liberty bodice.

'Can yer take that off, Mabel?'

She sat up to pull the bodice over her head. And then his hands were upon her breasts, cupping them, stroking, gazing and exclaiming in wonder.

'I've never seen anythin' so beautiful, never. Never.'

His skin no longer cold but flushed with the heat of his desire for her, his fingers no longer bone-thin but firm and strong upon her flesh, he now worshipped her with eyes and hands and lips. 'How beautiful, how utterly beautiful,' he said again, the Salvation Army officer who had become a corporal in the British army. 'Such happiness, Mabel. I'm in heaven – sheer heaven.'

She sighed and murmured, her heart swelling with love and pride because of his delight in her. And was she also happy? Was she too in heaven on this April afternoon in Maud's Lambeth lodgings? Not quite, because however hard she tried to live the present moment to the full, the future still intruded. She could not forget the parting they would soon have to face, the agony of farewell again. And the fearful uncertainty that would follow.

'Sweet – oh, so sweet, Mabel, every inch o' yer,' he breathed, revelling in the feel of her soft flesh, holding her, touching her as never before. She too felt her body's response, the throbbing, the moistening of her woman's part, getting ready to receive him as an honoured guest. And she knew by the hardness beneath the rough material that he was just as ready to enter her: only four small buttons kept his erection out of sight.

'Yes, Harry, yes.' She answered the question he had not asked in words. And so the buttons were undone and she held in her hand the proof of his passion for her, proud and firm.

'Ah, this is too much for me, Mabel,' he muttered under his breath as she took his member in her hands, stroking it between her fingers. She lowered her head to touch it with her lips.

'Ah, Mabel – ah – I'm afraid o' makin' a mess –'

She told him it didn't matter, she had a handkerchief.

'But I'll make a mess – I'm going to – ah!'

He groaned, cried out and gushed forth his stream on to her white petticoat. She hadn't realised that her skirt was up above her knees. The top of her corset was digging into her uncomfortably, its row of hooks and eyes still securely fastened. Her drawers were on and her suspenders gripped the tops of her stockings. He had not come close to her and they had only done what lots of couples did, as she knew from the secret whispers between nurses at the Infirmary. Girls had to face the age-old problem of avoiding the disgrace of pregnancy, with all the agony that must follow: banishment to a mother and baby home and the heartbreak of parting with the child: or the danger of abortion, the risk of poison, damage, even death. Mabel knew all about it from what she had seen at first hand of other women's lives.

But Harry Drover had not been that close to her, though he now lay gasping out the last shudderings of the climax he had reached between her hands. Mabel found that she was extraordinarily moved by the stream of life that had flowed out from him. She leaned over and breathed in the scent of it on her petticoat, kissed the dewy dampness of what should have been hers; she knew she would not want to wash it away.

His breathing slowed to normal and he nestled his head against her breasts; she knew he was smiling, though his face was hidden. After a while she became aware of his weight upon her, for he had gained two stones since his convalescence began. She hadn't the heart to ask him to move, but closed her eyes and waited. She needed to empty her bladder, but that too could wait until he stirred. She had given him what he had asked of her, the memory he needed to carry away to the war with him, and in so doing had found a deep satisfaction herself.

And it had all happened so quickly: they still had an hour and a half. After using the chamber-pot, Mabel shyly suggested that they both remove their outer clothes – and she thankfully divested herself of corsets and stockings – and got properly into the bed, between the sheets. With her back to him, she lay closely curled in the convexity of his body, his knees behind hers, her head tucked beneath his chin – 'like a small letter "c" inside a big "C",' she said. With his arms around her they talked a little, dozed a little and pressed themselves ever closer together while the minutes ticked away towards four o'clock and the time when they must go their different ways.

'I love yer, Mabel. Whatever happens, I'll love yer for ever.'

And there was no need for regret, no asking for forgiveness, because there was nothing to forgive. Only thanks and gratefulness, a deeper bond of intimacy and understanding – and a memory for Mabel, too, to sustain her during the coming separation.

The call came two days later, and by the end of the week Corporal Drover had left with his platoon for Victoria Station and the train that would take them to Dover, from where they would be silently spirited across the Channel by night, with lights dimmed because of the U-boats. Once in France they were to be taken to a region of sloping hills and woodlands, of high ridges overlooking a green valley where the River Somme meandered through Picardy on its winding way to the Channel.

'There's goin' to be a massive bombardment o' the German trenches, Mabel,' Harry had told her, 'followed up by a tremendous forward thrust o' men, British north o' the river, French south of it, to drive 'em back to the Rhine, what's left of 'em, after all that night 'n' day shellin'. It'll wipe the poor devils out.'

The look of revulsion in his eyes and the set of his mouth showed how he felt at the prospect of such carnage, and Mabel remembered what Ada Hodges had said: *Anything to get the hateful business over.*

She said, 'But if this big push, this Somme offensive, as yer call it, brings the war to an end, Harry, well then – won't it be for the best?'

His expression was curiously blank and he closed his eyes. 'This hideous war, Mabel, my love. Whatever's it doin' to our lives?'

'Now, now, this won't do, Norah, I won't let you spend all your time at Pinehurst,' declared Aunt Nell. 'Albert must take you out for some sunshine and fresh air. Besides, Daisy says that you're never here when she comes home from school. I shall speak to Kate about it.'

Albert was only too pleased to have Norah all to himself and on the Thursday the couple spent a day in Belhampton, dining at the old Wheatsheaf Hotel, formerly a coaching inn on the London-to-Portsmouth road. They wandered round the cattle market, the ancient church and adjacent almshouses, they gazed up at the fine eighteenth-century mansions with their well-kept gardens. Norah was enchanted by everything she saw in Albert's company.

And there were dress shops and a milliner's where he told her to choose anything that took her fancy.

'I never 'ad a chance to bring yer a present, Norah, so let's make up for it now,' he said with the traditional open hand of a sailor in port. 'See that one over there wiv the lace on – the green one? It'd suit yer dahn to the grahnd – er, the ground,' he corrected himself.

Down to the ground this particular model was *not*, being in the newer, shorter style that came up to a lady's knees; but while Norah hesitated, Albert asked for the dress to be wrapped up for her, along with a more conventional gown in dark-blue with puffed leg-o'-mutton sleeves.

'D'ye want a hat to go wiv 'em? There's some big, flowery ones in the shop across the road. C'mon, let's get a couple o' them an' all.'

'For heaven's sake, Albert, whatever will yer aunts say, spendin' all yer money on me!' she remonstrated, but that wasn't all. In a little dark jeweller's shop off the main square, Albert asked to see rings and the man brought out a tray of glittering precious stones.

'Choose yer engagement ring, Norah. What abaht an emerald, to match that green dress?'

Norah flushed in embarrassment, horrified by the prices.

'Sure an' a little plain one'd do me fine, Albert,' she protested, and in the end settled for a single pearl in a pretty gold setting. Albert had to agree that it looked right on her and remembered a saying he'd once heard, 'as pure as a pearl'. When it was put on the third finger of her right hand it fitted perfectly, so the matter was settled.

'Now I feel as if we're prop'ly engaged, Norah,' he said with an odd mixture of pride and shyness. 'I'll fink o' yer wearin' it, an' – an' that'll keep me goin', like, when I'm back at sea.'

Seaman Court had had little practice in the language of love, but his devotion was as true as any poet's, and Norah thought him the wisest and wittiest speaker she had ever heard.

They walked back slowly along the Beversley Road between green hedgerows bursting with an abundance of new growth. On the banks cool yellow primroses gleamed and shyly peeping dog-violets. Albert was carrying the packages, but set them down at a spot

199

where the road passed over a stream. Standing on the little bridge he took his Irish rose in a gentle embrace.

'This is the happiest I've ever been in me 'ole life, Norah,' he told her gruffly. 'I don't deserve yer, but ye've made all the difference to me.'

She trembled in his arms like a fluttering bird. 'Yer sister knows the difference ye've made to *me*, Albert,' she answered softly. 'I *belong* to somebody at last, y'see.'

'Yeah, I know, she told me. An' you belong to *me*, darlin' Norah, for ever an' ever.'

His kiss upon her mouth was as light as the touch of a butterfly's wing. He would have loved to take her in his arms and kiss her as a pretty girl should be kissed, but there was something about Norah's trusting innocence that put an unfamiliar constraint upon him; she was like a being set apart, to be adored but treated with the greatest care.

'Ye're that precious to me, Norah – me own sweet little darlin' –'

He took her right hand and lifted it to his lips, kissing first the back of it and then turning it over to kiss the palm, pressing his mouth hard against it with all the passion he dared not show in a more intimate way.

'Yer know I got to go back to sea soon, Norah,' he whispered. 'I'd marry yer tomorrer if I could, only I got to get through this war an' learn to be more worvy o' yer.'

'But Albert, ye're dearer to me than all the world.'

And so he was, this man who had been saved from the sea by her prayers. Norah McLoughlin's heart soared with love and thankfulness, and she considered herself the happiest, luckiest girl in the world. With his hand still holding hers she offered him her rosy mouth again, all smiles and shy invitation, impossible to resist.

'Oh, my Gawd, Norah, I'm in 'eaven,' he gasped when at last they drew apart to take breath.

On his return from Belhampton Seaman Court was ordered to report to the SS *Galway Castle*, one of the Union Castle fleet patrolling the eastern Mediterranean and carrying men and supplies to the Eastern Front. Norah was dismayed, having hoped that he would remain in home waters, keeping guard over the Channel ports and the North Sea, though he assured her that no place was safer than any other in wartime.

In the Rising Sun on the corner of York Road he ran into an old friend and fellow striker from railway days, Sam Mackintosh, now a train driver and married, the father of a baby girl. Caught by the Military Service Act, Sam downed a few glasses and put a brave face on being drafted into the 13th London Rifles.

'Won't be so much as a bloody rat left alive in them Jerry trenches after the poundin' we're gonna give 'em!' he boasted.

Arthur Hodges, newly drafted into the same platoon, tried to be equally sanguine, but could not forget the sound of his wife's hysterical screams, imploring him not to leave her and the children. Her parents had sent for Dr Knowles who prescribed tincture of laudanum and told her gravely that his own son had already returned to the Front with the RAMC. He did not add that Stephen was preparing to take charge of a casualty clearing station behind the lines in preparation for the 'big push'. Arthur felt wretchedly guilty at leaving his wife in her condition, and the frightened faces of little Arthur and Jenny haunted his dreams.

On a sunny afternoon in May Mabel and Norah stood at a window on Men's II and waved to a battalion of

201

marching men in the street below. There were cheers and shouts of 'Come home soon!' from the onlookers, and the soldiers grinned as they hoisted their rifles and sang:

'Pack up yer troubles in yer old kitbag and smile,
     smile, smile!
While ye've a lucifer to light your fag – smile, boys,
     that's the style!
What's the use of worrying? It never was worth
     while –
So – pack up yer troubles in yer old kitbag and
     smile, smile, smile!'

Later – much later – Mabel was to marvel that men had actually sung those words on their way to the Somme – the bloodiest episode in the history of the British Army.

Chapter Eleven

Young Daisy Somerton was feeling distinctly aggrieved. Everybody seemed to be taken up with important matters to do with the war in one way or another and nobody was interested in her, not even her very best friend Lucy Drummond. Her twelfth birthday had come and gone without making any difference to her life, and certainly no improvement. If she walked over to Pinehurst she was told she was too young to be of any use to the men who were recovering from war injuries there, and if she played at the edge of the pond down by the green, scooping up frogspawn in a jar, she was scolded for dirtying her clothes like a child. Once it had been fun to keep frogspawn and watch the little black dots turn into commas that would one day be new frogs if they survived, but now it seemed pointless. Even her dear little kitten had grown into a cat and had kittens of her own. Uncle Thomas said that if she had any more they'd have to be drowned, otherwise Pear Tree Cottage would be overrun with the creatures, and when Daisy cried, Aunt Nell had told her not to be silly when there was so much worse trouble in the world.

Like the trouble at the Rectory where Mrs Drummond did nothing but cry because the eldest boy, Cedric, had been conscripted to go to the war like Harry and Albert and Gerald. Lucy cried about Cedric, too, and had nothing to say to Daisy about the things they'd been talking about lately: the business of growing up and what happened to girls when they were twelve or thirteen or fourteen. A lot of secret whispering went on among the girls at school, about how you got bigger and rounder in the chest, like Alice, and hair suddenly appeared under your arms and down there where you did number ones and number twos, things that were never mentioned out loud. And there was something else that happened to girls as they got older and bigger: Aunt Nell had spoken to her rather awkwardly about monthly periods and what had to be done to conceal the mysterious flow of blood. Daisy already knew from Alice that ladies had to wear strips of cloth between their legs, attached to belts round their waists, rather like babies' napkins, when these 'periods' were on, and that it was in some way to do with what happened later on when you got married and had babies. Daisy thought it sounded very messy. And there were some silly, giggly girls at school who whispered unbelievably vulgar things to each other about how and why babies began to grow. Daisy had no wish to hear the rude words they said, yet at the same time she felt left out of some secret knowledge. Her teacher said she was a very bright girl and she usually came top of the class at the end of term; yet silly girls at the bottom of the class seemed to know more than she did about certain things. It was no good asking Alice who was twittery and cross these days because Gerald was in France as an air pilot, and hadn't been home since the middle of March and now it was June. And Mabel hadn't been to see them at all this year, though it had been lovely when Norah came for the week in April and Albert had brought her all those presents. Now *that*'s what being in love should be like, thought Daisy, not giggly and rude like the things whispered about by those girls at school.

She picked up her sunbonnet and wandered out into

the lane which continued southwards over rich farm-land owned by the Savage family of Houghton Hall. Fields and woodlands lay shimmering in the blaze of a summer afternoon; the ripening corn was turning from green to gold, and fine dairy cows stood motionless in lush meadows. Daisy had heard the cuckoo that morning, but now all the birdsong was hushed, and the only sound was the tiny whirring of innumerable insects in the grass and on the still air.

Suddenly the quiet was broken by the clatter of a motor car engine, and Daisy stepped over to the side of the lane. Into sight came a dusty cloud containing the open-topped car from the Hall, all polished metal bodywork and leather upholstery. Young Sir Guy Savage was at the wheel and conscientiously sounded his horn long before he reached the young girl idling beside the lane. The lady beside him lowered her dark head and put a hand up to steady her hat, which was tied in place with a strip of white muslin as a motoring-veil, essential protection against wind and dust. But Daisy knew the blue flower-trimmed hat and, with a shock of surprise, realised the lady was her sister Alice who clearly did not want to be recognised.

The car roared off up the lane in its accompanying cloud and disappeared around the next bend. Alice hadn't said anything to Daisy about going out for a drive, but then Alice didn't say much about anything to her sister these days. Perhaps old Lady Savage had invited her up to tea at the Hall with those two daughters. What did it matter, anyway? If only Mabel would come to see her again! But Mabel was always so busy at that infirmary, and she and Norah were also in the middle of their final examinations; Albert had gone back to the dangers of the sea, which must be a terrible worry for Norah, just as Mabel worried about Harry. Nothing was the same as it used to be and all because of this horrible war. It was supposed to have been a great adventure and everybody had been so excited at the beginning, but now it was spoiling everything, and Daisy wished that it could all be over and done with.

'I thought you were at Pinehurst this afternoon, Alice,' said Mrs Somerton at teatime. 'But Kate says you haven't been there since Monday.'

Daisy's ears pricked up as she spread strawberry jam on her bread-and-butter.

'I took a walk over by Parr's Wood, Aunt Nell. Er – I thought I'd call at those cottages on the corner there, where the – er – what's the name of the people –'

'The Potters?'

'Yes, that's it, the Potters. There's been trouble there this spring – the children have had whooping-cough and I thought I'd enquire how they were.'

Elinor Somerton frowned. 'Mary Potter's girl had a cough during the winter, Alice, but it's all right now, she's back at school. But only last week they heard that the eldest boy, Mary's brother Billy, has been killed in France. Mary's heartbroken and somehow or other she's got to comfort the poor old parents. *That's* the trouble at Potters' cottages and I'm surprised you didn't know about it. I'm sure I told you.'

Aunt Nell's tone held a question and she looked straight at her eldest niece.

'Er – yes, well, Aunt Nell, I didn't actually reach the cottage. The sun was so hot and I had a headache, so I thought I'd rest a while in the shade by Parr's Wood, and then I came home.'

Alice spoke confusedly and looked flustered. When Daisy looked up she caught Aunt Nell's eye and blushed crimson, just as if *she* had told a lie, not Alice. In the

206

awkward silence that followed Mrs Somerton pressed her lips together to stop herself from saying more.

'I needed to be alone by myself, Aunt Nell. For heaven's sake, I needed to *think*,' said Alice irritably, using attack as the best form of defence.

'Very well, Alice. I realise how difficult it must be for you, with Gerald away in France,' said Mrs Somerton quietly, though Daisy felt that she would have questioned Alice further if they had been alone.

Sitting out in the central courtyard on that same sunny June afternoon, Mabel and Norah were joined by Maud, who had bought a chocolate cake for them and begged for a cup of tea in return. She sat beside them on the bench and fanned herself with a newspaper.

'So, that's your exams over, girls. When d'yer get the results?'

'Couple o' weeks,' replied Mabel wearily. 'And either we'll pass or we won't. Either way, we'll be stayin' on here for the time bein'.'

'Phew, i'n't it 'ot?' Maud went on. 'Wonder 'ow the boys are likin' it over there? Must be better 'n that rain an' mud they 'ad all winter. Alex reckons the big push is comin' up any day.'

Mabel nodded. 'That's what everybody's sayin'.'

'Harry an' all?'

'Harry never writes about that sort o' thing in his letters.'

'Well, they're not allowed to, are they? What *does* 'e say, then, apart from the love an' stuff?'

Mabel took the latest letter from her pocket. 'Not a lot, really, Maudie.' She opened it out and read a few sentences; there was only one page. 'The men are in good heart, and I am full of admiration for their courage and cheerfulness,' he had written.

There is a great sense of fellowship in a common purpose, and we are sure that the Lord will give us victory. The French have suffered heavy losses at Verdun, but so have the Germans. We always look forward to getting our rations, and it is funny to see bacon and eggs frying in a pan at the side of a trench, and water boiling in a billycan for tea!

Mabel paused, and Maud raised her eyebrows. 'Ooh, don't 'e write a lovely letter! Sounds as if it's come straight aht of a book!'

'The next bit's just for me alone,' said Mabel with a shy smile, for Harry had gone on to write, 'I carry the memory with me that we share, my dearest girl, and it never fails to renew my strength. You are ever in my thoughts and prayers, as I know I'm in yours.'

'Sure he's a grand writer, better than Albert for the spellin', but they all have their own ways o' sayin' things and isn't it grateful that we are to get their letters!' said Norah with feeling.

Mabel smiled. 'He says, "Give my kindest regards to your good friends Maud and Norah and say I thank the Lord for them. And my love to Daisy and all at Belhampton."'

'Well, 'e can't say fairer than that, can 'e? It's more 'n I get from Alex,' said Maud, though Mabel's impression was that the letter withheld more than it told. Corporal Drover's letters from the Front, so eagerly read, were full of praise for the men who lived and fought in the trenches behind the battle lines, and Mabel treasured every word, yet they were curiously unreal; apart from his brief, loving personal messages, they told her nothing of his true feelings about the warfare as he was now experiencing it.

'The staff nurse on Men's I showed me a letter from

her young man, an' he told her that the worst part was the noise o' shellfire all day an' sometimes all night as well,' Mabel told them with an anxious frown. 'He said it got on their nerves even more than the lice. Y' know, it must be far worse out there than any of us can understand.'

''Arry don't want to upset yer, Mabel, that's why 'e don't go into details,' said Maudie. 'I mean, d'ye tell 'im abaht the latest Zeppelin raids?'

'Oh, for God's sake, the great monsters, don't they scare the livin' daylights out o' me!' Norah shuddered, and indeed it was true that Mabel told Harry little about the terrifying raids when Londoners looked up to see the cigar-shaped airships humming in the night sky, manoeuvring to avoid the searchlight beams. Their bombs left random scars across the city and the last raid had set a row of warehouses ablaze down by the docks.

'So there y'are, Mabel, yer both try to save each other from worryin',' Maud said reasonably, and turned to ask Norah for news of Albert. The terrible naval battle of Jutland at the end of May had left the sea awash with bodies and both the British and German dreadnoughts had claimed victory after a night of mutual destruction. Mabel had shared Norah's thankfulness that Albert was in the Med on the *Galway Castle*, well away from the North Sea – but the loss of over six thousand British sailors had shaken the nation, and Norah wept as she knelt and prayed for the bereaved families. The tragedy had helped her to put into perspective a more personal matter that she had to bear: a painfully divided loyalty as an Irishwoman. The Easter Rebellion in Dublin against British rule had been forcibly crushed within twenty-four hours and a Royal Navy gunboat had shelled the rebel headquarters from the River Liffey.

All the leaders who had signed the proclamation of independence were arrested and executed, not even being allowed burial in consecrated ground. Anti-Irish feeling was bitter at a time when England was fighting for her life in a bloody European war and Norah had been subjected to pointedly harsh remarks against her countrymen. She had remained silent, saying nothing about centuries of British oppression, nor of the letter she had received from Mother Patrick, telling of the death of the Mayor of Cork while on hunger strike, and the British troops now occupying the city; but now she allowed herself the relief of confiding in her two dearest friends.

'The fact is that I'm here now, y'see, and not over there. I've thrown in me lot wid the English for better or worse, an' I'm goin' to marry an Englishman. If I was to stand up for me own people, there's them who'd tell me to go back there – an' I can't go back, not now.' She drew a deep breath. 'I just hope the Sisters o' Mercy don't think the less o' me for turnin' English. Mother Patrick says there's no love lost between the Cork people an' the British troops keepin' the peace there. Sure an' that's not my fault now, is it?'

'Of course it isn't, Norah, but we're sorry, just the same.' Mabel felt for her friend's divided heart in much the same way that she sympathised with Ruby Swayne who was finding life very difficult as the wife of a conscientious objector. Matthew and Mark had to endure ridicule and ostracism at school, and Ruby had been shouted at in the street and spat upon by a woman who had taken to drinking after her son had been killed in action. She told Mabel that Herbert had lost weight and looked wretched after three months of solitary confinement and a diet of mainly bread and water at Wandsworth Military Prison. His fingers were rough and sore from sewing mailbags, though he had refused to stuff canvas bags with cork to make make fenders for ships.

'He's to go before another tribunal at the end o' June, Mabel, and I pray to God that he'll agree to join up as a non-combatant,' Ruby confessed, though what the Drovers thought about their son-in-law's stance they kept to themselves, but the strain showed.

Norah brewed the tea for the three of them, and brought it out on a tray with a knife to cut the cake. Maud grinned as she raised her cup. 'Guess what, girls, I'm in the chorus o' *Chu Chin Chow* – and understudyin' for Ali Baba's wife *and* 'is son's little bit o' fluff, Marjanah. So ye'll 'ave to come an' see me doin' me stuff at 'is Majesty's – we open at the end of August – an' please Gawd, let the boys be 'ome to see it 'fore it finishes. Goin' to be good. Cheers!'

She gulped her tea with relish and held out her cup for a refill.

'I'm afraid there's no gin, Maudie.'

Maud gave her friend a sharp look. 'So? That don't worry me, gal, I can take it or leave it. An' besides, I can't 'ave me little bruvver gettin' into them sort of 'abits already.'

Mabel smiled and poured out another cup for her. When Teddy Ling had begun to turn up more and more frequently at his sister's lodgings, she had flatly refused to give him money and ordered him back to the Waifs and Strays home. But Teddy, now fifteen and a bright lad, had found himself a variety of jobs – first as a newsboy, then a messenger in a newspaper office, where he made himself both popular and indispensable. And when he moved into a tiny room at the top of the same lodging house as Maud, he used her gas ring to heat water and do his simple cooking, sometimes for them both. He was there for her when she got in late at night from wherever she was playing and he let himself out in the mornings while she was still sleeping. Maud complained that he got in her way and was a big responsibility, she never knew what he was up to, and suppose Alex was to appear on the doorstep? But she had also admitted that she quite liked having 'the little bleeder' around, and Mabel suspected that Teddy had noticed his sister's gin-drinking habit and that was the reason he had moved in with her. The brother and sister had been through bad times together as children, and the bond between them was deeper than might appear on the surface; when Maud complained that she had to keep an eye on him, Mabel felt pretty sure that Teddy might be watching her too. And that, she thought, was all to the good.

'Any ideas abaht what ye're goin' to do when they tell yer ye've passed?' asked Maud.

Mabel and Norah exchanged a look. They had already talked about this and come to no conclusion so far.

'Matron wants us to stay on as staff nurses and says we'll be in line for Sisters' posts this time next year if we do,' began Mabel without enthusiasm, but Norah cut in quickly.

'And she's been so good to us, it'd be a sin to let her down, so it would.'

'But Mrs Spearmann wants me to go to the Midway Babies' Home as Assistant Matron to Mrs Lovell –'

'Cor!' Maud was impressed. 'That's pretty quick promotion, ain't it? An' ye've always wanted to be wiv children. Are yer goin' for it?'

'Oh, Maudie, I don't know. I went there on me half-day last week and it always breaks me heart to see 'em, though Mrs Spearmann's done a lot to brighten the place up. They're not exactly *sick* children, poor little lambs, just short o' lovin' – and it'd be good trainin' for runnin' a Salvation Army children's refuge when Harry and me – oh, whenever this *wicked* war's over. I just can't seem to see me way ahead at all.' Mabel shook her head helplessly.

'Nobody can, darlin',' soothed Norah. 'An' shouldn't we stay here an' wait for our dear men to come home before we think o' movin'? An' stay together wid each other,' she added in a lower tone, for she dreaded separation from Mabel.

Maud glanced from one to the other and saw how tired they both looked, older than their years. She nodded. 'That's right, if yer can't make yer minds up, better stay put till yer can. Only trouble is, ye're sloggin' yerselves into the grahnd 'ere, that's what worries me.'

'I got a week's holiday comin' up in July,' said Mabel, brightening a little. 'It's been such a long time since I last saw Daisy an' the family. Oh, wouldn't I just *love* to take half a dozen little mites from the Midway for a holiday in the country!'

'Didn't yer say there was one poor little gal there 'oo'd wet'er drawers, an' yer wished yer could take 'er 'ome wiv yer?' asked Maud.

'Yes, dear little Mary.' Mabel nodded, brightening. 'There's a bit o' good news about her now, at least I hope so. Yer know I told yer Mrs Spearmann's been askin' friends o' hers to invite children to tea with 'em, to give 'em a treat – well, Mary got taken out to tea with these two spinster sisters who live together, quite well off, said they wanted to do somethin' for the war effort, an' Mrs Spearmann told 'em that this was one way o' doin' it. An' now Mary goes to stay with 'em overnight and they've really taken to the poor little soul.'

'Go on! D'yer think they might take 'er on? Adopt 'er, like?'

'Who knows? It seems they've got this maid, Kitty, who's about eighteen and came from an orphanage herself – she loves lookin' after Mary. Mrs Spearmann says it's changed all their lives, an' she's ever so pleased 'cause it was her idea in the first place.'

'Nice to 'ave the money to do it. 'S'easy enough to do good works if yer got the necessary,' said Maud the cynic.

'But Mrs Spearmann didn't *have* to take on the Midway, did she? It was Mr Poole's doin' in the first place, gettin' her interested – and yet I thought he was a hard man. Yer never can tell with people.' Mabel spoke thoughtfully. She had not finally made up her mind whether to take up Olive Spearmann's offer or not. It would be an opportunity for her to do some good and enjoy doing it, for it had always been her dream to look after childen in need of love and care.

But there was Harry who also needed her and, as Norah had hinted, they were not in a position to take on new commitments while their menfolk were fighting a war.

The examination results were published on the first of July and all the finalists had passed as general nurses. Five of them, including Nurses Court, Davies and McLoughlin, were also entered on the register of the Central Midwives Board.

But this news passed almost without comment at Booth Street. That first day of July was also the first day of the long-planned Somme offensive. While the nation held its collective breath for news, the reports that filtered through at first seemed to be encouraging; in fact, the first day was presented as a victory, and losses were described as by no means excessive.

THE BIG PUSH: A GREAT BEGINNING ran the headline in the *Observer*. The heroism and self-sacrifice of the men was extolled, and hopes ran high at home where families waited for news of their own sons, husbands and brothers taking part in the great conflict: until they had news of their own men they could not allow themselves to rejoice.

Within a matter of days the dreadful truth began to emerge with the casualty lists taking up whole pages in all the newspapers, national and local. Extra pages had to be added to make room for the thousands upon thousands of names in column after black column: the dead, the wounded and the missing. Whole batallions had been wiped out; complete units had been mown down in the advance on the German lines, for the enemy had not been dislodged by the week of bombardment upon their deeper, better organised dugouts. As the British soldier obeyed the order to move forward with his bayonet fixed, Jerry shot him dead.

Mabel frantically scanned the casualty lists under D, but found no Henry W. Drover among the twenty thousand British dead on that first day, or the forty thousand wounded; but among the fallen were the names of Arthur Hodges and Sam Mackintosh.

Chapter Twelve

Mabel could not remember nursing a more demanding sick child than five-year-old Timmy Baxter. He came into Women's II from the Midway in a semi-comatose condition, with a high fever and a swelling behind his left ear that had been treated with hot poultices. The battle for his life dominated July 1916 and it took another two months before he was fit to be discharged; in time to come Mabel could never separate Timmy's illness and recovery from the other events of that fateful quarter. As soon as he was admitted, the duty doctor sent for the surgeon who looked at the boy and gravely shook his head.

'Abscess of the mastoid process and probably clotting of the lateral sinus – which means that the infection could be all over him by now. We'd better get it drained, though it's probably too late – he could be brewing a brain abscess and meningitis, I shouldn't wonder. Still, get him ready for theatre straight away.'

Mabel accompanied the porter who carried the boy in his arms to the operating theatre where his limp body was routinely strapped down on the table. Mabel held his hand and talked to him in a low voice while the anaesthetist sprayed chloroform on to a gauze and cotton-wool pad gripped in the metal cage of a hand-held Schimmel-Busch mask. She knew that Timmy was unaware of her, or his surroundings, but she talked quietly just the same until he gave a choking moan and passed into merciful unconsciousness; the knife was inserted and a large quantity of pus under pressure was drained off; dressings and bandages were applied, and Timmy was returned to Women's II with a small chance of survival.

He survived the next forty-eight hours, but then came days of agony that wore down the nerves of staff and patients alike. He screamed at the top of his voice for hours on end, and clawed at the bandages round his head and neck. His arms were splinted to his sides to stop him doing this, but Mabel could not bear to see him rendered so helpless, and she made tubes out of rolled cardboard to encase his arms, which meant that he could at least move them from the shoulder, though unable to bend his elbows. She fed him drinks from a feeding cup, but anything semi-solid was spat out, and he would not take the cup from anybody else. It was next to impossible to get him to swallow the bitter opium-based sedative that was prescribed for him, or the equally nasty-tasting syrup of chloral. An injection of morphia was ordered to be given at night, and Mabel felt treacherous as she dissolved the tablet in boiled water on a spoon and then drew it up into the glass syringe. The needle was jabbed into Timmy's tiny buttock and his yell of pain caused every patient to wince.

'Omigawd, can't yer do anythink to shut 'im up, Nurse Court?' pleaded the women, and Mabel would once again lift Timmy out of his cot and walk up and down the bare boards of the ward with him.

'Hush, hush, Timmy, ssh-ssh, Mabel's here, never fear,' she would croon softly, over and over again until he fell into an exhausted slumber for an hour or two.

And slowly, slowly, his temperature began to fall and the foul-smelling discharge lessened.

*   *   *

Every day Mabel hurried to the dining-room for the post, but there was no word from Harry, and the Drovers had not heard from him either since the horrific first of July. Ruby Swayne's anxiety for her brother was aggravated by her husband's continued absolute refusal to take any part in the war, and he received more rough handling at the second tribunal before being sentenced to imprisonment in Dartmoor for the next five years.

'I shall have to get work, Mabel,' Ruby said. 'I can't look to my parents or the Salvation Army to support me and the boys for all that time. I shall have to give up our house and find somewhere smaller.'

In the event, she stayed at her home in Deacon's Walk, and continued to work as a Salvation Army officer during school hours while offering emergency overnight accommodation for homeless women and girls when the Army called upon her services. She could have earned more money in a munitions factory, but this would have gone against all the ideals that Herbert was now upholding as a prisoner of conscience.

Doris Drover could not conceal her indignation on her daughter's behalf. 'How much more use Herbert could be as a non-combatant!' she burst out in a moment of exasperation. 'Our poor Harry could be in need of a stretcher-bearer and an ambulance driver while Herbert's spendin' his time breakin' stones at a place too far away for his wife and children to see him – an' his poor old mother breakin' her heart, an' them two poor little boys bein' shunned at school – it's too bad of him!'

Mabel sent a note of sympathy to the bereaved family at Rectory Grove in Clapham where the blinds were permanently drawn, expecting no reply and getting none. Maud Ling was very sorry for all that she had said about Ada Hodges and sent her flowers. It was from

Olive Spearmann that Mabel learned of Ada's pathetic state, the terrible wails heard by the neighbours when the telegram arrived; her parents moved in to look after her and the children, but Ada, whose third child was expected in September, took to her bed and turned her face to the wall, refusing to be comforted. A polite note arrived at the Infirmary from Mrs Clay, thanking Ada's friends for their kind wishes to her daughter, but saying that Ada had been totally crushed by the death of Arthur and did not wish to see anybody.

'His poor parents are also grieving, but they find some solace in our grandchildren,' she wrote. 'Ada will not take any interest in life, and we fear for her future and the unborn child.'

Mabel tried to imagine how it would be if she and Harry were married and had children – and then if he'd had to go to the war and been killed, as Arthur had, she knew without a shadow of doubt that his children would be her greatest comfort; she thought of Timmy Baxter who would be waiting for her on Women's II, his hollow eyes brightening at the appearance of his Nurse 'Maby' again. How much more would Harry's child give her reason to go on living! Poor little Arthur and Jenny, deprived of both parents – and poor Ada, not to see where her consolation lay . . .

'Hey, girls, let's go to Charing Cross Station to meet the troop trains comin' in!' said Nurse Tasker. 'Everybody's buyin' up all the flowers to throw at the war heroes!'

Mabel shook her head, but Norah had an afternoon off and agreed to accompany Betty to join the crowds of cheering Londoners who congregated at Charing Cross and Victoria Stations to meet the trains coming in with men who had landed at Dover and Folkestone.

Mabel settled on the bench in the central courtyard

with several pairs of stockings to mend. She had always dreaded confronting the agony of the war wounded and when Norah returned her face confirmed Mabel's worst fears.

'Oh, 'twas dreadful, dreadful – ye should've seen the ambulances lined up to meet the train – a dozen of 'em at least. God in Heaven, Mabel, there never were so many fine young men laid low. Ye could hear the people sighin' instead o' cheerin', an' women were cryin' out names, askin' for their sons, wonderin' if they were there, 'cause yer couldn't see close up.'

Mabel shivered. 'I'm thankful I wasn't there, Norah – I was afraid it'd be like that. But surely there were *some* men walkin' off the train? They can't all've been stretcher cases.'

'No, there were men walkin' on their two legs, but ye should've seen 'em, Mabel – filthy they were, uniforms covered in mud, boots that looked as if they'd been on for weeks – and the *faces* of 'em, Mabel, that was the worst of all, their eyes. There was one young boy, must've been the same age as Albert, nothin' wrong wid him as far as I could see, but his eyes were starin' at somethin' only he could see. His poor mother was there to meet him, but he didn't speak a word, just went on starin' at nothin', God save him!' And Norah McLoughlin burst into tears at the thought of one young man's horror, while Mabel stared at her, thinking of Harry.

At the beginning of August Mabel was greeted on her entry into the staff dining-room with the longed-for news: 'A letter for yer, Nurse Court – from France!'

She tore open the envelope with trembling fingers. The letter was brief, only half a page, and as she read it her heart sank and she put her hand to her mouth.

'My dearest Mabel,' said the uneven scrawl that was in Harry's hand and yet seemed unfamiliar. 'Pray for me and all of us here in the Hell.' The word spelt with a capital H could have been Hell or Hill. 'All the dear men of my platoon that were in my care are lost and their Blood is on everything I see everywhere. This world will never be again the same without them, LOST FOR EVER. I trust I shall see you again my Angel in the Land of the living. Pray for us all that He Who is All-Merciful will bring me up out of the horrible Pit the miry clay.'

Mabel recognised the jumbled quotation from Psalm 40, but the general tone of the letter was different from any she had previously received from Harry, and clearly reflected a mind in turmoil, if not torment. That evening she changed her plan to go to the cinema with Ethel Davies, and got on a Battersea bus, which dropped her at the end of Falcon Terrace, where she found that Ruby and her two sons were also visiting at number 8.

The Drovers had had no news, but on hearing that Mabel had a letter, Harry's father at once asked to see it.

'Oh, my poor boy,' he muttered under his breath as he read the short scribble. 'May the Lord help him, my poor boy.'

'Let me see it!' Doris practically snatched it from him. 'Oh, Harry, my son! This can't be from him!' She began to cry. 'He never wrote this!'

'Yes, he did, Mother, but he's badly shocked,' answered her husband. 'He tells yer there, he's lost every one o' the boys in his platoon, the ones he helped to train at Wandsworth. And he's blamin' himself; in fact, he says he sees their blood everywhere. The poor boy's sufferin' from shock.'

Ruby Swayne glanced at Mabel, then took the letter from her mother's hand. On reading it through she looked up with tired eyes. 'I think he was drunk when he wrote this,' she said quietly.

'How dare yer say such a thing!' cried her mother. 'My boy never touches a drop o' that stuff, never in his life.'

'But somebody might've offered him a drink and he's not used to it,' persisted Ruby, and John Drover sighed heavily.

'Ruby may be right, Mother,' he said. 'These are terrible times and we can't picture what it's like over there. Thank yer for bringin' it to show us, Mabel, and the best thing we can all do now is what he asks of us – to pray for him. Here, now, just where we are, let's ask the Lord's help for our son.'

In the little living-room the family knelt down, and Mabel fell on her knees with them. For a minute the only sounds were Doris Drover's stifled sobs, then her husband cleared his throat and began to pray aloud for Harry and all those caught up in fighting a war they had neither sought or wanted. 'If it be Thy will, O Lord, return our son to us in soundness o' body and mind,' he ended. 'And now let's join together in sayin', "Our Father who art in heaven" . . .'

They all recited the Lord's Prayer and Mabel realised that Drover had not once mentioned Herbert Swayne, now forced to labour from dawn to dusk in the stone-breaking sheds of the prison on the bleak moor. With hands sore and roughened, isolated from his loved ones, inadequately fed and labelled a coward and a traitor, his lot was not enviable, as she knew from Ruby. But he had clearly lost the sympathy of his in-laws.

Another brief letter arrived ten days later, in which Harry said he was on three days' leave in France, billeted in a village some twelve miles from the front line. He and three other men were resting in the blessed

222

quiet of the country, he wrote, adding that he did not join his companions on their trips into the nearest small town at night. 'I look up at the sky at night where I see your face my own beautiful Angel.'

Reading between the lines, Mabel guessed that the oblivion offered by alcohol and available women was too great a temptation for most men to resist when the next week they might be lying dead in no man's land. But Harry had his angel and the secret memory they shared.

Against all odds, Timmy Baxter overcame the ravages of a virulent infection and was pronounced to be out of danger by the time Mabel was due to go on her holiday. He was still pale and sunken-eyed, and would always have some loss of hearing in his left ear, but his life had been saved, and he could feed himself and play with the battered toys kept in the wooden box at the bottom of Women's II. Mabel hated leaving him, but the surgeon praised her for her part in his recovery.

'You saved his life just as much as I did, Nurse Court,' he told her, and the Ward Sister remarked on her patience with the boy, the extra time she had put in to give him the care and attention he needed. And so said the women who had watched his progress.

'Ye're a brick, Nurse Court, a bloody marvel! 'E'd've driven us all crazy – we'd've throttled 'im!' they told her with alarming candour. 'Nearly drove us orf our chumps, 'e did!'

But Mabel smiled and hugged Timmy Baxter, who had done exactly the opposite for her. Far from driving her mad, his demands had saved her sanity at a time of agonising worry over the fate of the man she loved.

'Nothing's the same any more, Mabel,' said Daisy sadly.

'Everybody's busy with things to do with the war, but they won't let me do anything. Aunt Nell and Alice go every day to help look after the men at Pinehurst, but I've got to stay here and help Cook in the kitchen and tidy the bedrooms and do the dusting because there's only one maid, poor Margery with the harelip. It's been the dullest summer holiday I've ever had.'

Mabel hardly knew how to answer her discontented younger sister. She and Daisy were sharing a bedroom at Pear Tree Cottage, and her aunts absolutely forbade her to visit Pinehurst while on her week's holiday. The war had touched Belhampton since her last visit and a strange quietness lay over the countryside, now largely bereft of men. A group of young women had come to work on the farms, which had caused quite a stir among the locals. Mabel had seen the posters advertising the Women's Land Army, showing a bonny girl wearing boots beneath her skirt and sporting a hat. The real ones wore men's trousers tied round the waist with string and scarves round their heads. They drove the dairy herds down the lanes to and from milking, raked out cowsheds, stables and pigsties. In the evenings some of them went to the village inn and downed their mugs of ale alongside the older men.

'They smoke cigarettes, too, and laugh out loud and don't care what anybody says about them,' reported Daisy, adding in a wistful tone, 'I wish I could be a land-girl, Mabel.'

Thomas Somerton had to put in long hours at Chalcott Draperies, just like Ada Hodges's father at Lipton's, because of the absence of young men. Aunt Nell confessed to Mabel that she was worried about him. 'He's fifty-five, now, and gets so tired.' She sighed. 'Sometimes he comes home looking quite grey-faced, and makes me think of my own dear father who was only a year older when he had that fatal seizure.'

Mabel sympathised and refrained from mentioning that old George Chalcott's death had been blamed on her mother, Anna-Maria, his beloved youngest daughter who had run off with the improvident Jack Court and shamed the whole family.

'We've had some very sad cases at Pinehurst lately, Mabel,' went on her aunt one evening when they were alone. 'Some of them are very difficult to nurse and Kate has had to employ women to sit up at night in case of disturbances. Some have terrible dreams, shouting out and sleepwalking; in fact, Kate's had to get up herself in the night to talk to men who've broken down and wept like children because of their injuries, the loss of a hand or foot, you know.'

Mabel was horrified. 'Oh, Aunt Nell, how dreadful. Don't they go to special hospitals?'

'They have to wait their turn because there are so many. We get much worse cases now than at first and I've got a better appreciation of the things you have to do at that Infirmary, Mabel. We can't afford to be too ladylike any more.'

'So that's why Daisy's not allowed to go with you?'

'Oh, dear me, no, it's no place for a child. And Alice has had to overcome a lot of her reluctance, not that she's any the worse for that, it's opened her eyes to what this dreadful war is doing to the men fighting in it.'

'Has she heard from Gerald lately?' asked Mabel.

'She gets a few letters, but it's been night and day flying for his squadron for months with no home leave, poor Gerald. It's good that she's got this work at Pinehurst to keep her occupied.'

'Yes, work's a great help – in fact, it's a life saver,' agreed Mabel, thinking of Timmy Baxter. 'And I admire

Alice so much for looking after the wounded, because it's something I've always dreaded having to do.'

But whenever Mabel attempted to talk to Alice about Pinehurst, or anything else for that matter, she found her very difficult to approach. She longed to be closer to the lovely girl she had looked after as a child in Battersea, but her sister seemed embarrassed by her overtures.

'Alice, dear, it seems such a pity, with both of us bein' engaged to men fightin' out there, that we can't share more with each other,' pleaded Mabel. 'Y'know what I mean, we're both goin' through the same thing, wonderin' about 'em all the time, lookin' out for letters. Couldn't we –'

Mabel's words tailed off into silence as Alice gave a little shrug. 'I'm sorry, Mabel, but it isn't really the same, you know. I don't think you can compare our situations.' After a short pause, she went on, 'Did Aunt Nell tell you that Lady Savage visited Pinehurst last week with her two daughters? She was most impressed by what Aunt Kate's doing there and she's talking of turning over part of Houghton Hall as a convalescent home for wounded officers.'

Which effectually checked any attempt to draw closer. There was a barrier between them that prevented any real intimacy and Mabel regretfully came to the conclusion that Alice preferred it to be that way.

When the next day brought them an invitation to tea at Houghton Hall, Alice was suddenly transformed. Her dark eyes sparkled and she seemed to be brimming with suppressed excitement. It was not just one of Lady Savage's At Homes, but a special invitation to Miss Chalcott and Mrs Somerton, Miss Somerton and Miss Daisy.

'I expect she wants to consult with you, Aunt Kate,' said Alice with a satisfied air.

Miss Chalcott sent a polite reply up to the Hall, adding that their eldest niece was staying with them, and back came an immediate invitation to Mabel, at which Alice's heart sank. She fervently hoped that Mabel would mind her 'p's and 'q's and not bore them all to death with tales of that tiresome child she had nursed after an ear operation. She found her sister's jarring London twang was nearly, though not quite, as bad as Albert's.

Tea at Houghton Hall was in the drawing-room, with its casement doors open on to the terrace, and Lady Savage's daughters shared hostess duties with her. The elder girl, the Honourable Mrs Rosamund Bennett, had been recently married to a younger son of Sir Thomas Bennett; her husband was newly appointed as a major in the 18th Hampshire Fusiliers and she had come on a visit to her mother with a happy secret to impart. Miss Georgina Savage was the same age as Alice and had been told to converse with the three sisters.

Mabel looked around her with interest, impressed but not overawed by the grandeur of the Hall and the Her Ladyship's condescension. The daughters of the house were pleasing enough and she smiled politely as she accepted a cup of tea from Miss Georgina who asked how the war had affected life in London.

'Well, life's not what it was, that's for sure, Miss Georgina. Everythin's sort o' shabby, y'know, 'cause of all the shortages, an' no lights on after dark 'cause o' the Zeppelins.'

'Oh, do tell us about those horrid airships – have you seen one?'

'Yes, great big things dronin' away in the sky an' movin' at a fair rate. People either come out o' their houses to look at 'em, or hide away under their stairs in case a bomb drops on 'em! Only last week there was one came up from over Tilbury way, an' the guns were firin' full blast tryin' to shoot it down – but it turned and went back down to Mersea. And the week before –'

Alice had sat with closed eyes as if praying for strength, willing her sister to be quiet. 'I believe your mother wishes to discuss the conversion of part of the Hall as a convalescent home, Georgina,' she interposed, cutting Mabel off in mid-sentence.

'Oh, er, yes, we enjoyed our visit to Pinehurst,' Georgina replied. 'Mamma greatly admires Miss Chalcott's work for the wounded.'

Mabel felt herself to be silenced and tried not to be hurt, though Daisy glared and shook her head when Georgina offered her a slice of cake. Alice was humiliated by this display of bad manners, but Daisy stuck out her lower lip and continued to glower.

This awkward situation was saved by the arrival of the son of the house, the newly qualified Flying Officer Sir Guy Savage. He kissed his mother who greeted him fondly.

'Guy! How good to see you, just as we have guests from Belhampton this afternoon.'

'So I see, Mother.' He smiled, turning his attention first to the older ladies.

'How d'ye do, Miss Chalcott? Please allow me to congratulate you on your wonderful work at Pinehurst – my mother talks of little else! And Mrs Somerton, I know that your time is much taken up there, too.'

He was a fresh-faced young man of middle height with fair hair and light-coloured eyes, who had the easy charm of one raised and educated to be the heir of Houghton Hall. Having done his duty towards the older ladies he turned to the younger ones, and Mabel saw how his eyes were drawn to Alice.

'Always a pleasure to see you, Miss Somerton – and, er, Miss Daisy,' he added to the scowling younger sister. 'I hope Georgie's taking care of you. May I pour myself a cup of tea?'

As he helped himself to tea and cake, Mabel sensed Alice's interest beneath her demure exterior, her consciousness of the young officer's presence.

'Georgie, you are failing in your duty,' he said, indicating Mabel. 'You have not introduced me to the other young lady.'

'Oh, I beg your pardon, Guy. Mabel, this is my brother Guy. And Guy, this lady is Miss – er – Mabel, the elder sister of Alice and Daisy.'

'Alice's sister? Then why have we not met before, Miss Somerton?' he asked, holding out his hand. 'Alice has never mentioned another sister!'

Alice blushed crimson, and before she could reply Mabel interposed, 'The name's Court, sir. I'm Mabel Court.'

'Then good afternoon, Miss Court, I'm delighted to make your acquaintance. I take it that you are a half-sister to Alice and Daisy, then?'

'No, we're the same family, sir,' said Mabel. 'I've taken after me mother for looks and me sisters are dark like our dad.' He raised his eyebrows and Alice looked as if she wished that the floor would open and swallow her up.

Elinor Somerton hastily came to the rescue. 'My husband and I adopted Alice and Daisy after the death of their mother, Sir Guy. Mabel was older and preferred to stay in London where she has just completed training as a nurse.'

'How absolutely splendid, Miss Court!' he exclaimed. 'Which hospital are you at?'

'The Booth Street Poor Law Infirmary, sir.'

'Booth Street? Now where have I heard that? Is it in Lambeth?'

'Yes, not far from the Elephant and Castle.'

'That's the one! I heard about it from a chap I know, a flying ace who came to speak to us at Upavon. He's friendly with an actress who took him to visit this place last Christmas – a most frightful hole he said it was – but this splendid girl entertained on all the wards, singing and dancing like a trooper. She properly livened the place up, he said – ah, I see that you're nodding, Miss Court.'

'Yes, I was there!' Mabel told him eagerly. 'The actress was my friend Maudie Ling and her young man's called Alex Redfern. It made all the difference to Christmas, havin' them come to visit an' entertain.'

'But this is amazing, Miss Court! Redfern has been an inspiration to us all, the man simply lives for flying. And for the lovely Maud Ling, of course – she's a friend of yours, then?'

'Yes, ever since we were children. She used to –' But Mabel checked herself. The days of Maudie begging in the streets were long gone. 'A very good friend she's been to me and I reckon she'll make a big name for herself one o' these days.'

'Ah, that's exactly what Redfern says. Why haven't you told me all this, Alice?'

'When have I had the opportunity?' she countered quickly, and Mabel's sharp ears caught the note of warning in her voice. There were undercurrents here that her aunts clearly knew nothing about: something was going on between this young man and her sister.

'You should be very proud of your sister, Alice,' he said.

Alice nodded and managed a smile, though her discomfiture was painful to witness. 'Of course I am.'

Daisy caught Mabel's eye and gave her a very unlady-like wink, which had the effect of restoring Mabel's sense of what was important and what was not. She tried to imagine what Maud would have said about this afternoon's visit to the gentry, and the very thought made her smile to herself. The pretentious tinkling of teacups and exchanging of polite nothings with Lady Savage and her daughters – how trivial it all was compared with the real world she knew at Booth Street, the value of friends such as Maud and Norah!

And yet . . . this young man was about to find out the true horror of war at first hand. He would experience the danger and the terror faced by Alex Redfern and Gerald Westhouse. His mother and sisters would share the same daily anxiety endured by tens of thousands of families with a loved one away at the war. This war that had levelled the differences of class and status in a common bond of suffering.

So Mabel smiled civilly and bowed to their hostesses and Sir Guy when it was time to go.

The letter from France was waiting for her on her return to the Infirmary. Her name and address on the stained envelope were in an unfamiliar hand, and she felt the blood drain from her face when Norah handed it to her.

'D'ye want me to open it for yer, darlin'?'

Mabel sank down on to a dining-room chair, her blue-grey gaze fixed on Norah who slit the envelope open with a knife and drew out a single sheet of paper. She looked at the signature.

'It's from Captain Knowles, Mabel.'

'Oh, my God.' Mabel's first thought was that Stephen had written to break the news of Harry's death in action. She could not speak, but sat with open mouth and imploring eyes.

231

'He says, "Dear Miss Court,"' Norah began. '"I am writing to let you know that Corporal Drover is on his way to – to –" Oh, Mabel, he says Harry's on his way to Folkestone!'

Mabel gave a cry. 'Oh, thank God! Oh, heaven be praised!' She put her hands to her face and heads turned in the direction of the two girls in the dining-room. 'Go on, *go on*, Norah, do!'

With a voice that shook with relief, her friend read on. '"He has sustained a wound of the right shoulder from a bullet which has shattered the scapula and dislocated the head of the humerus. It will need immobilisation for some time –"'

'So he'll be home to stay this time!' cried Mabel, laughing and crying. 'It'll take *months* for that to heal – oh, thank God! Sorry, Norah, go on.'

'"– and it is not possible at this stage to assess the long-term effects. There may be permanent loss of movement of the shoulder."'

Norah paused and looked at Mabel's shining eyes, the tears on her cheeks.

'He says there's somethin' else he must tell ye, Mabel.'

'Does he? Here, Norah, I can read it meself now.'

And taking the letter she scanned the page, down to where Norah had stopped.

But there is something else I must tell you, Mabel. Harry is badly affected by *war shock* due to the terrible pressures of trench warfare and the loss of his whole platoon. It has taken the form of an acute melancholic state and loss of speech which even without the wound has rendered him unfit for service. The shoulder injury is a blessing in a sense, strange as that may sound, as victims of war shock are not considered as casualties, though since the beginning of the Somme offensive there has been a marked increase in these distressing cases.

I have to warn you, Mabel, that he will need all your care and patience, because no man who has seen and survived what has taken place here will ever forget it.

The letter ended with the signature 'Stephen Knowles'.

'Oh, Norah, where will he be by now?' cried Mabel, hugging her friend in her relief. The date of the letter was two days ago. 'I must go round to his parents and see if they've heard anythin',' she said. 'And maybe Dr Knowles – Stephen's father – can find out from the Red Cross where he's gone – oh, my Harry! Comin' home after all he's been through!'

'But Mabel, darlin', ye saw what the doctor said – Harry can't talk, an' he might be like that poor young fella I saw at Charing Cross who didn't seem to know his own mother –'

'Oh, Norah, he'll know me! He's probably in England already, praise be to God!'

By the following day all the next of kin of the latest batch of casualties had been notified of their arrival and destinations. Corporal Drover had been taken by ambulance straight from Charing Cross Station to the Tooting Home, now renamed the Church Lane Military Hospital. By the time Mabel arrived at his bedside, his parents and sister were already there, painfully trying to understand a man who had lost touch with reality.

Chapter Thirteen

Day and night the pounding of shells. The screams of pain, the obscenity of young, healthy bodies torn apart. The open, dying eyes of men he'd known and loved as brothers, all gone, all dead, and he alone left to slither in their blood. Night and darkness, pain, always pain. Dawn and sunlight, blood, always blood. Not for him the quiet earth where the dead find peace at last, not for cowards and betrayers, cut off out of the land of the living.

Voices come and go, hands come and touch, lift, carry. A voice he knows, saying his name: 'Harry.' This voice makes him think of Mabel. Is it a friend? He doesn't know, he's not sure.

'Steady on, Harry. You've got a nasty injury to your shoulder.' A wet cloth, a bandage, a sharp prick – a bayonet? 'It's a Blighty one, Harry. We're sending you home.'

He doesn't understand, the words don't make any sense. Jolting movement, pain, a stifling railway carriage with shelves instead of seats. The warm smell of bodies. Thirsty.

A ship, rocking, night and darkness. Day and night, another train carriage, a long journey and good God, a London ambulance – people walking, talking, real people, a real house, a real room, big, a real bed. Quiet. Drink. Pain. Voices near and far. Another night.

Another day. Voices, faces, getting closer, a woman with tears on her face, a man's gentle hand over his own. He opens his mouth but no sound comes out. They stare at him – good God, his mother and father! They're saying something, but he can't make it out; and there's another woman he ought to know. Somebody says 'Ruby'. Are they real or in his dream? The nightmare closes in on him again and he tries to shout: Help, help me! But there's no escape, no place to hide from the wrath of God. Done for, damned, cut off from the land of the living.

But wait, look, here's another face, pale and beautiful, the face of an angel. Her eyes, her hair, her smiling mouth – she *is* an angel, his own beloved Angel, come to save him! He opens his mouth to say her name: *Mabel, Mabel, my own Angel, come to me at last*!

But she can't hear him. He holds out his hand but he can't reach her, so pale, so far away.

Cut off out of the land of the living.

All hands were needed in the field from dawn to dusk when corn-cutting began, though the land-girls had told Daisy Somerton and Lucy Drummond in no uncertain terms to get out of the way of the workers; this was a farmer's field, they said, and you either worked or cleared off. Hot, tired and itching, the girls made for the shade of the oak-hanger on the edge of Parr's Wood. There the ground shelved steeply down from a bank where the bracken was shoulder-high, and here they sat to fan themselves and talk of the men whose absence left such a sad gap in village life.

'Cedric's learning how to pilot a flying boat,' said Lucy. It appeared that there were aeroplanes that could land on the decks of ships, and Cedric Drummond, in the Royal Naval Air Service, was bound for the Mediterranean.

'Gerald Westhouse has shot down five German planes,

so that makes him an ace pilot,' countered Daisy, and they both fell silent. Mr Clark, the local butcher, had lost a son in the Somme offensive and it had turned his wife from a big, laughing woman into a pale shadow who walked with her head down. Daisy thought of Harry, now home but ill in hospital; Aunt Kate wanted him to come and stay at Pinehurst.

'Papa says we must put our trust in God, to keep them all safe,' said Lucy.

'He didn't keep Rob Clarke safe, though, did he? Or Billy Potter – so what's the good o' praying for any of them?' asked Daisy.

There was no ready answer, for the question was echoed all over the nation.

When Mabel got back to Booth Street after that first visit, she wept in Norah's arms.

'He's been sent back to me, Norah, but only half alive. It's much worse than when he came back from the Dardanelles. Stephen did warn me, but I didn't pay proper heed as I should've done – I was just so thankful that he was comin' home.'

'Did he know ye, Mabel, darlin'?' asked Norah gently.

'Yes, 'cause he tried to say "Mabel", but it wouldn't come out and he went into a sort o' fit, shakin' all over an' – not exactly foamin', but the spit oozed from the side o' his mouth an' dripped down his chin, like the poor imbeciles we get in here sometimes. Oh, it was awful!'

She clung to Norah who soothed her as well as she could. 'What about his parents, Mabel?'

'His mother tried to talk to him, but yer could see he wasn't takin' it in – an' poor Major Drover was really sufferin'. Ruby was tryin' to comfort them both.'

Mabel released herself from Norah's arms, wiped her eyes on a handkerchief and blew her nose. 'If I could have him to meself, Norah, I might be able to bring him round. Aunt Kate says he'd be welcome at Pinehurst, and that's where I'd like to take him. After all, me trainin's finished now and I can take a bit o' time off.'

'B-but ye won't be earnin', Mabel, not if ye're not workin',' Norah pointed out.

'Aunt Kate's always said I could count on her,' Mabel replied. 'I've never taken anythin' from her before, but now I'll accept her hospitality. I've got to put Harry first in me life now, Norah – it's about time. As soon as he's discharged from Church Lane, he's goin' to Belhampton and I'm goin' with him!'

A drowsy hush hung over the land. Down in the shady hollow the grass was dry after a long sunny spell and in the hawthorn above the reclining couple the wild clematis flowers tumbled in a cascade over the thick hedge. It was a perfect bower for lovers, and the girl in the white dress and straw hat was a royal princess, to grant or withhold her favours. But her face was hidden by the straw hat, and the man was not sure how he should approach her. Time was fleeting . . .

She knew that he wanted her, he showed it in every lingering look. And yet he hesitated and she revelled in her sense of power over him. What happened next was for her to decide.

'When do you have to leave?' she asked in a low voice, breaking the silence.

'I have to report at Brockwith on Monday,' he replied quickly. 'We're flying to Cambrai, actually a place called Bapaume – my French was never up to much.' He laughed briefly and took her hand. 'It'll be a baptism of fire by all accounts.'

She gave him a sidelong glance from under the hat. 'I'll be here, thinking about you.' She smiled and lowered her face. His heart thudded in anticipation.

'You know I shan't be able to see you again before I go.'

So, it had to be now. She let him draw her down beneath the trailing feathery fronds of the wild clematis. She took off her hat and laid it aside. Which meant she was his for the taking.

'Alice.' His hands were upon her and she allowed him to do what he wished. The buttons of her light-green summer dress were undone, the drawstrings of her white underwear were untied. His breath was upon her face, his mouth was upon her lips, his hands were upon her lovely body, discovering secret places never before explored.

'Alice, you beautiful girl.' She shivered with delight at his passion: she gloried in his adoration of her body. At nineteen Alice Somerton had been admired by a number of men, but it was to this man that she yielded up her virgin womanhood. A sudden stab of pain, a sharp intake of breath, a long sigh. And his shuddering gasps as he claimed his pleasure from her. She could have laughed out loud as she lay beneath him, savouring her moment of triumph. She had given herself to Sir Guy Savage of Houghton Hall.

And she was completely unaware of the two girls staring down from the bracken-covered bank above them, open-mouthed and unbelieving.

'I don't believe it! How could they be so cruel – so *wicked* after all he's been through – look what it's done to him! How *dare* they!'

Mabel was as horrified as she was indignant when Ruby Swayne told her what the RAMC Colonel in charge at Church Lane had said to Major Drover. *Court martial?*

'It's 'cause of him not speakin', yer see, Mabel – they think it's to avoid answerin' questions,' said Ruby wretchedly. 'And we know he blames himself for the loss of his platoon, poor boy.'

Colonel Tressider was a hard-faced, grey-haired man who had seen service in the Boer War, and he now questioned Corporal Drover's conduct in the face of the enemy; there was an underlying accusation of cowardice, of deserting his post.

'There've been *thousands* o' men killed on that bloody Somme, an' more dyin' every day!' cried Mabel. 'Harry could've easily been one of 'em – he's been shot in the back –'

She stopped speaking, flushed and defiant, as Ruby looked at her meaningly.

Shot in the back. The splintered shoulder blade was evidence of it. How had it happened? Could he have been running away, leaving his men to be mown down by enemy gunfire?

'*Never!*' she almost shouted and Ruby put her finger to her lips, as they walked together in the hospital grounds. 'Never would he have turned his back on his platoon!' She burst into angry tears. 'Oh, Harry, Harry, my love, what've the buggers done to yer?'

Whatever happened had turned Harry Drover into a pasty-faced invalid, unable to speak, mysteriously separated from his loved ones. If he recognised his parents and sister, it gave him no pleasure, for he never smiled. When Mabel came to his bedside he sometimes held out his left hand, but if he tried to speak her name he could only slaver and grimace, at which she would soothe him gently, though her heart was breaking within her. 'Ssh-ssh, Harry, don't try to talk, just breathe in and out, nice an' slow, that's better – good boy.'

She thought of Timmy Baxter who was now much better and came trotting down Women's II to greet her, his little face all smiles: 'Maby, Maby!' She prayed that Harry too would be cured and emerge from the black pit into which he had been thrown by the horrors of war.

The next they heard was that Harry was to be sent to the National Hospital for the Paralysed and Epileptic in Queen Square.

'There are too many of these sort of cases and we have to sort out the genuine from the malingerers,' said the Colonel with brutal frankness. 'He'll see a specialist who's been getting good results by using electrical stimulation. They'll make him talk, you'll see!'

Ten miserable days passed in which Harry was allowed no visitors while under observation and treatment at Queen Square, at the end of which he was returned to Church Lane, Tooting, diagnosed as 'war shock, due to repressed war experience', and there would be no court martial. He could now talk a very little, with a stammer so severe that he seldom completed a sentence. It was recommended that he be transferred to the Royal Victoria Military Hospital at Netley, near Southampton, which had a special block for his kind of case.

Mabel at once made her wishes known, against Doris Drover's vigorous protests.

'I'll take him to Pinehurst Convalescent Home at Belhampton,' she declared. 'It's run by my aunt, an' he'll have peace an' quiet in the country, an' I'll nurse him meself, round the clock.'

She was supported in this by Major Drover, who could see only too clearly that his wife would not be able to cope at home with Harry in his present state. It was therefore arranged with Miss Chalcott that Harry would travel down to Belhampton by train with Mabel in the last week of September, and meanwhile he was to take exercise and practise talking.

'M – M – M – M – Mab – Mab – Ma-bel,' he managed as he shuffled down the ward, clinging to her with his left arm. 'M – m – my – an – an – an – an-gel. An-gel.'

'Well done, Harry, dear. That's very good,' she told him, smiling at his pitiful attempts to recall their former closeness. She was the only person with whom he could make any contact.

'It's as if he's cut off from the land of the livin',' said John Drover, unknowingly expressing his son's own bleak experience.

Daisy had never know Alice to be so 'twittery'. She jumped at every sound and snapped at everybody, even Aunt Nell who had made her apologise to the laundrywoman for her bad temper.

'I'm sorry, but I haven't been sleeping well lately,' muttered Alice and indeed, her usually blooming complexion had a muddy tinge, and there were dark circles under her eyes.

'Is that why you were so late getting up this morning?' asked Mrs Somerton. 'I noticed that you didn't take breakfast, which was very silly. You need to keep up your strength for working.'

'I think I'll take this afternoon off and walk up to Houghton Hall,' said Alice suddenly. 'Mrs Bennett's there visiting her mother, and I want a word with Georgina.'

'Well, you might tell that young lady that she's welcome to lend a hand at Pinehurst any time she likes,' replied her aunt sharply. 'So far it's been all talk and no action on that front.'

After her niece had flounced out of the room Mrs Somerton sighed and told Daisy that she really didn't know what to do about Alice. If only there was news of Gerald . . .

At the Hall Alice found Lady Savage deep in conversation with Mrs Bennett, now three months into her first pregnancy, and Georgina had a friend with her, a Miss Delmont. The talk seemed to be all of maternity matters, from suitable clothing and diet to the relative merits of local midwives.

'It must be so exciting to be an expectant mother for the first time!' gushed Miss Delmont.

The words sent a shiver down Alice's spine. Oh, please, God, *please*, let it not be – but there was no doubt about it, she had missed her September period. Was the queasiness she felt due to worry, or was it – oh, no, let it not be – she'd heard that it couldn't happen the first time. Her heart was pounding and she could keep silent no longer, so without being invited to speak, she broke in on the ladies' talk to ask the question foremost in her mind.

'Er – has there been any news from G— Sir Guy yet, Your Ladyship?'

Lady Savage looked up in surprise at being interrupted while talking with her daughter. 'What? Oh, just a card to say that he'd arrived at – what's the name of the place, Georgina?'

'Bapaume, Mamma.'

'Well, whatever it is, these French towns with their difficult names. And he's made his first flight out over the German lines. He says it's frightfully exciting, but there's very little time to rest, let alone write letters.'

The lady smiled at her daughters, and poured out another cup of tea for the young mother-to-be. 'And how is the morning sickness now, Rosamund? Are you able to take a little tea and toast at breakfast time?'

A wave of faintness passed over Alice, and she fanned herself with a parish magazine that lay beside her, hoping that the others would not notice her discomfiture. She need not have worried on that score, for they were not paying her any attention. After taking a few breaths, she looked at the French clock on the mantelpiece and rose to her feet.

'If you'll excuse me, Your Ladyship – Mrs Bennett – Miss D-Delmont – Georgina – I'd better be getting back. I'm on duty at Pinehurst this evening.'

Lady Savage looked up briefly. 'Very well, Miss Somerton. Good afternoon.'

No invitation to call again. No offer to get out the pony trap to take her back to Belhampton. By inviting herself up to the Hall, poor Alice realised that she had made a social blunder.

But if her suspicions were correct, that was the least of her worries. Whatever would she *do* if . . . but it didn't bear thinking about.

At Pear Tree cottage Daisy's heart rejoiced at the latest news from Mabel. Harry was improving and would be coming to convalesce at Pinehurst as soon as he was discharged from Church Lane – and Mabel was coming with him!

Miss Chalcott and Mrs Somerton were happy, too. 'This time Mabel will stay at Pinehurst, to be on hand for him,' said Aunt Kate with satisfaction. 'After all, she's his fiancée.'

'Oh, heavens, I suppose there's going to be the most

enormous fuss over them now,' muttered Alice when the aunts had left the breakfast room.

'What d'ye mean, fuss?' demanded Daisy. 'Aren't you glad to know that Harry's home and getting better?'

Alice's pale cheek flushed crimson. 'Of course I am, but there are plenty of men still out there fighting a war.'

'Can I ask you a question, Alice? Are you going to marry Gerald Westhouse? Or Sir Guy Savage?'

'What?' Alice rounded on her young sister. 'What are you talking about?'

'Well, seeing as you ask, I'm talking about *you* – and Guy Savage down in the hollow below Parr's Wood on the first day o' corn-cutting.'

Alice's stomach seemed to turn over. 'W-what? What did you say, Daisy?' she whispered, her hand on her throat.

'You heard what I said, Alice. Lucy Drummond and I saw you. I know what he was doing.'

'Lucy Drummond? Oh, my God. Oh, merciful heaven.'

'It's all right, Alice. She said she wouldn't tell anybody and neither have I.'

'You must never breathe a word to a soul, Daisy. Not a word. Promise me you never will.'

'I promise. Only – won't you have to marry Sir Guy now, and live up at the Hall with that old lady, instead of marrying Gerald?'

'I – I don't know, it's very difficult for me – you're only a child, Daisy, you don't understand. It's this hateful war, it makes it so much harder to – to know what to do.' Alice closed her eyes and held her head between her hands, her elbows on the table. 'For heaven's sake, you mustn't tell a soul, Daisy – not ever.'

Daisy promised again with her hand on her heart. It

was strange to see Miss high-and-mighty Alice reduced to pleading. And she looked so scared that Daisy felt a little scared, too.

Alice now felt herself to be in the grip of a nightmare. Was it possible that Lucy Drummond might say something at the Rectory? She could never be quite certain, whatever Daisy said . . .

Two events took place before Harry was transferred from Church Lane to Pinehurst. Mrs Ada Hodges was delivered of a little girl she called Anne, and when Mabel and Norah went to visit they found that childbirth had been a turning point for her, setting her upon a journey of recovery. Arthur and Jenny were once again gathered up into her maternal arms and, although she remained a sad-eyed widow who vowed that she would never recover from the loss of her husband, she began to take an interest in people again. She even went with Mabel to visit Harry at Church Lane and, seeing his useless arm and hearing his mumbling stammer, she actually put her arms around his neck and whispered that he must get better for Mabel who loved him as she had loved Arthur. Maudie Ling came visiting, too, with a bottle of port wine and fruit for the invalid.

'*Chu Chin Chow*'s a winner!' she told them happily. 'Make sure yer come an' see it some time – it's goin' to run an' run 'til after the end o' the bloody war!'

'Then I'll wait to see it wid me future husband.' Norah laughed. 'When the *Galway Castle* comes home!'

The other event was a tragic one. Gerald Westhouse was shot down over France and, although he managed to bail out of the blazing craft, he suffered burns over the left side of his face, neck and shoulder, with the loss of the left eye. He was taken to a base hospital and from there across the Channel and by train to a special surgical unit at Aldershot, not so far from Belhampton.

His parents at once offered to take Alice Somerton to visit him there, showing her all the kindness and consideration due to a future daughter-in-law.

The country night was darker and more silent than anything Harry Drover had ever known. Apart from the occasional call of a night bird or the distant yelp of a fox, the only sounds were occasional grunts and moans as his three companions stirred and snorted in their sleep. The door was ajar and a lamp burned beside the night-sitter dozing in her armchair. He longed for a cigarette, but could not light up with only one hand; if Mabel was here she would light it for him and sit beside him while he smoked it, but she was asleep somewhere else in the house. Mum and Dad would be surprised to see him smoking, not to mention drinking his daily pint of porter, the dark, sweet ale that the doctor said was strengthening for invalids. It was directly against Salvation Army rules, but the war had changed him as it had changed everything.

It was calm and quiet here. Everybody was kind. He didn't have to think about that specialist doctor in London who'd put a metal rod in his mouth and sent an electric shock through him.

'Say *ah.*' His whole body had jumped each time the doctor touched him with it: 'Ah! Ah! Ah!'

'What is your name? You are to answer me.' Ah! the electric shock again.

'D – D – D – D – Dro – Dro – Dro – Dro-ver. Dro-ver. Ah! Ah!'

Only the thought of Mabel, his own sweet guardian angel, had kept him from breaking down under the torture. In his dreams he held her in his arms, curled around the soft warmth of her, his face buried against her beautiful breasts: two bodies one, closer than close – safe, safe . . .

Miss White was a rather nervous, fidgety woman in her forties, who wanted to do something useful for the war effort, which was why she had volunteered to help out at Pinehurst. Tonight it was her turn to 'sit up' and she accordingly settled herself in the armchair on the landing between the three dormitories. She had a copy of *Woman's Weekly*, but by one o'clock her eyelids were beginning to droop. Her head nodded and the magazine fell to the floor.

She did not know what time it was when she felt something touch her shoulder, and a clammy hand groped around her head: it seemed to Miss White that it was over her face, stopping her breath. She rose up from the chair with a shriek of terror.

By the light of the oil lamp on the oak chest against the wall, Miss White saw the figure of a man standing in front of her, 'barring her way', as she said later. *And he was completely naked.* He was leaning over her, touching her with stone-cold fingers like a dead man's, and making hideous noises in his throat: 'M – M – M – M – Ma – Ma – Mab – Mab –'

He was pinning her down! He was about to ravish her!

Miss White's blood-curdling screams raised the whole house. Men sat up in their beds with shouts and oaths. 'Who's there?' – 'What the bloody hell's going on?' – 'Blimey!'

Kate Chalcott leapt out of bed and threw on a dressing-gown; Mabel thought she was at Booth Street with Zeppelins overhead. Shaking herself free of sleep,

247

she thought some woman was being attacked and rushed after her aunt.

Within two minutes Miss Chalcott had taken charge of Miss White and Mabel led Harry back to his bed, to the accompaniment of sympathetic noises from the other three men. She replaced his pyjamas and re-bandaged his shoulder, tucking in his white and life-less right arm. She kissed him, she soothed him and told him that everything was all right, it had only been a dream, a silly woman making a fuss about nothing. Miss Chalcott brewed tea for everybody and settled Miss White on the couch in her office, while she herself took over the night-sitting. This would be told all over Belhampton, she thought crossly, and would lose nothing in the telling. She blamed herself for taking on a hysterical spinster for such a responsible task, but her heart ached for the young couple and their blighted hopes. She decided to ask Dr Forsyth, the general practitioner, to arrange for Harry to be seen at a Military Hospital at Aldershot, for another opinion.

When Harry had fallen asleep, Mabel rose and went back her room where she beat her head with her fists and bit her pillow to stop herself crying out aloud at such injustice.

If Harry was an object of sympathy, so was Alice, who was clearly under great strain. She had lost weight and was 'a bundle of nerves', as her Aunt Nell remarked. Although Mabel's time was taken up with Harry, she was of course concerned for her sister and Gerald.

'How did yer find him this afternoon, Alice?' she asked gently. 'Was he talkin'?'

'Yes, of course he was, there's nothing wrong with his *brain*. It's just that – all those bandages, and that one eye staring at me – oh, leave me alone, Mabel, for God's sake!'

Mabel drew a deep breath and spoke quietly to the unhappy girl. 'Alice, dear, if yer don't want to marry Gerald, yer don't have to. Just be kind an' see him through this bad patch, and when he's better yer can talk it over.'

Alice turned to her with a face full of misery. 'Thank you, Mabel, I know you mean well.' And disappeared before another word could be said.

She was desperate. Her October period had not arrived and something would have to be done – and there was only one person she knew who might be able to do it: she would have to pocket her pride and appeal to the sister she had despised.

And yet she put off the moment from day to day, hoping against hope that it would not be necessary.

Visiting Gerald at the Military Hospital with his parents was a recurring ordeal for her.

'Hello, Gerald.' Her voice sounded thick, unfamiliar even to herself.

'Alice. I'm sorry, you've waited so long, and now – this.' He too sounded different.

'Is it very painful?'

'Not so bad now. Thanks for coming over. I'd kiss you if I could.'

'Can you walk, Gerald?'

'I have done, yes. They're going to get me up and trotting around before the skin operation.'

'So it won't be long before – before you can come home, then?'

'Don't really know. This Gillies chap is talking about a graft of some sort – from my thigh.'

'Gerald, I – oh, Gerald –'

'Hey, steady on, old girl, can't have you crying! I'll

be all right, you know – face won't ever be the same, I dare say, but nothing wrong with the rest of the works. Alice – dearest Alice –'

When Mr and Mrs Westhouse tentatively entered the room, they found both their son and Alice in tears, and an air of constraint between them which was hardly reassuring.

The army surgeon at the Cambridge Hospital in Aldershot shook his head after examining Harry. In spite of daily massaging by Mabel, there was wasting of the muscles of the right arm.

'The scapula was so broken up that there's no socket for the head of the humerus to fit into,' he told Mabel. 'And there's damage to the nerve supply.' Lowering his voice, he added, 'I think he should go back to the military hospital, my dear. I'll write a letter to Colonel Tressider.'

A little later he passed her in the corridor, talking in low tones to a colleague, and Mabel's sharp ears overheard a chilling remark.

'Never be any more good, that poor devil. God, what a waste of a life. Terrible, terrible.'

And she had to smile brightly for Harry.

Miss Chalcott was very sorry to lose them both, but there was an element of relief too in knowing that Harry was to receive expert attention. He had been at Pinehurst for over a month without any noticeable improvement and she felt that the sooner he was back at Church Lane, the better.

On the evening before they were due to leave Pinehurst, Mabel went into Miss Chalcott's study to make a list of everything she had to do. There was a knock at the door.

'Mabel – may I speak with you for a minute?'

'Alice? Oh, come in, dear – how was he this afternoon?'

At the sight of her sister's face she held out her arms and Alice flung herself into them.

'Oh, Mabel, Mabel, you've got to help me, or I don't know what I'll do!'

'Hush, hush, dear, tell yer big sister all about it – ssh-ssh, ssh-ssh.'

And as Mabel stroked the dark head on her lap, her heart sank and she braced herself for what she was about to hear. Never before had she seen the haughty, imperious Alice Somerton in such a hysterical state. If she had changed her mind about marrying Gerald Westhouse, there was no real problem: it would be a nine-day wonder and Alice would be labelled a cold-hearted jilt, but it would blow over. No, this was something worse and Mabel prayed that her sister might be spared the terrible disgrace that would befall her if . . .

But when Alice raised haggard, tear-filled eyes, Mabel's worst fears were confirmed.

'Oh, yer poor girl, me poor sister – ye're expectin' a child.'

'Yes, Mabel, this is the second month I've missed – how did you know?'

'I knew it couldn't be anythin' else. Was it young Savage?'

Alice stared aghast, her hand to her mouth. 'Who told you that?'

'Nobody told me anythin', I saw for meself that afternoon we went up to the Hall for tea. I'm not daft, yer know, Alice.'

'I was so sure he loved me and wanted to marry me, Mabel – but I haven't heard a word!'

'Hush, don't start cryin' again. Listen, ye're not the

first, an' yer won't be the last. I'll do what I can for yer, dear, an' to start with I'll break the news to our aunts –'

'What? No, no, for heaven's sake, they mustn't know, not ever!'

'My dear, they'll have to know, o' course they will. And I can get yer into the Agnes Nuttall Home nearer the time – y'know, the Women's Rescue off Lavender Hill, where I worked –'

'No, no, Mabel, not that!' Alice cried. 'I don't want to have it, I want to be done with it, *finish* with it, have it taken *away*, and you're my only hope, can't you see? You're a midwife and you used to work for Grandmother Court, you must know what to do!'

Mabel straightened herself up. 'Yer don't know what ye're talkin' about, Alice. Grandmother Court was a bad woman and yes, she did abortions for women who could pay her charges. I know of one who died and another nearly bled to death – I could tell yer stories that'd make yer hair stand on end. D'ye know that a doctor can be sent to prison for performin' an abortion? An' so can a chemist for supplyin' a drug to cause one – and risk killin' the woman as well as the child? No, Alice, I can't help yer in that way, but I'll do all I can to get yer into a home where ye'll be looked after and delivered –'

But Alice had got to her feet, her eyes blazing. 'No, don't say any more. I might have known you'd come over all holy and righteous. And don't you ever breathe a word to the aunts, do you hear me? Not a *word*!'

'Alice, I beg yer, don't go and find some woman to do it for yer – it could be yer death. Let me help yer!'

'I don't want that sort of help. And I don't want anybody else to know. Forget I ever asked.'

For Alice Somerton had thought of another way out.

It would need a lot of nerve and stamina, but she was desperate enough to give it a try.

Both aunts and Daisy accompanied Mabel and Harry to the station on a chill, misty morning, packed into Thomas Somerton's car.

'You'll let us know what happens, won't you, Mabel?' said Aunt Nell, while Daisy blinked back tears of disappointment that poor Harry was was no better than when he had arrived, and now he was taking Mabel away again. There seemed to be nothing to look forward to any more.

'Remember that whatever happens, you can always bring him back to Pinehurst, Mabel,' said Aunt Kate in a low voice. 'While the war's on and after it's over, he'll always be welcome here, as long as I'm alive.'

'God bless yer, dear Aunt Kate!'

And Katherine Chalcott saw again her lost sister Anna-Maria in the face of her niece.

Chapter Fourteen

'I'm very sorry about Captain Drover, Nurse Court, but my concern has to be with the patients here. You've taken four weeks of unpaid leave and now I need to know that I can rely on you to stay on my staff.'

'Yes, I can stay for the time bein', Matron, until I know what's happenin' to him.'

Matron frowned. 'What exactly do you mean by that, nurse?'

'I've taken him back to the military hospital at Church Lane, Tooting, with a report from a specialist at Aldershot. The sooner somethin's done about his right arm the better.'

'And where will he go when he's discharged from there, Nurse Court? His parents' home?'

'That's what his mother wants, Matron.'

'I see. And until Captain Drover's future is assured, you intend to remain here at Booth Street?'

'If ye'll let me, Matron,' Mabel said anxiously.

'Good. Tomorrow you will report for duty at seven thirty on Women's I. And get a good night's rest. All our wards are stretched to capacity and you look very tired.'

'Yes, Matron. Thank yer.'

After the girl had left the office, Sarah Brewer sighed and rubbed her aching forehead. Sympathy for her nurses must not be allowed to come before her duty to the patients. A year ago she might have been more flexible in such a case, but the staff problem was now so acute that even trained nurses could only take one day off per month.

Norah was overjoyed to be reunited with her best friend, though naturally very sorry to hear of Harry's lack of progress and the condition of his arm. 'Sure an' they'll get it sorted out in hospital, darlin',' she said, pouring a cup of tea. 'An' how are all the dear people at Belhampton?'

'Me aunts and uncle have been very kind, Norah, but I didn't see much o' Daisy, and I know she did her best with Harry – but it's hard for a twelve-year-old to understand such a – such a change in somebody they've known and loved for so long,' said Mabel sadly. 'It isn't always easy for grown women,' she added, thinking of the unfortunate Miss White.

'Ah, God love her.' Norah shook her head. 'And Alice? D'ye think she'll cope wid that poor young airman who's been burned?'

Mabel hesitated. 'Better not ask about me sister Alice. I don't think she'll marry Gerald now.'

But there she was wrong. A rather bewildered letter arrived from Aunt Elinor to say that as Gerald Westhouse had to wait for six weeks before a skin graft could be attempted, Alice had begged his parents to ask if he could come home for a short time. And the next thing to take place after that was a very quiet wedding at a Belhampton church, by special licence because of the groom's condition. No banns had been called, and only Gerald's parents and Mr and Mrs Somerton had been present; nobody else had been invited. Afterwards the bride had taken up residence at her in-laws' home as young Mrs Westhouse. Her devotion to Gerald in his affliction, and her eagerness to become his wife as soon as possible, had taken them all by surprise, wrote Aunt Nell.

Mabel's first thought on reading the letter was that Alice had imposed secrecy upon her and, whatever came of this marriage, she was bound to keep her knowledge to herself. When the pregnancy became apparent, and a child was born a full two months ahead of its expected time, whether or not the Westhouses suspected a deception – and what a deception! – Mabel must remain silent. Of course there was always the possibility that Alice had confided in Gerald and that he had agreed to the quick, quiet ceremony for her sake; perhaps he loved her enough to forgive her and save her public shame, even to the point of calling another man's child his own. Alice had not written, so there was no need to write to her; nor was it Mabel's place to judge her sister who had proved herself a true granddaughter of old Mimi Court.

And in any case she had other matters on her mind. Long days on a crowded ward with stints in the theatre, and rushing off to visit Harry whenever she could was hard enough, but at the end of that dark November came another blow. Colonel Tressider suddenly informed John Drover that Harry's right arm had deteriorated, and he was to be transferred immediately to the Royal Victoria Military Hospital at Netley – 'where he should have gone in the first place, instead of that convalescent home, in my opinion,' added the Colonel with a dash of spite.

'It's a splendid place, overlooking the Solent,' he told Harry's father. 'He'll have the very best of care, they treat every kind of war injury and there's a special block for luna— for these cases of so-called war shock. He's very fortunate to be able to go there.'

Not surprisingly Mrs Drover turned on Mabel for taking Harry to Belhampton against her wishes and she also blamed the Church Lane doctors for not taking earlier action. 'Our son's been shamefully neglected and badly managed,' she said bitterly.

But worse was to come. When the Drovers travelled down to visit their son on the day after his transfer, they were told that his arm was to be amputated the following day, to prevent the spread of the gangrene that was affecting his fingers.

Ruby wept on hearing this, and John Drover covered his face with his hand as he reported it. Mabel had been half expecting it, but still felt that the Lord had forsaken her and the man she had promised to marry. Not to be able to write, except with the clumsy left hand; nor do something as simple as wringing out a facecloth, tying up a shoelace: so many everyday actions needed two hands.

And he would never play the trombone again.

Major Drover tried to put a brave face on this latest calamity. 'He could join the Post Office as a sorter o' letters, and deliver 'em as well,' he said. 'He'll still be able to help out at the homeless shelters and soup kitchens – or maybe work with other injured ex-servicemen. He could learn to type with one hand. There's all sorts o' possibilities.'

'And as soon as they let him out, he's comin' back here to be properly looked after in his own home,' declared Doris Drover. 'Our boy'll recover when he's back in the fold o' the Salvation Army!'

Mabel kept her own counsel, for the future seemed dark and unknowable. Her heart ached as she pictured Harry being wheeled to the operating theatre and the merciful oblivion of the anaesthetic – from which he would awake without his right arm. And without her at his side to comfort him in his crippling loss. She would not be able to visit until December the twenty-second, a Wednesday, when she was due for her day off. There were trains running directly from Waterloo to Southampton, from where, John Drover told her, a special branch line of 'Netley carriages' took visitors right to the hospital grounds.

Norah did her best to keep Mabel's spirits up and Maud came to take her out to tea one Sunday afternoon at a Lyons Corner House café. Alex Redfern was with her, 'off operations' for the weekend.

'Sunday's me only day off from the featre, so 'e's spendin' it wiv me,' said Maud happily, pouring out tea. 'An' I says to 'im, "'Ere, let's take Mabel aht for an hour, get 'er aht o' that 'ole!"'

Redfern silently chain-smoked as she chattered and Mabel thought his face had coarsened since she had last seen him. There was a tension in his jaw and deep lines running from the corners of his mouth; it was clear that he still adored Maudie and was happy to indulge her for this hour with Mabel. Towards the end of it he joined in their talk of Harry, which was not only about his amputation, but his strange alienation from family and friends.

'We get them in the Flying Corps as well, poor bastards who've broken under the strain,' he said bluntly, and when Maud shushed him he shrugged. 'The best of us can only take so much of it.'

Maud cleared her throat, glanced at Alex and said tentatively to Mabel, ''Im an' me 'ave been talkin' abaht 'Arry, an' Alex says 'e can understand the poor ol' boy feelin' cut orf from everyfin' after what 'e's been frough. The only ones Alex can talk to are the ones 'oo've been frough it as well.'

'That's right,' agreed Redfern. 'It separates you from all the rest – your family, your friends left at home, they can't have any idea of what it's like to face death day in, day out, and they talk such utter bollocks. I've given up on my parents and brother and sisters – they'll never understand and it cuts me right off from them.'

He spoke harshly, yet Mabel was grateful, for it was clear that he could indeed understand Harry's lonely isolation.

Maud winked at her. 'If yer was to ask me, gal, I'd say your 'Arry's better orf wiv ovver men 'oo've gorn frough it, an' there'll be plenty o' them at Netley. *Time*'s what 'e needs, not a lot o' fussin' an' faffin' from 'is muvver an' that. 'E's got to get over it in 'is own way, in 'is own time.'

'And it could take a very long time, Mabel,' added Alex grimly.

The approach of Christmas brought little festive cheer. The so-called Battle of the Somme had ground to a halt in mud and misery, and for the thousands of lives lost, only a small advance had been made. The navy was having better success in that British ships were now blockading German ports in retaliation for the losses caused by the U-boats, and it was causing real hardship to the civilian population.

'We're getting our own back now,' wrote Albert. 'Starving the buggers out.'

While the newspapers rejoiced over the success of the blockades, Mabel as always thought of the children who would suffer by it: the German mothers who would go hungry so as to give their children what meagre rations they could lay their hands on. What an evil thing war was, killing husbands and fathers, damaging healthy young men! Mabel began to have more sympathy with the pacifists, the Herbert Swaynes who chose imprisonment and disgrace rather than take part in it, though she kept such thoughts to herself.

Suddenly, out of the blue came an unexpected letter.

'Dear Miss Court,' wrote Captain Knowles. 'I'm on Christmas leave, staying with my parents. Father tells me that Captain Drover has had his arm amputated at the Royal Victoria at Netley, which I'm very sorry to hear. I'm planning to visit a couple of friends there next week, and could offer you a lift there and back if you could manage to get away on the twenty-second or twenty-third of December. Will you let me know?'

Would she! It was like an answer to prayer and Mabel eagerly accepted, naming the twenty-second.

When Stephen Knowles called at Booth Street in his Ford Model T, Mabel was ready and waiting, carrying a shopping bag filled with Christmas presents from herself, Norah and Maud.

'This is really good o' yer, Dr Stephen.'

'It's no trouble, seeing that I'm going there anyway. I'll be glad of your company, Mabel.'

He looked older and leaner in the face; his blue eyes had dulled, and the hollows around them were seamed by a network of fine lines though she reckoned he could be only thirty-two or -three. Like Alex Redfern he seemed to have hardened: there was no humour, no relaxed ease of manner such as she remembered from their brief earlier acquaintance, and as she got into the car she decided to stay silent unless he spoke to her. But he at once asked her about Harry, and she gave him a brief summary of what had happened over the past four and a half months. When he fumbled in his pocket for a cigarette, she took the matchbox and lit it for him.

'Damnable business, Mabel. No man who's been through the Somme and come out alive will ever be the same again. *I* won't, and I haven't been subjected to the day and night shelling that Drover had to put up with. Lost every man in his platoon.'

'I know, Stephen. It's what's preying on his mind. He blames himself for them.'

'So does every other survivor, Mabel – it's part of the picture. In fact, I'd go as far as to say that *all* men who've come through the Somme have got war shock to some degree, some much worse than others, of course.'

He paused and she asked about his father.

'Whacked out – doing far too much for a man of his age. Ought to be retired, but his caseload's bigger than ever before. A lot of his patients should be in hospital, but everywhere's been taken over by the military.'

'Except for Booth Street,' said Mabel with a wry smile. 'It's terribly overcrowded and patients don't get the care they should. It's heartbreaking, really, especially for the children.'

He drew on the cigarette, blew out a cloud of smoke, coughed and glanced at her. 'Didn't you want to nurse children at one time?'

'Oh, yes, and I *will*, too, one day – only Harry has to come first at present.' She smiled. 'As a matter o' fact, I've been asked if I'd like to be Assistant Matron of a babies' home.'

'Ah! Now, would that be a godforsaken hole called the Midway? Been taken under the wing of a do-gooder Jew, name of Spearmann, currently making a fortune in service uniforms?'

Mabel was quick to defend Mrs Spearmann. 'It's his wife, not him, and ye'd never believe how much she's done for them poor little children, thanks to Mr Poole who got her interested. I think that if somebody does that much good, people ought not to look too hard at where the money comes from.'

'Didn't know you were such a little Machiavellian! All right, Mabel, I'll give your Lady Bountiful the benefit of the doubt. But *you*'d be better off getting on the staff of the East London Hospital for Children at Shadwell. They're feeling the pinch now, not enough doctors, nurses rushing off to be ministering angels to the wounded – they'd welcome you with open arms, Mabel, and you'd love it.'

'Oh, yes, I would, it would be what I've always dreamed of,' she said, her eyes lighting up. 'But Harry's got to come first with me now, y'see.'

He did not reply and after a moment she enquired about Mrs Knowles.

He shook his head. 'She and my father worry about each other. Always tired these days, and her hair has turned completely white. I suppose they worry about me, like all parents.'

Mabel cleared her throat. 'As a matter o' fact, I was askin' about yer wife.'

'Oh, I see. Yes, poor girl.' Again that shake of the head, and he raised his right hand briefly from the steering wheel in a non-committal gesture. 'Not the marriage we'd planned, obviously. Disappointment on every side, you could say, like hundreds of other couples, Mabel, like you and Harry – waiting until it's all over before we can start from the beginning again. She's with her parents at Northampton and I'll be going up there some time over Christmas.'

He lapsed into silence and Mabel fell into a doze. The road was narrow and winding, but there was very little other traffic and they made good time. He nudged her to point out the massive Victorian edifice with its central dome and arcaded windows, built for victims of the Crimean War. Standing in spacious grounds above the Solent, its pavilioned wards were joined by wide corridors where patients could sit in wicker chairs among a forest of pot plants and spend their time talking, smoking, reading, playing cards and board games. To Mabel it seemed palatial, yet she was full of apprehension.

'I'll come with you to see Captain Drover before I go to see the others,' Stephen told her, lightly taking her arm.

Harry was in a ward of thirty beds, sitting in an armchair wearing regulation blue hospital pyjamas and a dressing-gown. He looked thin and frail, and did not smile as Mabel kissed him. Knowles had to conceal his shock beneath a show of bonhomie.

'Well, well, Captain Drover, we meet again. Better than last time, eh? So how are things, old chap?' He grasped Harry's left shoulder, but there was no response at all.

'Yer know Dr Stephen Knowles, don't yer, Harry. He kindly drove me down here.'

Harry turned his eyes mutely upon Mabel. Stephen caught her eye, and with the briefest of nods he turned on his heel and left the ward. Only then did Harry's features soften a little and he held out his left hand to her. She kissed him again.

'Look, I've brought yer some presents – an' lots o' love from Norah and Maudie!'

She sat down beside him and opened the bag. There was a bottle of brandy and Woodbine cigarettes from Maud, and a tin of McVitie's mixed biscuits from Norah. Mabel had got him a picture-book of paintings of English views, from the Thames at Westminster to Land's End.

'Ye'll be able to look at 'em again and again, Harry, an' pretend we're walkin' together in all those places!' she told him, smiling. 'I'll have to hand in the drink and the fags, but yer can keep Norah's biscuits on yer shelf, see?' The men had shelves on the wall behind their beds as well as small tables between them.

He hung on to her hand like a drowning man, but made no other response. Alex Redfern was right, she thought sadly, it was going to be a long time. Well, she could wait.

At three o'clock the lamps were lit and a tea trolley was brought in, with bread-and-butter. An Anglican army chaplain also arrived, and opened a book to read a shortened form of Evensong. Mabel held Harry's hand as they listened, and was struck by the way his eyes brightened at the words of the psalm. It was No. 116, a prayer for aid in time of trouble, and included the words: 'I will walk before the Lord in the land of the living.'

'M – M – M – Ma-bel – Mabel –' he muttered, pointing to the book in the chaplain's hand. Not sure what he wanted, Mabel's instinct guided her to ask for the psalm to be read again when the prayers were finished. The clergyman willingly obliged and Harry listened with an attention that touched Mabel's heart. Afterwards she pressed her warm lips to his pale cheek.

'The land o' the livin', Harry. Hold on to those words, dearest love,' she whispered and for a moment she saw his eyes come alive with recognition. On his part he saw and heard her close at hand instead of far away – the voice and the touch of his own guardian angel, the woman he had loved for so long: *Mabel!*

'Mabel,' he said and smiled directly into her eyes.

'Ready, Miss Court?'

Stephen had appeared beside them and spoke with brisk formality, looking at his watch.

'I think I'd better get going now, if you don't mind saying goodbye to Captain Drover. It's a long drive in the dark and I promised my wife I'd be back by eight.'

Mabel remembered that Stephen had said his wife was in Northampton, but then realised that he was reassuring Harry. He tactfully turned away while she gave Harry a last kiss and whispered a final loving word, but the moment had passed and he had returned to his lonely isolation, blank-faced and mute.

Stephen hardly knew what to say to his passenger on their return journey, for he felt he should not encourage her to hope. On the other hand, it was not for him to intrude upon the special relationship she had with Drover.

'How was the Captain at your aunt's home, Mabel?' he asked conversationally, and this simple question led to an outpouring of all that had happened at Pinehurst, Harry's nightmares and the incident with Miss White, the consultation at the Cambridge Hospital and her regret that she had insisted on taking Harry to a convalescent home instead of letting him go to Netley when it had first been mentioned.

'My dear Mabel, he was going to lose that arm whatever happened and wherever he was. Don't fret over regrets, just be thankful they amputated in time.'

That word 'regret' led Mabel into confiding her thoughts and feelings about Harry's state of mind, his remoteness. She said again that she was sure it was due to his guilt, however unjustified, over the loss of his platoon. She spoke bitterly of the Colonel's attitude, the mention that had been made of a court martial. Her voice broke on a sob and Knowles gripped the steering wheel as if it was the Colonel's neck and he was throttling the man.

'Oh, what crimes are committed in the name of patriotism!' he burst out. 'I couldn't begin to tell you what hell it is out there, Mabel. The line between courage and cowardice is a very fine one and depends largely on how long a man has had to endure it – the shelling and the sleeplessness, danger, fear, seeing his friends fall down dead – Christ! I'd never call a man a coward who'd been through that lot. We all have a breaking point, and I may reach mine one of these days and gibber like an idiot, turn into a raving monster as I've seen some men become – or be half drunk most of the time. I've had to ease off on the whisky since I've been home. Some poor chaps have been charged with desertion and shot, while others have been awarded medals for gallantry – I'll tell you, Mabel, it's very difficult to tell them apart sometimes.'

He had not realised how furiously he was ranting on until he noticed that Mabel was crying.

'My dear girl, I'm sorry. I hadn't intended to get carried away like that. I never speak of it as a rule. Please, Mabel, don't cry. I'd stop the car, only I might not be able to get the damned thing started again, and we don't want to be stuck out here on a country road in the pitch dark –'

Mabel wiped her eyes. 'Don't worry, Stephen, I'm glad yer said what yer did. Let me light yer a cigarette.'

When they reached Booth Street he got out of the car and came round to the passenger door. 'Here we are, Mabel. Give me your hand.'

She reached out and he steadied her as she climbed down from the seat. He took her arm and carried her bag, leading her to the short flight of steps at the front entrance of the Infirmary. It was cold, dark and deserted.

'I'd like to take you somewhere for a hot meal,' he said apologetically. 'It's rather late and you're tired, but if you like we could go –'

'Oh, no, no, yer parents'll be waitin', Stephen, and ye've already been so kind. All I want is – is – oh, for Harry to be well again! Back in the land o' the livin'!' And she burst out crying again.

'Mabel, Mabel, my dear – you poor, brave girl.'

She felt strong arms around her, warming and supporting. It was so long since she had been held close like this. She let her head rest on his shoulder and realised that she was shaking from head to foot. For a few minutes he stroked her head and murmured to her, 'Hush, Mabel, hush, there's a good girl – ssh, ssh –' until she quietened. And then he spoke firmly to her, not unkindly, but with emphasis.

'I'm going to say something to you, Mabel, so please listen, because it's for your own good. Harry's going to be at Netley for a very long time, perhaps for – well, the foreseeable future, and I think you should consider your own life and go for children's nursing while you've got the opportunity. It's what you've always wanted and you'd be helping the war effort in the best possible way. Apply to Shadwell, that's my advice – they'll be only too glad to have you. You could still go and visit Harry, but he's going to need time and he's better off with the other amputees at present.'

It was exactly what Maud Ling had said. She knew in her heart that he was right and was aware of an extraordinary sense of relief. She had stopped trembling and was still standing enfolded in this man's arms – the sense of security that it gave made her reluctant to draw apart from him.

'Oh, Mabel,' he muttered at last. 'This bloody war.'

Slowly, slowly he released her and without another word she passed through the doors.

'I'm applyin' to the East London Hospital for Children, Norah.'

'Ah! An' haven't I been waitin' for yer to say so – an' dreadin' it, for surely I can't be stayin' on here widout ye. D'ye think they'd have me, too?'

'I don't even know whether they'd have me, Norah, but is it what yer really want? Ye're goin' to marry Albert as soon as the war's over, so d'yer really need to start a new trainin'?'

'That's what I've been thinkin', Mabel, and maybe the Blessed Mother o' God put it into me mind about them poor little mites at the Midway, 'cause I can't get 'em out o' me head.'

Mabel stared at her in astonishment.

'That Mrs Spearmann asked yer to go there, didn't she? D'ye think she might settle for me instead?'

'Norah McLoughlin! Just wait till she hears this!'

Matron Brewer resigned herself to the inevitable and sent a glowing reference with Mabel's application to the East London. At her interview with Matron Rowe, Mabel said that she eventually hoped to run a children's refuge for the Salvation Army, but said nothing about marriage. Within a week a letter arrived from the hospital secretary to say that she had been appointed as a junior staff nurse, commencing on the first of February.

Mrs Spearmann, disappointed at losing Mabel, joyfully pounced on her Irish friend and took her on an afternoon visit to the Midway Babies' Home. Norah's heart was immediately won by the love-starved children and she was appointed as resident Sister-in-Charge, to be the only fully trained nurse on the staff. Mrs Lovell was transformed into the Domestic Superintendent, in charge of catering, cooking and all housekeeping duties, while being relieved of direct responsibility for the children. Sister McLoughlin was to commence her new duties on the first of February, too, so both she and Mabel could work out their month's notice at the Infirmary.

On the day that Mabel said goodbye to Booth Street

Harry Drover's parents removed him from the Royal Victoria Hospital and brought him home to number 8 Falcon Terrace. Once more the little front parlour became a sickroom for an invalid.

Chapter Fifteen

Mabel's first posting at the East London Hospital was to the Outpatients' Hall, where a stream of women and children poured through the double doors every day with a variety of afflictions to be seen, advised upon and treated. Along one wall were the doctors' consulting rooms and opposite these the treatment cubicles; medicines and applications were issued from the dispensary opposite the doors and the body of the hall was filled with rows of forms. Tea and biscuits were given out by members of the Ladies' Association, a voluntary body with a long history of service to the hospital; they had also supplied the pictures on the walls, one prominently showing Jesus with a group of children at His knee, and the title *For Theirs is the Kingdom of Heaven*.

Sister Colledge in navy-blue was in charge of outpatients, assisted by two staff nurses in royal blue, of whom Nurse Court was the junior, and three probationers in blue and white striped dresses. All wore 'Sister Dora' caps, with two rows of frills for the Sister and one row for the staff nurses. All wore starched white aprons, collars and cuffs. Mabel felt a little awkward at first, not only because the probationers knew the routine better than she did, but also because their accents were far more refined. However, as soon as the doors were opened and the mothers and children surged in, she relaxed and gave them a welcoming smile – which made her a target for all their hard-luck stories.

'Up all night we bin wiv 'er, nurse, fightin' for 'er breff, she was, wiv the croup!'

'Look 'ere, nurse, 'e's caught this nasty imbertiger rash off them dirty kids rahnd 'ere!'

'She's still bein' sick as a dog, nurse, an' 'er farver reckons that medicine's made 'er worse!'

'No time for chatting, nurse,' said Sister Colledge. 'There are a lot of daily treatments to be done before the doctors arrive – I'll go over the basics with you and then you can ask if there's anything you're not sure about.'

For the next hour and a half Mabel applied dressings to boils and abscesses, cleaned discharging ears, rubbed sulphur ointment into the shaved heads of ringworm sufferers and painted fungal rashes with tincture of iodine. There were several cases of impetigo associated with head-lice and both had to be treated. Cuts, burns and scalds had to wait to be seen by a doctor, unless very slight.

When the doctors arrived at ten to take their clinic, Mabel was sent to assist Dr Dunn, a chest physician.

'I've put the medical student, Mr Green, with him, Nurse Court,' said Sister Colledge. 'Make sure the next patient's ready to go in as soon as the last one comes out – there are a lot to see!'

Mabel soon discovered that Dr Dunn disliked the word 'croup', constantly used by the mothers. 'It can mean anything from a simple dry cough to acute bronchitis, whooping-cough or diphtheria,' he told her and Mr Green. 'A mild condition or a killer disease – don't ever let me hear you using it.'

Mr Green respectfully took note, but Mabel grinned to herself, being used to doctors and their bees in their bonnets; on the whole she found Dr Dunn a caring man, if a little impatient with the mothers. He remarked that the mortality rate among children had risen since the war.

'We do what we can for them here, and then send them back to the conditions that caused their sickness in the first place,' he said ruefully. 'It's the same way that we treat our wounded servicemen, when you come to think about it.'

Between twelve and one the nurses had to take turns to go for their midday dinner; the clinics went on until the last patient had been seen at around four or five o'clock. As the hours progressed and the noise of howling children and women's chatter continued, Sister Colledge stood like a lighthouse in a turbulent sea, calm and reassuring towards all comers, including a girl of about ten who had brought in her little brother, aged two, who had cut his head.

'Me mum's ill, see, so I 'ad to bring 'im in,' she told the Sister, holding the whimpering toddler in her arms and rocking him to and fro. ''E's frightened yer goin' to take 'im in, y'see.'

'But shouldn't you be at school?' asked one of the probationers.

'I've 'ad to stay orf again, me mum's pretty bad,' said the girl, and Mabel remembered the times in her own childhood when she had missed school through having to be a 'little mother'.

And yet she was aware of a lifting of her spirits: she was at home among these children, it was like breathing her native air. She knew with certainty that she had done the right thing in coming to Shadwell.

At one point Mr Green wrinkled his nose and remarked about the smell of some of the women and children going in and out of the consulting-room. 'Haven't they ever heard of washing?' he said to Mabel in a low tone, and was taken aback by her reaction.

'*You*'d smell an' all if yer had to live in a crowded hovel with no runnin' water for cookin', let alone washin',' she snapped. 'I know the smell o' poverty, I trained at a Poor Law infirmary.'

He stared back in astonishment and she later overheard him saying to another student, 'Watch your step with that staff nurse with the cockney accent; she's one of these reforming socialist types. Or possibly a Bible thumper.'

'Is she? I thought she was rather a peach,' said the other young man. 'Nice eyes.'

Sundays were a day or half-day off for outpatients staff, and at the end of her first week Mabel set out for Battersea in the afternoon, anxious to find out if Harry was better for being at home. Doris Drover received her coolly, but the Major gave her a smile and led her into the front parlour where Harry lounged on the sofa.

'Here's Mabel to see yer, son – ah, I thought that would cheer yer. Ye'll stay for tea, Mabel? Mother and I'll be goin' up to the Citadel later on.'

Which told Mabel that she would be alone with Harry for an hour or two.

Mrs Drover made no remark when Harry reached for a packet of cigarettes which he handed to Mabel for her to take and light one for him. It was clear that compromises had been made: half a dozen cigarettes a day had a calming effect on Harry, as did the daily jug of porter, which John Drover fetched from the Falcon Arms each morning before he put on his uniform. He attended to Harry's personal needs, encouraging him to dress and undress with the minimum of aid, feed himself and practise writing with his left hand.

Alone together, Mabel was not short of stories to tell him; the Outpatients' Hall provided her with endless incidents to recount, and amusing things that the children had said or done.

'L – love ag-again, M – M – Mabel,' he murmured, reaching out to touch her. She held his head against her blouse and let him put his arm round her; after his parents had left the house she undid the buttons and let him lay his face against the soft warm flesh. How could she deny him that much?

'Harry – oh, Harry, my love.' She yearned over him like a mother with her child: her sick and injured child. She loved him still and always would, though she recognised that her love had changed; the war had changed everything. This harmless intimacy which meant so much to him would be their special secret for as long as the present situation continued. Meanwhile her work with the children at Shadwell satisfied to some extent the longing in her heart.

From the Midway Norah McLoughlin reported that she too had settled in well and enjoyed her work with the children there. At first she had found it difficult to deal with recalcitrant members of staff who threatened to leave and join the newly formed Women's Auxiliary Army Corps; her youth counted against her in a position of authoriy, but she had the backing of Mrs Spearmann and by the end of her first month was much more confident. Three years of training in a Poor Law infirmary had given her knowledge of the world without affecting her natural sweetness, and young nurserymaids found that they could tell her their problems and she would listen like an older sister.

'So ye see, it's all worked out well,' she said when Mabel called one evening. 'I know I'm in the right place for the time bein' – until Albert comes home for good an' we can be man an' wife together – oh, Mabel darlin', I'm sorry – your poor dear Harry –' She bit her lip and put her hand over Mabel's.

'It's all right, Norah. If I can't marry him, I shan't want anybody else. And haven't I just been tellin' yer how much I love it at Shadwell? And to think you're here for these poor little souls – yer know, Norah, we've got a lot to be thankful for.'

Letters arrived from Belhampton, with the news that young Mrs Westhouse was expecting her first child. Her husband was back in hospital and Mr Gillies had carried out a skin-graft operation on his face.

'It sounds very uncomfortable,' wrote Aunt Elinor, 'and he is taking a long time to recover. It must be such a help to him, knowing of the happy event due in July. We do not see much of Alice, unfortunately, living at opposite ends of Belhampton.'

'I cycled over to see Alice last Saturday,' wrote Daisy. 'She said she was feeling very tired and had to lay down to rest. Mrs Westhouse is crochering a shawl for the baby to be chrisened in. Aunt Kate has had some bad cases at Pinehurst, like poor Harry. Please give him my love, and Norah too. Have you heard from Albert. I am pleased you like the children's hospital.'

Alice must be five or six months by now, Mabel thought, and surely feeling the strain of having to pretend to be earlier. She had not written a word to Mabel, the only person who knew her secret.

Or did anyone else suspect? Mabel could not help wondering. Neither Mrs Somerton nor Miss Chalcott had experienced childbirth, but Gerald's mother had and, living at such close quarters, might she have her doubts? And what would happen when Alice was delivered of a full-term baby two months prematurely? Would the little boy or girl be accepted by its alleged father and grandparents? Mabel worried about it, but could confide in no one.

The days lengthened and spring returned again to London: a sadder, shabbier London of increasing shortages both of food and fuel. The new Prime Minister, Mr Lloyd-George, praised the work being done by the women of England and exhorted the nation to press on with every kind of war effort. The newly formed Ministry of Food encouraged the growing of vegetables, especially potatoes, in gardens and allotments, but in the mean and overcrowded streets of the East End this was a poor joke. Women, some with children in their arms, would start forming queues before six o'clock in the morning for such necessities as bread, sugar and margarine, and as supplies lessened, prices rose.

No sooner had the Zeppelins vanished from the skies than a new terror appeared over the south-east coast: the twin-engined Gothas like great silver insects flying in over the Channel, soon to be followed by the four-engined Giants, dropping bombs that left a trail of destruction. Once more under attack from the air, the civilian population listened in dread for the menacing hum, the woe-woe-woe-woe-woe of the Gothas and the doom-doom-doom-doom-doom that warned of the approach of Giants.

At the beginning of April Mabel was sent to Enfield Ward, mainly surgical. Post-operative care was largely a matter of keeping the children adequately nourished and Mabel taught the probationers how to tempt capricious appetites, such as when young children had hernias repaired and were nursed flat with roller towels across their tummies, weighted down with sandbags on each side. She was adept at pretending that sweet lemonade was ginger beer, mashed potatoes with gravy was meat pie, and steamed fish was fried fish with chips. Bread and jam, that standby of the poor, was cut into fingers and dipped in milk to make it soft to munch and swallow. She slyly introduced a competitive element at mealtimes, wondering aloud who would be the first to finish.

Enfield was a lovely ward, light and airy with a handsome stained-glass window, and each cot carried an individual brass plaque with the name of the donor on it: this might be the Duchess of Portland or a prosperous manufacturing firm. When the probationers grumbled at having to polish them, Mabel told them to be grateful for such generous patrons.

'Oh, Lord, Nurse Court, you're not going to start lecturing us again about that Infirmary!'

Mabel knew that they mimicked her accent and and giggled over her little homilies, but she took no notice, for her only concern was for the children.

'If ye've finished polishin' them brasses, nurse, yer can give me a hand with Oliver.'

Eight-year-old Oliver was recovering from removal of a badly inflamed appendix. He had to be nursed sitting up, with a bolster under his knees, so that the pus could drain downwards. He moaned when the nurses hauled him up the bed and Nurse Court examined his dressing; the discharge was still quite heavy and foul-smelling. Opposite him was another boy, Toby, with osteomyelitis of his right leg. He had been saved from blood poisoning in the nick of time, by having his tibia bone opened and drained. A bed cradle protected the swollen limb, and Nurse Court was constantly pressing him to drink the sweet and slightly salted 'lemonade' that was daily prepared in the kitchen.

A junior surgeon came into the ward, smiled at the

two boys and announced to the nurses that there had been a victory at Arras. 'The Allies have captured Vimy Ridge,' he said. 'It sounds like a new spring offensive, especially now that the Americans have come in at last. Another big push and the balance could be tipped.'

While the others enthused, Mabel shuddered at the very mention of the terms 'spring offensive' and 'big push' with all their remembered horrors of last year, the men killed, wounded, burned, gassed and blinded – and for a moment she felt physically sick. Thank heaven she was here in a children's hospital, away from the blood and carnage of war!

Later, as she stood at the servery in the staff dining-room, she heard two Sisters talking.

'You must remember, Dr Knowles!' said one. 'Trained at the London and came here to get sick children's experience – found his niche and started to specialise in surgery.'

'Of course, I remember him now.' The other nodded. 'Lovely with the children, wasn't he? And didn't he marry just before he was called up? Oh, no, don't tell me he's –'

'No, he's alive but badly wounded in the thigh and might have to lose the leg, so Mr Cowell was saying. He's in the London. Isn't it awful?'

'Why, Nurse Court, you've gone as white as a sheet,' said the girl standing behind Mabel in the queue. 'Is anything the matter?'

Somehow Mabel managed to conceal her shock at what she had just overheard. But she had to find out what had happened to Stephen, whether he was really likely to lose his leg. Dear God, whatever next was to happen in this horrible war?

It was a Thursday and she had an evening off. Could she walk up to the London Hospital in Whitechapel

Road, no great distance, and wait around for his visitors? His parents would be seeing him and his wife would surely be at his side; she might get a chance to speak to her old GP and express her sympathy.

And yet – why should she trouble the Knowles family? It wasn't as if Stephen was a relative, which would give her the right to enquire. No, she mustn't intrude. She would go to see Harry instead and wait until further news of Stephen came her way.

She did not have to wait long. As soon as she got off the tram at Lavender Hill that evening, she met Mrs Lowe, the midwife who had attended her mother at Daisy's birth, a well-known figure in Battersea and always well up with local news. She sympathised with Mabel about Harry and then asked if she'd heard about Dr Knowles's son.

'Only that he's been wounded in the leg – oh, Mrs Lowe, have yer heard how he is?'

It appeared that Stephen had been struck by a piece of exploding shell that had torn into his left thigh.

'Dr Knowles says it'll finish him for the RAMC, Mabel, and he makes no secret that he's thankful for it, says it's probably saved his son's life by gettin' him out o' the fightin'. And – er –' She hesitated for a moment, then went on, 'And seein' as it's *you*, Mabel, I'll tell yer as one midwife to another – it means that Captain Knowles'll be home when the child's born, if she don't miscarry again. Let's hope it's third time lucky, eh?'

'Oh, I – I didn't know,' faltered Mabel.

'Yes, must've been when he was on leave at Christmas, so it's due in September. She's havin' to rest up, that's why she's stayin' with her parents up Northants way. They don't want to take any chances this time – well, yer can understand it, can't yer?'

Mabel took in this unexpected news, which was after

all not so surprising. Stephen and Phyllis Knowles had been reunited at Christmas and now she was expecting again. It was wonderful news, of course. Only . . .

'Ye'll keep that to yerself, won't yer, Mabel? She's just about four months and could still lose it. It's a shame she can't come to visit him in hospital, though – that couple've spent more time apart than together. Still, they're not the only ones, are they?'

When Mabel reached Falcon Terrace she found that just about everybody in Battersea had heard about the old doctor's son, but she instinctively felt that the less said about Stephen in front of Harry, the better. As usual their talk was of Oliver, Toby and the other children in Enfield Ward, and Harry did not mind as long as he could look at her and hold her hand; anything more was not possible with his parents looking on. She felt that Doris Drover tolerated her because she was 'good' for Harry and he visibly brightened in her presence; but this time she had to make an extra effort to smile and hide the new anxiety in her heart.

Maud Ling was not a pretty sight when Mabel called at the lodging house in South Lambeth Road on the following Sunday morning. Her eyes were so puffy that she could hardly open them, her hair was unkempt and her nightgown distinctly grubby.

'What, not up yet, Maudie, on a lovely spring day?' Mabel chided, then drew back sharply from a whiff of sour breath.

'Bloody 'ell, Mabel, no need to shout, me poor 'ead's frobbin' fit to kill. Yer wouldn't like to put the kettle on for a cuppa, would yer?'

Mabel obliged and Maud laid her head back on the pillow and closed her eyes. While the kettle boiled on the gas ring, Mabel went to the window and threw up the sash to let some fresh air into the room.

'Gawd, Mabel, 'ave an 'eart, them bloody bells go frough me 'ead like 'ammers,' Maud complained. 'Next fing we'll 'ave the Salvation Army raising their oompahs just under me winder – ooh, sorry, Mabel, I'd put up wiv 'em for hours on end if only poor ol' 'Arry could blow on 'is trombone again – aargh!' She winced as a shaft of pain stabbed her behind the eyes. 'What I need is a drop o' the 'air o' the dog that bit me last night – fetch the brandy out o' the corner cupboard, will yer?'

Mabel reluctantly peered among the tins of tea and cocoa, jars of pickle, jam and Bovril.

'There's no bottle here, Maudie. Yer must've finished it. No wonder ye've got a headache!'

'I never finished it! That little bleeder must've took it, damn 'is eyes. Wait till I get me 'ands on 'im – ouch! 'Urry up wiv that tea, Mabel, I'm dyin'.'

'D'yer mean Teddy?'

'Yeah, 'oo else?'

Mabel supposed that Maud's young brother had removed the bottle to prevent her from finishing it off. Poor Maudie, what a mess she looked, not at all the smart and cheeky girl she liked to show to the world.

'Did yer have friends in last night, Maudie?'

'Nah, I was on me own. Teddy must've come in an' put me to bed. Sat'day night,' she added with a shrug. 'This is the one day I don't 'ave to go to the featre, yer see.'

'Look here, Maudie, this won't do,' said Mabel who was quite upset by the thought of the sixteen-year-old boy heaving his dead-drunk sister into bed. It was not a pleasant picture. 'Yer know the way yer father an' mother went, and yer don't want to go down that road, do yer?'

281

'But I ain't got kids to look after like they 'ad.'

'Ye've got Teddy, who wouldn't be alive today if it wasn't for the way yer looked after him when he was a baby. Now the poor lad's tryin' to save yer from yerself. Just think, Maud, s'pose Alex was to turn up suddenly and find yer like this, it'd put him off for good. Wouldn't yer feel ashamed?'

'Oh, don't start gettin' on at me, Mabel, gal. It's only Sat'day nights I get really drunk. I'd never risk losin' me place in *Chu Chin Chow*, it's the one fing that keeps me sane.' She covered her face with her hands. 'They're 'avin' a terrible time out there, the Flyin' Corps, losin' good boys all the time, an' every day I fink it could be Alex next. 'Nuff to make anybody drink.'

Her voice quavered and Mabel was filled with pity. 'Oh, Maudie – Maudie, dear, I'm sorry.'

'Yeah, they're at it all hours rahnd the clock, 'ave to sleep when they can, eat when they can. They lorst a whole batch o' new fellers in one day last week – one of 'em was a right toff an' all, Sir Somebody or ovver from dahn 'Ampshire way, rollin' in money, all the wimmin was after 'im, Alex said – all over now, burnt to a bloody cinder when 'is plane was shot dahn.'

'Yer don't know his name, Maudie?' Mabel's heart had given a great thump.

'Alex did say, but I can't remember. There's been so many of 'em gorn.'

'Was it – Savage?'

'Yeah, that was it, Savage – like the fightin' out there. Why, did yer know 'im?'

'Only by name,' Mabel muttered. 'Here's yer tea, Maudie.'

'Cor, fanks, gal. I'll take a coupla aspirins wiv it.'

Mabel went over to the window. She felt cold all

over, and fortunately Maud was too woolly-headed to notice her sudden silence as she stared across the roofs of London, the church spires that rose up out of a city of sorrows, a nation mourning an ever-increasing number of young men killed. How would the women at Houghton Hall take the news? And Alice, how would *she* react at hearing that Guy Savage was dead? She'd have to hide her feelings and say nothing.

Mabel turned from the window. 'That's better, Maudie, ye've got a bit o' colour in yer cheeks. Come on, get up and have a wash, do yer hair an' go out to get a bit o' fresh air an' sunshine.'

Maud gave a hollow groan.

Letters from Belhampton confirmed the utter desolation at Houghton Hall.

'Lady Savage has not left her bed since she was told the news,' wrote Aunt Nell.

It was feared that Mrs Bennett might miscarry with the shock, so she too has been confined to bed and cannot visit her mother. Miss Georgina is left to run the house as well as she can. They simply cannot believe that this has happened to the heir of Houghton Hall, the last baron of the line, dead without issue. We do not see much of Alice, but she is keeping well and is a good size for the time she has reached, almost six months. Gerald is out of hospital and we hear he is making progress, helped by Alice's devotion, I'm sure. How thankful the Westhouses must be that their son was spared and that a little one will soon be here to add to their happiness.

Mabel could not help wondering just *how* soon the little

one would arrive – and whom would he or she most resemble?

The work on Enfield continued to be an endless source of interest and satisfaction. Surgery was making new strides with the correction of birth defects, and conditions like harelip and cleft palate could be operated on with a fair guarantee of success. Mabel quickly learned how best to handle the tiny babies who had to be fed with teaspoons or special teats with flanges that were supposed to fill the gap in the child's upper lip; it was a messy business which led to swallowing of air and consequent windy colic. Club-foot was corrected by division of the tendons and, as with all surgical operations, the ever-present danger was septic infection. Once this set in it was virtually untreatable except by the three principles of nourishment, rest and cleanliness. Oliver took nearly three months to recover from his appendix operation, but Toby's septic leg refused to heal and, when acute blood poisoning threatened again, the leg was amputated just below the knee. Toby would have to learn to walk with a wooden 'peg-leg' until he was older and could be fitted with a proper artificial limb that could 'wear' a sock and shoe – and nobody would know it wasn't real, Mabel told him and his anxious parents.

Meanwhile she had made a friend, the senior staff nurse on Enfield, a well-built girl whose plain features were redeemed by intelligent grey eyes that always softened when she was attending to a child. Violet Stoke-Marriner had taken up sick children's nursing in defiance of her family's wishes, bored by the social round enjoyed by her mother and sisters.

'Their kind of life never interested me, Nurse Court. I wanted to do something for children, especially those at the lower end of society, and at last I had to stand up and say so,' she said. 'My mother threw a fit, but my father saw that I was in earnest and he agreed to pay for my training. I chose to come here rather than Great Ormond Street, because it's such a poor area. I think I've picked up just about every kind of infestation that there is – lice, fleas, scabies – not threadworms, though, not yet!' She gave a booming chuckle.

'What d'yer family think o' yer now?' asked Mabel, fascinated by the story.

'Oh, they look upon me as a freak. But think, Nurse Court, what a farce it would have been for a big creature like me to be presented at Court! I'd have probably keeled right over when I curtsied to Their Majesties!' She laughed again. 'But this – ah, Nurse Court, *this* is real life.'

She spooned up another helping of milk pudding to push into the mouth of a flushed little girl whose tonsils had been removed and who whimpered every time she swallowed because of her sore throat. 'Come on, dear, it'll be better soon – good girl.'

Yes, thought Mabel, she's right, this is real life. What a privilege it was to care for sick children and see at least *some* of them get better: it was what she tried to share with Harry when she told him stories about Shadwell.

Nurse Marriner was asking her a question: 'Have you seen this show that everybody's talking about, Nurse Court? This *Chu Chin Chow*? All the soldiers on leave are being taken to see it, and everybody's singing the songs – would you like to go one evening?'

Mabel longed to accept, but there was Harry who could not go with her. 'I'd've liked to go and see it with me young man – yer know, the one who's badly shell-shocked an' lost an arm – but he can't go,' she said sadly.

'Why not? Can't he get to the theatre?'

'No, not the way he is, Nurse Marriner. And he's very much under his parents' thumb, and they're Salvation Army people and don't really approve o' the theatre, y'see.'

'I don't quite understand, Nurse Court. Hasn't he got a mind of his own at all? If I were to hire a taxicab for us, is there any reason why we couldn't call for him and take him to the theatre one evening when we're both off duty? And take him home again afterwards?'

Mabel remembered how much Harry had enjoyed sitting beside her at the Canterbury to see *Cinderella*. It would be such a wonderful change for him – a treat for them both. She suddenly made up her mind.

'Thank yer very much indeed, Nurse Marriner, an' yes, it's marvellous idea, and I've got a friend who's in the show an' she can get us tickets!' She was becoming more enthusiastic by the minute.

'And what about that other friend of yours, Nurse Court, the one who's in charge of a babies' home?' asked Violet Stoke-Marriner. 'Wouldn't she like to come, too?'

'Oh, it's no good askin' Norah, she won't go to anythin' unless me brother takes her,' replied Mabel, shaking her head. 'And the Lord only knows when he'll be home from sea again.'

And so a decision was made, and a delighted Maud produced four tickets. 'Just in case my Alex can get over, then 'e can sit an' flirt wiv yer posh friend while you enjoy yerself wiv 'Arry!'

Harry and the Drovers were duly told of the treat in store, and the Major soon agreed to his son having an evening out with Mabel and her friends, especially as he would be fetched and brought back in a cab. It was to be on the eighteenth of May, a Friday.

*   *   *

And then, on the Thursday before the outing, a miracle occurred: the reappearance of the proverbial bad penny.

'*Albert!*' Ecstatic hugs and kisses from his sister were followed by a dash to the Midway and the sight of Norah's blue eyes lighting up with joy. And she was not entirely surprised.

'*Albert!* Sure an' didn't I see yer last night, smilin' an' wavin', on yer way home to me.'

'Gawd, ye're more beautiful than ever, Norah.' As always, he was somewhat tentative about embracing his 'little nun' at first, and only when she put her arms round his neck and planted her soft, warm lips on his weatherbeaten cheek did he show how much he had been longing and living for this moment.

'Got shore leave while the ol' *Galway Castle* gets patched up – she's been knocked abaht a bit this year,' he explained, his words muffled as he withdrew his lips for a moment to take a breath. 'Oh, Gawd, to be in 'eaven again . . .'

Maud was hastily consulted, seats in the circle were rearranged and the theatre party was increased to six.

Chapter Sixteen

They were in the middle row of the circle. With Harry on her right side and Albert on her left, Mabel was flanked by the two men she loved most in the world. Next to Albert sat Norah and next to Harry, Violet; beyond her sat Alex Redfern, waiting to admire and adore Maud's every move on the stage as a dancer and a slave-girl: every movement that she made would be for him alone, and tonight after the show they would melt into each other's arms. Everything had worked out so well, Mabel thought, had fitted like pieces of a jigsaw puzzle, and with perfect timing, to bring them all together on this May evening at His Majesty's, thanks to Violet Stoke-Marriner for suggesting it in the first place. Three hours of sheer exotic enjoyment stretched ahead, and such romantic songs as 'Any Time's Kissing Time' and 'I love Thee So', as well as the haunting melancholy of 'The Cobbler's Song'.

At the moment the lights went down and the curtain rose on the wealthy merchant Kasim Baba being carried on his purple palanquin, the audience sighed with delight and settled down to be entertained. Mabel clutched at Harry's hand in the darkness and gave her full attention to the scene before her.

Harry longed to lay his head on her beloved bosom, to bury his face between her breasts where he knew he was safe from the dreams and fantasies that lay below the surface of everyday life, festering in the dark of the unconscious. Here all was brightness, music and magic, like the pantomime they had seen together – how long ago? – when Maud had sung 'You Made Me Love You' and everybody had cheered and clapped. That had been in another life, before the killing began. This was different, an eastern tale of romance between Ali Baba's son and the beautiful Marjanah . . .

But as the first act went on, a sinister sound broke in: a steady thump-thump-thump-thump of marching feet, of boots striking the ground in military formation, getting louder, thump-thump-thump-thump! And now there was singing, the sound of a whole battallion raising their voices in chorus:

'We are the robbers of the woods,
And we rob everyone we can –'

Robbers! Robbing men of blood and health, time and life itself. *Thump-thump-thump-thump!* Harry began to sweat and tremble: gripping Mabel's hand tightly, his breathing got shorter and shallower until he was panting in time to the rhythm of the 'Robbers' Chorus'. Panic was rising up in his throat to choke him – but here was Mabel, sweet and understanding as always.

'All right, Harry, it's all right, don't worry, it's just a story on the stage,' he heard her whisper close to his ear. 'Just breathe slowly, dear, in and out – in and out, that's right – that's better, well done. Close yer eyes and just breathe in and out.'

She kept as quiet as possible, though Violet was aware of her low whispering. Albert and Norah were too absorbed in the play and each other to notice, and Alex Redfern either didn't know or pretended not to see the effect of the 'Robbers' Chorus' on a member of their party.

Listening to her, holding her right hand and feeling

her left hand gently stroking his arm, Harry gradually quietened. She was right, it was only actors on a stage – though he'd enjoyed *Cinderella* more. Everything was different now, the world had changed and become frightening: even a story on a stage could take on a sinister note.

But the first act was over now, and everybody was talking and laughing, saying how good it was. Norah leaned over to say wasn't Maud surely lovelier than the girl playing Marjanah!

'All right now, Harry, dear?' Mabel whispered, and he put his one arm round her shoulders and nuzzled against her neck as the lights went down. He was feeling tired now – fear always wore him down – and he closed his eyes against the brilliantly lit stage. He'd wait for 'The Cobbler's Song' which Mabel said was the best tune in the show.

But 'The Cobbler's Song' was not until Act Three and first there was Act Two to be got through. It was full of scheming plots and intrigues to do with getting into Kasim Baba's palace and stealing all his treasures – and then, oh, God help them all, the horrible robber chief appeared again with his fiendish chorus. And he was singing, or rather yelling, a truly terrifying song.

> 'When I draw my short, sharp scimitar –'
> 'His scimitar! His scimitar!'

echoed his followers, their grey helmets gleaming.

> 'To end thy maudlin mutterings,
> And close thy senile stutterings –'

Harry had never heard anything so menacing since –

help! He leapt in his seat as a sudden burst of gunfire echoed across the space betwen them and him: he saw the glitter of bayonets bared and raised!

> 'Carve thee up, carve thee down,
> Slice thee through from heel to crown –'

Half blinded by the sun flashing on the cold steel, the one-armed soldier struggles to rise to his feet. But the enemy has seen him and is after him – look, look! Here they come!

Help me, he's coming for me, there he is, he's out to kill me – can't yer see him?

> 'See his scimitar, see his scimitar,
> Ha, ha, ha, ha, ha, ha!'

The shouting of the advancing enemy and the screaming of his own poor, annihilated platoon is now all around him. He tries to get down below the parapet, down into the trench – *ugh!* It's all dead flesh, stench, mud and great, slimy rats.

> 'Carve him in, carve him out,
> Whilst with pride we robbers shout,
> See our scimitars, see our scimitars!
> Ha, ha, ha, ha, ha, ha!'

Oh, help me, God, if there is a God who saves – help me, help me!

'All right, I've got him – easy there, steady on, don't struggle with him, he's trying to crawl along the row – good God, what a racket!' Alex Redfern is down on his hands and knees.

A man in evening dress appears. 'What the hell's going on?'

'Chap's gone berserk.'

'Has somebody sent for the police?'

'Reckon it's an ambulance we need here.'

'Oh, Albert, whatever can we do?' It is Mabel's voice.

'Don't get in a state, gal, 'e just fought 'e was back in them trenches, poor ol' beggar. Wotcher, 'Arry? What's up, then, mate?'

And then uniforms and men's voices, friendly and reassuring. Hands are touching him, not roughly but kindly. Not out to kill him. A whole lot of different voices, all jumbled up together, making no sense.

'All right, mate, we'll soon get yer away from here.'

'What about the young lady?'

'Are yer comin' with him, miss?'

'Look, Mabel, I'll come along wiv yer bofe. Alex'll look after Norah an' Violet.'

'No, Albert, you stay with Norah. *I'll* go with them,' says a woman in firm, well-bred tones.

'Oh, thanks, Violet. Where're yer takin' him?'

'Springfield Asylum, miss, they'll settle him down and sort him out there. What d'ye think set him off?'

He hears Alex Redfern answer, 'The poor devil was in the Somme, and got badly shell-shocked as well as losing an arm.'

'Gawd, what a shame – what a tragedy, eh?'

'We'll see him all right, don't worry.'

And voices and more voices, rising and falling, a journey lying on his back, a destination, other voices, further away, getting quieter, fading into silence. Night, a faint light and silence. Cut off out of the land of the living.

*   *   *

Doris Drover was furious about Harry's public humiliation and maintained that the incident had been a judgement for taking him to see a show of such depravity. Everybody who witnessed his abject terror was haunted by it and even Alex Redfern, entwined with Maud in passionate lovemaking that night, could not blot out what he had seen and heard.

'It was weird, Maudie,' he panted while still lying on top of her, gripped by her thighs around his trunk. 'That damned robber chief with his scimitar – *I swear I saw what Harry saw.*'

Corporal Drover stayed at Springfield Asylum for three days and Albert spent a precious half-day of his leave visiting him there. At his parents' request he was discharged home; otherwise he would have been sent back to Netley. Miss Stoke-Marriner visited him at 8 Falcon Terrace and accepted all responsibility for persuading Miss Court to take him to the theatre. She said that she should have made more enquiries into the kind of show that it was, the scenes likely to disturb a man returned from the front line. The fact that it was a very popular show among servicemen on leave had misled her, she said, and apologised unreservedly to his parents. Harry appeared to have recovered from the experience, but withdrew even further into a world of his own where he comforted himself with daydreams centred upon Mabel; her visits to Falcon Terrace were coolly received for a week or two, though John Drover suggested that if Mabel called once a week at a pre-arranged time, he would see that she and Harry were left alone for an hour, simply because 'it did the boy good', like his daily ration of tobacco and ale.

And Albert was back at sea, having spent most of the daylight hours of his leave at the Midway Babies' Home where he had played with the older children, and charmed Mrs Lovell and the other members of staff. Norah had been grateful for every moment spent with him and had not cried when they had to say goodbye again; she had held him close and assured him that he was in the care of the Sacred Heart of Jesus. Privately she reproached herself that he had seen so little of his sister.

As always, it was her work that provided Mabel with a safety valve, though her transfer to Heckford Ward the following week introduced her to some of the saddest cases in the hospital. It contained mainly medical conditions and had a high mortality rate. The East London was in the forefront of research into 'marasmus', a blanket term to describe a variety of little-understood wasting diseases, mysterious intolerances of the digestive system, and even when a cause was discovered, as in diabetes, the cure was not necessarily forthcoming straight away. Most of Mabel's time seemed to be taken up with feeding and replacement of body fluid in a last-ditch attempt to halt the muscle wasting, but all too often her final task was to wrap the pathetic skeletal bodies into tiny white shrouds, which then had to be stitched and labelled for the mortuary.

'It was for children dying of cholera that Dr Nathaniel Heckford founded this hospital, Nurse Court,' said the middle-aged Sister, traditionally called Sister Heckford, after the Ward in her care. 'He began it in an old warehouse at Ratcliff Cross, just a dispensary for women and children, and he never lived to see the building we have here today. We like to think that we're still carrying on his tradition of caring – towards recovery if possible, but if not, well – we're here beside them to the end.'

Sadly, the war had brought about many cuts and

curtailments to the work of the East London. The glass-fronted summer house known as the Pavilion at the back of the hospital building was closed for the summer months due to staff shortage, and its tubercular patients transferred to long-stay sanatoria.

'It's a pity we can't use it for the bronchitics and asthmatics who need all the sunshine and fresh air they can get.' Sister Heckford sighed. 'But of course they're not such a problem in the summer. You should see Heckford in the winter, Nurse Court, with fish kettles going full blast and steam tents all down one wall! And of course the fires in the wards cause a lot of dust. But this warm weather brings enteric fevers and gastroenteritis, like poor little Annie Reeves in bed 4, getting weaker every day before our eyes. It makes us all feel so helpless.'

And as Mabel gazed upon the pinched grey face and sunken eyes of the three-year-old girl, she could only pray for a miracle.

On the whole she got on well with the other ward staff, though there was a section of the medical students and probationers who joked about her constant preoccupation with replacements of body fluids in sick children. 'Never miss a chance to give a drink to a dehydrated child. As soon as they wake up from sleep, when ye're makin' their bed, or if they want the potty – any time is drinky-time! And don't just put the feeding cup by the bedside – make 'em *drink* it!'

'I can't get little Annie Reeves to take anything, no matter how much I try,' said a third-year helplessly. 'She doesn't respond at all, poor little thing.'

At that moment Dr Lamarr, the senior house physician, appeared on the ward, accompanied by two medical students. He nodded briefly to the staff nurse, and turned down the corners of his mouth at the sight of Annie, prostrate and semi-conscious in her cot. 'Hm – what have we here?' he asked.

The question was directed at the students, but Mabel did not realise this and answered promptly. 'She was brought in with enteritis, Dr Lamarr, and everythin' goes in one end an' out the other,' she said, handing him the cardboard folder with Annie's details. The students exchanged a look.

'Have you tried a slow rectal infusion of saline?' asked Lamarr.

'No good givin' rectal saline or anythin' else while she's passin' these liquid stools, doctor,' Mabel said somewhat impatiently. 'Better try subcutaneous Ringer's solution.'

'Hm-mm, I suppose so, then.' The doctor's tone was not hopeful.

'D'ye want to give it, or one o' the students – or shall I?' asked Mabel, who had already prepared a large sterilised syringe containing two ounces of the special preparation of saline and glucose. When Lamarr did not answer, she proceeded to clean the skin of Annie's right armpit, then carefully injected three or four drachms. A swelling appeared beneath the site, and Mabel withdrew the needle and gently massaged the area. The swelling disappeared fairly quickly as the fluid dispersed, and the procedure was repeated into the left armpit while doctor and students looked on.

Lamarr proceeded with the ward round, and on returning to Annie the effect of the injection of fluid was noticeable. She stirred and whimpered.

'All right, Annie dear, Mabel's here – have a nice little drink, there's a good girlie.' The spout of the feeding cup was put to Annie's dry lips and she sucked a few drops from it.

'Right, well – it seems to have done the trick for

the time being, anyway. I hope you'll remember what you've seen and learn from it,' Lamarr said to the students as they turned to leave the ward. 'It's a relatively simple procedure that a trained nurse can do, as you saw.' The truth was that Lamarr disliked giving fluid by direct subcutaneous injection and, if the site should become infected, he did not care to take the responsibility for it. The staff nurse with the jarring voice had obviously wanted to show off her skill and in any case the child was not much longer for this world.

'Hasn't he got the most gorgeous dark eyes!' whispered the third-year as he left.

June came in with sunshine and clear skies; the windows of the East London were opened to their fullest extent and cots were taken out into the courtyard at the back of the main building, behind the closed Pavilion.

Two important items of news arrived one Monday morning. First there was a letter from Aunt Nell and Mabel put it beside her place to read during the first sitting of dinner, for surely it must contain news of Alice, now two or three weeks past the true expected date for her baby's birth. As Mabel was about to rip it open she became aware of a group of nurses at the table next to hers exchanging the latest hospital gossip.

'I say, have you heard the news?'

'No, what about?'

'Guess who's come back on surgery and anaesthetics, starting from today, looking ten years older and walking with a stick!'

'Go on, tell us!'

But Mabel knew at once and her heart gave a sudden lurch. Stephen Knowles's army service might be ended, but he had lost no time in returning to the place and the work he loved, and where he was so sorely needed.

Mabel thought quickly: if he was back on surgery, she would not be likely to see much of him on Heckford Ward. And his wife would be between five and six months by now, and presumably had not miscarried this time, which must be a great relief to them both, she thought. And wondered why her hands shook as she opened her letter.

It drove all other thoughts from her mind for the time being, for she had become an aunt.

'My dear Mabel,' wrote Mrs Somerton.

Prepare for a happy shock! I know that you will rejoice to know that your sister Alice was safely delivered of a son in the early hours of this morning, Saturday, the second of June. She went into labour on Thursday, but her pains were not recognised as such by the midwife who said it was far too early and must be indigestion. So poor Alice lay in pain all Thursday night and on Friday the midwife had to admit that the birth was soon to take place, and sent for the Westhouses' doctor. After a long and very painful ordeal she was delivered this morning, and little Geoffrey weighs six and a half pounds. The midwife says he would have been eight pounds at least if Alice had gone the full time, so I suppose we must be thankful that the birth was several weeks premature, not being due until the end of July. Their vicar was called to christen him at midday because of this.

Both mother and child are doing as well as can be expected, though poor Alice is exhausted after such a long labour, and I understand that little Geoffrey is rather slow to suck. The midwife says this is quite usual in premature babies, and has been giving him a little boiled milk and water in a bottle to tide him over until Alice's milk comes in. Thomas and I are so relieved, and of course the Westhouses are overjoyed to be grandparents, though it was a shock! And Daisy, like you, is an aunt. Geoffrey is a sweet baby with blue eyes and fluffy fair down all over his dear little head. I hope it will not be too long before you can visit us again, Mabel, and see your nephew for yourself.

Mabel set the letter aside and offered up a silent prayer of thanks that the ordeal was over and that the baby was relatively small. He would go through life never knowing that he was the only issue of the last baron of Houghton Hall – and Alice, who had pulled off her daring deception, aided by Nature, must be feeling the greatest relief of all. Mabel noticed that her aunt had said nothing at all about Gerald, the new father. What were *his* thoughts about the baby?

Mabel was at the office desk when the surgeon limped into the ward the following afternoon.

'Good afternoon, staff nurse. I've been asked to see a boy brought in on Monday – oh, good heavens, Mabel Court! My dear girl, how are you?'

'Oh, er – good afternoon, Dr Knowles.' Mabel rose hurriedly to her feet. 'Very pleased to see yer after yer – er –' She faltered, shocked at his appearance, so much aged since she had last seen him at Christmas; his hair had turned completely grey. 'Oh – d'ye need a chair?'

She brought forward the chair she had been using and he winced as he lowered himself on to it, placing his walking stick across his lap. 'Trouble is, Mabel, it hurts my thigh when I stand up and still hurts my backside to sit down. A right pain in the arse, you could say, begging your pardon.'

'Let me fetch yer a cushion –'

'I can't tell how glad I am to see you, Mabel. I heard about Harry and what happened at the theatre – these stories get around and I was very sorry. How's the dear chap doing now?'

Mabel had no sooner begun to speak than Sister Heckford bustled in and claimed his full attention, having known him before the war. She took him to see a boy with a high fever and swollen glands of the neck, possibly tubercular, in which case he would need surgery for their removal. Mabel got on with her observation round, taking pulses and giving drinks, but before Knowles left the ward he sought her out and spoke briefly to her again.

'There's a lot I want to ask you, Mabel. When are you next off in the evening? I'm not driving yet, and still a bit creaky on the left leg, but we could go down to the Prospect of Whitby and share a glass by the river if that's all right for you. Thursday any good?'

She nodded, and saw Sister's eyebrows shoot up.

On Heckford Ward there was also cause for rejoicing, marked by the grateful tears of little Annie Reeves's parents. Against all the odds the child had recovered from a severe attack of gastroenteritis and Dr Lupton, the consultant physician, was fulsome in his praise of Dr Lamarr and the Ward Sister, though the latter quickly pointed out that her junior staff nurse had spent literally hours giving fluids by subcutaneous injection and by mouth, so preserving Annie's life over the crucial days of the acute infection. Dr Lupton then asked Nurse Court personally about her impressions of Annie's progress and recovery.

'D'ye know, I began to think that it *might* clear up,

sir, by the smell o' them stools!' she told him with a confident air. 'It wasn't yer usual marasmus smell, nor cholera, it was more like as if she'd ate somethin' that'd gone off an' given her food poisonin'. And another thing – she had that acidy smell on her breath that they get when they're short o' fluid, d'ye know what I mean? Yer can tell a lot from usin' yer nose!'

The physician listened and nodded politely as her eager, unselfconscious words carried down the ward to the group of medical students accompanying the great man on his round. It was impossible for them to keep straight faces.

'Good enough for our concert party!' murmured one young man with a mischievous look.

'You could write a song for us, Thompson, and Tim and I could fit it to music,' said another amidst suppressed laughter. 'What about something from *Chu Chin Chow*?'

'*Yes!* "Any Time's Drinky-time"!'

'Ssh! Here comes Sir – straighten your tie and shut up.'

'Ah, there you are, Mabel! What a pretty dress, just right for an evening like this.'

Stephen took her arm, leaning on her slightly, holding his stick in his left hand. And of course that made her think of Harry.

'Now, you must tell me all about what's been happening,' he said, smiling, 'especially about Harry and that rapscallion Albert.'

'Me two favourite subjects, Dr Stephen! Well, Albert leads a charmed life, thanks to Norah McLoughlin's prayers to the Sacred Heart, or so she says – did yer know she's at the Midway Babies' Home now, and don't yer *dare* say a word against Mrs Spearmann, 'cause what

301

she's done for those dear children is nothin' short o' miraculous!'

'I wouldn't dream of contradicting anything you say, Mabel Court. Just go on talking to me.'

And so she chattered away happily as they walked down Glamis Road, past the old fish market on the opposite side to the hospital, and on reaching the Highway they crossed the bridge to Wapping with its wharves and warehouses. Work was almost over for the day, but a group of dockers were still unloading the diminished cargoes of tea, sugar, tobacco and other commodities that had evaded the German U-boats; an exotic mixture of smells wafted to them on the slight breeze from the water. The river was full of small craft, the barges and lighters that nipped in and out among the larger vessels unable to pull into the shallows. A few gulls wheeled round above them in the clear sky.

She suddenly fell silent and he saw her gazing downriver.

'I don't suppose Albert's leave was very long,' he said quietly, and she shook her head.

'Just Thursday to Monday, while the *Galway Castle* was being refitted. Oh, it isn't that I begrudge one minute o' the time he spent with darlin' Norah, but – I miss him too, y'see.'

'I know, my dear, and I'm so sorry. Come on, here's the Prospect of Whitby. Let's go in and sample the casks!'

It was still early evening, before the rougher element had arrived, the dockers and watermen. Babies sat in battered prams outside the door and bare-footed, gap-toothed children waited at the kerbside, sharing a few chips or eating a slice of bread smeared with jam.

Stephen nudged her. 'See those little girls with nothing on their bottoms?'

302

'Saves the washing,' she promptly replied. He smiled to himself. Always practical, this girl.

The sun-browned faces of the children looked up at the couple and a small boy suddenly grinned and called out, ''Allo, Nurse Cork!'

She recognised him as an outpatient who had come for daily treatment of impetigo and sore eyes back in her early days at the hospital, and she was touched that he still remembered her. The sight of these cheeky, ragged urchins in all their dirt and poverty stirred something deep within Mabel and a tender, reminiscent smile played about her mouth.

'Harry and me always said that one day we'd run a children's shelter for the Salvation Army,' she told him, clasping her hands together. 'Oh, how I used to hope and plan and dream about what it'd be like, and the things we'd do for 'em!'

How lovely she looks, the poor darling, he thought involuntarily, and immediately frowned at himself. 'Come on, let's go in and sit in the back parlour.' He took her arm, at the same time fumbling in his pocket for a cigarette.

After the daylight the smoke-stained old inn seemed very dark. Its small round windows were not designed to let in much light, and the flagstoned floors and cast-iron hearths, now empty, gave a sense of its murky past merging with the present troubled times, as if to remind them that this war too would become history. Settled by the window overlooking the waterfront, Mabel poured out her heart to this man; tears welled up when she spoke of Harry Drover and Knowles produced a large handkerchief, which he handed to her in silence.

She told him that she no longer had any expectations of Harry's recovery.

'I clung to those hopes for so long, Stephen. There was

a time when he seemed to be comin' back to the land o' the livin', but now I don't think he even wants to.'

'Because the real world has been too cruel for him to cope with, Mabel. That's why he's turned his back on it.'

'He just wanders in a world of his own, dreamin' about –' She hesitated, for this was very private territory, shared by no one else, not even Norah or Maud.

'Can he talk with you, Mabel?'

'No, he stammers so badly, I do most o' the talkin'. He loves me to sit beside him – close, so's he can – touch me.'

Stephen drew on his cigarette and exhaled deeply. 'Ah, yes. Oh, God, poor Harry. And you don't mind, Mabel?'

She raised her eyes to his and looked straight at him. 'O' *course* I don't mind! Harry and me loved each other as soon as we met, all them years ago when I was sixteen. We've waited an' waited, our marriage plans've been put off again and again, and it breaks me heart to see him like this –' Her words ended on a stifled sob. 'It's all very well for *you*, Stephen, ye've got yer wife an' soon ye'll have a child – that's somethin' Harry an' me'll never have!'

She wept afresh, stifling the sound with the handkerchief.

He leaned towards her, putting a hand lightly on her shoulder. 'Oh, Mabel, Mabel! My dear girl. You're right, of course, and I don't blame you for saying so, but it isn't as easy as it may appear. I blame myself for what happened at Christmas – should have kept off the drink, it was damned irresponsible. I could have been knocked off in France and she'd have been landed with a fatherless child.'

'But ye're *home* and ye're *safe*!' Mabel protested, impatiently shrugging off his hand.

'I know, I know, but the war's spoiled so much that was good and hopeful – I mean, look at me, I'm not the man Phyllis married. I wasn't joking when I said I was a pain in the arse, a bad-tempered swine who drinks and smokes too much, and can't ever tell Phyllis what I've seen – or what I've done. Can't tell anybody. There are some things I'll always have to keep to myself – and never be free from the memory of them, not till the day I die.'

There was a long silence: his eyes were averted from her, staring out of the window.

At length she straightened herself up and gently placed both of her hands over his.

'Why don't yer tell *me*, then?' she asked softly.

He turned to look into her blue-grey eyes that were willing him to speak. Which at length he did, after first lighting another cigarette. 'We see some sad sights at the East London, Mabel, and it was no picnic for you at Booth Street, either,' he began. 'But Mabel, you should have seen that casualty clearing station close to the Somme in the middle of winter. Cramped, cold, dirty, only the most basic of equipment, not enough room for all the wounded who kept pouring in. It was *hell*.'

'Didn't the ambulances get 'em away to base hospitals as soon as they could?' Mabel asked, awed by the bleakness of his expression.

'As fast as they could, yes, but often I had to say who was to go and who was to stay and die. We had a "moribund ward" – a wretched place where we put the men who were going to die. There were a few Red Cross nurses who stayed with them. We didn't bother to splint a broken arm or leg, you see, if the man had lost more blood than he could afford – we saved our time and supplies for those who stood a chance. And it was never easy to judge the hopeless ones against those

305

who just might survive.' He lowered his voice. 'And I made mistakes.'

'Oh, Stephen, yer poor man.' What words were there for her to say? Nothing that was half adequate in such circumstances.

'But that wasn't all, Mabel. I had to – I had to despatch a few of my own men when there was no help for it – nothing else to be done.'

Mabel's mouth fell open, aghast at what she was hearing.

'Yer own men? Yer mean British soldiers?' she said incredulously, remembering Harry's fear of killing Germans.

'Yes. What else could I do, listening to a man dying in agony, calling out for his mother all night until he choked on his own blood? I wonder what *you*'d have done?' His voice was low and harsh. 'One night I shot two Tommies in no man's land for the same reason that I shot dying horses – and there were plenty of those pitiful creatures, I can tell you!'

He put his mouth close to her ear and she closed her eyes. 'I pushed my .45 revolver muzzle against the back of their neck, first one and then the other, and I said I was sorry and fired. Death was instant, at least there was no doubt about that – the whole of the front of the skull came away and there were their brains, just blown out – oh, Christ. Oh, Mabel. Oh, Mabel, I was a doctor. A *doctor*.'

He covered his face and again turned towards the window with his back to her. She handed back the handkerchief and prayed for the right words to say, what to do for this tormented man. Her instinct was to take him in her arms and cradle his head against her shoulder, as she did with the children; but she could hardly whisper 'All right, ssh-ssh, never fear, Mabel's here' to Dr Stephen Knowles. She could only rise and place her hands upon his shoulders waiting until the storm passed over. At least he knew that she was there as a friend he could trust.

After a minute or two he brought himself under control, wiped his eyes and blew his nose.

'Thank you. I won't apologise because – oh, Mabel, I've told you what I've never told before, not my own father, not anybody – let alone my wife, poor girl. Thank you, my dear. Thanks more than I can say.'

'And it'll never go any farther, yer know that, Stephen.'

'I know. And I know it's upset you, but –'

'No, I'm glad yer said it to me and nobody else. I'm glad I was the one yer could tell. It was a good deed that yer did, Stephen. Only God could give the kind o' courage ye'd need to do that.'

'Bless you, Mabel. I couldn't have gone on much longer out there, though.' He grimaced, shaking his head. 'We'll both stick with our sick children here at Shadwell, Mabel – and it's time we were going back there. Come on!' He rose stiffly from the seat and took her arm, picking up his stick.

Outside the evening was still clear and they stood and looked across to the East London Hospital towering above the Shadwell Basin. They walked slowly back over the bridge and up the gradual ascent of Glamis Road. A sound of movement, talk and laughter could be heard from the Outpatients' Hall.

'The staff are allowed to play badminton after hours,' he remarked. 'It was passed at the last Board meeting. Not that I'll be leaping about bashing a shuttlecock,' he added ruefully.

'And I wouldn't have the faintest idea how to play,' she replied. 'I'll leave that to the poshies!'

'Poshies?'

'Yes, the medical students and lady probationers who think that all Poor Law infirmaries are workhouses!'

'Oh, Mabel.' He was about to say something, but changed his mind and just joined in her quiet chuckle. He felt somehow released from the horror that had separated him from the life and the people he had known before the war. He had been able to tell this girl what he had not told to another living soul. She had understood, because of Harry. And Stephen was grateful.

'Goodnight, Mabel. Thank you for – this evening.'

'Thank yer too, Stephen. Goodnight.'

On his way up to his room in the medical quarters, Knowles heard loud male laughter coming from the students' lounge; it sounded as if young Thompson was at the piano and practising with his friends for the concert party they traditionally held at the end of their time spent at Shadwell. The door was ajar, and Knowles heard one of them ask for another run-through of a song.

'Can you do "Taught by Court" again? It's so priceless when we come in for the chorus!'

Stephen Knowles's ears pricked up and he stopped outside the door to listen.

A few opening bars were played, and then Thompson began to sing with an exaggerated cockney accent, in the style of a music hall ditty.

> 'If ye're seekin' information,
> To en'ance yer reputation,
> Let ev'ry eager student come along –
> Though she never went to college,
> She's a fountain'ead o' knowledge,
> An' 'er nose is always sniffin' aht a pong!'

Another male voice chimed in,

'So don't complain if bedpan smells ain't quite as
   sweet as roses –'

Thompson came back with,

'But take a sniff, a good ol' whiff, to aid yer
   diagnosis –'

And together they sang with gusto,

'Yer know to use yer eyes an' ears, but *don't forgit
   yer noses*!
We was taught – pooh! – phew! –
By Staff Nurse Court!'

Howls of laughter greeted the final two lines and somebody begged for another verse, to bring in *halitosis* and
proboscis.

Knowles's first reaction was one of furious indignation, and he was about to burst in on the young men
round the piano and tell them that their so-called wit
did them nothing but discredit; but second thoughts
restrained him. Better not to make an issue out of
thoughtless high spirits; he didn't suppose the silly oafs
had intended malice towards a young woman whose
shoes they were not fit to tie up. He'd have a private
word with Thompson, though, and tell him to remove
that tasteless item from the programme forthwith.

Stephen Knowles even managed a grim little smile to
himself as he slowly ascended the remaining stairs to
his room. Later he was to be thankful that his common
sense had prevailed.

Chapter Seventeen

The sight of the little children happily playing out of doors on a sunny Sunday afternoon was a joy to behold. The small open space – it could scarcely be called a garden – at the front of the Midway Babies' Home had been transformed by three bench seats, two new swings and a see-saw, all supplied, like the two large perambulators, by Mrs Spearmann's Friends of the Midway, a charitable association which not only held fund-raising events but encouraged its members to befriend individual children and invite them into their homes.

'Some o' them get on well from the start, like little Mary with those two sisters and their housemaid Kitty,' said Norah. 'But others take longer, and sometimes it just doesn't work out at all. The great thing is, y'see, they know they can always come back to Sister Norah at the Midway!'

Mabel, who was sitting on a swing with a toddler on her knee, remembered Albert's words about Norah being 'like a little nun'. Infants swarmed around her, trying to sit on her lap and clamber on her shoulder, forever clinging and clutching in the way of young children starved of affection; in Sister Norah they recognised a mother-figure who always had time to spare for them.

'How're ye gettin' on over there, Maudie? Is he takin' it?' she asked.

Maud Ling had been presented with a yelling baby and a boat-shaped feeding bottle of milk. Seated at the end of the bench that Norah occupied, she was concentrating hard on the task in hand. Once the eager little mouth had gripped the rubber teat, the milk rapidly disappeared, to the accompaniment of encouraging noises from Maud.

'Ain't done this since Ted was a baby – whoops! I fink it's got blocked – 'e's stopped suckin'.'

'Try bringin' up some wind.'

''Oo, me?'

'Here, let me show ye.' Norah laughed, and when the baby had given a loud, satisfying burp, Maud took him back and gently pushed the teat towards his rosy mouth again. There was a tender, thoughtful look on her face as she fed the child, and although her skin was pale and her eyes shadowed, Mabel felt fairly sure that she was making a big effort to keep her drinking habit under control. It had been a terrible spring for the Royal Flying Corps, with the loss of three hundred British airmen in April.

'I wish ye'd say a few o' yer prayers to the Sacred 'Eart for my Alex, Norah, same as yer do for Albert,' said Maud sombrely.

'Oh, but I *do*, Maud darlin', I *do*!' replied Norah at once. 'I say a Rosary for *all* o' the dear men, every single day, and hasn't it kept Albert safe all this time?'

There was no reply, because both Maud and Mabel were thinking of Harry, safe from enemy action now, but tragically crippled in mind and body. There was no point in dwelling on it and Mabel now passed on the news of Alice's baby Geoffrey.

'Cor, that was quick, wa'n't it?' Maud grinned. ''E may 'ave 'ad 'is face burned, but there can't be much wrong wiv 'is ovver bits!'

Norah lowered her long lashes modestly in front of the children, and Mabel stayed silent. Maud looked deeply abashed. 'Oh, sorry, Mabel, that was an *awful* fing to say. If my Alex had been – oh, Gawd, yer wonder 'ow much longer it can go on for, don't yer? S'pose it should be better now that the Yanks've come in.'

'How's Harry's brother-in-law?' asked Norah.

'Still in chokey on Dartmoor,' answered Mabel. 'Ruby took the boys down to see him on the train. She said he looks thin as a rake, but he gets on well with the other chaps, and they're all determined to stick to their principles.'

'Reckon 'e's got the right idea, if yer ask me,' said Maud dourly. 'At least 'e'll come aht alive, which is more than can be said for – wonder 'ow yer friend Ada's gettin' on, Mabel – whevver she's copin' on 'er own.'

'She's got her children and her parents – and Arthur's parents to help. She's better off than Sam Mackintosh's young widow,' Mabel said sadly, remembering Albert's friend from railway days, killed on the Somme.

'Hey, did yer see that poster about the Waifs an' Strays? Five fousand poor kids they got now to look after.' Maud sighed. 'They did a jolly good job for me an' Teddy, but it must be 'arder than ever now. Yer know, *you* ought to do summat like that, Mabel, after the war. Seein' as poor ol' 'Arry –' She bit her lip and there was a silence before Mabel replied.

'Yes, Maudie, I've thought about it,' she said softly. 'Get this horrible war over, an' then it'll be children for me – other people's, seein' as I shan't have any o' me own.' She got up and smiled round at the children. 'Who's comin' to have a swing?'

A circle of four- and five-year-olds immediately surrounded her, clamouring to be first; it was so good to see them smiling, shouting and running around in the sunshine, in contrast to the pale-faced, dull-eyed mites she had encountered on that first visit to the

Midway eighteen months ago with Mrs Spearmann. And what a difference that lady had made, with her money and determination! And Norah was ideal as Sister-in-Charge, calm and sweet-natured, never in a hurry. *It was right that she should come here and that I should go to Shadwell*, reflected Mabel; *and perhaps – who knows? – when Albert returns to marry her and take her away from the Midway, I may be the one to take her place* . . .

For Mabel now knew – and in fact had known in her heart for some time, that her future would not be with the Salvation Army, much as she admired its aims and achievements.

The arrival of Mrs Lovell with a tray of tea, bread-and-butter and scones put an end to further exchanges. Two nurserymaids brought out drinks and rusks for the children who gathered around them with hands outstretched. Mabel left the swing and picked up the little girl who had been clinging to her skirt. Two soft arms at once went round her neck.

'She's prop'ly taken to yer, Mabel, poor little fing,' said Maud. 'Ain't it a shame, so many kids an' not enough love to go rahnd!'

The following Wednesday dawned clear and bright, and when Mabel wrote the date on a bed chart, she realised it was June the thirteenth. A shiver ran down her spine, for it was five years exactly since that unforgettable day when she had come home to find her father dead at the hand of his young son: she saw again the glass flower vase, the marguerite daisies strewn around on the carpet, the wet tablecloth that Jack Court had dragged off the table as he fell. And dear old Dr Knowles had put his own career and reputation at risk by conspiring with her to make it look like an accident, and then arranged to get George away to Canada. And how good Harry

313

had been, faithful and loving through it all, even when he knew the truth of what had happened – oh, Harry, Harry, best of men! She had a sudden longing to see him, but today she only had a morning off, from ten to one thirty, which meant that there wasn't really time. But . . .

'You needn't come back until two, Nurse Court,' said Sister Heckford. 'You were on late last night, so get out and enjoy the sun for a few hours.'

Four hours of freedom – and there *was* time. It was just the day to take Harry out for an airing, and if she got a bus from Cable Street to take her over Tower Bridge and down to the Elephant and Castle, she could get another bus along the Wandsworth Road to Battersea. Only she'd have to get a move on, so without stopping to change out of uniform she put on her scarlet cloak and ran for the bus.

Before eleven she was at Falcon Terrace, helping Harry into his jacket, while his mother looked on without enthusiasm. 'I don't want him tired out, Mabel. John took him too far yesterday.'

'I'll take good care o' him, we'll go on the bus to the Park and sit by the boating lake,' Mabel answered with determined brightness. 'An' we won't need yer walkin' stick, Harry, 'cause I'll be holdin' yer arm.'

But Doris Drover picked up the stick and handed it to her. 'Better take it,' she said, pursing her lips. 'Yer never know.'

Mabel did not see the point of lumbering herself with the stick in her left hand while supporting Harry with her right, but not wanting to argue with his mother, she did as she was told.

'Goodbye, Mrs Drover! I'll bring him back by one at the latest!'

What a relief it was to be out in the open air and on

their own, she thought thankfully. They reached a bus stop just in time to get aboard for Battersea Bridge, and within another fifteen minutes were walking under the trees.

'Like old times again, isn't it, dearest Harry?' she said, squeezing his arm, and he responded with his slow, faraway smile. 'L – love ag – again, M –'

'Just like when we were first courtin'. Look, there's a grey squirrel runnin' across the path – there he goes, shinnin' up that tree, see, with his bushy tail up!'

She laughed, pointing with the walking stick. The war might have changed their lives and this dear man had been to hell and back, yet here they still were on a summer morning, the green of nature all around them, the London sparrows chirping. But Harry's steps were slowing.

'I don't think we'd better go as far as the lake, Harry. We'll have a rest here if ye're tired.' She led him to a bench seat, and Harry obediently sat beside her, feeling for her hand. The sunlight filtering down through the leaves made little round circles of light on the path, and Mabel closed her eyes, savouring the moment: it was a brief idyll of peace and calm, happiness of a kind, but alas, the time was passing.

'I just heard it strike twelve back there, Harry, so we'd better start makin' tracks for the bus.'

He shook his head in protest, but she reluctantly rose and gently pulled on his arm. 'I've got to be back for two, dear. We've had a lovely mornin', haven't we? Come on, give me yer arm.'

Tucking his walking stick under her left arm and linking her right in his, they retraced their steps and reached Battersea Bridge Road where a bus was due to arrive.

But suddenly there was tension in the air, the threat

of approaching danger: people were pointing up into the cloudless blue sky, and when the bus appeared the conductor was hanging on to the rail and bending backwards, staring up at something above the city.

Then Mabel saw them, high and silvery, like great gleaming insects coming over in formation.

'Them are ours!' cried a woman.

'No, they ain't, they're Jerries!' shouted a man. 'Better take cover!'

The bus came to a halt and both driver and conductor leapt off, yelling the same message.

Mabel could now hear the noise of the bombers, the menacing woe-woe-woe-woe-woe of German Gothas. People were getting off the bus and standing around uncertainly, while Mabel wondered how on earth she was going to get Harry home and still be back on duty in time.

And then they heard the explosions, the sickening thuds as the bombs hit the ground some distance away: it shook beneath their feet.

'Lie down, keep low!' roared the conductor, throwing himself flat on the pavement, while others ran for the shelter of buildings, the shops, pubs, barbers – any cover from the air raid. Mabel dragged Harry into a newsagent's, where he made a tremendous effort not to show his fear, though he could not stop himself from shaking. It was only for a few minutes, and when the raid was over a police car slowed down and an officer told the gaping crowd that the danger had passed.

'Ye've missed it round here!' he said. 'They've copped it out Stepney and Poplar way – Jerry must've been goin' for the docks.'

Mabel froze. What about Shadwell? Oh, God have mercy, let not the children's hospital be hit, please, God, please.

'Harry, I'll have to go back straight away,' she said through trembling lips. 'Ye'll have to get home on yer own.'

'N – n – n – n – no!'

'Yes, Harry, ye'll have to manage,' she insisted, silently thanking Mrs Drover for the stick.

He clung to her arm and she looked wildly round as passengers re-boarded the bus.

'Can somebody take care o' him an' see him home to Falcon Terrace, Battersea?' she called out and the conductor, seeing her uniform, nodded reassuringly.

'What? Where's 'e goin'? The Falcon? Ah, an' 'e's lorst an arm, poor devil. Been out the Front, 'as 'e? Don't worry, nurse, I'll put 'im down an' see 'im right.'

'Thank yer, that's good o' yer, only I got to get back to me hospital at Shadwell,' gasped Mabel. She kissed Harry quickly. 'He'll take care o' yer, dear – here's yer stick – I must go.'

She had to wrench herself free of his arm and literally ran across the road to jump on a bus going towards Kennington Lane and the Elephant and Castle. Here she got on another bus which took her up to Tower Bridge, over it and into the Highway, past Wapping Docks and there, oh, *there* was the East London Hospital up on Glamis Road, above the Shadwell Basin, solid and untouched! Heaven be praised! She got off at the corner and began to run . . .

And then she saw the white vans with the red crosses on their sides, the police cars, the milling crowds around the building.

'They're all in the Outpatients' Hall, Nurse Court!' somebody called, and she found the side doors blocked by men and women shouting, weeping and calling out the names of their children. Policemen, firemen and Salvation Army officers were all caught up in the confusion, and everywhere she looked she saw grief and terror on faces; in dread of what might lie ahead of her, she elbowed her way forward.

'Excuse me – please let me through – I'm on duty!' she cried, raising her voice and pushing past the doors until she was in the familiar Outpatients' Hall. Only it was no longer familiar, for she was confronted by a scene such as she had never imagined possible, nor ever thought to set eyes upon.

It was a battlefield – or rather, the field after the battle. Except that the bloodied bodies were not men's but children's, spread out on the floor, more or less in rows, lying on mattresses, blankets, coats, some in their parents' arms. Some were still and quiet, others were screaming, some were wailing and moaning, and adults were talking to them, whispering, murmuring, men's voices, women's voices, an extraordinary orchestration of human sounds. Doctors and nurses walked among them, parents sat beside them, there were clerics from all the churches, Salvation Army officers of both sexes, members of the Ladies' Association with cups of tea, Matron Rowe and Mr Wilcox the hospital secretary, all trying to make some kind of order out of chaos. Everybody looked grimy, grubby, dirty-faced like chimney-sweeps, and a pervasive smell hung over the hall, a blend of blood, dirt, soap, carbolic and something indefinable, a smoky smell, the very odour of pain and fear, or so it seemed to Mabel, now seized with a sense of horror, of being caught in a nightmare from which there was no escape.

And there was Sister Colledge, the lighthouse in the middle of it all, holding a chart with names and numbers on. Her face was flushed and her apron blood-streaked, but apart from sounding slightly breathless her voice was steady as she spoke to Mabel. 'Ah, Nurse Court, there you are, good. You're to stay here for the rest of the day. We must all be strong and keep a cool head – think about Miss Nightingale at Scutari, how she rose above all the suffering around her – and we must do the same.'

'B-but – these are children,' stammered Mabel, white-lipped, but Sister Colledge was already telling her what had to be done.

'Now, these children here on this side have just arrived and need cleaning up a bit – yes, over there, please, beside the dressing-station –' she gestured to an ambulance man carrying a child in his arms, followed by a white-faced woman. 'Right, Nurse Court, Mr Cowell and Dr Dunn are seeing the worst injured, Dr Knowles and Dr Lamarr are doing assessments on the rest, and I've put you down to assist Dr Lamarr, with Nurse Watkins to help you. Put saline dressings on wounds until the doctors can attend to them. Keep the patients warm, keep air passages clear, report haemorrhage – and see that each child has a label with name and address and any medication given. They're mostly aged between five and seven, it was a direct hit on a school in Poplar. There are dressings, towels and saline solution for cleaning – and the dispensary staff are making up morphia injections in one-eighth and one-twelfth of a grain, ready to give straight away, only you must get a signed slip from Dr Lamarr if he orders one. Oh, and I've put Mr Thompson the student with you as well, so you're a team of four.'

Where to begin? Mabel faced the row of the latest admissions and saw Lamarr talking to the parents of the first one, a boy with a gash across his scalp and bruising of his chest. On his legs he wore calipers and his father was saying that these had saved his legs from being crushed.

'Dahn the cellar they was, sixty of 'em, poor little blighters, the bomb must've gorn frough three floors, doctor – they was bringin' 'em aht when we got there, an' the ambulance bloke said it was the calipers what saved 'is legs.'

'Right, let's get that scalp wound cleaned up – the skull's not fractured and we'll put some stitches in later.' Lamarr nodded. Nurse Watkins, a second-year, picked up an enamel bowl and they moved on.

An unnatural calmness descended upon Mabel. Her hands were steady and her voice clear as she spoke to the children and their relatives. The muscles of her face settled into an automatic smile as she approached the next case. It was another boy, his ribs crushed and his chest punctured. He was blue-faced and breathing with difficulty. Mr Thompson's face paled.

'Oh, dear.' Lamarr got down to look at the chest wound. 'Cover it over with a big square of cotton-wool gauze, Nurse Court – make a note for Dr Dunn to see him as soon as he's available.'

Mabel could see that the child was dying and touched the mother's hand. 'D'ye want to see a chaplain, dear?' The woman stared back with despairing eyes, her last hope gone. And they had to pass on to the next one, a girl with a dislocated shoulder and probable fractured collarbone. There was a lot of swelling over the area and she was in a great deal of pain.

'That will need a sling for the time being until we can reduce it under an anaesthetic. Can you get her arm out of the sleeve, nurse?'

'What about morphia, Dr Lamarr, say a twelfth of a grain?' asked Mabel.

'Well, yes –'

'Then will yer sign her card for it?' He did so and Thompson was sent off to the dispensary where he got the ready-mixed injection, and Mabel took it from him to administer to the girl; now was no time for students' fumblings.

'There we are, dear, ye'll feel better soon.' Mabel felt cut off from any kind of emotion and seemed to be following the dictates of reason alone, as if her heart had no part in it. She willed herself to consider each child in co-operation with Lamarr who glanced at her to see if she agreed with his recommendations before passing on to the next case. They looked upon terrible bruising, lacerations, splinters of wood embedded in flesh – and silent, beseeching eyes of children too badly injured to cry. She heard herself speaking in the same controlled tones and knew that if she allowed herself to think deeply about any one of these cases – these suffering children – she would not be able to leave them and pass on to the next one.

They stopped by a girl whose face had been cut by glass, all down one cheek. It extended up to her left lower eyelid which was split in two, revealing the lower part of the eyeball, except that because of the blood filling the cavity, the extent of the injury could not be estimated.

'Put a saline dressing over her face on that side and ask Mr Cowell to see her urgently,' muttered Lamarr and they passed on to a boy lying passively on his back.

''E can't move 'is legs, doctor,' said the old lady who was with the boy, presumably his grandmother.

Lamarr got down beside the boy. 'Hello, old chap. Does it hurt anywhere? Can you lift your head? Your arms? Can you feel this? And this?'

There was neither movement nor sensation below an identifiable point halfway down the back and spinal injury was all too obvious.

Lamarr stood up. 'Keep him warm, still and lying flat – and we'll get one of the specialists to see him as soon as one's available.'

The next patient was a boy with mouth injuries, with bleeding lips and broken teeth. Lamarr felt his jaw, and the boy screamed, literally bubbling through blood and mucus. Mabel rushed for a rubber suction catheter and a bowl from the dressing-station, and placing the end of the tube in the boy's mouth, she sucked at it until she felt the warm liquid matter in her own mouth, and spat it out into the bowl. 'Now fetch me some saline gauze to clean his mouth, Nurse Watkins,' she said. 'If his jaw's broken, yer still need to keep the air goin' in an' out.'

'Is he goin' to be all right?' asked the boy's mother with imploring eyes.

'Yes, dear, only he needs his mouth kept clear,' replied Mabel. 'Yer saw what I did just now – well, I'm goin' to ask *you* to do it if his mouth fills up again, just like I did, see?'

Lamarr and Thompson exchanged a glance and they passed on to the next child, a girl. She was pale and clammy, and her eyes stared up at them mutely, while the woman at her side introduced herself as a teacher. It was another shoulder injury and, on uncovering the towel that had been put over the child, the arm was seen to be almost entirely severed and the humerus bone was broken and visible. Lamarr gasped.

'The – er – books would say put a tourniquet round the upper part of the arm, Thompson,' he muttered, 'but I don't think – er –'

No answer came. Thompson had swayed, put his hand to his mouth and mumbled his excuses before lurching away to sit down, his face as white as a sheet. Mabel placed a clean towel over the child's shoulder.

'This little girl'd better have some morphia, too – can yer write it up for her, doctor?'

'Yes, yes – here –' Lamarr scribbled on the card. 'And we'd better ask for the surgeons to see her straight away.'

'Soon as they can,' murmured Mabel, seeing that the child was at the point of death and only wanting her to be free of pain.

Going from one injured child to the next, having lost all sense of time, was like walking through a scene out of hell. Mr Thompson rejoined them after a few minutes, shamefaced and apologetic, with a tell-tale whiff of whisky on his breath.

'I'd have had to give up my training if I couldn't cope with this, Nurse Court,' he muttered.

They reached the end of the row and met with the two other teams who had been assessing the forty-five children admitted. Mabel heard that twelve had been killed outright, their little bodies dismembered by the blast, and of those brought into the East London, thirty were considered seriously injured in various degrees. The rest had escaped with relatively minor cuts and bruises, though the mental scars would stay with them for life.

For the first time that day Mabel found herself face to face with Stephen Knowles, who like herself looked dishevelled, dirty and blood-smeared at the end of assessing injuries.

'So, Mabel, you've been called upon to nurse the wounded after all.' The words were said very quietly, for her ears only. Not daring to show the slightest sign of emotion, she merely nodded and turned her head away.

Decisions had to be made about the deployment of staff, and Matron Rowe held a hasty consultation with Mr Wilcox and senior consultants. A few patients were transferred to other hospitals and a small number were discharged home. The most serious cases stayed at the East London, though by the end of the day three had died. Extra medical and theatre staff were sent over from the London Hospital and at half past two operations began.

The worst cases, including eye injuries, were taken up to the theatre, but minor surgery such as suturing of lacerations was done in two examination rooms, using the couches as operating tables. Stephen Knowles spent the next few hours giving anaesthetics, sitting at the patient's head while the surgeons stood. One theatre sister came down to help and Staff Nurse Court acted as a second theatre nurse, cleaning wounds, handing sponges and threading catgut, snipping and tidying up after the surgeon's stitching, while Thompson assisted him, his confidence improved by having something definite to do. Mabel performed her tasks with armour-plated calm, unaware of fatigue, feeling neither hunger nor thirst, though Sister Colledge sent her off at some point that evening to have a drink and go to the lavatory. She came straight back and resumed her post, aware of Knowles's eye on her over the top of his face mask, his almost imperceptible nods of encouragement. The brief contact of eyes conveyed an alliance between them, a mutual acknowledgement of what they were being called upon to do.

'A lot of these wounds are going to get infected,' remarked one of the surgeons as he sponged and stitched. 'Can we open up the Pavilion and put a few in there? Get some sunlight to them?'

'I believe Wilcox is getting it organised,' answered Knowles. 'We've admitted seven to Enfield Ward and a couple to Heckford, but they've got nasal diphtheria on Mary, so that's off limits. Nine have been sent to the Queen's in Hackney Road.'

'And three to the mortuary, and another couple likely to follow, I believe.'

Knowles shrugged. 'We'll be left with about twenty-one or -two of the original admissions. All right, Nurse Court? You've been standing for a hell of a long time.'

By eight o'clock the operations were completed, and by nine the Outpatients' Hall was empty.

'Right, Nurse Court, you're off duty,' said Sister Colledge. 'Time to go over to the dining-room – there's a special late meal prepared for all of us.'

Mabel's head was swimming and her stomach churned. The very thought of food was nauseating. And yet she did not want to go to her room and her bed in the nurses' home. She wanted to get away, to escape – to 'take the wings of the morning', like the Psalmist, 'and fly to the uttermost parts of the sea' . . .

It was still light, being nearly midsummer, and she was tempted to walk out of the hospital and go down to the river. It would be frowned upon as foolish, for there were some very dubious characters around the Highway at this time of day, and besides, her knees were curiously weak. The sensible thing would be to go to bed: tomorrow would be another long and no doubt harrowing day on Heckford Ward.

Heckford! How many of the victims had been sent there? Two? She knew that the girl with the nearly severed arm had died, and so had the boy with the crushed chest. What about the girl with all the glass lacerations of her face? Would she lose the sight of her injured eye? Mabel knew that she had to see that girl again before she slept, and so made her way along the bottom corridor and up the stairs.

'Mabel!' Violet Stoke-Marriner was in charge of

Heckford that right and spoke in a whisper. 'Oh, Mabel, what a day. You've been in Outpatients', haven't you?'

Mabel managed to croak, 'The girl with the cut face – the cut eye – is she here?'

Violet put a finger to her lips. 'Yes, in the side ward. Only we have to be very, very quiet.'

She led the way to the small room where very ill and dying children were put for quietness. There were two small beds, both occupied. One held the girl Mabel sought and by the dim electric light on the wall, she saw that the child's head was swathed in bandages, though the right eye was left exposed so that she would be able to see a little, in spite of its being bruised and swollen. Her mouth and nostrils were free, though crusted with blood. She lay in a morphia-induced slumber, briefly and mercifully oblivious of the disaster that had over-taken her.

'Mr Cowell says that the eye should be all right,' whispered Nurse Marriner. 'He sewed the eyelid together with thin silk and says the blood will disperse in time from the socket. The eyeball may be bruised, but he's hopeful. Of course, her face will be scarred for life, but –'

They stood looking down at the sleeping child, not daring to disturb her short respite.

'And the other?' whispered Mabel.

'Another girl – fractured base of skull,' muttered Violet. 'We can't guess what her chances are, we'll just have to wait and see. Come away now, Mabel. It's time you went to bed.'

She led the way out of the room. 'I've got to go to check the others now, and see how the probationer's getting on with the hourly drinks. Will you be all right?'

Mabel nodded, and Violet glided away into the main

ward where the last of the daylight still persisted. At the head of the stairs Mabel hesitated, feeling that she was going to vomit. Where could she go?

The sluice-room was empty and she lurched into it, holding on to the door frame and then the edge of the wide enamel sink with its adjacent sluice, like a giant WC where excrement was flushed away and soiled sheets were sluiced before being sent to the laundry. A row of enamel potties hung on hooks, and flat enamel bedpans and urinals were lined up on a shelf, each with its covering cloth.

Mabel leaned helplessly over the sluice. In the half-light the waterhole appeared dark as if filled with blood. Her stomach began to heave and her whole frame shook as she retched again and again into the sluice, though only a trickle of hot, bitter bile came up. She heard herself sobbing spasmodically between retches as the events of the day were replayed before her inward eye. She took that walk through hell again and this time without the armour-plating: she saw and heard and touched and smelled the violation of the children's tender flesh. Her heart and mind were exposed to the full horror of what had happened at the school in Poplar on this day, and her mind reeled back five years to that other June the thirteenth in 1912 and the scene of a murder just committed. That picture had haunted her ever since, and yet how much worse had been the wickedness committed today! Where was good to be found? Where was God?

A long, low, despairing wail broke from her.

And then, like the answer to a prayer wrung from the heart, she found she was not alone. Two strong arms slid round her waist; two large hands met across the front of her apron as her body was firmly held, pressed back against a man's solid frame. Dr Knowles's chin came to rest on her left shoulder and she heard his voice softly speaking in her ear.

'For a girl who could never nurse the wounded, you've done wonders today.'

Limp as a rag doll, she let her head roll back and gave herself up to the sensation of being supported by his encircling arms. After such a long time of caring for others, for Harry, for so many children, she now felt her own need to be upheld – to be cherished and looked after. Just for a few moments she experienced that blessed relief before the tears began to flow.

'Ah, now, Mabel, there, there, we've all seen the worst that war can do today. We're all crying inside. I'm here, dear, I'm here for you.'

His voice was comfortingly familiar, for she had known it all her life.

'Oh, Dr Knowles, dear Dr Knowles, yer were *always* there for me – for us – for poor George on that terrible day when Dad was –'

'Ssh-ssh, my dear, I know, I know,' he said quickly, realising that she was addressing his father rather than himself.

She turned round within his arms and wept upon his chest, oblivious of their surroundings until a probationer came in for a potty and a bedpan. The girl gave a gasp of surprise, but Knowles gave her a conspiratorial look and put a finger to his lips. When she had left the sluice, he gently released Mabel.

'Come along, now, it's time you got some rest. When did you last eat? Did you get any of that late supper in the dining-room?'

'No, no, I couldn't – I was feeling so – so sick.'

'Yes, of course, but you need to get something in your stomach before you sleep. Come on, there'll still be something on offer – here, give me your arm.'

And together they carefully descended the stairs and made their way to the still open dining-room where a few tired-eyed nurses sat drinking tea and eating slices of bread with cheese and pickle. He poured two cups of rather stewed tea and stirred two teaspoons of sugar into each.

'There you are, drink that, and have something to eat if you can. We owe it to the kids to keep ourselves stoked up. God alone knows what tomorrow will bring.'

She looked up at him over the cup of tea. 'You're so like your father, Stephen. He was the best friend our family ever had.'

'And he thinks the world of you, Mabel. No, don't say any more, just eat up.'

And much as he would have liked to stay with her, he waited only until she had swallowed the tea and eaten a slice of bread and margarine.

'Promise you'll go straight to bed now, Nurse Court?'

'Yes, Dr Knowles.'

'Goodnight, then. And well done.'

329

Chapter Eighteen

The massacre of the innocents, as the Poplar incident came to be called, cast a long shadow. The communal funeral was a public occasion attended by Members of Parliament and local dignitaries, and marked by unusually violent displays of grief; grown men wept openly as the flower-strewn coffins were lowered into the ground.

Likewise a sombre atmosphere hung over the East London Hospital: the medical students' concert was never performed, and if Mabel had not been so taken up with her duties, she might have noticed a significant change in attitude towards her from some quarters. Gone were the giggles over her oft-repeated maxims and the mimicking of her accent. Dr Lamarr had lost his patronising air and Mr Thompson was almost embarrassingly deferential; lady probationers were now eager to listen to and learn from Nurse Court.

Stephen Knowles observed the change with quiet satisfaction and was glad he had not made an issue over 'Taught by Court'; but Violet Stoke-Marriner, who missed very little, began to have suspicions about another matter, of which Nurse Court seemed to be entirely unaware.

At Falcon Terrace Mabel had to face Doris Drover's wrathful indignation.

'Nearly out o' me mind with worry, I was, when he didn't get back till gone two. Some man had taken him to the Falcon, if you please, and the poor boy didn't know what was goin' on, you leavin' him like that to make his own way back.'

'I hadn't any choice, Mrs Drover. I knew – I just *knew* that I had to get back to Shadwell as soon's I could. And if ye'd seen what I saw in that Outpatients' Hall when I got there –'

'Yes, Mabel, we heard from some of our brother officers who were there,' John Drover interposed in a gentler tone. 'It was unfortunate that Harry was – er –'

Confused by Mabel's desertion of him, and having been brought to the Falcon by a man under the instructions of the bus driver, Harry had left the pub and had been found wandering around Clapham Junction by a neighbour who had brought him home. Mabel was very sorry, but could not apologise for her hasty return to Shadwell.

'O' course I can understand Mrs Drover resentin' me,' she told Maud Ling as they sat together on a park bench in the little Arbour Square Garden between Commercial Road and Charles Street. 'Her heart's been broken and she's got to blame somebody. But oh, Maudie, yer should see the way his dear brown eyes light up when I come through the door! His dad's got him a wheelchair from the Red Cross and I take him out in it whenever I can, but she doesn't really like me doin' anythin' for him.'

'Hah! I know all abaht trouble wiv parents,' replied Maud grimly. 'D'ye know, Mabel, I got a good mind to go an' see the Redferns at Elmgrove, an' tackle 'em 'ead on, know what I mean? Say we ain't seen Alex since 'e came to *Chu Chin Chow*, and Gawd knows when we'll see 'im again, so can't we just *pretend* to be friends, for 'is sake? D'yer fink I ought to?'

'Oh, I don't know, Maud.' Mabel was doubtful. 'S'pose they gave yer the cold shoulder an' yer lost yer temper with 'em? Yer could end up worse then before.'

'Oh, I wouldn't let Alex dahn, Mabel, no matter what they said. It'd mean such a lot if we could meet and be civil to each ovver.' Maud spoke wistfully and Mabel decided that she should be encouraged.

'Go on, then, Maudie, write a little note first, to give 'em a chance to put yer off, and if there's no answer, just march up to the front door and say ye've come to make yer peace with 'em for Alex's sake – yes, go for it, Maudie, and the very best o' luck!'

'Fanks, gal, that's what I'll do. It's good to 'ave a friend to talk to. Teddy's a good 'un, but 'e's only a boy, an' I can't expect 'im to know 'ow it feels.'

'How's Teddy gettin' on at the – Daily Chronicle, isn't it?'

'Ooh, 'e's proper puffed up wiv 'imself these days – there's this photographer bloke 'oo lets Ted 'elp 'im when 'e goes out wiv 'is camera, takin' pictures o' whatever's going on. 'Ouses wiv their roofs blown orf an' women policemen in uniform, faces to strike fear into the 'earts o' men, that sort o' thing. Ted reckons 'e'll get 'imself a camera one o' these days, an' do the same.'

'Hasn't Teddy done well, an' yerself, too, Maudie!' said Mabel admiringly. 'Ye're a good advertisement for the Waifs an' Strays. The more I think about it, the more I reckon that's what I'll do after the war – get a job in one o' their small homes for children.'

'Right up your street, gal. Talkin' o' which, I ought to shift me arse rahnd to the Midway more often, to play wiv them little kids an' give a few bottle feeds.'

'A very good idea,' answered Mabel at once, thinking of Maud alone in her cramped lodgings, tempted to turn to the bottle to ease her loneliness. 'Norah'd love to see yer.'

'But first I'm goin' to get meself up to St John's Wood an' turn the charm on Ma an' Pa,' said Maud, raising her chin in resolution. 'Just you wait, gal, I'll 'ave 'em eatin' aht o' me 'and!'

'There's another case of diphtheria confirmed on Mary Ward today,' said Sister Heckford and Nurse Court grimaced. Diphtheria was a killer, for there was no cure, though research was being done to develop an 'antitoxin' that might be given in the early stages of the disease to combat the deadly poisons produced by the diphtheria bacillus. An outbreak in a hospital had to be contained in strict isolation, and the staff of Mary Ward occupied separate quarters where they ate and slept, cut off like lepers from their colleagues and from the outside world, where the news seemed to get worse with every week that passed. July the seventh brought another big air raid over London, with fifty deaths; people were taking to the Underground stations as a refuge, and the blackout regulations were tightened.

And still the wounded continued to pour into the country. A new major offensive began on July the thirty-first and the third nightmare battle of Ypres commenced, to drag on for four months in which four miles were gained by the Allies in the advance to Passchendaele Ridge, at a cost of over three hundred thousand men. From some quarters there now arose a serious call for an end to the carnage, but still it dragged on.

There was a knock at Mabel's door just as she was taking off her uniform. It was late and she was tired, but Nurse

Stoke-Marriner wanted to see her and the gravity of her expression alerted Mabel.

'Come in an' sit down, Violet. What's up? Somethin' I've done?' she asked quickly.

'It's to do with you, Mabel, certainly. I'm sorry it's late, but this is the only place where we won't be interrupted.'

'Go on,' said Mabel, sitting on the edge of the bed.

'I've been trying to shut my eyes and ears for some time now, Mabel, but I can't ignore it any longer,' said Violet rather breathlessly. 'I must speak my mind to you as a friend. Mabel, there's talk about you in this hospital. Gossip.'

'*Gossip*? About *me*? Why, what're they sayin'?' Mabel was genuinely mystified.

'About you and Dr Knowles.'

Mabel flushed crimson. '*Dr Knowles?* What, Stephen Knowles, yer mean? But yer know that's ridiculous – he's married and his wife's expectin' a child in September!'

'Exactly. Which is why I reprimanded two probationers who were whispering about you. You were seen in a very compromising situation in Heckford Ward sluice on the night of the Poplar bomb, just after I'd taken you to see those two girls in the side ward. I thought you'd left after that, but it seems that Nurse Railton, the first-year, went into the sluice and saw you and Dr Knowles. And you were embracing.'

Mabel gave a gasp. 'We were *not* embracing! I'll tell yer what I was doin' – I was being sick in the sluice, throwin' up bile an' almost collapsin'. He heard me retchin' and came in to support me because me legs were givin' way. To tell yer the truth, I can hardly remember what happened, I felt so bad. What absolute *nonsense*, to say we were –'

'I'm sorry, Mabel, but Nurse Railton saw him with his arms round you, and she says he put his finger to his lips to signal that she was to forget what she'd seen.'

'So why did she go straight off an' *tell* everybody? I'll speak to her meself when I see her next, tell her she's caused a lot o' mischief by spreading false tales. And on such a day, too! If Stephen's heard any o' this stuff, I'll never be able to look him in the face again!'

'All right, Mabel, let's forget about Nurse Railton. You've been seen walking and talking on other occasions with Dr Knowles, inside and outside the hospital, and it's being talked about.'

'We went to the Prospect o' Whitby one evenin' in May or June, I can't remember – and what he told me there was no concern o' yours or anybody else's, Violet.' Mabel was by now thoroughly incensed. 'I've told yer before, I know his father well, God knows I've got reason to bless that dear man – an' Stephen knows all about my poor Harry, more 'n anybody else in this place does. He drove me all the way down to see him at the Royal Victoria Hospital at Netley just before Christmas, when yer could still get petrol.'

'Look, Mabel, I'm sorry. I apologise. I believe everything you say, I'm not questioning you, just giving you a bit of advice as a friend, to avoid these occasions of being seen alone with Dr Knowles. Gossip will do neither of you any good and as he's a married man –'

'To hell with gossip and nasty minds that spread it!' retorted Mabel. 'I'm surprised yer could think such a thing o' me, Violet. I'd've thought yer knew me better!'

'I'm sorry, Mabel.'

'So yer should be.'

'I hope we're still friends.'

'Yes, but – oh, all right, I s'pose yer meant well. But

next time somebody comes tittle-tattlin' to yer, I hope ye'll give 'em an earful. Now, if yer don't mind, I'm tired an' want to get to sleep.'

'All right, Mabel. Again, I'm very sorry. Goodnight, then.'

'Goodnight.'

Violet Stoke-Marriner went away, blaming herself for her blundering attempt at sounding a warning. She was totally convinced of Mabel's innocence and had been all along, but she still suspected her of naivety. Everybody saw the way that Knowles looked at the girl . . .

Violet sighed, hoping that she had at least sown a seed and that Mabel Court would have the sense to be more discreet in future.

'Darling, darling Maudie, I've only got tonight – I had to come over and hold you in my arms before we fly out over the lines again. Hold me – hold me now and for ever!'

He had been waiting for her outside the stage door. She thought at first that he was a vision conjured up by the intensity of her longing; but she soon discovered that here was no dream but her own Alex, her lover returned. He looked haggard and war-weary, yet he was impatient, almost running her back to South Lambeth Road through the empty streets under a full moon. Reaching the lodging house, they tumbled headlong up the stairs. His eyes held a feverish glint as she put the key in her door and he could hardly wait for her to lock it behind them.

'Hurry up, Maud, and get your drawers off, I have to get inside you straight away – look, here he is, ready to burst – haven't time to get my trousers down – quick! Ah – ah, God! Oh, Maud, Maud – come into the garden, Maud!'

'No, it's *you* comin' into the garden, Alex – that's it, there y'are, in yer go, darlin' love – deep, deep, deeper – aah!'

Passion leapt, to find instant mutual satisfaction; they needed to make love again within half an hour.

'And this time with our clothes *off*, Maudie – you still had your hat on when I did it first.'

'An' *you* tore straight frough me petticoat. What in God's name 'ad yer got in yer trouser pocket – a gun?'

'No, I keep my gun down here in front, and it's reloaded – oh, my own dear, sweet Maudie, I could lie with it inside you all night.'

'It'd soon go limp.'

'Then I'd put a finger in. Two fingers.' He rolled over to face her as they lay on the bed. 'Christ, Maud, you wouldn't ever go off with one of those fucking stage door johnnies, would you? One time when I'm not there to keep an eye on you?'

'Not unless yer said yer didn't love me any more.'

'Why the hell would I ever say a thing like that?'

'Yer might, after the war, Alex.'

'Don't talk such bullshit. God, if you only knew how much I've longed for this – come on, open up – wider, wider –' He spread her legs apart, then hoisted them up and held them one on each side of his head. 'Come on, put them up around my neck, that's my girl – give me a clear landing!'

'What d'yer think I am, a bleedin' contortionist?'

'No, no, you're just my own precious little darling Maudie – mine, and nobody else's – mmm! Come on, here we go again – and again –' He groaned as he thrust into her.

'An' again, an' again,' she echoed. 'Ouch! This is better 'n ever, Alex, better 'n ever – aah!'

So she said, exhausted as she was, uncomfortable and

sore, yet never would she have dreamed of diminishing his pleasure by a single word of protest. When at last he fell asleep, his head cradled on her right arm, his snores close to her ear, she lay awake and stared up at the patches on the ceiling shown up by the pale moonlight that filtered through the thin curtains. Her arm beneath his head became completely numb, but she would not move it.

Lying there, she could almost have wished for a Gotha or a Giant to come over and end their lives now, at this moment while they lay entwined. Not to be parted again. Not to have to face the uncertainly of tomorrow.

Over at the Midway Babies' Home, Sister Norah stood at her window, looking up at the moon and the clear sky; then she closed the curtains and knelt down beside her narrow bed.

There were so many things to pray about: Albert – Harry – Alex – and Mabel working so hard at Shadwell, and Maud going on stage every night, looking pale and puffy-eyed . . .

And Mabel's sister Daisy who had written her a woeful little letter. Now thirteen, she was finding life very dull in Belhampton. 'We have to creep about and not make a noise at Pear Tree Cottage because Uncle Thomas is ill in bed and the docter says he must not be disturbed,' she wrote.

> Aunt Nell will not let me go up to talk to him in case I tire him, so I go to Pinehurst to help Aunt Kate with the soldiers who are much worse than Uncle Thomas who has got both his arms and legs also his eyes. Georgina Savage has started to work at Pinehurst but she isnt much use and I think

its only to get away from Houghton Hall which is very gloomy because her mother Lady Savage says there is no God because Sir Guy Savage was killed and he was her son you know.

How are you dear Norah. I wish you wuold write to me as I do not get much from Mabel, only little notes about the poor children she looks after at Shadwell. I wish I cuold come and see you but Aunt Nell says I cant because of the air rades.

I have a little baby nephew who is called Geoffrey. His mother is my sister Alice who does not come to visit much. She has to care for her husband Gerald who has half his face covered with bandages and wont go to church or see his freinds.

Have you heard from my brother Albert. Oh Norah, when will this war be over and let us all be happy again like we were before. Even my best freind Lucy Drummond is sad because her brother Cedric is somewhere at sea and they have no news of him but read the casualty lists every day and hope his name will not be on them.

Please write to me Norah. I do not think that Mabel cares about her family any more.

Norah finished her prayers with a novena to the Sacred Heart, crossed herself and got into bed. Poor Daisy was too young to understand the pressures they were all under, but tomorrow Norah would write to her and explain why Mabel needed her love as much as ever.

'Mabel! Mabel, wait a minute! Nurse Court!'

She heard Stephen's voice calling after her as she left the hospital by the front entrance and quickly descended the three wide stone steps to Glamis Road. She could pretend not to hear and hurry on down to the Highway and the bus to Tower Bridge. He couldn't run after her, that much was certain.

'Mabel!'

She turned round. He was leaning on his stick and waved to her, then pressed forward with as much speed as he could muster. She stood still on the pavement before the imposing triple façade of the hospital, the late summer sun glinting on the tall, stained-glass windows.

He reached her side, his eyes lighting up. 'Where have you *been* these last weeks, Mabel? Every time I looked in on Heckford you were doing something vitally important, or you'd gone to dinner or supper, but could never be found in the dining-room. You're as elusive as the Scarlet Pimpernel – except that you're in blue, which suits you better.'

He was smiling down at her, the harsh lines of recent years softened by a bright, almost boyish look. He put out his arm to touch her shoulder, as if to stop her disappearing again.

'Hello, Dr Knowles.' She lowered her eyes, aware that she was blushing. 'I'm just on my way to Battersea to spend an evening with Harry.'

'Oh, say you've got time to raise a glass in the Prospect of Whitby first! We haven't talked since – that last time.' His blue eyes pleaded, but Mabel shook her head.

'I'm sorry, my bus goes in five minutes. They're expecting me at Falcon Terrace and I don't want to be late.' She began to move away. 'Harry needs me, yer know that.'

'But Mabel, I need – yes, of course, I understand, I'm sorry. But when will you next have an evening off? There's something we touched on that I'd really like to talk about further.' He smiled and assumed a mock-formal air. 'May I make an appointment with you, Nurse Court?'

She hesitated. 'I might be able to get away on Friday at five, but it depends on whether Sister wants me to do a split shift.'

'Good! Meet you here Friday, five sharp.'

'Better make it six, down by Wapping Bridge. I really must go now.' She began to walk away.

'Thanks, my dear,' he called after her. 'Friday at six, I'll be there. Remember me to Harry!' The smile faded from his eyes as he watched her retreating figure.

Mabel was annoyed with herself for being so easily persuaded and, taking her seat on the bus, she concentrated her thoughts on the evening ahead. She might take Harry out for an hour in the wheelchair, and then no doubt they would spend an hour, perhaps longer, in his parlour bedroom after his parents had gone out. And she would give him that special, intimate comfort he so craved.

'And you don't mind, Mabel?'

Of course she didn't mind, and of course she still loved Harry. Real love didn't change with changing times and it was the least she could do for him these days, for the sake of those other, better days they had known and shared.

Maud Ling turned up on the front doorstep of Elmgrove on a Thursday afternoon at three, preceded by a carefully written note – Teddy had helped her with the spelling. She was dressed in a neat, dark jacket and skirt with a plain white blouse, and a pretty little blue hat trimmed with daisies; her gloves, shoes and handbag were navy-blue. She rang the bell and waited.

The uniformed maid raised her eyebrows and asked Miss Ling to 'Come this way, please'. Maud followed her through to a smallish room at the back of the house, where Mrs Redfern interviewed staff and conferred with her cook. Left to herself, Maud waited for what seemed like half an hour, but was probably not more than ten minutes. When Mrs Redfern appeared in a black and white house-gown, she looked pale and unsmiling.

'Good aft'noon, Mrs Redfern. Thank yer for seein' me.' Maud managed a polite half-smile.

'I haven't much time to spare,' said the lady without preamble. 'Say what you've come to say and get the matter over.' She glanced at the clock on the mantelshelf.

Maud swallowed. 'Well, o' course it's Alex I've come abaht, as I said in that note I sent yer.'

Mrs Redfern's eyes hardened. 'As you said on that piece of paper pushed through our door, I gather that you want to make some kind of claim on our son, Wing Commander Redfern.'

'I ain't makin' no kind o' claim on 'im, Mrs Redfern. I've just come to say that I know 'ow worried yer must be all the time, wonderin' if ye'll ever see 'im again, 'cause I feel exactly the same. I love 'im too, an' I go frough just as much 'ell as *you* do, wonderin' where 'e is, an' what 'e's doin'.'

Mrs Redfern stiffened, drawing herself up and giving Maud a contemptuous look. 'Mr Redfern and I are quite aware of the danger and don't need reminding by the likes of you.'

'But that's just it, we bofe worry abaht 'im, so we – we shouldn't really be –' In spite of her determination to stay calm, Maud's voice shook and her eyes filled with tears.

Mrs Redfern's lip curled. 'Let's cut a long story short, shall we? Are you in some sort of trouble and do you intend to name Wing Commander Redfern? Because if you attempt to threaten or blackmail me or my husband,

342

I shall send for the police and have you thrown out of our house. Is that quite clear?'

For a moment Maud Ling's mouth hung open in disbelief, but she quickly regained her self-possession and anger gave her a certain dignity. 'No, I ain't in any sort o' trouble, as yer call it, and if I was, ye'd be the last person on earf I'd come to for 'elp. I just thought that we might at least *pretend* to – to get on wiv each ovver, for Alex's sake, seein' as we bofe love 'im. For *'is* sake, not mine. I'd do anyfing for 'im.'

There was a momentary flicker of response on the face of the older woman. Then she seemed to make up her mind to speak plainly.

'Very well. You say that you care for my son and would do anything for him.' Her eyes narrowed as she looked straight at Maud. 'There is one thing that you could do to prove to my satisfaction that you really do care about his life and his future.'

She paused, and Maud waited, steadfastly returning her look.

'Stop dragging him down into the gutter. Give him up. Keep away from him. Get out of his life and I'll believe you to be sincere.'

For a moment Maud's face was blank as the import of the woman's words struck her like a blow. Then her colour returned and she gave her answer.

'Fanks for nuffin',' she said in a low voice. 'I came 'ere for Alex's sake, not mine, I don't give a damn whevver yer like me or not. But I'll tell yer what, Alex loves me, an' comes to me first when 'e gets leave, 'cause I understand 'im better 'n you. An' until 'e tells me to me face that 'e don't want me any more, I'm 'is for the takin'. Is *that* quite clear? Nah, don't show me aht, missus, I'll use the trademen's entrance like I 'ad to when I was yer 'ousemaid.'

Mr Redfern appeared only just in time to see a girl with blazing eyes sweeping out of the back door with her head held high. His wife was flushed and disconcerted.

'Damned impertinence!' she hissed. 'Common little hussy! How *dare* she talk to me about my own son as if she knew more about him than I do, his own mother!'

'Sit down for a while and compose yourself, my dear,' said her husband rather helplessly. He had a somewhat better understanding of his son's needs, but could not explain this to Mrs Redfern, who burst out in a sudden torrent of tears.

'Oh, why does Alex go on associating with her? What can he possibly *see* in her?'

'Mabel! I thought you weren't coming. What kept you?'

'Busy afternoon,' she said, indicating her uniform, the scarlet cloak around her shoulders. It was a quarter past six, and his relief at seeing her was obvious. He linked an arm with hers and, with his walking stick in his other hand, began to walk with her along the waterfront.

'There are things I want to talk about with you, Mabel, questions I'd like to ask – if you don't mind, of course,' he said, glancing at her face to see how she reacted. 'On that last occasion you mentioned my father and how he helped you when you had that – the double tragedy. May I ask you a little more about that, my dear?' His hold on her arm tightened briefly and she hardly knew how to reply. How much did he already know from his father?

'Dr Knowles was a good friend to our family,' she said slowly, looking away from him, across the river. 'He was especially good to me mother, an' understood the difficulties of her life. Yer know we lost me little brother Walter, only two he was – an' Daisy was born the followin' spring, she was the last one. Me mother was never really well again after that – she was anaemic an' didn't go out much.' She did not add that Annie Court had taken regular consolation from a secret jam jar hidden behind her bedroom curtain, containing gin.

'Ah, and that's when you took over the running of the house and the care of your brothers and sisters, Mabel,' he said, nodding. 'My father told me how he used to worry about you and the number of schooldays you lost, because he always thought you were the brains of the family and a born nurse. How right he was! What did you do when you left school? Didn't you go to work at that Women's Rescue place off Lavender Hill?'

'Not straight away. I worked first at a nursery attached to Hallam Road school, and then I went as a ward maid at the Anti-Vivisection Hospital on the corner o' Prince o' Wales Road – an' lost me place there when Albert got into trouble over the Tower Hill riots. *You* were the doctor who saw him the night he was arrested, remember?'

'Could I ever forget! And good old Captain Drover of the Salvation Army came with you to take him home. It was the first time I met you – to speak to, that is.'

'It was then I got the job at the Rescue, an' Albert joined the navy – he was only sixteen.'

'Albert gave you quite a few headaches, didn't he?'

'Not as many as Dad gave us. He was a bookmaker, not really a bad man, but a weak one. He was a fair drinker and went with women, 'specially after Daisy was born.'

She stopped in her tracks and turned to face him. 'What did yer father tell yer, Stephen?'

'Well –' He hesitated. 'He was very upset over your mother's death, Mabel. He'd visited her that very day and must have wondered if he'd said anything to –

forgive me, Mabel, but why did she drown herself? Was it because she had cancer? So many women are terrified of it.'

'No, it was syphilis. Yer father tried to keep it from her, but she wasn't a fool, an' she put two an' two together. An' she couldn't live with it.'

He took a deep breath and exhaled slowly. 'Ah, yes. Yes, I see. The poor woman.'

'Yer father arranged for us all to have blood tests, an' I lost me job at the Rescue, though the test came up clear. Dad had disappeared – he was in the Lock Hospital, though we didn't know it. His mother offered us a home with her at Tooting, but me mother's sisters turned up from Belhampton an' took Alice an' Daisy.'

'But not you or George?'

'No, George didn't want to go and I stayed at home with him. Yer dad found me work with two old ladies in Clapham.'

Mabel was silent for a while, reliving that fatal summer. They passed the Prospect of Whitby and continued to walk further along beside the docks. He pressed her arm. 'Go on, Mabel.'

'And then – and then came that day I'll never forget, another June the thirteenth it was, when Dad turned up again. He'd been drinkin' and was talkin' about our mother. George had come home from school and couldn't stand listenin' to Dad sayin' how he never meant her any harm an' all that stuff – George couldn't *stand* it, an' he picked up a glass vase o' flowers off the table and brought it down on the back o' Dad's head. I came in just as he was fallin' to the floor o' the livin'-room an' I saw he was dead. I told George to go upstairs an' keep quiet, an' I dragged Dad's body out into the hall to the bottom o' the stairs, to make it look as if he'd fallen down 'em. Then I sent a neighbour's boy for yer father.'

'Oh, yes, my dear Mabel, I remember that. And didn't he rush him into the Bolingbroke Hospital immediately?'

Mabel looked straight ahead of her as she replied in a dull, flat tone, 'My father was dead when yours arrived at the house, Stephen. George killed him instantly. Yer father made out he could still hear a heartbeat, just so's to get the body out o' the house an' keep the police out of it for as long as he could. Dad was supposed to have died on the way.'

'My God, Mabel. What you must all have gone through – you and George –'

'And Dr Knowles, Stephen. He risked everything for us. He could've been struck off the Register for givin' false evidence at the inquest. He did it to save George who was only a child, and I was an accessory to it. An' we got away with it, yer father an' me.'

'Oh, my dear girl.' He tucked his stick under his arm and put a hand over hers as they stood on the quayside. 'And so that was why Father got George away to Canada on that child emigration scheme? I know he was very troubled at the time – oh, Mabel, my dear girl.'

'Yes, it was awful, Stephen – but it was nothin' like what happened here when that bomb hit the school, five years later to the day – oh, Stephen!'

She blinked back tears and he put his arm round her as they stood looking down at the water. 'You're right, Mabel – what happened in the past doesn't matter now, not any more. But I'll be able to tell Father that I know now, and understand. You've explained some things that I think I've half suspected. And after all, your father would have died anyway, wouldn't he, of –'

'Of syphilis, yes. Yer dad pointed that out to George an' me, though he didn't use that word, he just said a

347

fatal disease. Oh, he was wonderful, the very best o' doctors.'

They walked along slowly, retracing their steps past the old inn which Mabel's uniform barred her from entering. She shivered and drew her cloak around her; there was a touch of early autumn in the air, a change in the colour of the sky. Upriver the water gleamed with silvery reflections, while down towards Limehouse Reach it was flat grey, already fading into mist. The masts of small craft stood motionless, though the sound of boatmen's voices still drifted up, the endless activity of the river in all seasons.

'How's Phyllis?' she asked suddenly. 'That *is* yer wife's name, isn't it? She must be nearly due now.'

'Oh, yes, poor Phyllis. September twenty-fifth or thereabouts. I don't hear much from them.'

'So she's still stayin' with her parents?'

'Heavens above, they'd never let her come to London with these air raids! And I spend most of my time here, of course – I don't even see much of my own parents in Battersea.'

'But ye'll go an' see her an' the baby as soon as she's delivered?'

'Not very often, I suspect, not until this lot's over, anyway.'

Something about his tone discouraged her from asking further questions, not because he might resent it – after all, he'd asked her a great many – but because she was half afraid of what she might hear. For some reason she thought of her sister Alice whose marriage she suspected was less than satisfactory. A little warning bell began to ring in her head.

He tightened his arm round her waist. 'You don't know what you've done for me, Mabel. I know now why my father's so close to you. I might even be able

348

to tell him – what I've shared with you about what happened – over there. Mabel, my dear –'

'I'd better be gettin' back, Stephen. Violet's goin' to take me to –'

'*No*, not yet, please, we've only had half an hour!'

'Stephen, I think it's best if we didn't.' She broke off awkwardly and felt her face blush scarlet. 'Yer know how it is in hospitals, people are always talkin'. An' I don't want 'em talkin' about *you*.'

He looked at her blankly. 'What do you mean? Don't be ridiculous, Mabel! We're old friends – we've known each other for *years*, for God's sake.'

'Yes, but you're a married man, an' it's best not to give waggin' tongues a chance, so if yer don't mind, I think I'd better go back – on me own.'

'I can't believe I'm hearing this. I don't believe you're doing this to me. I need you, Mabel – yes, I *need* you, can't you see?'

'Ye're a married man, Stephen. An' soon ye'll be a father. I must go.'

She shook herself free of his arm, and without another word turned away and left him standing alone. She did not look back.

Tears blinded her eyes as she hurried up Glamis Road, telling herself that she was doing the right thing. In fact, the only thing to do.

Chapter Nineteen

Staff Nurse Court gave a gasp of dismay on hearing that she was to be posted to Mary Ward where the diphtheria outbreak was being contained.

'I'm sorry to take you from Heckford where you have done excellent work, Nurse Court,' said Matron Rowe, 'but a staff nurse on Mary has contracted diphtheria and the pressure on the staff is very great, so I really have no choice but to send you as a replacement for her. You may remove your belongings to the special staff quarters this afternoon and commence duties tomorrow at seven thirty. Thank you, Nurse Court, you may go.'

Mabel contemplated the disadvantages of this sudden announcement. She would only be allowed to leave the hospital on one day a week, after taking a bath and changing all her clothes. Her visits to Harry would have to be curtailed and she would not be able to go to the Midway Babies' Home at all. She would see even less of Maud than she did at present and – ah, yes, another thought came to her: Dr Stephen Knowles's work in surgery and theatre kept him away from Mary Ward and that at least was a relief.

As soon as she began her new duties, she was swept up into a tightly knit working team in which each member had a part to play.

'The earlier treatment is begun, the better the chance of recovery,' Dr Dunn frequently told the staff. Complete bedrest was essential, and the nurses had to observe and record pulse rates, swelling and tenderness of the neck, croupy coughs and running noses. They made regular examinations of the patients' throats, looking for redness and early patches of the dreaded diphtheritic membrane. Frequent small drinks had to be given – egg beaten up in milk was the staple food – and the air was kept warm and moist by fish kettles continually steaming at each end of the ward. The doors were hung with sheets soaked in disinfectant solution. Hands had to be washed before and after attending to each child, and became rough and sore; nurses were advised to smear Vaseline on them and put on cotton gloves before sleeping.

'Once we've nursed our child through the first week, he must remain on bedrest for a month before we can say he's cured,' said Dr Dunn. 'The two great complications are heart failure and paralysis.' So the children still had to be fed and toileted in bed, with the nurses constantly watching for blueness of the face, ears and fingers, drooping eyelids, limp legs and feet. And in spite of no other treatment being available, the mortality rate for diphtheria at the East London was comparatively low, thanks to strict adherence to these rules. During Mabel's first week on Mary there was only one death, a boy of five admitted in an advanced stage of the disease, the diphtheritic membrane having spread over the back of his throat.

It was the Ward Sister who casually mentioned one morning that Dr Knowles's wife had given birth to a daughter on September the seventeenth.

'I heard it from Sister Enfield yesterday. Let's hope it will help him to settle down. He's changed from the man he was before he went abroad, and not for the better,' said Sister Mary a little sourly, and Mabel wondered whether the words were meant for herself. It was good news, of course, and she could only echo the Sister's sentiments in her heart.

It was time for her first day off. She took her obligatory bath, put on clean underwear and her navy suit, and set off to visit Harry; but on the way she called in at South Lambeth Road to catch up with Maud Ling who welcomed her with a hug.

'Good to see yer, gal – it's been so long, I was wonderin' if I'd said summat to upset yer.'

'Oh, don't be daft, Maudie. I'm sorry, I've been on the diphtheria ward and it's ever so strict.'

'I'll put the kettle on, an' we'll 'ave breakfuss.'

'Haven't yer had it yet? It's nearly noon!'

'Yeah, well, I didn't feel like it. All right now, though.'

Mabel was at once alarmed. 'Are yer all right, Maudie?'

'Missed me August red-letter day, gal, that's what.'

Mabel stared at her aghast. 'Oh . . . oh, Maudie dear. How many days?'

'Free weeks. An' queasy wiv it. I know it in me bones, Mabel. I'm expectin'.'

Sorry as she was about her friend's predicament, Mabel was not really surprised. It was something she had been dreading ever since Maud's liaison with Alex Redfern.

'I've used the vinegar sponge most times, an' it's worked all right so far – but there wasn't a chance to put it in that last time,' said Maud gloomily.

'So what're yer goin' to do, Maudie – tell Alex?'

'Nah, not yet. Not 'til 'e can see for 'imself. Not before Chris'muss.'

'But ye'll be showin' by then, if ye're already a month gone. I mean, it'll be due in – er –'

'Some time next April, yeah. An' the war might be

over, or – yer know, I never wanted to trap 'im, gal. 'E don't 'ave to marry me, an' maybe 'e won't want to – but I'll 'ave 'is child to remember 'im by.'

Mabel was impressed by Maud's stoic realisation that she might find herself left alone. So much now depended on Redfern's loyalty towards his faithful cockney girl.

'Er – are yer goin' to say anythin' at Elmgove?' she asked tentatively.

'Don't make me laugh – what, after the way she spoke to me? I wouldn't go near 'em.'

'But his mother might feel differently if she knew yer were carryin' his child –'

'She won't get the chance – it's what she fought I was talkin' abaht, even before I knew it'd 'appened. No, Mabel, I'll carry on wiv *Chu Chin Chow* for as long as I can, an' then I'll 'ave to get some ovver job. It was a bit of a shock at first, but I won't be the first, nor yet the last. Ovver women've managed, an' so can I.'

'But Maudie –' Mabel decided to say no more for the time being. It was early days yet. A lot could happen before the spring: a miscarriage, perhaps, or even a hasty wedding, especially if the war ended. But it was a very uncertain prospect: a penniless unmarried mother with no parents to assist her would be a social outcast and the future of her child decidedly bleak.

'Now, listen to me, Maud Ling, I'm goin' to take yer in hand,' she said briskly. 'Yer got to start takin' proper care o' yerself. Get rid o' that gin bottle for good and drink milk instead. Make sure yer get enough rest, don't wear anythin' too tight an' keep yer bowels reg'lar.' She laughed, determined to be hopeful and optimistic in spite of her own misgivings.

353

'Oh, Mabel, yer always was a good 'un – best friend I ever 'ad.'

Maud's eyes were moist as she hugged her friend close again, hiding the fear in her heart.

Night, a three-quarter moon and silence over the river: from the south windows of Mary Ward could be seen the forest of masts in the Shadwell Basin. In the dimly lit ward the only sound was the painful rasp of little Tess Graves's laboured breathing. Nurse Court stood over the cot and regarded the child, not five years old and fighting for breath, her eyes looking up in mute appeal. Beside her sat her mother, Susan Graves, who had been snatched from the very jaws of death three years previously at the Booth Street Poor Law Infirmary. Now her daughter lay dangerously ill, a steam kettle hissing beside her cot; at first her breathing seemed to ease a little in the stream of warm, moist air, but now as Mabel looked into her mouth, pressing down the tongue with a spatula, she saw that the membrane had spread, an obscene, pale, leathery growth across the whole of the back of the throat.

Susan Graves looked up beseechingly at Mabel. Like the nurse, she was wearing a white cotton barrier gown and a face mask over her nose and mouth.

'Can't yer do *anythin*' for her, Nurse Court?'

Mabel straightened up. 'I'll send for the doctor on call, Susan.' She felt unable to give the young mother much hope. It was just after half past one. In an hour or two more, the diphtheritic membrane would close the airway completely. It was a dire emergency and the treatment was hazardous.

The telephones installed on each of the wards were a boon for summoning doctors, rather than having to send porters with messages.

'It's Mary Ward,' said Mabel to the woman on the hospital switchboard. 'Can Dr Cuthbert come at once? I think we're going to need a tracheotomy here.'

Having made the call, she quickly prepared a tray for the procedure, setting out the sterile silver tracheotomy tubes, inner and outer, on a huckaback towel. A bowl of antiseptic lotion, another of saline, gauze swabs and thin sponge holders were added – and the knife with its sharp new scalpel blade.

'Mabel.'

She jumped at hearing her name and looked up to see Stephen Knowles framed in the doorway of the treatment room.

'I see you're preparing my fate,' he said.

'G-Good mornin', Dr Knowles. I was expectin' Dr Cuthbert.'

'Has had to go home to his father, sounds like a stroke. I'm standing in as duty officer. And Dr Dunn isn't in the building. Have we got time to send for him?'

'I don't think so. Ye'd better come an' see little Tess Graves, five years old, diphtheria, third day. Her mother's with her.' Mabel was breathless with anxiety. 'I'm sorry, I should've sent for yer before, but an hour ago she wasn't this bad.'

'Hm-mm.' He tied a face mask on and donned a barrier gown. Mabel sketched in the child's history as she tied up the tapes at the back. She led him to the cot where he nodded to Susan Graves, drew in a long breath and let it out in an audible whistle.

'Tracheotomy straight away. Get her into the treatment room.'

Mabel lifted Tess out of the cot and Knowles spoke to the mother. 'You stay here while I see what I can do for your little girl,' he said.

'Oh, let me come, *please*, doctor, I'll hold her for

yer, she'll be better if I'm there – *please!*'

'I'll examine her first, and then let you know.'

He turned on his heel and followed Mabel who laid the child upon the treatment couch.

'Say a prayer for her, Mabel,' he muttered grimly. 'And for me while you're at it.'

'Have yer ever done one before?' she whispered after she had closed the door.

'No. Seen a couple, though. The trick is to avoid the major blood vessels, they're all over the place. Nick the jugular and that's that.' She knew that he was afraid.

Beneath the electric light, Tess tried to cry out, but only managed a faint wheeze. Her little face was blue, her eyes staring from their sockets.

The door opened and Susan Graves appeared. 'Let me stay with her!'

Mabel caught Stephen's eye and he shrugged, leaving the decision to her.

'All right, Susan, yer can hold her still,' she said, offering up a desperate prayer that the mother was not about to see her child killed like a sacrificial lamb.

Knowles picked up the knife. Tess's windpipe was visible under the skin, though the swelling of her neck on either side made it difficult to ascertain the exact position of the blood vessels.

'So easy when you look at diagrams,' Knowles murmured under his breath. 'There's the trachea, there's the thyroid gland, there are the arteries and jugular veins on either side . . . but when a kid's lying in front of you, swollen and gasping for air –'

'May the Lord guide yer hand.' Mabel stood on the opposide side to him, gauze swabs ready to mop away the blood. Susan Graves had one hand on her daughter's chest, the other on the top of her head.

Knowles placed two fingers on the windpipe and felt for the fourth and fifth rings of cartilage. Keeping exactly to the middle line, he quickly cut a small vertical slit in the skin. A little blood oozed out, and he then drove the knife through the hard cartilage: immediately there was a soft hiss as air was sucked in through the opening just made. Mabel dabbed at the oozing blood, and he put down the knife and picked up the curved silver tracheotomy tube, inserting it into the hole so that it curved downwards. The rasping noise had stopped, to be replaced by a regular whooshing sound as air passed in and out through the tube.

'Done it.' He almost groaned. 'Mabel, we've done it.'

They raised their eyes and Susan Graves sobbed with relief. 'Thank yer, doctor, thank yer, Nurse Court, thank yer, thank yer!'

Mabel handed him the inner tube which he thrust inside the one already *in situ*. The whoosh-whoosh-whoosh of air flowing in and out of Tess's lungs was music in their ears.

'Good girl. Got the tapes ready? And a dressing to put round the tube. Old Bob Parker must be looking down from the stars at us.'

Mabel smiled. The distinguished surgeon Robert Parker was one of Shadwell's great names and his work on tracheotomy a milestone, along with the tube he had designed and perfected.

Mabel put a gauze dressing over the tracheotomy and threaded white cotton tapes through the flanges of the outer tube, to tie round the neck and keep it in position.

'Thanks be to God.' Mabel's silent prayer rose straight from her heart.

'Couldn't have done without you,' she heard him

mutter. 'Wouldn't have had the nerve.' He was wet with perspiration and strands of grey hair clung damply to his forehead. He raised his arm and wiped the moisture away with his elbow.

'Better keep her here under observation for a bit.' Turning to Susan Graves, he spoke solemnly. 'Your little girl stands a chance now, but she's by no means out of the woods. You do realise that, don't you? She's very sick with diphtheria and the next forty-eight hours will be critical. I can't make any promises, Mrs Graves.'

'Oh, but she's breathin', doctor, an' she's sleepin',' whispered Susan, her eyes shining through tears. 'She's goin' to get better, thanks to you an' Nurse Court, I know she is, I just *know* it – she's been spared to me.'

What answer could there be to that? Mabel told the second-year to go and put the kettle on for tea. They could only hope and pray that Susan was right, and that her little girl would indeed recover. Without the tracheotomy she would certainly have been dead before morning, but now there was hope.

Twenty minutes later Mabel carried the sleeping child back to her cot.

'Ye'll be wantin' to get back to yer bed, Dr Knowles,' she said.

'Is there another cup of tea?' He was in no hurry to leave. She refilled his cup and passed it across the kitchen table. 'An' how's *your* little girl?' she enquired.

'All right from what I've heard. It all went off well, apparently.'

'What're yer callin' her?'

'My wife has called her Lilian, so I suppose she'll be Lily.'

'And don't yer want to see her, Dr Knowles?'

He ran his fingers through his hair. 'I can't picture any life apart from here, Mabel. To go careering up to

Northampton on a short trip wouldn't be worth it, I simply wouldn't belong. My wife's parents don't think a lot of me and it might do more harm than good. I'm going to have to wait until after this war to start building on the life I had before. If that's possible.'

'But – yer own little daughter –' Mabel began, but he cut her short.

'Is in the care of her mother and grandparents. Especially the latter. Everything's changed. Well, you know something about that, Mabel – look at poor Harry Drover, the way *his* life's been destroyed.'

'Don't say that,' she said sharply.

'I'm sorry, Mabel, but I'm tired of pretending. Listen, I couldn't have done that bloody tracheotomy without you, I was half paralysed with terror in case I killed her. I need you, can't you see, can't you understand? Oh, for God's sake, girl, don't turn away from me, I can't carry on without you. Mabel, *help* me!'

He had seized her shoulders and was almost shaking her as he spoke in a tone that was both angry and imploring. 'You listened to me when I told you what I'd done out in France. It made you a part of me, more than anybody else I've known. I can't tell you what it meant –' He broke off and stood before her, his eyes fixed on hers so that she could not look away. 'Mabel, please, just for the duration of this bloody war, I'm begging you, my dear, my darling – I'm lost, I need you – help me, for Christ's sake.'

She was never sure of what exactly happened next. With his back against the kitchen door his arms were round her, holding her with fierce possession. She put up her hands to fend him off, but her arms seemed to lift of their own accord, resting on his shoulders and then sliding up around his neck until her hands met at the back of his head.

'Mabel, Mabel –'

She opened her mouth to speak, but his lips closed upon hers, taking her breath away. Unable to speak or move, she clung to him, swaying in his arms, his mouth fastened to hers in a hungry kiss, a selfish kiss that had no thought for anything else but his own overwhelming need. His hands roved over her back, one holding her shoulders, the other tracing the downward curve of her spine and coming to rest on her buttocks, pulling her thighs against his hardness. She felt her body soften, seeming to melt in the heat of his desire. It was an indescribable sensation.

When at last he took his lips from hers to let them both draw breath, she whispered his name: 'Stephen, Stephen.' For a moment, for just one moment of madness she experienced a wave of desire such as she had never known before. She trembled in his arms as they clung together, hearing each other's heartbeats, conscious of nothing else. The world stood still and for the length of that moment out of time Stephen Knowles was all she knew: he was her life, he was everything.

And then the real world returned with all its duties and responsibilities. What had seemed like an eternity had been less than half a minute. Staff Nurse Court remembered where she was.

'I must go,' she said.

'But you won't leave me, Mabel?'

'You must let me go – now, this minute.'

'You'll see me again tomorrow?'

'*Let me go*. I must see to Tess – and all the other children.'

So he had no choice but to release her.

When the sun rose at the end of that fateful night on Mary Ward, little Tess Graves had turned the corner in her fight with the poisons of diphtheria. Allowed to breathe freely again and aided by rest and nourishment, the following day brought unmistakable improvement in her condition, and at the end of a week her mother's firm prediction of recovery was seen to be justified. Although strict bedrest had to continue because of the possible after-effects, Tess Graves would not die: her life had been saved by the emergency tracheotomy performed by Dr Knowles.

But Mabel Court had to escape from him. She knew that the moment of revelation in the kitchen of Mary Ward would stay with her for ever: she would always remember his arms around her, his body against hers, his kiss: a kiss to drown in. *Stephen, Stephen* . . .

But he was a married man with a newly born child, and she was committed to Harry Drover who had loved her faithfully for seven years, even though broken in mind and body by the war. So she would have to separate herself from Stephen Knowles; if she stayed she would be unable to resist her own heart's longing, and would betray all her lifelong beliefs and principles.

So she had to leave the hospital she had come to love and look upon as home. There was simply no other way.

Part Two

Women Alone

Chapter Twenty

'But *why*, Nurse Court? I simply fail to understand,' said Matron Rowe, shaking her grey head in bewilderment. 'You've shown yourself to be an excellent children's nurse in every respect. Why, only last week Dr Dunn told me he would support your early promotion to a Sister's post. Are you not happy here?'

'It isn't that, Matron. I've been very happy here,' replied Mabel wretchedly.

'Then why –' Miss Rowe hesitated, and then her features softened beneath her tall lace cap. She leaned across her desk towards Mabel, speaking as one woman to another. 'There *must* be a reason for this sudden decision on your part, Nurse Court. Is it something personal, my dear? Can you confide in me?'

Mabel had to fight back tears, for she did indeed long to tell Matron that her heart was breaking; but to mention a doctor's name in connection with her departure was of course out of the question. She swallowed and cleared her throat.

'I – I'd like to be nearer to my fiancé, Matron, Captain Drover o' the Salvation Army,' she faltered. 'He lives in Battersea, and he's a – an invalid. He lost an arm at the Somme.'

'My dear Nurse Court, I'm very sorry.'

'An' I – I thought I'd better get some more midwifery experience in,' Mabel added lamely, thinking of Maud and her promise to keep a close eye on her.

'But Nurse Court, you are such an outstanding *children*'s

nurse and I really don't see why you need to be a mid-wife.' Miss Rowe paused and looked at Mabel's set face, stonily resolved. 'However, if you have made up your mind, I will of course give you a good reference, though I deeply regret losing your skills as a sick children's nurse. Very well, you may go.'

'Oh, Mabel, *no*! There's no need for you to leave the hospital!' cried Violet Stoke-Marriner.

'There's no alternative,' Mabel almost snapped back. 'If I'd paid more attention to what yer said in the first place, I might not be in this – this – what d'ye call it now.'

'You don't mean that Dr Knowles – that he's made some kind of – that he's said anything untoward?' gasped Violet.

'Yes – that's about the long an' short of it. An' if I stay here, there's no tellin' where it'd end.'

'Mabel!'

'Please, Violet, I don't want to talk about it. Let's just say ye've been proved right, and I've been a complete and utter fool.'

'But Mabel, whatever will you *do*? Where will you *go*?' wailed her friend.

'I've got me midwifery certificate from Booth Street, an' thought I'd apply for a district job for a change – get away from hospitals for a bit.'

'Oh, I'm just so sorry, Mabel – more than I can say.' It gave Violet no pleasure at all to have her warning vindicated.

It was Doris Drover, of all people, who pointed Mabel in the direction she was to take. It had been difficult telling the Drovers that she had given in her notice at the East London, and when they heard that she was thinking of applying to the LCC, Doris remarked that there was a need for a reliable midwife in Kennington. 'Some sober, respectable woman prepared to be on call round the clock, to get up an' go out in the night to a poor woman labourin' in pain, whether she can afford to pay or not. I wonder *you* don't go for good work like that, Mabel.'

Kennington: it was within easy cycling distance of both Harry Drover and Maud Ling. Mabel decided to call on Ruby Swayne to ask if there was in fact such a need for a midwife there.

'Oh, there certainly is, Mabel. There've been some shockin' cases o' women givin' birth with only neighbours to help them, and some old handywoman turnin' up with a stained apron to see to the baby. Why, are yer lookin' for a job, then? I thought yer were so well settled at Shadwell.'

If anybody else says that I think I shall scream out loud, thought Mabel; but she composed herself and considered what Harry's sister had just told her.

'I wonder what sort of accommodation the LCC provides for its district nurses,' she said.

'The last one lived in her own house, but her relief used to lodge with the dressmaker on Kennington Park Road – a poor widow who was glad of the extra money.'

They both sat in silence for a minute, drinking the tea that Ruby had brewed. Mabel contemplated lodging with a stranger, having to tiptoe up and down stairs when she went out to cases in the night; Ruby was thinking of the last girl she had sheltered for the Salvation Army, who had repaid her hospitality by absconding in the night with the contents of Ruby's purse.

They both looked up and began to speak in unison.

367

'Ruby, would yer fancy takin' a lodger who had to work all hours –?'

'Mabel, if ye're thinkin' o' takin' on the job o' midwife in Kennington, what about –?'

They both stopped speaking and stared at each other, then exclaimed together, '*Yes!*'

And so it was settled; the application to the LCC was duly made and accepted, and Mabel prepared to move into the home of the woman who was to have been her sister-in-law.

'I don't know why ye're leavin' the East London, Mabel, and I won't pry into what isn't my business,' said Ruby in her direct way, 'but it'll be good for us all to have yer here. Life hasn't been much for the boys since we've been on our own.'

Which proves that it's an ill wind that blows nobody any good, thought Mabel as she worked out her month's notice on Mary Ward, thankful to be hidden away from the nurses' home and staff dining-room where she might meet Knowles, and also be subjected to a barrage of questions from her colleagues.

Her last day arrived and she ordered a taxicab to transport her few belongings to number 3 Deacon's Walk on the Friday before she was due to take up her post on the Monday, October the eighth. A letter from Aunt Nell suggested that she take a holiday at Belhampton before beginning her new job on the district, but Mabel wanted to get started on it straight away, rather than spend her time brooding over her situation and trying to evade her aunts' questions. Aunt Kate had responded with a generous cheque towards the inevitable expenses of the change and Mabel put it to good use at the cycle store on the Brixton Road.

Ruby and the boys exclaimed when they saw the brand-new bicycle with a basket attached to the handlebars in front, and a rear bracket for her midwifery bag. Lights with batteries were an additional purchase, and the boys' eyes gleamed as Mabel mounted and pedalled along the Brixton Road in the Saturday traffic, not that there was much of it: a few horse-drawn carts and the trams. She wobbled a little at first, but the skill soon returned, with an exhilarating sense of freedom.

'Can I have a go, Miss Court?' asked Matthew longingly and, when they were back in Deacon's Walk where few vehicles appeared, Mabel let Matthew climb up on the saddle and try his skill at keeping upright.

'And please call me Aunt Mabel,' she told the boys. She was beginning to realise that life with the Swaynes would have its compensations; for one thing Ruby understood only too well the situation with Harry, his gradual decline into further dependence, though Mrs Drover continued to pray for his recovery and restoration to active membership of the Salvation Army.

They were all invited to tea at Falcon Terrace on that first Sunday afternoon, and afterwards Mabel accompanied the family to a meeting of prayer and worship at the Citadel. Harry clung to her hand when she kissed him goodnight, and slowly, painfully stammered that he would see her more often now that she lived with Ruby and the boys.

This, then, was to be her life for the foreseeable future, she thought. She must not look back to the past and especially she must not think about *him*. The Lord had directed her to this new line of duty, and she must give it all her skill and energy.

And it began sooner than expected.

Ruby was making cocoa at twenty to ten that night, when a hammering at the front door made them all jump. 'It's the police, missus, an' we want the midwife!' roared a male voice.

369

Ruby unlocked the door, to reveal a burly police constable on the step.

'Mrs Thornton's started,' he informed her. 'Haberdasher's in Brixton Road, the husband's goin' frantic. Can't track down ol' Mrs Cummings, an' some woman said there was a midwife here. So can yer come? It's her third.'

Mabel felt her knees go weak. To be called out in the dark to a woman she had never met and whose history she did not know . . .

'Yes, o' course, I'm the midwife, an' I'll come straight away,' she said, catching Ruby's eye and nodding quickly. 'Just let me get me bag – me bicycle's in the shed – an' me hat an' coat.'

'I'm on me bike, so I can show yer the way,' said the policeman, clearly relieved at having run her to earth.

'I'll say a prayer for you an' the mother an' child,' whispered Ruby as Mabel left the house.

Cycling along beside the policeman down the Kennington Road, past the headquarters of the Waifs and Strays Society, into Kennington Park Road and round into Brixton Road with its closed shopfronts and no street lighting, Mabel also prayed that the delivery might be normal and straightforward.

When they reached the shop, Mr Thornton was waiting at the door. 'Thank God ye're here, nurse – our neighbour's with her and thinks it won't be long.'

Mrs Thornton lay in their double bed, hanging on grimly to the brass rails behind her. A heavily built woman stood over her with her sleeves rolled up. She eyed Mabel doubtfully.

'We was expectin' Mrs Cummin's.'

Mabel pulled off her coat, put her bag on the dressing-table and advanced to the bedside.

'Hello, Mrs Thornton, I'm Nurse Court, yer midwife,'

she said with a smile. The mother stifled another cry of pain as Mabel drew back the sheet and put a light hand on the board-hard abdomen. 'All right, dear, I'm here to look after yer. Is there some hot water ready, Mrs – er –?' she asked the big woman. 'And is there a washing bowl to use before I examine her?'

The neighbour was politely put in her place and her services engaged as assistant. To Mabel's great relief, the internal examination revealed that the cervix was fully dilated – a gush of cloudy water followed the withdrawal of her two probing fingers.

'Very good! Not long to go now,' she assured the mother. 'Come on, me dear, let me help yer to sit up, put yer hands behind yer knees – like this – and as soon as yer feel the pain comin' on, take a big breath in an' hold it – that's right – hold yer breath an' push – push – push – push – *push*! Good girl, that's the way to do it!'

The midwife's air of friendly authority gave new confidence to Mrs Thornton and she duly pushed with all her strength – to be rewarded by the birth of a baby girl less than ten minutes later. Mabel received the child's slippery little body into her hands and, as the piercing cry of a newborn baby filled the room, she felt again the sense of witnessing a miracle, that wonderful moment when the pain of childbirth turns to joy at the sight and sound of a new human being.

'Ye've got a girl, a dear little *girl*, Mrs Thornton! Just listen to her – isn't she beautiful? D'ye want to hold her?'

The afterbirth quickly followed and Mabel asked the neighbour who was wiping her eyes on the corner of her apron if she could make tea for them all. 'What are yer goin' to call her, Mrs Thornton?'

'Little Margaret, that's her name,' whispered the

mother, gazing down at her baby. 'Can me husband see her, nurse?'

Mr Thornton was duly summoned, and a wide-eyed little boy and girl were brought in to see their new sister. Mabel's heart swelled with thankfulness to be part of this family event, sharing in their relief and joy. Even the belligerent neighbour had been won over and nodded her approval over the strong, sweet tea she had brewed.

When Mabel took her leave at nearly midnight, Mrs Thornton had given baby Margaret her first breastfeed, and the two other children were asleep.

Mr Thornton was overwhelmed with gratitude for his wife's safe delivery. 'We can never thank yer enough, Nurse Court,' he said as Mabel mounted her bicycle, feeling something like happiness again; certainly it was satisfaction. Her new job had started well.

And so it was to continue. Pedalling through dark October nights and morning mists, the tang of autumn in the air and the pavements slippery with fallen leaves, Mabel took pleasure from getting to know her mothers and their families, the smiling faces of the older children and the proud grandmothers. As the weeks passed, local doctors recognised her as a trustworthy professional woman, even though young, unmarried and without the personal experience of childbirth that many women considered a necessary qualification.

The growing closeness between herself and Ruby Swayne helped to ease Mabel's relationship with the family, especially with Mrs Drover who came to realise that Mabel had no intention of coming between her and her son. Sometimes Mabel joined the Drovers and Ruth at a prayer and praise meeting, though she always had to leave a message to inform callers where she could be found. Matthew and Mark were very useful as messengers in this respect, and she soon became a familiar part of their lives, a friendly aunt whose work took her out at highly unusual times to do all sorts of mysterious things in other people's houses. They began to take a pride in the fact that Nurse Court actually lived with them: it gave them a sense of importance, in contrast to the absence of their father who was far away in a place they could not bring themselves to name.

Forbidden love might be banished, but duty was always there to be done and had its sunny side. Time, Mabel told herself, would cure a broken heart, whether hers or somebody else's.

And, of course, there was Maudie, now within easy cycling distance down the South Lambeth Road, and happily claimed as a booked patient of Nurse Court's.

'Are yer gettin' enough rest, Maud?' Mabel enquired, her eyes appraising her friend, now at three months. She was definitely looking better, her skin was clearer and her eyes brightened whenever Mabel appeared at her lodgings.

'Makes a difference, knowin' ye're me own midwife, an' goin' to take care of Alex's baby,' she said trustfully. 'Makes it seem all official, like.'

'Yes, an' ye'd better do as ye're told, or yer midwife'll give yer a right dressin' down,' Mabel answered. 'And I'm not jokin', Maud. Have yer got yerself a doctor?'

'Yeah, Dr Swift, lives up the posh end o' Souf Lambeff Road, by Park Mansions. Alex bin payin' 'im sixpence a week for Teddy an' me to be on 'is panel. But I won't need a doctor for this, will I? I got *you*!'

'Yer never know, Maud, I tell all me mothers to get a doctor, just in case,' said Mabel lightly, not wanting to go into any details about obstructed labour, haemorrhage or her own greatest dread, a limp and silent

373

'blue baby'. She wrote down Dr Swift's name on Maud's record card.

'I know I'll be all right wiv you, gal. An' Teddy'll come an' fetch yer, 'e's a good lad.' There was a calm, confident look on Maud's pretty face, and Mabel felt less anxious about her now, but still wished she would tell Redfern of her condition.

'I'll maybe tell 'im next time 'e turns up,' said Maud, a saucy smile curving her lips. 'Tell 'im 'e's got to go a bit more careful now!'

And there was Norah. The Midway was out of Mabel's district, but well within pedalling distance, and with the freedom she now enjoyed, away from the constrictions of hospital life and the tyranny of forever reporting on duty, she was sometimes able to drop in on Sister Norah and her brood. Mrs Spearmann told them that there were plans to pull down the Midway after the war and build a better home in healthier surroundings, but at present it seemed as if the war was never going to end. A fearful rout of Allied troops in northern Italy had resulted in further long lists of dead and wounded, and Mabel was thankful that Stephen Knowles was out of it, though she caught herself up sharply as the man's name flashed into her head. Neither of her friends had the slightest idea of the real reason why she had left Shadwell.

And of course they talked about Maud.

'I don't think we need worry too much about her, y'know, she's lookin' much happier, sort o' contented, like. She says she'll probably tell Alex next time he turns up, and then who knows? You an' me might find ourselves at a weddin', Norah!'

But Sister McLoughlin's blue eyes were sombre. 'There's nothin' sure in the world, Mabel, not any more. I thank God that Maud's got yerself to look after her an' love her, the poor darlin'.'

Mabel stared. This did not sound like Norah with her simple faith and hopeful outlook.

'We can only wait an' hope an' do the best we can for her,' she replied. 'Any news o' that brother o' mine?'

'Not lately, but I'm hopin' he might turn up at Christmas or round about, ye know the way he suddenly jumps up from nowhere.' Norah smiled, though Mabel doubted that he would. The blockading of German ports was having a terrible effect upon the morale of the starving civilian population, and in some quarters it was said to be more likely to shorten the course of the war than the continued carnage on the Western and Eastern Fronts.

Then came a letter from Violet Stoke-Marriner, full of news of the East London and saying how much Nurse Court was missed by everybody. 'And by the way, Mabel,' she wrote at the very bottom of the page, 'Dr Knowles came and brought the baby to show us last week, such a dear little thing. He came into the dining-room at lunchtime, and held her up in his arms. He looked so proud of her. I thought you would be pleased to know this, Mabel.'

And of course Mabel was pleased – for Stephen's sake, for his wife Phyllis and most of all for their little daughter who now had a loving daddy. It was happy news, and how thankful she was that she had done the right thing . . .

But that night her treacherous subconscious mind caused her to dream that she was again in his arms, reliving that one and only moment, that single kiss. In a transport of joy Mabel awoke suddenly and found only the vaporous fragments of a dream.

The curtains moved softly, as if love had flown out of the window, and Mabel despised herself for her weakness.

October gave way to dark November and fogs that hung around all day. Londoners looked shabby and careworn, and more and more women wore the black of mourning. Theatres still did good business offering escape to a world of colour and romance, and *Chu Chin Chow* was being rivalled by *The Maid of the Mountains* at Daly's Theatre and *Peg o' My Heart* at the Globe. On the silent cinema screens Mary Pickford was bringing in the crowds.

Maud Ling woke at ten o'clock, yawned, stretched and got out of bed to put the kettle on. The morning sickness had passed, and she felt fit and well in her fourth month. She patted the little swell at the bottom of her abdomen and whispered, 'Our baby, Alex, darlin'. I'll 'ave to tell yer soon, won't I?'

She took her breakfast of tea and bread and marmalade back to bed with her. She felt that she ought to go out and take a sniff at the moist air, maybe stop for pie and mash at Wilcox's Dining Rooms. She might even look in discreetly at the *Daily Chronicle* and see if young Ted was around – ask him out for a bite in his dinner hour. She dressed quickly in the cold room, put on her winter coat and jaunty green hat, and went downstairs.

'Mornin', Mrs Hiscock!' she called to the landlady whose ground-floor door stood open.

'Mornin', miss!' came the reply, almost drowned out by a crashing of pots, pans and cutlery. The woman did not show herself and Maud wondered if there had been just the slightest emphasis on the *miss*. She gave a little grimace; sooner or later the old girl would have to be told, and then would she, Maud, be able to stay? She'd never been behind with the rent, like some, and Teddy was a very useful messenger and errand boy when occasion rose.

And how much longer could she stay in *Chu Chin Chow*?

Out in the street she ran into Madge, a pert blonde of twenty, who was in the chorus of the show.

'Ye're lookin' pretty good these days, Maud,' she said. ''Ow's that young airman o' yours? Officer, i'n't 'e?'

Maud nodded. 'Yeah, Royal Flyin' Corps. 'E's a wing commander.'

Madge raised her thin eyebrows. 'Coo! Was 'e the one 'oo was waitin' outside the featre that time when 'e dragged yer away soon's yer showed yer face at the stage door?'

'Yeah, that was my Alex.'

Madge's light-blue eyes travelled over Maud's figure. ''Scuse me askin', but are yer engaged to 'im?'

'Er – yeah, unofficial, like.' Maud glanced down at her ringless fingers.

'Got a date for a weddin'?'

Oh, my Gawd, she's guessed, thought Maud. Well, everybody's got to know sooner or later.

'I reckon I'd better be gettin' along, Madge – get back in the warm an' put me feet up before goin' on tonight.'

'Yeah, ye'd better make sure yer get yer afternoon rest, Maud,' said the girl, and Maud thought she saw a meaningful look in her eye, cheeky little cow.

The front door of the lodging house was open, in spite of the all-pervading fog, and Mrs Hiscock stood in the hall, looking curiously flustered. Something had happened.

'What's up?' asked Maud sharply.

'Yer got a visitor, Miss Ling. An officer.'

'*Alex!*' shrieked Maud, looking wildly around her. 'Where is 'e?'

'I let 'im into my sittin'-room – 'ere, 'alf a minute, miss, wait! 'E ain't that Redfern bloke – 'ere!'

But Maud had dashed through into Mrs Hiscock's ground-floor flat and was calling out to the man she loved. 'Alex! Alex!'

And then she saw the unfamiliar officer standing in the middle of the room. He had removed his peaked cap and held it in his hand. 'Miss Ling?' he asked without smiling.

By refusing to acknowledge him, by not listening to him, Maud tried to make him disappear.

'Alex – ye're not – yer 'aven't – where is 'e?' she babbled, her words a senseless jumble.

'Squadron Leader Dobson,' he said, introducing himself. 'I'm a – I was a friend of Wing Commander Redfern – Alex – and I've come to inform – to tell you that – I'm sorry, Miss Ling.'

There was no getting rid of this messenger. He refused to disappear. The colour drained from Maud's face and her eyes seemed to grow larger; her mouth dropped open and she put up her hands as if warding off a blow.

Mrs Hiscock came to her side. It seemed that she and Dobson had already spoken.

'Miss Ling, I very much regret to say that Alex's de Havilland 4 was shot down over enemy lines two days ago, Tuesday, November the thirteenth. His relatives have been informed by telegram from the Air Ministry. I knew Alex, he told me about you, and I promised him that I would let you know if – if this happened. I'm very sorry, Miss Ling, but Alex Redfern is dead.'

The howl that broke from Maud's throat was like that

of an animal in pain. And then she spoke. 'But there's the baby,' she whispered. 'I ain't told 'im. 'E don't know about the baby yet.'

She swayed on her feet and Dobson put out a hand to steady her. He caught her in his arms as she fell.

'There's a woman askin' for yer downstairs, nurse,' said the patient's mother. 'Salvation Army uniform. I told her you were attending to my daughter.'

Mabel was immediately alert. 'Oh, heavens, it'll be my landlady and friend. Just stay with yer daughter while I see what she wants, will yer?'

When she heard Ruby's message she clung to the newel post of the banister.

'Oh, my God. *Alex*. Oh, no, no, no, no, it can't be. And I'm stuck here, Ruby. I can't leave.'

'I told her brother you were out on a case, Mabel, but I said I'd let yer know. He said she was in a bad way. Has she got any other friends or family?'

'No, only him, he's a good lad but only sixteen. Oh, Ruby, whatever can I do?'

'Let me go to her, Mabel. When she sees me uniform, she'll know I'm yer friend and her friend. I'll stay with her till yer can come.'

Upstairs the bedroom door opened and the patient's mother called down urgently, 'Nurse, she's pushin' down – come back up at once, d'ye hear?'

'All right, I'm comin', don't worry!' Mabel called back. The demands of a woman in labour overrode all other considerations for a midwife and she had to make a decision at once.

'Thanks, Ruby – an' if yer can get in touch with Sister McLoughlin at the Midway Babies' Home an' tell her – tell Maud I'll be there soon's I can. Bless yer, Ruby. All right, all right, I'm comin'!'

It was seven o'clock that evening when Mabel was finally able to leave her patient and the seven-pound baby boy she had delivered, and without stopping to eat she set out again on her bicycle for South Lambeth Road and Maud's room on the second floor of the lodging house. She found Norah sitting beside a wax-pale Maud, trying to get her to drink tea and eat a boiled egg with toast, 'for the baby's sake'. Young Teddy Ling had gone up to his own room, a fugitive from women's talk and tears.

'He's comin' down to stay wid her tonight, after we leave,' explained Norah in a low voice.

'Maudie, dear – I'm so sorry I couldn't come before,' Mabel whispered, embracing the friend of her childhood.

'It don't matter, there's nuffin' left for me now, gal,' came the dull reply.

Both her friends protested that she had the baby to think about and live for: Alex's baby that only today she had felt kicking inside her for the first time.

'Did Mrs Swayne tell yer, Norah?' asked Mabel in a low tone.

Norah hesitated. 'No, I was already here, y'see. When I was gettin' the children ready for their dinner, didn't I see Maudie's face in front o' me, clear as I'm seein' it now,' she said quietly. 'An' I knew it wasn't good, 'cause me heart went cold inside me an' I knew I had to go to her straightway. Mrs Lovell was frightened when she saw me face, she said 'twas white as death, like seein' a ghost.'

Mabel shivered.

Maud moaned and sat up in the bed. 'I'll 'ave anuvver cup o' tea if ye're makin' one,' she muttered.

'Good girl!' said her friends in unison and Mabel rose to put the kettle on.

'Ye've got to look after yerself, Maudie dear, for the baby's sake,' she said.

For the baby's sake. It was to be an oft-repeated rallying cry in the cold, dark, desolate months ahead.

Chapter Twenty-one

It was only after the news of Alex's death that Maud Ling noticeably began to 'show'. Until then she had concealed her condition by wearing loose jackets and coats, but from mid-November she seemed suddenly to become obviously pregnant and made no attempt to hide it – except when she went on stage, for to her friends' amazement she returned to *Chu Chin Chow* on the following Monday.

'Need all the cash I can lay me 'ands on, gal,' she told Mabel grimly. 'Ever so good to me, they are at 'Is Majesty's, lettin' me wear them baggy trousers an' a couple more veils floatin' arahnd. Reckon I can keep goin' till the New Year, an' then I'll look aht for anuvver job where me shape don't matter.'

She gave her bulge a tenderly possessive pat. *Her baby*.

Mrs Hiscock turned out to be unexpectedly sympathetic and Maud was suitably grateful for this, though knew she would have to tread carefully with the landlady.

'She could turn rahnd an' say I was givin' 'er boardin'-'ouse a bad name – an' I reckon she *would*, too, if I gave any ovver cause for 'er to complain. But I pay me rent in full on time, don't make no noise, no followers – she used to turn a blind eye to Alex 'cause 'e tipped 'er well – an' she knows if she frew me aht, Teddy'd go too, an' she finds 'im useful, bringin' in the coal, goin' dahn to the 'Orns for 'er pint o' porter, fetchin' the newspaper – so I reckon we can stay. It's 'ome, near enough.'

Mabel nodded, thinking of the memories the dingy little room held for them both, and made a point of speaking to the landlady on her visits, for which she now had an official reason. But when she tentatively mentioned the Redferns, now in mourning and uncomforted by the knowledge of an expected grandchild, Maud's mouth hardened.

'No, Mabel, they don't care, not them. She fought I was expectin' when I called on 'em that time – "in some sort o' trouble", that's what she said, an' freatened to 'ave me frown out. They ain't goin' to get a second chance. No fear!'

Sadly, in these times of men's lives lost, Maud Ling was not the only unmarried girl on Mabel's books. Many of these unfortunates went into rescue homes of one kind or another, but some stayed with their parents and faced the neighbours and local busybodies.

'This has been a great sorrow to us, Nurse Court,' said Mrs Clegg, a stalwart of the Kennington Methodist Chapel where her husband was treasurer. 'But Catherine would have been married if her father and I hadn't told them to wait until after the war. That was before we knew that she – and now his ship's gone down and she's having his child, so the least we can do is stand by her.'

'Of course, Mrs Clegg, she's yer daughter,' said Mabel gently, though she could see that both mother and daughter were full of regret about the situation.

'I mean, take that girl down the street, that Beasley girl, well, Mrs Sands she is now, only seventeen and married in a hurry before the man went away. She'll be confined about the same time as Catherine, and if she's widowed she'll get a pension, even though –'

'All right, that's enough, let it rest now,' broke in Mr Clegg irritably. 'No need to parade all our business in front of strangers.'

383

'Nurse Court isn't a stranger, Frank.'

'Maybe not, but it's bad enough having to walk down Kennington Park Road with everybody gawping and talking behind their windows. Our daughter's shamed her family.'

There was a brief, awkward silence. Mabel smiled at Catherine, a listless, ungainly figure at eight months.

'Let's go up to yer room, Catherine,' she said, and the girl silently led the way upstairs. Mabel told her to lie down on the bed so that her tummy could be felt and the baby's heart heard through the 'ear-trumpet', as Mabel called the foetal stethoscope.

'It's very sad, losin' yer young man, Catherine, but o' course ye're not alone,' she said kindly. 'The war's changed so many lives. But the important thing now is the new life on its way. How're yer feelin' in yerself? Are yer sleepin' all right? Is the baby kickin' a lot?'

The pale, dispirited girl who had not so far uttered a word, now looked up with heavy eyes. 'Nothing will ever be the same as it was before, nurse.'

Mabel took hold of her hand and searched for some words of comfort. 'Yer baby'll bring a lot o' love with it, dear, an' yer mother an' father'll cheer up when they find 'emselves grandparents, just yer wait an' see. The important thing now is the new life inside yer. That's what yer got to hold on to, Catherine.'

'Mother's asked us all to spend Christmas Day at Falcon Terrace,' said Ruby. 'Dad's got an open-air meeting in the morning and we could join him there with the boys while mother cooks the dinner. I don't know whether Harry'll be able to come out in his chair. What about you, Mabel? Will yer be able to come?'

'It depends what calls come in, an' Christmas could be busy,' Mabel answered. 'An' I'll be lookin' in on

Maud an' Teddy at some time.' She sighed. There seemed to be so many things to worry about, or be sorry for, or both. Things that should have made her happy, like the cards, gifts and letters that arrived from Belhampton, only brought more bad news. Aunt Nell sounded worried about Uncle Thomas's continued shortness of breath and swollen legs; the doctor said it was to do with his heart and had prescribed the traditional extract of foxglove. Aunt Kate's letter was short, and told of the tragic suicide of a legless man who had managed to tip himself from an upstairs window at Pinehurst. Daisy wrote that Lucy Drummond's brother Cedric was reported as being badly wounded and likely to lose a leg, so there was no Christmas joy at the Rectory. By separate post came a plain Christmas card with the message, 'From Gerald, Alice and Geoffrey Westhouse.'

Mabel felt guilty about her sister Daisy, now nearly fourteen; they had missed so much of each other's lives in the past three years. She promised herself a visit to Belhampton in the spring, then immediately thought that she could not leave Maud until after the delivery, expected in April.

There was a scrawled, creased postcard from Albert, dated the sixth of December, which contained no real news, only that he missed his two sweethearts and sent regards to Harry.

Of George there was no word, and Mabel feared that all contact was lost with the brother who had been so swiftly despatched to a strange land. It was time for his eighteenth birthday, and Mabel never thought the day would come when she would be thankful that George was safely out of the way. Out of the war . . .

*   *   *

385

As it turned out, Mabel did not see either Maud or Norah on Christmas Day. A summons at three in the morning called her to a woman in labour with a third child and progress was rapid. By ten to six she was pushing and, to Mabel's horror, the fleshy protuberance that she had thought was a head was in fact a bottom, embellished with testicles and penis. An undiagnosed breech! She felt herself gasp in alarm, for breeches could be difficult to deliver and if the head was stuck in the vagina for too long after the body was born – or if it was delivered too quickly – brain damage could be the tragic consequence. What should she do? It was too late to send for a doctor.

She need not have worried, for in another thirty seconds and a good hard push from the mother, a small baby boy slipped out, weighing scarcely five pounds. His small size and the fact that he was a third child saved him from danger, and Mabel sighed with relief as he lay squirming between his mother's thighs, bubbling at the nose and mouth in his efforts to cry. Thankfully she seized a twist of cotton wool to clear the air passages.

'That was the quickest I've ever 'ad, nurse!' said the mother in admiration, and Mabel smiled, feeling that the less said, the better, though she sent up a silent prayer of thanks.

Back at Deacon's Walk for breakfast with Ruby and the boys, there was another knock at the door. Mr Clegg, unsmiling and clearly embarrassed, stood on the step with a request from his wife that Nurse Court would come to see Catherine who was 'getting a lot of backache'. Swallowing her piece of toast and taking a last quick gulp from a cup of tea, Mabel said she would come straight away.

*   *   *

Catherine lay flushed and restless in her bed, and her abdomen hardened at Mabel's light touch. The baby's heartbeat was regular and there was no 'show' of blood or sign of the waters having broken.

'She's probably goin' into labour, but it'll be some time yet,' Mabel told Mrs Clegg. 'She'd be better gettin' up and walkin' around the room for a bit, to help bring the baby's head down.'

She left a dose of 'mother's mixture', an opium-based sedative with aspirin for pain relief, and said she would return later that morning.

Ruby and her sons were ready to leave for Falcon Terrace at ten and Mabel joined them. There were greetings, kisses and exchanges of small gifts.

'Happy Christmas, Harry! Look, I've brought yer this,' she whispered, producing a cosy woollen dressing-gown, not wrapped up as it was difficult for him to unwrap with one hand. 'Remember that Christmas when I gave yer a pair o' socks an' yer gave me a silver cross on a chain? – I've still got it, look!' And she undid her top button to show that she was wearing it under her uniform.

Ruby, Matthew and Mark accompanied Major Drover to the Park, but Harry preferred to stay indoors. Mabel sat and held his hand for a while, before cycling back to Kennington to check on her patient.

'How's she doin'?'

'Oh, the pains are definitely worse, Nurse Court.' Mrs Clegg had spent the morning at home with her daughter, while her husband had gone to the service at their chapel.

An internal examination showed that the cervix was 'three fingers' open in the midwives' jargon, or about half dilated.

'Good girl, Catherine, ye're well on in labour,' Mabel told her.

387

'How long d'you think it will be, Nurse Court?' asked Mrs Clegg: the eternal question.

'Ye'll have yer baby before the day's out, Catherine, I can tell yer that much.' It was never wise to predict times, especially with first babies. 'I won't leave yer now, I'll stay here till it's born,' Mabel reassured the girl and her mother, thinking she would miss dinner at Falcon Terrace, but knowing that she was more needed here. Mrs Clegg had cooked a small roast beef rib, served with roast potatoes, cabbage and gravy, and followed by home-made Christmas pudding, which Mabel was cordially invited to share. The drawback was that she and Mrs Clegg had to take it in turns to join Mr Clegg in the dining-room while the other stayed with Catherine, which meant that she had to eat with a morosely silent man, unable to give vent to his mixed emotions of pity for his daughter and shame on her behalf.

Being young, with supple muscles, Catherine made good progress during the afternoon and, as darkness was falling, Mabel was happy to tell her that the neck of the womb was fully open, and some good, hard pushes were now needed to bring her baby into the world. Mrs Clegg had the cot all ready, warmed by a hot-water bottle.

'Come on now, Catherine, sit up and take a big breath in, hold it and *push*!' ordered Mabel, using the time-honoured words of midwives throughout the ages.

The girl gazed imploringly at her mother who gripped her hand and whispered, 'Just go on doing what Nurse Court tells you, Cathy – good girl – oh, my little girl – my poor little girl!'

'Ssh, Mother, we don't want any tears just now, only hard work,' said Mabel, though her own heart ached for them both. 'Come on, Catherine, another push – it's not called labour for nothin', yer know!'

And sure enough, with a last, long-drawn-out groan from the mother, a baby girl emerged at a quarter past four.

'It's a *girl*, Cathy, a dear little girl, oh, thanks be to God!' cried Mrs Clegg, leaning over to kiss her daughter in a shower of tears and endearments.

'A daughter on Christmas Day.' Mabel smiled, wrapping the new arrival in a towel. 'What're yer goin' to call her?'

'We'd thought of Rhoda, after my husband's mother,' said Mrs Clegg. 'But she's a Christmas baby, so shall we call her Carol?'

'Yes, Mamma, let her be Carol,' murmured Catherine. And for the first time since Mabel had met her, she smiled. A look of pure love spread over her face as she held out her arms to receive her child from the midwife.

Neither Mabel nor Mrs Clegg could speak as they gazed at the mother and child. Mabel reflected that life would not be easy for Catherine: she would have to face setbacks and rejection, and almost certainly loneliness later in life, for she was unlikely to marry in a world drained of its young men. But for now, on this Christmas Day, she was the mother of a lovely child and Mabel rejoiced with her.

'I'm sorry to be late, but I've delivered two babies today,' Mabel told Mrs Drover when she eventually returned to Falcon Terrace as they were finishing tea. Taking the cup she was handed – she had lost count of the number of cups of tea she had downed that day – she noticed Harry looking at her with something of the old understanding they had shared in the past.

'N – N – N – Nurse D – D – Dro – Drover!' he managed to say, nodding to emphasise that she should be bearing his name: a dream that would never be fulfilled now.

'Oh, Harry. Oh, Harry, my dearest love.' And she leaned over him as he sat in his chair and kissed him full on the lips, not caring that his parents, sister and nephews saw her. In spite of everything, this was the right place for her to be: this was reality, anything else was a dream.

On Boxing Day, having visited her two newly delivered mothers and their babies, Mabel cycled over to South Lambeth Road where she found Maud sitting up in bed, looking as white as the sheets and being waited on by Teddy. She had collapsed after the Christmas Eve performance of *Chu Chin Chow*.

'Oh, Maudie! And I didn't get over to see yer at all. I had two confinements – oh, I'm so sorry! How are yer?'

''S all right, gal, I spent yesterday in bed, I was that whacked aht,' said Maud with a wan smile. 'I meant to go over to see Norah an' the tots, but –' She shrugged.

'Is the baby all right?' asked Mabel anxiously. 'Yer know yer can't go back to the show.'

'I know, I was leavin' at New Year anyway.' Maud closed her eyes momentarily. 'Don't worry abaht me, gal. Ted looks after me a treat, don't yer, little bruvver?'

'I do me best,' he answered with a wry grin and Mabel warmed to him, a wiry lad with dark curly hair and a cheeky expression.

'Yer could've lost the baby, Maud,' said Mabel seriously.

'Yeah – an' there's them 'oo'd say it'd be for the best, an' all. But I want Alex's kid now, Mabel – it'll be all I got left of 'im.'

Before she left, Mabel had a word with Mrs Hiscock to find out her reaction.

'I don't mind keepin' 'er 'ere, nurse,' the woman told her with a self-consciously generous air. 'But wouldn't yer think '*e*'d 'ave made some provision for 'er – left 'er a few 'undred in 'is will? Yer ain't 'eard nothin', 'ave yer?'

Mabel hadn't and did not want to discuss Maud's affairs with the landlady. She was not surprised that Redfern had left his faithful sweetheart penniless; she had always suspected that he had used the girl and never given a thought to her future. But then she told herself that perhaps she was being unjust, and in any case they would never know now; like Catherine's sailor, he was one more life lost in this most terrible of wars.

When Maud asked Mabel to look out for a vacancy for temporary domestic service with one of her clients, she was doubtful that she could oblige. 'Somebody 'oo's just 'ad a baby, an' might be glad of an extra 'and wiv the 'ousework, like,' said Maud hopefully. In fact, most of Mabel's patients did not employ domestic help, but relied on relatives and neighbours to help out. Those who could afford paid help usually engaged a private maternity nurse.

Ruby Swayne offered to find a place at one of the Salvation Army's women's refuges, where Maud would be alongside other girls in the same situation; but Maud wanted to stay at her lodgings with Teddy.

It was Norah who had the brainwave. 'Sure and aren't we always havin' trouble findin' an' keepin' good staff at the Midway! And Maudie's so good wid the babies – an' doesn't mind what jobs she does – an' sure the dear children aren't goin' to gossip about her, are they?'

Mabel seized on this suggestion with enthusiasm. 'Oh, that's wonderful, Norah!'

'I'll have to ask Mrs Spearmann, o' course, but that shouldn't be any bother, she'll rely on me bein' acquainted wid Maud – an' yerself, too.'

Maud at once agreed. 'But d'yer really fink she'd take me on?' she asked doubtfully, looking down at her increasing girth.

'Ah, won't she be glad to have ye, Maudie!'

Norah spoke with blithe certainty, but received a sharp and unexpected setback from Mrs Spearmann.

'This home is run for the benefit of homeless children, Sister Norah, not fallen women like this, er, singer. Does she intend to leave her child here and go back to the stage after the birth?'

'Oh, *no*, Mrs Spearmann,' exclaimed Norah, surprised by such hardness from the patroness. 'Ye can ask Nurse Court, Miss Ling has a very good character, I'm tellin' ye.'

'Hm, her conduct tells a different story. What about the father's family – this flying officer who was killed? Can't his people do anything to help Miss Ling?'

'I don't really know,' replied Norah, who found this question difficult to answer. '*Please*, Mrs Spearmann, we're short o' good, reliable staff who'll turn a hand to anythin' – if ye'd just see Maud for yerself an' maybe give her a trial?'

Olive Spearmann sighed deeply, for she was having a difficult time. She was aware that the work and money she had put into the Midway Babies' Home was looked upon in some quarters as a sop to her conscience, for there was now open hostility towards manufacturers who had made money by supplying arms and equipment towards the war effort. Amos Spearmann's textile works was now entirely given over to uniform material, buttons and accessories, and on occasion he had been followed by shouts of 'Profiteer!' and 'Dirty Jew!' as he travelled between home and factory in his chauffeur-driven car. His wife felt these public accusations very keenly and to hear her charitable work belittled was hard to bear; it was the wrong moment to ask her to employ an unmarried expectant mother as a favour. In the end she reluctantly agreed to take Maud on trial for a month, but at the brief interview Maud had to swallow hard when she faced Mrs Spearmann in the role of a penitent magdalen.

'Why cannot the grandparents of this baby help you, Miss Ling? Surely it is their duty?'

Maud bit her lip. 'I wouldn't go to them if they was the last people on earf, ma'am. They upset Alex by what they said abaht me, an' I want to be independent of 'em.'

'Well, I think they should at least be told about the baby and given a chance to make up their own minds. However, we will leave that for the moment. What kind of work will you be able to do in your condition?'

'Anyfing that needs doin', ma'am, sweepin', dustin', scrubbin', washin' an' lookin' after the children – I ain't afraid o' work.'

'And what about when you get larger and slower? How long to you expect to be useful?'

Maud drew herself up. 'I can't say exactly, ma'am, but I'll keep goin' as long as I can. Me midwife finks I got a good free monfs o' workin' time to go.'

'Your midwife being the excellent Nurse Court, I believe. Very well, I'll take you on for a month's trial, starting on Monday next. You will report at eight o'clock as a general domestic assistant at eight shillings a week.'

'Yes, ma'am. Fank yer. Good aft'noon.'

*   *   *

393

And so began 1918, with no prospect of peace on the horizon. The queues lengthened and food rationing was begun, first for sugar and then meat, bacon, butter and margarine. Prices remained high, but food was more equally distributed and Ruby's household benefited from the four ration cards that were issued to her. The news of the war on the Western Front grew worse as the spring advanced: in March a new major offensive was launched by the Germans and there were rumours of an invasion of Britain. Casualties continued to pour in and fresh battalions of young men were sent off to take their places; the British commander-in-chief tried to rally the nation with a speech about 'fighting with our backs to the wall', but in truth the fighting spirit had faded from hearts wrung by the sorrow of bereavement. Hardly a family in the land was untouched by the massacre of a generation, and one of Mabel's patients had lost her husband and three brothers; the desolate grandparents on both sides were scarcely cheered by the arrival of a little grandson, their only surviving male issue. Cycling round her district in the lengthening daylight, the young midwife was aware of a general weariness and melancholy that the spring sunshine and early daffodils could not lift.

Maud soon proved her worth at the Midway, vindicating Sister Norah's recommendation. Olive Spearmann had to admit that she was a hard worker, good with the children and liked by the staff. She was duly re-engaged for a further month and her wages were raised to ten shillings, which helped with her bus and tram fares. Nevertheless, she began to find the work more tiring, and Norah tried to help by giving her sewing jobs, cot sheets to hem and repairs to the children's clothes; Maud thankfully sat down in the nursery or playroom with her needle and cotton, keeping an eye on the little ones as she sewed. As time went by she was sometimes white with exhaustion, dragging her heavy body from one room to another, and when possible Norah would send her to lie down for an hour, summoning her quickly if Mrs Spearmann appeared. On arrival back at her lodgings in the evening, she was almost too tired to climb the stairs; Teddy would get supper for them both, but Maud was often unable to eat and simply collapsed into bed.

'I really don't think I can engage her for another month, Sister Norah,' said Mrs Spearmann, who had missed her own February period and had ominous digestive disturbances. 'She looks almost due to be confined.'

And she was proved right. Maud was supposed to be due in April, but on Friday the twenty-ninth of March, she awoke at half past five in a soaking wet bed. She tried to get up, but was seized by a pain in her back so sharp and intense that she could not move until it had somewhat subsided; then she eased herself slowly off the side of the bed and felt her way to the door. Opening it, she stepped out on to the landing and called up the stairs to the attic, 'Teddy! Can yer come dahn, Ted? *Teddy!*'

Her cry brought Mrs Hiscock from downstairs, panting as she tied her dressing-gown. 'What's up, Maud? 'Ave yer started?'

'Yeah, I fink so. Me waters've broke. Sorry.'

Teddy came running downstairs, rubbing the sleep out of his eyes. 'Did yer call, sis?'

Maud Ling's hour had come and she was in labour.

Chapter Twenty-two

'Come on, Maudie, breathe *hard* when yer get the pain, that's the way!'

'Gawd, Mabel, I'm goin' to die.'

'No, ye're not, ye're goin' to have a baby.' Mabel's tone was bright, but she could not shake off a feeling of disquiet. Maud's baby was in a 'back-to-front' position: its head was coming first but was facing the mother's front instead of her back, which made for a long, slow labour and possible obstruction if the head became jammed in the pelvis while rotating round as it descended. This was a potential danger to mother and child, requiring the use of the delivery forceps. A skilled obstetrician like Mr Poole had long practice in the use of instruments, but Mabel had no idea what experience Dr Swift had. She knew she would not be happy until Maud was delivered.

'I'm that glad that ye're wiv me, Mabel.'

Mabel hid her unease beneath a smile. After sending Teddy to the Midway with a note for Sister McLoughlin, she took the early precaution of sending him out again with a scribbled message to Dr Swift, to give him fair warning of what might lie ahead. She gave Maud an enema to clear her bowels, and got her to sit on the chamber-pot regularly to keep her bladder empty. Small drinks of tea, water and fruit cordial were given throughout the day as the hours went slowly by: midday, afternoon and evening. Maud bore the pains stoically, helped by doses of 'mother's mixture' and Mabel's constant attention; but twelve hours into labour, she began to lose heart and was not helped by a visit from Dr Swift who shook his head and said there was nothing to do but wait for nature to take its course.

'I have to attend a dinner for the Royal College of Physicians tonight,' he told Mabel grandly. 'She'll probably dilate up and be delivered by the time I get back, but leave a message at the surgery if you're worried. There's a GP standing in for me, but try not to bother him as he's getting on a bit. Nice old chap, but –'

Seeing the look on Mabel's face, he patted her shoulder. 'Remember that old Mother Nature knows her job better than we do, Nurse Court, and we have to be patient at this game. "Masterly inactivity", as my old tutor used to say!'

Mabel could have kicked him.

Day became night: eight o'clock – ten – midnight. Mabel told Mrs Hiscock to go to bed and Teddy was also despatched to his attic room. The contractions had become weaker and Mabel encouraged Maud to sleep in snatches if she could. Such pauses in a long labour were said by some midwives – and Dr Swift, obviously – to be nature's way of giving the mother a rest, but Mabel knew that without contractions the baby could not continue its journey; she also knew that if Mr Poole were here, he would be talking about sending the patient into hospital for a Caesar . . .

She laid her head on the bed and dozed while Maud slept fitfully, stirring and moaning at intervals. Two o'clock – four – six. Then, as dawn was breaking over a grey wartime London, Maud started up in bed with a cry.

'I got a feelin' dahn there, gal, as if I wanted to 'ave a good turn-aht on the lav,' she groaned. 'Elp me, Mabel, I don't want to make a great stink!'

Mabel rose at once. 'Don't worry, Maud, it's not yer bowels, it's the baby's head pressin' down. Come on, dear, put yer knees apart an' let me see –'

The cervix was indeed fully dilated, but to Mabel's dismay the baby's head was still high and its heartbeat was slowing. They were going to need help.

Teddy was sent to fetch Dr Swift, and Mrs Hiscock came bustling up to say she had plenty of hot water on her kitchen range. The minutes ticked by to half past six – twenty to seven.

Teddy returned to say that Dr Swift was out on another case, and that another GP had been telephoned and was on his way. Mabel's heart plummeted.

''Ow much longer d'ye reckon, Mabel?' asked Teddy, putting his head round the door.

'Not long now, Ted, just waitin' on the doctor.'

He rolled up his eyes, glancing at Maud who lay exhausted on the bed, her face mottled, her eyes blood-shot. 'I'm dyin', ain't I?' she muttered. 'Dyin' wiv me poor baby not born.'

Mabel bit on her knuckles as her courage faltered. Was Maud truly going to die with her child? Where the hell was that damned doctor?

Help us, Lord. Help me to help her. In thy mercy send us help quickly, Lord.

The doorbell rang again and Teddy went down to let in Norah McLoughlin, her nurse's cloak wrapped round her against the chill wind. She came into the room, her blue eyes wide.

'Mabel, darlin', how's she doin'?'

'*Norah*! How did *you* get here?'

'On me own two feet. I been tossin' an' turnin' all night, then I sez to meself, for God's sake get up an' go to 'em, wumman! So I've left Mrs Lovell in charge o' the Midway and here I am.'

Mabel began to speak in a low, rapid tone, able to express her fears at last. 'We're goin' to need help here, Norah. She'll never push it out herself, an' we're waitin' for some old relief doctor who should be here by now.' Lowering her voice still further she added, 'She thinks she's goin' to die.'

'Ah, ye're both tired out, God love ye.'

Norah sat down beside Maud. 'Listen, darlin', ye're not goin' to die at all. Ye've got yer friends to look after ye and Holy Mary's prayers to help ye. Hang on to me hand till the doctor comes.'

The Irish girl's fresh and hopeful presence was like a breath of cool air in the staleness of the room and, as Mabel felt her courage reviving, they heard the longed-for knock at the door. Mrs Hiscock flew down to let in the doctor who came up and entered the room, carrying his black Gladstone bag. And he was Dr Henry Knowles. Mabel could have wept with relief. He had aged since she had seen him last, though his delighted smile of recognition lit up his tired face.

'Mabel Court! I couldn't wish for a better nurse. And good morning, to you, my dear,' he said to Maud, touching her forehead and feeling her pulse as he took in her condition.

'Now, what have we here?'

'My friend Maud Ling, first baby, cervix fully dilated at least two hours, no progress in second stage,' replied Mabel at once. 'An' this is Sister McLoughlin, the one who's engaged to me brother Albert. She's come over to help.'

He smiled and nodded. 'Ah, yes, Maud Ling, of course I remember. Well, Maud, we're all here to help deliver your baby. Now, I'll just open my bag and get everything ready.'

His findings agreed with Mabel's and the atmosphere

in the room became one of purposeful activity. He put on a rubber apron, donned rubber gloves and spread a towel over a tray provided by Mrs Hiscock. He sent her for a bowl of hot water and took out another towel containing his instruments.

'First of all let's turn her round so that she's lying across the bed with her bottom right at the edge and her legs raised. Sister McLoughlin, will you take her left leg and Mrs – er – the right one, thank you. Let's put this pail down on the floor and I'll sit on this chair, facing her – so.'

With a pillow under her head and her legs raised aloft, Maud had the curious sensation of reliving the night when this child had been conceived: when Alex had hoisted up her legs and pulled them over his shoulders. She could hear the doctor talking in a low voice to Mabel.

'Stephen assures me that you're capable of administering this, just while I do the necessary. The spray nozzle goes on the bottle like this, you see, and –'

'Yes, yes, I know, doctor, I can do it,' whispered Mabel. 'And is there a pad or something?'

'Yes, a square of cotton wool between muslin. Would you like me to start it?'

'No, no, you get on with yer job, doctor, I can see to this.'

She got on to the bed behind Maud. 'Maudie, dear, I'm puttin' this soft piece o' muslin over yer nose an' mouth like this, see, don't worry, I'm here with yer, just keep on breathin' in an' out, in an' out – ye'll smell this stuff, don't worry, just go on breathin' in an' out – good girl!'

The light spray began to fall upon the pad, filling the room with its odour. Maud screwed her eyes tightly shut and put her trust in Mabel, resisting the urge to struggle. The vapour penetrated her air passages as she breathed in and out, and the sounds and voices faded away as she drifted into the merciful oblivion of chloroform.

'All right, Mabel?'

'Yes, Dr Knowles, she's away.'

He took scissors and made a long cut in the vaginal entrance at the back, extending it out to one side. Picking up one of the long-handled forceps blades, he passed it up beside the baby's head; then he took the other blade and passed it up on the opposite side, so that the two blades closed together, clicking into position and forming a protective cage around the head.

'Say a prayer for her and for me, Mabel,' he said very quietly to his emergency anaesthetist.

'May the Lord guide yer hands, Dr Knowles.'

And then the pull. The pull and the pull and the pull and the pull. Mabel dropped her chloroform bottle and pad, to grip Maud under her shoulders to prevent her from being pulled right off the bed, while a horrified Mrs Hiscock and breathless Norah held on to the legs.

'Coming now,' gasped Knowles. 'Coming, coming – chin, mouth, nose, eyes – ah!' The head was born. Knowles dropped the forceps into the pail and guided the shoulders as they rotated. One arm was freed, then the other, and the rest of the body followed at once. A son was born to Maud Ling at twenty minutes past seven on Saturday morning, the thirtieth of March 1918. It was Mabel's own twenty-fourth birthday.

Knowles clamped and cut the umbilical cord, and handed the limp, bluish-white baby to Mabel. The expulsion of the afterbirth was followed by a great gush of blood.

'You see to the infant, Mabel, I'll deal with the mother.'

They were faced with two dreaded, life-threatening emergencies: a flat, lifeless baby and a post-partum haemorrhage.

Mabel judged the baby to be between seven and eight pounds. He had a livid purple weal over one side of his face from the forceps blade and his head was elongated by the pressure it had sustained on its long, slow journey. He was a pathetic sight. Mabel laid him on a towel spread over the other side of the bed. She placed a thin rubber tube into his mouth and throat, sucking at the other end of it, to remove obstructive fluid and mucus. She blew upon his chest two or three times and felt for his heartbeat with a forefinger: she was not sure that it was there. Laying him flat on his back, she let his head fall back over her hand, extending his neck, and then put her open mouth right over his tiny nose and mouth. She blew gently into his lungs, once, twice, three times.

She saw him give a gasp. His chest jerked. He gasped again, his nostrils flaring. He gave a weak grunt and then another. He jerked again, his little arms and legs flexing convulsively. He gave another grunt, bunching his tiny fists as if fighting; he arched his back, his chest heaved, and air was sucked in through his open mouth and nostrils. The blue skin turned to white and then to dusky pink. Mabel felt for his heartbeat again and there it was, pit-a-pat-pit-a-pit-pat-a, the beginning of a lifetime of beating. He lived and breathed!

She looked up. Dr Knowles was concentrating his whole attention on arresting the bleeding. 'Get her further back on to the bed,' he told his two assistants. 'And keep her legs raised.'

He clenched his left hand into a fist and thrust it into the vagina. He put his right hand on the abdomen, compressing the slack womb between his hands for a full minute. When he withdrew his fist, a thin stream of blood trickled forth.

'A pack, I'll need a pack,' he said. 'Open my bag and take out the big roll of gauze and the packing forceps. Bring her legs down – slowly! – and keep them far enough apart for me to put in a pack.'

Norah produced the pair of long, round-ended forceps that he used to push the whole length of gauze into the vagina, inch by inch, foot by foot, yard by yard until it was all used up.

Maud stirred and a faint tinge of colour returned to her face as she uttered one word 'Alex'.

'Ye've got a little boy, Maud,' whispered Mabel.

'Alex,' said the mother again.

Knowles looked up, his face grey with the effort he had made. 'How is he, Mabel?'

'Alive an' breathin', Dr Knowles,' and as if in confirmation a tiny, mewing cry was heard from the towel-wrapped bundle in her arms. She and Norah exchanged a look of mute thankfulness, and Mrs Hiscock blinked and sniffed.

It was the landlady who saw the doctor sway and she grabbed hold of him, her stout arms round his waist; Norah helped her to heave him on to the bed beside his patient. His skin was pallid and sweating, and he scarcely appeared to be breathing. Norah felt for his pulse and for one unspeakable moment they thought he was dead. Norah quickly loosened his clothing, unbuttoned his shirt and put her hand on his chest. The heartbeat was there, but weak and rapid, and his breathing was shallow.

'We need an ambulance,' said Norah. 'Can Teddy run down to the police station and ask them to telephone for one?'

Teddy was called and sent out straight away on his

errand. Mabel told him to ask for a police message to be sent to Dr Stephen Knowles at the East London Hospital.

By midday the old doctor lay in the London Hospital in Whitechapel Road and Maud Ling, refused admission at the General Lying-In Hospital, was in Women's II at the Booth Street Poor Law Infirmary. Baby Alexander Ling was installed in Sister McLoughlin's own room at the Midway Babies' Home and Mabel Court lay asleep at number 3 Deacon's Walk; Matthew and Mark were warned by their mother not to disturb her on any account.

It was five o'clock and Ruby Swayne crept into Mabel's room. 'Mabel – Mabel! I'm sorry to wake yer, but there's a visitor for yer an' I think ye'll want to hear his news,' she apologised as Mabel started up, her eyes unfocused.

'Who? Who is it?'

'It's young Dr Knowles, yer know, the son. He's been to see his father. I've put him in the front parlour.'

'Oh. Oh, yes. I – I'd better see him.' Mabel started to get out of bed. 'Better put me uniform on – an' Ruby, please stay in the parlour with us, will yer?'

Stephen rose as the two women entered; Mabel sat down and Ruby stood rather awkwardly beside her.

'Mabel, my dear – Miss Court – I've just come from seeing my father and I thought you'd like to know that he's going to be all right.'

'Thanks be to God.' She closed her eyes briefly. Even after all that had happened in the last thirty-six hours, the sight of the man and the sound of his voice made her heart leap.

'Yes, I think there's every reason to hope that he'll recover from this heart seizure and at least it means he'll have to retire now. He's been working much too hard for a man of nearly seventy.' Stephen clasped his hands behind his back as he continued, 'He sends you his – his love, and says he couldn't have managed without you.'

'And I was never so thankful to see anybody in my life as I was when he arrived this morning,' she answered. 'Maudie would've died with her child unborn, most likely, and if – oh, my God!' She suddenly covered her face with her hands. 'I thought we were goin' to have three deaths in that room this mornin'!'

Ruby put an arm round her shoulders as she relived the nightmare. 'An' then the General Lyin'-In wouldn't take Maud 'cause she was already delivered, so she had to go to Booth Street an' hasn't even got the baby with her – he's at the Midway.'

'Yes, and that's all for the best,' he said gently. 'His mother won't be able to care for him for some time. I've been to see her, too.'

'Ye've seen Maud?' She stared at him.

'Yes, after seeing my father. I thought you'd want to know how she is and I'm afraid it's not good news, Mabel. She's running a high fever and there's bound to be infection after all that internal handling. Now, I believe the baby has grandparents, Mabel, the father's people. Can you tell me their name and where they – do they know?'

Mabel was at once defensive. 'No! They're not to be told anything at all,' she said, colouring. 'She has nothin' to do with 'em – and they're nothin' to do with her!'

There was no mistaking her strength of feeling. Glancing at Ruby, Stephen attempted to calm her. 'All right, my dear, don't be upset, I wouldn't do anything against your wishes. But we have to face facts, Mabel. If the girl should succumb – forgive me, but puerperal fever is a killer – the grandparents surely have a right – the *child* has a right to some sort of family life?'

'No! Wait an' see how Maud goes on, an' when she's well enough, she can be asked – an' she won't agree!' retorted Mabel, refusing even to admit the possibility that Maud might yet die. 'The baby's in good hands with Sister McLoughlin, an' he's not to be taken away from her!'

Knowles was somewhat taken aback. 'Very well, Mabel. As I said, I'd never go against your wishes.'

'It's Maud's wishes, not mine. And what about *your* baby, Dr Knowles?' she asked suddenly. 'I was pleased to hear from Nurse Marriner that *she's* got some sort o' family life!'

He flushed. 'Yes, Mabel, I'm deeply attached to Lily now that I've seen her and held her. She'll be staying with her mother and grandparents until after the war, and then I hope to be a proper father to her.' He glanced at Mrs Swayne again, and Mabel also turned and caught her eye with a look that said, *stay*.

Knowles cleared his throat. 'I'm more sorry than I can say that you left Shadwell.'

'There's no need to be, Dr Knowles. I've settled down very well in Kennington with Harry's sister, and I was there for Maud and her baby. I have no regrets at all.'

'How long do you intend to stay here?' he enquired.

'Like you at the East London, everythin's got to wait till after the war. I'm takin' Harry to Belhampton soon for a breath o' country air, but I can't leave London while Maud's poorly.'

She rose from the chair and smiled for the first time. 'Thank yer for comin' to tell me about Maud an' yer father. I'm very glad he's better and please remember me to him when yer see him again.'

She offered him her cool fingers to touch, and Ruby

406

Swayne saw him out. When she returned, she reminded Mabel that they were invited to tea at Falcon Terrace.

'Oh, Ruby, not tonight!' Mabel groaned, putting her hand to her forehead. 'All I want is to go back to bed with a cup o' tea an' a couple of aspirins. Me head's killin' me.'

'But Mabel, Harry's expectin' yer! He's got a present for yer birthday – yer hadn't forgotten, had yer?'

Stephen's prediction of puerperal fever proved only too true. For two weeks Maud lay barely conscious in a screened-off corner of Women's II, sweating and burning as the fulminating infection of her pelvis destroyed her fertility and came near to claiming her life. The organisms in her bloodstream carried the poisons to every part of her body, erupting in boils and septic spots. Her flesh wasted away, her bright hazel eyes sank deeply into their sockets and her hair fell out in handfuls. Mr Poole shook his head at her bedside and nobody expected her to live.

'They said she'd had a baby,' muttered one nurse to another as they changed her sheets and foul-smelling pads. 'Some baby! Anybody can see she's had an abortion an' it's gone septic.'

And this was the opinion of the patients near to the corner bed. 'No business to be in 'ere wiv 'er dirty diseases,' they muttered. 'Bloody disgrace, puttin' 'er along o' respectable wimmin.'

Even Matron Brewer failed to recognise the vivacious music hall star who had entertained in this very ward more than two years earlier. However, the new Ward Sister of Women's II, Ethel Davies, was alerted when she received enquiries about Miss Ling from her former colleague Nurse Court, the district nurse who had sent the girl in. She spoke to Maud's young brother when he visited and mentioned her discovery to Matron.

'Of course I remember the pantomime and Prince Charming,' recalled Matron, 'but surely this poor creature can't possibly be –?'

'She *is* the same one, Matron,' insisted Sister Davies and from then on she took a special interest in this patient who clung so stubbornly to life. She fed her drinks of milk and the sweetened, slightly salted barley water which had proved beneficial when no other form of nourishment could be tolerated. Teddy began to look more hopeful, and reported on his sister's progress to Mabel and Norah who could not visit such a highly infectious case.

Then came the day when Maud's temperature dropped, and she opened her eyes and asked for her baby. 'Where is 'e?' she wanted to know. 'I wanna see 'im. Will somebody take me to see my baby?'

In another couple of days she got out of bed and shuffled down the ward. Mabel was allowed to see her, and could hardly control her emotion at seeing her friend so gaunt and emaciated. Against all expectations Maud had pulled through, and the question now was where would she go when she was discharged?

Teddy and Mrs Hiscock wanted her back at South Lambeth Road, but Norah flatly refused to let baby Alex go there.

'Sure an' she's nowhere near fit to look after him round the clock, Mabel. I'm keepin' him wid me at the Midway till she's a lot stronger than she is now.'

'But she's pinin' for her baby,' Mabel pointed out. 'Can't she come to the Midway just one afternoon to see him an' give him his bottle?'

And by arrangement with a sympathetic Matron Brewer and Dr Henry Knowles, now recovered and retired, Maud was taken by the old doctor in his car to be introduced to her son, who was five weeks old. She held out her thin arms for him and gazed in wonder. 'Alex,' she whispered. 'I got me little Alex to remember 'im by.' She kissed his downy head reverently while Norah fluttered anxiously over them.

'Ye can come an' see him, Maud, ye can give him his bottle, but ye can't take him away wid ye,' she said firmly, inwardly shuddering at the thought of this precious baby cooped up in Maud's dingy, airless room.

A pattern of weekly visits to the Midway became established, but Mrs Spearmann, now three months pregnant, pursed her lips at the sight of the gaunt, hollow-eyed woman sitting with her baby among the other children, an incongruously saucy straw hat pulled over her hairless head. And the most annoying part was that this baby had no need to take up room in the hard-pressed, overcrowded home. 'If we get any more admissions, that baby will have to go, Sister Norah.'

At last Mabel was free to spend a few days at Belhampton, though Harry's mother was very doubtful whether he would be able to stand the train journey and change of routine. A taxicab was ordered to take him and Mabel to Waterloo Station, and a friendly porter assisted them with the wheelchair and their luggage. He found the journey tiring and when they arrived at the country station Aunt Elinor had to hide her shock at his appearance.

'We've got the three-wheeler outside, with old Shadow,' she said. 'We got rid of the car, because Thomas won't ever drive again.'

'How is he, Aunt Nell?' Mabel asked when the three of them were settled behind the shafts.

Elinor flicked the reins and the old horse moved off. 'Not so well, I'm afraid. He gets very breathless and can't walk far without having to stop and rest. But we're all so happy to be seeing you both again at last, Mabel – and dear Harry!'

The fifteen-minute drive took them between lush green fields, the trees freshly decked in tender new foliage. Mabel exclaimed at the riot of wayside flowers, the lacy meadowsweet and purple loosestrife that grew in abundance at the side of the lane. 'It's just like heaven to be here again after so long.' She sighed. 'Isn't it, Harry?'

But he had eyes only for her and indeed, he took up most of her time on this visit. They both stayed at Pear Tree Cottage on this occasion, Pinehurst being too full of war wounded for a man needing peace and tranquillity. He needed more help with dressing, washing and feeding, and very quickly tired when Mabel took him out in the chair. Guiltily she began to realise how much Doris Drover had to do for him each day and understood why she had been doubtful about him going on holiday.

However, there was one happy surprise: her sister Daisy at fourteen was no longer the child she had been on Mabel's last visit and was willing to give all the help she could with the two invalids, for Uncle Thomas was only a shadow of his former genial self. She even confessed to writing that self-pitying letter to Norah.

'I told her I thought you didn't care about your family any more because you hadn't been to see us for so long and your letters were so short – and she wrote back and told me about your life at the children's hospital and that dreadful bomb on the school – and now Harry – oh, poor, dear Harry – oh, Mabel, I'm sorry, I'm sorry!' And Daisy burst into tears.

410

'Don't think about it any more, dear. We're together again an' that's all that matters,' Mabel whispered as they clung to each other, all restraints dissolved in an uprush of sisterly love.

But Mabel's relationship with her other sister was very different.

'We'll go over to see the Westhouses on Monday, Mabel,' Daisy announced. 'Aunt Nell says she'll look after Harry for the afternoon, because she doesn't like leaving Uncle Thomas. In fact, we don't see much of Alice or baby Geoffrey and she only tells us what she wants us to hear. He drinks, you know,' she added conversationally.

'What, Gerald, d'ye mean?' asked Mabel in dismay. 'How bad is he?'

'Nobody actually says so, but we all know he does.'

As it turned out, Mabel was thankful for her little nephew, now nearly a year old, to fuss over and play with in the uncomfortable atmosphere of the Westhouse home. Alice's manner was polite but guarded, and there was clearly tension between herself and Mrs Westhouse senior.

Gerald greeted Mabel with apparent joviality, holding out his hand. He wore an eyepatch and the right side of his face had healed but was, of course, badly scarred.

'Delighted to see you again, my dear Mabel! I've always thought you an absolutely splendid girl, and so did poor Alex Redfern – bad job about him, eh? D'you see anything of that little actress he was so keen on?'

Fortunately he did not seem to expect a detailed answer and Mabel simply said that Maud Ling had been deeply grieved by Alex's death.

'Yeah, I seem to be the only one of the old gang left and I'm no more good.' He gave a mirthless bark and nodded towards young Geoffrey on the carpet by her

411

feet. 'What d'you think of our son and heir, Mabel? Grand little chap, what? Eats like a wolf cub and grows like a little savage! Doesn't he, Alice?'

Mabel caught that word *savage* and did not dare meet Alice's eye. By the time the visit was over she was convinced of two things: first, that while Gerald was not actually drunk, he was one of those constant tipplers who were seldom completely sober. And second, she was sure that he knew that the delightful fair-haired toddler was not his own.

She managed to seize a few moments alone with Alice in the garden before she and Daisy took their leave.

'Are yer keepin' well, dear? Are yer all right?' she asked, her grey-blue eyes anxiously scanning her sister's face.

'Yes, Mabel, we're very well, as you can see,' came the cool reply. 'Though things will be even better when we have a home of our own. It's not ideal to live with one's in-laws.'

'No, I shouldn't think it is,' replied Mabel with feeling. 'Has Gerald – have yer got any plans for movin'? There's no reason why yer shouldn't, is there?'

Alice replied lightly, 'When Uncle Thomas goes, I know that Aunt Kate intends to move in with Aunt Elinor – when this damned war is over and Pinehurst is empty, that is. And then Gerald and Geoffrey and I will move into it. It will be ideal for us.'

'Oh.' Mabel stared in surprise. 'Has Aunt Kate said as much?'

'Not in so many words, but of course she'll be very glad of a buyer in the family. Gerald can offer the full market price for it.'

'Well, I'm sure we all want Uncle Thomas to live for many more years to come,' said Mabel a little reproachfully. She said no more, for she sensed a deep discontent in her sister's life and felt sorry for them all.

No further invitation came from the Westhouses and Aunt Nell did not seem surprised.

'Alice has a difficult path to tread,' she said diplomatically. 'And Gerald does seem genuinely fond of little Geoffrey. We can only hope that things will be better for them after the war.'

For the rest of the week Mabel spent most of her time with Harry. At the back of Pear Tree Cottage there was a hawthorn hedge beyond which lay a meadow where sheep grazed. A gate opened into it from the garden and it was to this sheltered spot that Mabel took him for a few hours each day. Blankets, books and little picnics were carried out to the hidden haven where, safe from intrusion, they rediscovered something of the happiness of their early courting days. The weather was fine and warm, and on their last evening there was a glorious sunset over Wychell Forest.

He put his arm round her shoulder and she let her head rest lightly on his chest. He smiled into her eyes and although he said nothing – for he seldom spoke now – she knew that he was giving thanks for the love they had shared over eight years. Nothing on earth could ever take it away from them and in the silence of evening there was peace in their hearts.

Before the end of the week, Aunt Kate took Mabel aside and questioned her about her plans for the future, what she intended to do after the war. 'Of course I realise that your work on the district is convenient for you at present, Mabel, being able to visit Harry quite often, and he has to be your first consideration,' she said. 'But I wonder if you still hope to run a children's refuge one day?'

Mabel admitted that she still clung to her dream, but in her present circumstances she could not possibly make any plans; her work as Kennington midwife was rewarding and likely to continue for the foreseeable future. Miss Chalcott smiled and kept her own counsel, but when she and Mrs Somerton had seen Mabel and Harry off on the London train, she remarked to her sister that they would not see poor Captain Drover again.

'Mabel will live a single life as I have done, Elinor, but I believe that she will put it to good use,' she said. 'And she'll be happier than Alice in the long run, you mark my words.'

When Harry and his wheelchair had been safely deposited at number 8 Falcon Terrace, Mabel got a bus to Kennington Road and carried her suitcase from the bus stop to Deacon's Walk. Already her mind was occupied with what had been happening on her district while she had been away, which mothers had been delivered and which were still awaiting her.

Ruby greeted her fondly, but pointed straight away to a note on the mantelpiece with Mabel's name scrawled across it. It had arrived the day before, Ruby said, and was from Sister McLoughlin. With a sense of foreboding Mabel tore it open.

'For the love of God come as soon as you can, Mabel,' she read. 'Alex has been taken away and I cannot tell Maud. Please help me. Norah.'

Mabel's hand flew to her throat: the Redferns!

Chapter Twenty-three

'Norah, Norah, what happened? Was it the Redferns? When did they come? Who told them? Was it Stephen Knowles?'

If Mabel was distracted by the news of the Ling baby's disappearance, Norah McLoughlin was completely distraught. Never before had Mabel seen the quiet Irish girl in such a tearful, emotional state.

'This mornin', this very mornin', it was – one o' the nursery girls comes runnin' to me to say this man an' wumman are at the door all dressed in black like a pair o' crows, an' they're tellin' her they want to see baby Redfern. "But we haven't got a Redfern," she says, an' they say maybe the child's called Ling, an' then – an' then they push past her an' start openin' doors till they get to the nursery – oh, Mabel, I was out o' me office like a bat out o' hell – an' there they are bendin' over the little darlin' fella, an' she's sayin', "That's him! That's our son's child!" An' then she grabs him up an' runs away wid him, out o' the door and across the yard – I try to foller, but the man bars me way until she's out o' sight – an' then he's off after her, an' there's a big car waitin' outside – an' meself shriekin' like a banshee, an' Mrs Lovell cryin' – oh, Mrs Spearmann, what am I goin' to do? How can I tell Maud I've let her baby go?'

Olive Spearmann, summoned from Maybury Place on a Saturday afternoon, had appeared on the scene looking both annoyed and anxious. Now four months pregnant, she was feeling the strains of being a philanthropist, a wife to an alleged war profiteer, a mother with a household to run, and any number of other people's problems to deal with, and all without any thanks or appreciation. And now here was Sister Norah having hysterics and Nurse Court furiously angry.

'Who told the Redferns, Mrs Spearmann?' Mabel demanded as if they had changed places in the social scheme of things. 'Was it Dr Knowles – the younger one, I mean? I can't think that his father would do such a cruel thing. Tell me!'

'Kindly do not adopt that tone with me, Nurse Court. I'm not accountable to you for my actions,' retorted the lady, though her colour deepened and she did not meet Mabel's eyes.

'No, but ye're accountable to poor Maud Ling who nearly died havin' that child, and now he's all she's got left in the world.' Mabel raised her voice in accusation. 'Who told the Redferns?'

There was a moment of quivering silence, broken by the babble of children upset by the loud altercation going on.

Then Mrs Spearmann burst out defensively, 'Oh, for heaven's sake, the grandparents had a perfect right to know about their son's child! They can give him a good home and a proper upbringing. How was I to know that they'd come straight here and take the child without any discussion or permission? Don't forget they've lost *their* son, and it seems that their other son has had to go to the war, so they could lose him too. They must be frantic. And doesn't this just show the strength of their feelings? I still say that –'

Even in her anger Mabel felt a measure of relief that it had not been Stephen who had betrayed Maud. 'How *could* yer?' she cried. 'Takin' away the one thing she's got left in life – it'll kill her, that's what it'll do when she hears this – it'll *kill* her!'

Olive Spearmann suddenly collapsed in tears. 'I did it for the best!' she sobbed, her plump shoulders heaving. 'It would have had to come out one day, sooner or later. That girl should be thankful that her child's got grandparents with a decent home – he'll have everything money can buy – he'll be so much better off than the poor, unwanted babies we've got here. I'm tired of being blamed for doing my best for everybody!'

Mabel was beginning to see an awful inevitability in what was happening. Mrs Spearmann was right: there was no way that this could have been prevented. At some point the bereaved Redferns would have discovered that they had a grandchild. A single, penniless cockney girl could never challenge a wealthy, influential couple who were able to call upon the support of friends in the right places to back their right to the boy. Maud's only hope now was that in claiming him they would acknowledge her as his mother and allow her to visit him.

'Very well, Mrs Spearmann, I'll have to go and tell her, then. An' I'll get in touch with Dr Knowles as well. He delivered her and knows her circumstances. I'll see yer later, Norah.'

At the lodging house Mabel rang Mrs Hiscock's bell.

'I've come to see Maud. Is she in?'

'Yes, Nurse Court, come in. What's up?'

'Is Teddy in?' asked Mabel.

'No, he's down at the newspaper office. He'll be in early today, bein' Sat'day.'

'The sooner the better, 'cause I've got very bad news for Maud. Will yer put the kettle on?'

'Yeah, an' I'll get the brandy out, an' all, Nurse Court. Is it about the baby?'

'Yes. I'll go on up, then.'

She found Maud resting on the bed in which her son had been conceived and born. Her hair was beginning to grow again and she was putting on a little flesh, but remained a shadow of her former self. Her hollow eyes widened at the sight of her friend.

'Why, 'ello, Mabel, gal! 'Ow was yer 'oliday?'

'Lovely, thanks, Maudie.' Mabel heard her voice shake slightly and her heart twisted within her at the thought of what she was about to inflict on her oldest friend; her hands were clasped together so tightly that the knuckles whitened.

Maud raised herself up on one elbow. 'Hey, what's up, then, gal? Yer look as if ye've 'ad a kick in the teeth. What's 'appened? Is it 'Arry?' She looked into Mabel's face and her voice took on a note of fear. '*What's 'appened to Alex?*'

'Maudie, me poor friend – he's gone to the Redferns.'

The low moan that escaped Maud's throat was the most despairing of sounds. She fell back on the pillow, too weak to rail against fate.

'Yes, I can see what yer mean, Mabel, it's a tragedy for her, isn't it – on top o' losin' her young man an' all.' Ruby Swayne had listened in sympathy to Mabel's account of Maud's loss, but like everybody else who knew of it, from old Dr Knowles to Mrs Spearmann, she had to point out that baby Alex's best interests would probably be served by being adopted by his grandparents and brought up by them in a comfortable home. He would go to a good school and be given every opportunity in life; and now that Olive Spearmann had personally approached the Redferns and obtained an assurance that the child's mother would be allowed to visit him once a week, there seemed to be no real objection. Even Norah had agreed that it was a good compromise and best for little Alexander, as his doting grandparents called him.

'Has the poor girl got a job yet?' asked Ruby.

'No, she's not fit to go back to *Chu Chin Chow*. She could do with somethin' to earn a little money, and there's plenty o' places in service – but she's got no interest in anythin', poor Maudie. Oh, poor Maudie!'

'What about helpin' in a Salvation Army Women's Shelter, then?' suggested Ruby. 'We're always wantin' suitable assistants an' some of our girls are in the same sort o' trouble as Maud. Would yer like me to talk to her, Mabel?'

'That's good o' yer, Ruby – yes, if ye'd put it to her, it'd be up to her to take it or leave it. It'd tide her over until she was better an' able to move on. An' she could visit Alex once a week without havin' to go on her knees to beg for the time off. Yes, Ruby, the more I think about it, the more it seems like a good idea.'

'Good. I'll go round to South Lambeth Road and have a word with her, then. Don't worry, I'll be very careful with the poor girl.'

The sunny garden behind Elmgrove was a picture on a June afternoon, with the rose bushes in bloom and the trellises covered with dainty pink climbers. The big perambulator had been put out on the lawn under the watchful eyes of Nanny and Grandmother who sat together on a cushioned garden seat nearby. Maud Ling was a separate, solitary figure who walked to and fro across the grass, stopping every so often to gaze hungrily at the sleeping baby. He was now two months old, a fine, healthy child, and under the intensity of his mother's longing gaze he stirred, woke and gave a little cry. She leaned over him as if to pick him up and soothe him, but both the watchers rose at once to prevent her.

'Can't I give 'im 'is bottle, Mrs Redfern – ma'am?' she begged.

'He was fed at two,' replied Nanny firmly. 'He's not due again until six.'

'Can't I see if 'e needs changin'? If 'e's got wind? I used to be good at bringin' up the wind for them poor babies at the Midway 'Ome.'

Mrs Redfern shuddered at the very mention of that awful makeshift place where this dear child had spent the first six weeks of his life. 'Mr Redfern and I agreed to Mrs Spearmann's request that you be allowed to visit Alexander once a week, Ling, but you have to observe Nanny's rules,' she said icily. 'She has full charge of him and he is not to be handled without her express permission. Otherwise the concession will have to be withdrawn.'

The Maud of earlier days would have protested loudly, but now she stood still in mute submission while inside her head she heard herself yelling for the right to hold her son.

I'm 'is muvver – I'm 'is MUVVER – Alex loved me an' gave 'im to me – to ME, not this ol' cow of a Nanny – 'e's mine, 'e's mine, 'e's MINE!

But these were silent screams and only the trembling of the brown straw hat perched on the newly growing hair betrayed the inward agony, the desperation beneath the surface.

A housemaid appeared with a tray of tea for three and a plate of buttered scones. She set it down on a small table and Mrs Redfern proceeded to pour out three cups. She handed one to the Nanny and one to the maid to take to Maud.

'Put Ling's cup on that chair over there,' she ordered. 'She's to sit down to drink it.'

Maud stood with clasped hands looking down upon her lovely child in his pram. Everything that money could buy, that's what that Spearmann woman had said. The contrast between the handsome villa in St John's Wood and the cheap Lambeth lodging house was plain enough for anybody to see, and not even the stricken mother could deny it. And there was no doubt of the grandparents' love for Alex's son.

She couldn't go on with this miserable farce. The decision had to be made. Again she leaned over the pram and looked down at the baby, yearning over him with all her heart.

Goodbye, my dear little son, my Alex – goodbye, my only happiness.

Having made the silent farewell, Maud wrenched herself away. Slowly she left the pram and somehow made her way across the grass towards the side gate that led round to the front of the house and Hamilton Terrace.

The old Maud would have picked up the cup of tea and flung it in the faces of the pair who sat silently watching her go; but with her spirit now broken, she crept away without a word.

'There's some post come for yer, Mabel,' said Ruby. 'One o' them brown typewritten envelopes, more stuff from the LCC, I expect. Nothin' from Albert, I'm afraid,' she added, seeing the sudden light in Mabel's eyes, which quickly vanished.

It was not until after her evening visits that Mabel got round to opening the large, official-looking envelope that had been addressed to her at the Booth Street Poor Law Infirmary. Matron Brewer had sent it to the

Lambeth Borough Council, Maud's present employers, and it had been sent on to number 3 Deacon's Walk. At first she could not make head or tail of the contents. There was a folded document printed on thick, creamy vellum paper and an accompanying letter with the heading Jestico & Fox, High Street, Egham, Surrey. She spread the papers out on the table she used for writing up her register of cases and began to read the letter, which seemed to be about matters unrelated to her; she had never heard of Jestico & Fox and had never been to Egham.

'Dear Miss Court,' the letter began.

> As the trustees of the estate of Prudence Mary Lawton, late of 3 Ferryside Gardens, Egham, Surrey, we beg to inform you that following her death on the twenty-seventh of May, 1918 . . . we respectfully draw your attention to the enclosed copy of the Last Will and Testament of the said Prudence Mary Lawton . . . dated fifteenth July 1916 . . . in which you are named as the chief beneficiary thereof . . . we would be greatly obliged if you will contact our offices . . .

Mabel found it difficult to follow the jargon and the circuitous approach of solicitors. Her head swam as she took in the fact that Prudence Lawton, her grandmother, her father's mother, was dead. As Mrs Mimi Court she had practised as a midwife in Tooting for years, but it was her undercover activities as abortionist to the gentry which had built up her fortune and finally brought about her downfall and disappearance in 1913.

And now she was dead, having parted in bitterness from Mabel, disgraced and friendless. She had offered Mabel a home with her and to pay for her nursing training at one of the voluntary teaching hospitals, but Mabel had retorted that she would not touch Mimi's money with a bargepole, knowing how it had been made. Her grandmother had then sworn not to leave her a penny and had never contacted her again. Yet now here was this peculiar letter telling her that Mimi had bequeathed her the money after all.

Three thousand pounds, it said, £3000. The words and the figures were printed there before her, as meaningless as if in a foreign language. Mabel could not imagine such an amount of money, she who now earned £150 per annum, plus an allowance for her lodgings and uniform.

Suddenly she pushed away the papers and pictured her grandmother who had gone without a word of farewell or forgiveness, who had died in some strange place without Mabel's knowledge. Who had attended the funeral? Who had followed the lonely coffin? Mabel guessed that Mimi's dour-faced personal maid Elsie would be the other beneficiary, having endured her mistress's scolding ill humour ever since she had been taken from an orphanage to be trained as Mimi's assistant in her secret work. In spite of everything the maid had always remained stubbornly loyal.

And now three thousand pounds were waiting for Mabel in the London and Provincial Bank. It just didn't make sense. Mabel had never entered a bank in her life and could not take in what this meant. She needed to talk to somebody. If only Albert were here to advise her!

Albert. How long had it been since his last brief visit? A whole year. What would she give to see his face again, to hear his good-natured teasing! How Norah must yearn for the day!

For the time being Mabel decided to tell nobody. She

needed time. There was much that could be done with the money, for instance, Maud could be helped – but Maud was at present living at the Salvation Army's Women's Shelter in Victoria Street, working among fallen women, and finding some consolation in giving and receiving care. There were some things that money could not buy . . .

No. She would consult Albert at least by sending a letter that he might or might not receive, and wait for his reply that might or might not arrive.

Sister Norah's July birthday brought a totally unexpected surprise. A delivery van arrived from Arding & Hobbs's department store in Battersea and a big package was carried into the Midway, which when unwrapped turned out to be a *gramophone*, a splendidly constructed oakwood box with a detachable horn to augment the sound and a handle to wind it up. Several small boxes of needles were included and half a dozen gramophone records to start a collection. It was directed to Sister Norah McLoughlin of the Midway Babies' Home, Newington, and the sender was Able Seaman A. E. Court on board the SS *Galway Castle*. Heaven only knew what methods he had used to order and pay for this wonderful object, but here it was, in time for Norah's twenty-third birthday. She was completely overwhelmed.

'Did ye ever see the like of it, Mabel? An' the records, look here, "The Teddy Bears' Picnic" for the children, an' "You Made Me Love You" – an' this one, here, wait now while I show ye, look – "Let the Great Big World Keep Turnin'" – he's already mentioned that song in a letter, an' copied out the words for me, 'cause he said it was exactly what he wanted to say. Oh, Mabel, isn't it grand? Isn't he the best o' men? Aren't I the luckiest o' girls?'

Mrs Spearmann, looking flushed and rather bloated at six months, arrived at three o'clock with an iced cake, a tin of biscuits and half a dozen small jars of meat and fish paste to make sandwiches for a special birthday tea. She also brought news of Mrs Ada Hodges who had formed a War Widows' Association.

'It's the best thing that's happened to that poor woman since the birth of little Anne,' she said, sinking down on to a bench seat in the yard and discreetly mopping her face with a handkerchief. 'She holds the meetings at her home in Rectory Grove and the only problem is lack of space. I suggested that she might hire a church hall for one afternoon each week, but she said it wouldn't have the same welcoming atmosphere as her drawing-room.'

The lady sighed and looked almost furtively towards Mabel whose features were expressionless. 'Er – how is your poor friend getting on, er – Mabel? I understand that she no longer visits at Elmgrove and perhaps that's for the best, really. She knows that her son is getting all the care and attention that – er –'

The utter blankness of Mabel's face caused Olive Spearmann's conventional words to peter out into an awkward silence. Eventually Mabel's sense of fairness overcame her resentment and she told herself it was time to stop blaming this woman for Maud's situation.

'She's workin' in a women's shelter. It's not the first time that Maud's turned to the Salvation Army for help in time o' trouble,' she said briefly. 'And I'm very pleased to hear about Ada, though I reckon she's goin' to need that church hall, and a big one at that – there'll be so many of 'em – widows, I mean.'

'Now, then, we're goin' to bring out the gramophone an' dance!' said Sister Norah gaily. 'First we'll put on "The Teddy Bears' Picnic" an' we'll all join hands in a ring – come on, darlin's, hold handies! Mabel! Mrs Lovell! Where are the rest o' the girls? Come on, let's have a big, big circle – everybody's to join in!'

Squeals of delight filled the air; little legs tottered forward and little star-shaped hands reached out as the music began and a man's voice sang:

'If you go down in the woods today, you're sure
  of a big surprise –
If you go down in the woods today, you'd better
  go in disguise!'

The July sun shone down on the slowly revolving circle, and Mabel found herself thinking of the reforms that Olive Spearmann had brought about in this place and how fortunate she had been in acquiring Sister Norah, now singing along to the record.

'See them gaily gad about – they love to play and
  shout, they never have any cares –
At six o'clock their mummies and daddies will
  take them home to bed,
Because they're tired little teddy bears!'

Sadly there would be no mummies and daddies arriving for these little children, reflected Mabel, but there was a good tea waiting for them, and kind ladies and girls to take care of their basic needs. At the end of the song she saw that it was nearly five o'clock and time to return to Kennington for her evening visits.

'Oh, no, wait! Just wait while I put on Albert's special record!' cried Sister Norah and held out her hands to her friend. 'Let's dance together!' she said with shining eyes. 'Let's pretend he's here with us!'

426

So the pair of them held each other in the conventional ballroom manner, with Norah taking the gentleman's lead because she was the taller. On went the record and the music began, a man and a woman singing together:

> 'Let the great big world keep turning,
> Never mind if I've got you;
> For I only know that I want you so,
> And there's no one else will do –'

Norah pressed her right hand against the small of Mabel's back, while Mabel let her head fall on to Norah's shoulder as she joined in softly with the words of the song:

> 'You have simply set me yearning,
> And for ever I'll be true –
> Let the great big world keep on turnin' round,
> Now I've found someone like you!'

'Albert, me darlin' love – oh, God save ye, me own dear man,' whispered Norah and Mabel's eyes filled with tears as she circled round the yard with Albert Court's Irish rose, while far away on the SS *Galway Castle* a war-weary seaman longed for home.

> 'Let the great big world keep on turnin' round,
> Now I've found someone like you . . .'

It was consolation of a kind and the last they were to know for a very long time.

'Thank heaven ye're back, Mabel! We've got trouble at Falcon Terrace. Mother's been taken bad and Dad's called the doctor.' Mabel was at once alerted by Ruby's obvious concern.

'What d'ye think's the matter with her?'

'She's so *tired* – I mean, we all are, but she's in her sixties an' completely worn out. She says she just can't keep goin' any longer.'

'I'll go an' see her straight away.'

'Thanks, Mabel. I'm goin' to have to call in there every day to see to Dad an' Harry.'

'Don't worry, Ruby, we'll share it between us. I'll go an' see what I think and we'll sort somethin' out together.'

All the fight seemed to have gone out of Doris Drover. She lay passively in the double bed, her grey hair in two loose plaits on the pillow. The unbuttoned neck of her plain cotton nightgown exposed her wrinkled throat, usually covered by high-necked blouses with collars. Suddenly she looked an old woman and Mabel's conscience stabbed her. She felt Doris's pulse and then held the hand of this woman who should have been her mother-in-law.

'All I worry about is my Harry,' said Doris in a small, weak voice. 'What's he goin' to do if I'm laid up?'

'Don't worry about him, dear,' said Mabel, realising with a pang that the woman was simply exhausted with caring for her invalid son. 'Ruby an' me – we'll look after him till ye're better. Yer can rely on us.' She smiled reassuringly, but Doris did not respond.

'It's hard work, though, Mabel. He's been goin' down-hill these last weeks.'

The words fell on Mabel's ears like a knell. Never before had Mrs Drover admitted that her son was losing the battle with the damage done to his mind and body at the Somme. She had always insisted that he would one day recover his strength and speech, however long it took. Now she could no longer continue the struggle to keep up that illusion.

'Listen, Doris, dear, Ruby an' me can look after Harry. We'll take him to Deacon's Walk an' he can stay with us there until ye're better. I'll speak to Dad about it, an' we'll get him moved with his bed an' his wheelchair an' all – we'll take care of him, don't yer worry.'

It was the first time she had referred to Major Drover as 'Dad' or called Mrs Drover by her Christian name.

The following day a horse-drawn van was hired to take the invalid and all his necessary equipment from the front parlour of number 8 Falcon Terrace, Battersea to the corresponding room in Ruby Swayne's home in Kennington.

'We'll share the work between us, Ruby, an' fit it round our jobs – like when I'm out on a case, you an' the boys can help Harry with dressin' an' washin', an' when I'm in I'll do it,' Mabel said confidently. 'An' we'll take turns to pop over an' visit yer parents, though Dad says he can cope with the housework an' cookin'. Yer mother'll be better when she's had a good rest.'

But life at number 3 Deacon's Walk turned out to be much harder than either Mabel or Ruby had anticipated. Harry had become a lot less mobile and when sitting up he had a tendency to fall towards his right side. Mabel pushed a small cushion firmly down the side of the wheelchair, but sometimes the boys came home from school to find the cushion on the floor and Harry leaning over the side, his head lolling. Mabel had to be ready to go out at a moment's notice when a call came to attend a woman in labour, and sometimes she could be out for most of a day and a night with a confinement; Ruby cut down on her Salvation Army duties, but still had to visit her mother daily, and Harry spent too many hours alone. Mabel rushed from one job to another, never saw Norah or Maud and was always tired. Doris's recovery was slow.

July gave way to August and while the boys were out of school the situation was somewhat eased. It was their daily task to push Uncle Harry out in his chair to Kennington Park and Matthew, now almost eleven, was reliably observant, noticing when Harry was tired and needed to be taken home.

But it became more difficult to heave Harry from the bed to the chair and back again; there were times when his legs buckled beneath him and he dropped to the floor.

It was Ruby who finally spoke the words aloud, on the day before the boys were due to return to school. 'He'll have to go into hospital, Mabel.'

Mabel put a hand to her forehead and closed her eyes. 'Yes,' she admitted. 'Just for a week or two. I wonder if they'd take him at the Tooting Home? I'll speak to the doctor about it.' But looking into Harry's adoring brown eyes, she could have wept for what she saw as a betrayal.

Her brief interview with the doctor resulted in a visit from another doctor, the now retired Henry Knowles. 'This is a sorry business, Mabel, my dear,' he said as they stood in the kitchen, out of earshot of Harry. 'Though I must confess I've seen it coming, as I'm sure you have too. Anyway, I've done some asking around and so has Stephen, but I'm afraid there's only one place that will take your Harry. You see, he's classed as a chronic case.'

He did not add, 'without hope of recovery', which was the term used in Stephen's correspondence with the military.

Mabel took a breath. 'Netley?'

'Yes, my dear, the Royal Victoria.'

'And he'd go into D block, wouldn't he?'

'Not necessarily and certainly not at first. He'd go for assessment and then wherever they'd got a bed.' He sighed. 'I'm very sorry, Mabel, but you can't go on like this. Netley's a good place, you've been there and seen it, he'll be well looked after among other men who've suffered in the same – the same terrible battles. Talk it over with his sister and parents, and let me know when you're ready to send him there. Stephen says he'll take Harry down to Southampton himself – they'll go by train, you know they run these special ambulance trains now, the "Netley coaches". Whenever you decide, Mabel.'

She began to cry silently. 'Oh, Dr Knowles, how shall I ever tell him? It's so far away.'

'Yes, my dear, I know. But it'll be for the best in the long run.'

'Yes, an' it was all for the best when poor Maudie had to part with her baby and go to a women's refuge,' she said bitterly.

Knowles put a hand on her shoulder. 'Yes, dear, I know,' he said again. 'And I'm so sorry.'

There was something else that troubled Mabel, something she could not mention to Dr Knowles. She was not happy about Stephen's involvement in Harry's fate. No doubt he wanted to be of practical assistance in this crisis, but she knew that Harry had always sensed a rival in young Dr Knowles – and, she had to admit to herself, not without reason.

'I'll arrange for a day off – the relief midwife can take over – an' I'll go down to Netley with Harry meself,' she declared.

The Drovers and Ruby were deeply dismayed when they heard that Harry was to return to Netley, though they all maintained that it would be a temporary measure and that he would be home again by Christmas. The date was fixed for Thursday, the twelfth of September, and Stephen and his father were to arrive at Deacon's

Walk in their car at ten, so that they could accompany Mabel and Harry to Waterloo Station and see them on to the special carriage of the ten thirty train.

On the Wednesday night the Drovers came to say goodbye and sat for an hour with their son; John Drover said a prayer for a safe journey and a happy outcome for Harry after his two years of affliction. They kissed him and his mother gave him a small engraved text to put above his bed at Netley: *I will walk before the Lord in the land of the living*.

After they had left and the cases were packed and the wheelchair folded ready for the journey, Mabel told Ruby that she would sleep downstairs in the armchair in Harry's room, to be on hand if he needed anything in the night. In fact, she undressed, put on her rightgown and got into Harry's single bed, cuddling close against him with her arms round his thin frame, her warm face pressed to his cheek. He flung his arm across her, trying to speak, but she put a finger on his lips.

'Ssh-ssh, dearest Harry,' she whispered, kissing him. 'I love yer, remember that – we'll always love each other.'

He breathed a long, contented sigh. 'L-love again. Love.'

Mabel soon drifted into sleep and dreamed that they were walking out together on a fine, sunny day, arms linked and chattering happily as in their courting days. She smiled in her dream and her eyelids fluttered. The parlour was in darkness, but the curtains stirred a little at the open window as a light breeze blew them to and fro. The clock ticked, but Harry could not see the time, nor did he want to: he wished the night to go on for ever and ever, feeling her warm body beside him, listening to her soft, regular breathing like a lullaby, soothing him into sleep – a deep, deep sleep without dreams . . .

All of a sudden he awoke. The breeze was now pouring into the room, a healing stream of deliciously scented air that bathed him in its fragrance, pervading all his senses. Every ache and discomfort had gone, and his body had become as light as a feather, for he was floating up above the bed towards the window. He could look down and see himself lying there beside Mabel, curled in her arms: Mabel, dearest of girls, the only girl he had ever loved.

But now he knew that it was time to leave: time to go on that journey he had made once before when in the hospital on Malta, three years ago. He remembered it all as he saw again the night sky, the stars whirling around him as he ascended up and up, leaving the world behind, speeding onwards and upwards to that blessed realm of light, happiness and peace.

The first light was just beginning to touch the eastern sky when Mabel woke with a sudden chill. She started up in the bed and looked around her. The room was very silent. 'Harry!' she cried aloud. And then she saw that he had gone.

Mabel Court had looked upon death many times at the Infirmary and at Shadwell; she had seen both her mother and father in death, and it held no terrors for her. She got out of the bed, closed the half-open eyes, straightened the body, pulled the sheet up over the empty face.

There would be weeping and mourning for the loss of a good man 'promoted to glory' in the Salvation Army tradition, but in this quiet hour at sunrise Mabel knelt alone beside the bed and gave thanks through her tears that for Captain Harry Drover, that faithful soldier and servant of the Lord, the war was over; this cruel world would trouble him no more.

Chapter Twenty-four

Albert's letter – the longest he had ever written to his sister – arrived on the day of the funeral at Wandsworth Cemetery. The news of Harry's death had not reached him, and Mabel found his comments about his former workmate and friend all the more poignant.

'So the old girl come up with it in the end,' he had written on torn-off sheets of paper filched from some office cupboard.

And you diserve it Mabel after all you put up with from her. Its yours and not to give away do you understand me. Not for Alice or Daisy they are aright and so am I and we may never here from George agen so its yours Mabel.

But you coud help out poor old Harry and his family if they need ready cash but Mabel I think that he will have to go into one of these homes for servicemen there going to need a lot of them places I reckon. Also poor old Maudie you coud give her a helping hand. That was a terible shame about losing Alex and the kid as well. I hope she can go back to the thetter stage.

But Mabel you have you own life to think of and my advise is to look round for a nice big house in a nice part and buy it for children down on there luck. You always said you want to well now you got the means so do what I say. Spend it on a home you can be your own boss and not be holden to some lady de la Posh telling you what to do. You coud take in who you like and not who you dont like.

Escuse the spellng mustakes I am writing this on watch and cant see very much light.

Your loving brother Albert.

And then he had added an almost indecipherable scrawl at the bottom: 'I know youd take care of my little Norah if she was on her own Mabel.'

'Merciful God, Albert, never say so,' she whispered, folding the two sheets of paper back into the envelope; she put it in her pocket when they left Deacon's Walk for the funeral, so that she could touch it and feel his presence near her. But she'd never be able to show it to Norah, not with that last bit: why on earth had he written it?

A large crowd of mourners and well-wishers turned out to pay their respects to a much loved neighbour, supported by the Battersea and Clapham Corps of the Salvation Army with their bands leading the cortège. Ruby and her sons joined Major and Mrs Drover at the graveside, while Mabel was flanked by Sister Norah on her left and a wan-faced Maud Ling in black, holding her right arm. Teddy Ling stood a little way off, and one or two familiar faces from Booth Street and Shadwell gathered around in silent sympathy. Dr Henry Knowles was there, but Stephen was not, for which Mabel was thankful.

Harry's cap was placed on the coffin, and she felt her two friends' arms tighten around her as it was lowered into the earth to the sound of a single muffled drum-beat and his mother's anguished sobs; and then the bands joined to lead the singing of 'The Day Thou

Gavest, Lord Is Ended' Mabel trembled and thought of a passage from *The Pilgrim's Progress* that she had read many years ago at school: 'And so he passed over, and all the trumpets sounded for him on the other side.'

Only in Harry's case it'd be trombones, she thought inconsequentially and touched Albert's letter in her pocket, for it was just the sort of remark that the cheeky rascal would have made; but at the same time she made up her mind to follow his advice and put Mimi Court's ill-gotten fortune to good use. Without poor Harry to consider, there was nothing to stop her from handing in her notice to the LCC and applying to the Waifs and Strays Headquarters for work in one of their small children's homes. And then after the war – if it ever came to an end – she would buy that 'nice big house' and start her own refuge for children, fulfilling a lifelong dream. And it would be a memorial to Harry.

Afterwards she sat down with her two friends to talk. She was particularly glad to see Maud Ling after several weeks with no news.

'Dear Harry's brought us together again today, Maudie – you an' me an' Norah. How're yer gettin' on now, dear? Doin' all right at the – er –'

'At the shelter, yer mean? Yeah, they been very good to me, Mabel, and there's ovver poor girls there worse orf 'n me. But I can't stay there and I'm movin' dahn Twickenham way as soon as Teddy's found us lodgin's. 'E's got a job in a film studio there.'

'Oh, isn't he with the *Daily Chronicle* any more?'

'Nah! 'E's learnin' to be a cameraman, workin' with that photographer 'e met on the *Chronicle* – they're wiv a team makin' movin' pictures. Some bloke's bought up the ol' skatin' rink at St Margaret's an' turned it into a studio. Teddy reckons there's a big future in it.'

'My word, Maudie! Are yer gonner be in films like

436

Mary Pickford?' joked Mabel, though she sadly noted how pale the girl looked, with the pain of loss still shadowing her hazel eyes.

'Ha! Very funny, I'm sure!' said Maud, making a face. 'Nah, Teddy reckons 'e can get me a job doin' somefing arahnd the place, runnin' messages, makin' tea an' sammidges or summat. Don't want to go back into service again.' Her mouth tightened. 'I'm grateful to the Sally Army, Mabel, but I ain't cut out for that sort o' life, not permanent, like. No, I'm orf to Twickenham.'

'But ye'll keep in touch wid us, won't ye, Maudie, darlin'?' said Norah shyly. 'Ye won't be lost to yer old friends?'

Maud looked away without answering. Mabel knew that she could not forget how Norah had insisted on keeping baby Alex at the Midway – from where he had been stolen. She hoped that the coolness would pass in time, for the friendship between the three of them was too precious to lose.

Over tea and fish paste sandwiches the talk turned to the latest news from the battlefields, where it seemed the tide was at last beginning to turn. Another German advance on the Western Front in the spring had received a sharp setback in July, and in August a massive British attack using hundreds of tanks ploughed into the enemy lines and effectively broke up all but a few pockets of resistance. On the Eastern Front Germany's allies Bulgaria and Turkey surrendered, and then Austria. Newspaper headlines blazed with predictions of an end to the fighting, but by this time war-weariness had caused widespread cynicism; people no longer believed what they read of Allied advances and enemy retreats: they had heard it all before and been disillusioned. Worn out by austerity, shortages of food and fuel, crushed by the sorrow of the sacrifice of so many men's lives, the British public could see no end to the misery of war. They were for the most part unaware of the negotiations for a peace settlement, instigated by the German generals who, faced with military defeats, a half-starved population at home and mutiny in their navy, were now calling upon the Allies for an armistice.

When Maud and Teddy Ling had left, Norah spoke of Mrs Spearmann, now nearing her confinement. 'Sure I didn't like to mention her in front o' Maudie, but she's not at all well, y'see. She's blown up like a balloon wid the dropsy, an' gettin' blindin' headaches –'

'Oh, Norah, that's very bad – she could start havin' fits!' cried Mabel. 'What does Mr Poole say?'

'I don't know, except that he's visitin' her, an' keepin' her in bed wid the curtains drawn an' a private nurse livin' in at Maybury Place. It'd be terrible for the Midway if – I mean she's been the guidin' light o' the place, made all them reforms – God forgive me, Mabel, I should be prayin' for her husband an' two little ones dependin' on her.'

Mabel could follow Norah's train of thought and her fears for the future of the Midway Babies' Home if . . .

On the first of October Olive Spearmann was delivered of a stillborn son and came close to death herself. While she slowly recovered her husband fell victim to a new and deadly menace: a virulent epidemic of influenza had broken out in Europe and had reached Britain in late 1918, where it become known as 'Spanish flu'. It found an easy foothold in a population ravaged by four years of war and civilian deaths rapidly mounted, adding to the casualty lists of men lost in battle. Amos Spearmann's undernourished workforce was decimated by it and the resultant death toll included Spearmann himself.

Against this grim background rumours of an end to the war began to be taken seriously. All through October hopes rose and became openly expressed: people hardly dared to imagine that there could be light at the end of such a long, dark tunnel.

And then, suddenly, out of the blue, there was Ruby Swayne's stricken face waiting for Mabel to come home from her afternoon visits: she was holding the *Evening Standard* in her hand. Darkness was falling as Mabel read the report of the sinking of the SS *Galway Castle* – torpedoed in the Mediterranean – only a few survivors . . .

'I must go to Norah.'

Closing her mind to the full import of the news, Mabel leapt back on to her bicycle and pedalled furiously towards the Elephant and Castle and on to the Midway Home hidden among the backstreets to the north of the New Kent Road.

Breathless and perspiring, she wheeled the cycle down the passageway and stood it up in the yard that did duty as a playground in good weather. She rang the bell and a nurserymaid answered.

'Why, Nurse Court!' she said in surprise, but her smile froze on seeing the look in Mabel's eyes.

'I've come to see Sister McLoughlin. Where is she?'

'Down with the in-betweens, givin' 'em their tea.'

The in-betweens were aged from around six months to two years, making the transition from babyhood to toddling. There were about a dozen of them.

'Er – is summat wrong, Nurse Court?' asked the girl.

'I must see Norah,' replied Mabel, already walking down the corridor in dread at what she had to tell her dearest, closest friend.

Norah looked up from feeding a wriggling infant on

439

her lap when Mabel entered the room. Another helper was giving a bottle feed. Whimpers and gurgles filled the air in equal measure.

'Now, now, Charlie, ye got to learn to take it off a spoon. Why, Mabel, ye've cycled over here in the dark. Is it 'cause ye've had a telegram?'

Mabel stared blankly at Norah who had asked the question so matter-of-factly, patting the little boy as she spoke.

'No, Norah, not a t-telegram – not yet. But it's here – in the evenin' paper, see – the *Galway Castle*'s been torpedoed – an' sunk. Only a few – only a few survivors.' Her voice sounded thin and strained. When Norah remained silent she added, 'But ye've heard already, then? Yer *know*?'

'No, Mabel, I haven't heard anythin', it's just a feelin' I've had these two days past. I can't pray, y'see. Come on now, Charlie-boy, take another spoonful – open yer mouth – whoops, there's a good boy.'

She smiled at the child as he spluttered over the rusk softened in milk and Mabel stared in bewilderment, unable to comprehend Norah's apparent lack of emotion.

'There were survivors, Norah, it says so – he got picked up before when the *Christina* –'

Norah wiped Charlie's mouth on his bib. 'No, Mabel, darlin', not this time. I've seen him in a dream, y'see, like many a time before.'

Remembering how Norah's dreams of Albert had so often been followed by his actual reappearance, Mabel broke in eagerly, 'But if yer saw him in this dream, Norah – didn't he – did he say anythin'?'

Norah rose from her chair, lifted Charlie and held his face against her cheek briefly before placing him in a wooden pen with other 'crawlers'. She stood and looked at Mabel with enormous pity in her blue eyes. 'No, Mabel, darlin'. He just smiled – he was walkin' away from me – from us. He won't be comin' back. That's why I thought ye'd had a telegram.'

'Oh, no, Norah – oh, God, I never thought to lose him – not me brother!' cried Mabel as the truth at last struck her like a blow between the eyes. Her voice rose on a long, despairing wail.

'Hush, Mabel, not in here. Come wid me – watch the children, Izzie,' Norah ordered the open-mouthed nursery assistant, and taking her friend's arm she led her out into the corridor and along to her office where Mabel collapsed on a chair and laid her head upon the table.

'Albert! Oh, *Albert*, me brother, me own dear boy – oh, God, oh, *God*!' The words were wrung out of her; she beat her fists on the table in a kind of helpless rage.

Norah stood beside her and laid a hand gently on her head. 'Mabel, dear, yer brother's safe in God's keepin', we've got to believe that. Think of all the good times ye shared together wid him – how good he was to yer dear mother – how generous he always was wid his money – how funny he could be – he always made us laugh, didn't he? Sure an' he was the best o' men – the dearest man in all the world.'

Norah stroked her friend's head and went on murmuring softly about the man who was to have been her husband, the rough and ready sailor who had so adored her; who had been changed by his love for her. 'Meetin' himself made all the difference to me, Mabel, an' the memory o' him'll stay wid me for the rest o' me life, just as he will wid yerself. An' he thought the world o' ye, Mabel – told me ye were a bleedin' angel, so he did!'

Norah allowed herself a half-smile, picturing Albert's laughing face, his swarthy complexion and jet-black

441

brows – and those dark, dark eyes worshipping his 'little nun'.

But Mabel, his sister, she who had so stoically watched Harry Drover's gradual decline and prayed alone beside his deathbed, was now utterly crushed by this latest loss. When the door of the office opened and Maud Ling joined them with the evening paper in her hand, Norah beckoned to her without a word and the three women held each other in a triple embrace, giving mutual support in the unity of their shared sorrow.

'All three of us've lost the darlin' men we loved, an' we've only got each other left now,' whispered Norah, her dark head on Maudie's shoulder as they clung together.

But when the telegram arrived from the Union Castle line to confirm that Able Seaman Court had been lost at sea, Mabel felt that life could have nothing worse to inflict upon her. She truly felt that there was no consolation to be found anywhere. When Norah McLoughlin played her record of 'Let the Great Big World Keep Turning' Mabel could not bear to listen. In her ears she only heard Albert's voice growing fainter and farther away as he sang that other song:

'Mar-ri-ed to a mer-ma-id at the bottom o' the deep blue sea!'

It was her work that saved Mabel at that time of desolation. The Kennington midwife's duties did not stop for a period of mourning: women continued to need her, to call her to their homes and bedsides to comfort them in their pain and perform the most intimate service of all for them. At such a time in a woman's life it is not possible to remain detached, and Nurse Court had to smile as she soothed and reassured; she had to explain and instruct, sometimes with a degree of firmness, and keep her own unhappiness hidden.

People were sorry and many a hand was placed in Mabel's at a time of widespread loss. Ruby did all she could to provide tasty treats from meagre rations, and the boys willingly ran errands for their Aunt Mabel, keeping quiet in the house when she was resting after being out on a night call. She was touched by all the kindness shown to her, but found her best relief in the course of her work: the cry of a newborn baby, a mother's face on receiving her child in her arms, the first breastfeed. The great big world did indeed keep turning, though the two men dearest to Mabel had been sacrificed with countless thousands of others. It was not exactly consolation, more a kind of awareness of time moving forward, a hope that there might still be a future. The words of Albert's last letter echoed in Mabel's head and deep down in her lonely heart she let herself dream again of a home for children. Every time she passed the headquarters of the Society for Waifs and Strays in Kennington Road, she wondered if her future lay with that charity, in becoming a house-mother at one of their countrywide small homes for the sad children who had neither parents nor a roof over their heads. And now she had her grandmother's money . . .

But then, suddenly and unexpectedly, taking the whole country by surprise, came news of the Armistice, the end of the war at the eleventh hour of the eleventh day of the eleventh month of 1918, a Monday. A dazed nation awoke to the realisation that *the war was over*: four years and three months of carnage had come to an end, though a generation of men had been lost. A huge universal sigh of relief turned to shouting and singing, people danced in the streets under November skies, bands played, there was every kind of rejoicing to

443

celebrate the return of peace. Union Jacks were pulled out of musty drawers and cupboards, to be flown from windows, and crowds surged outside Buckingham Palace as they had at the beginning of it all, calling for the King and Queen to appear. After dark there were bonfires lit in spite of the drizzly rain and once again the church bells rang out to call congregations in to give thanks. But for Mabel, Norah and Maud the pain of loss was too recent and their grief too deep to be thrown off, even for a few frenzied days.

On the Tuesday of that memorable week, Mabel had a visitor at Deacon's Walk, a rough-looking youngish man with bloodshot eyes and two or three days' growth of stubble. He gave off a rank smell of drink and unwashed clothes, and Mabel felt a little uneasy about showing him into Ruby's parlour when he introduced himself as Able Seaman Smith, one of the few survivors of the *Galway Castle*.

'Me an' Albert made a promise when we was at sea, that if one of us was lorst the ovver'd go an' see the next o' kin,' he explained, seating himself on the sofa.

'Thank yer, Mr Smith, it's good o' yer to come,' Mabel said cautiously. 'Can yer tell me anythin' about how – how me brother died?'

'Yeah. Poor ol' Albert was on watch at the time we was 'it, Miss Court, an' never stood a chance. I'm sorry, 'cause 'e was a good 'un, one o' the best. Talked abaht yer a lot, an' an Irish girl called Norah. Bloody shame to get all frough the war an' then be scuppered. Too bad, that was. Too bad.'

Mabel shook her head slowly in agreement. 'Would yer like a cup o' tea, Mr Smith?'

'Tea? Yer ain't got nuffin' stronger, I s'pose, miss?'

'No, I'm afraid not,' replied Mabel, for this was a Salvation Army house.

'Er – I s'pose yer couldn't let me 'ave me fare up to Manchester, Miss Court?' he went on, his eyes narrowing to a foxy glint. ''Ad a bit of a set-to las' night, an' when I woke up 'smornin' I'd bin fleeced – them bitches'd cleaned me right aht. Me own fault, should've gorn 'ome soon's I docked, but what wiv the Armistice an' everyfink – if yer could – er, for Albert's sake, like –'

Without a word Mabel went out of the room and returned with five one-pound notes which she put into an envelope and handed to him. It was all that she had saved for buying Christmas presents.

'Crikey, Miss Court, that's good o' yer! Fanks – fanks a lot, Albert said yer was a good 'un, an' 'e was right an' all. Ta!'

'Ye'd better be gettin' on yer way, Mr Smith, if ye've got to go all the way to Manchester tonight. Yer don't want to get robbed again.'

She stood at the window and watched his uncertain progress down to the Kennington Road; in spite of the damp, foggy air she threw up the sash to freshen the room.

Poor devil, she thought. He was about the same age as Albert and not unlike him in looks. Suppose there had been no Norah with her gentle, sweetening influence on that rapscallion brother of hers, smoothing his rough edges, loving him, praying for him . . . who could say how he would have turned out? But now he was gone and she wept afresh for the pity of it.

'But I'll do as yer said, Albert – I'll buy a nice house an' make it into a home for children!' she vowed, though as yet she had little idea of how to set about it.

Chapter Twenty-five

The first Christmas of peace brought more sadness than festivity as families counted the cost of the war in terms of the men lost for ever, the spaces at Christmas dinner tables, the empty beds and lonely hearts. There was no word from George in Canada and, after three years of silence, Mabel had to face the fact that she had now lost touch with her remaining brother, no longer the boy she remembered but a young man who had become a Canadian with no wish to look back on bad memories.

The influenza epidemic raged on, continuing to claim lives: theatres and other public buildings were closed, and people were advised not to travel unless it was really necessary.

From Belhampton came the news of Thomas Somerton's death from a heart seizure on Boxing Day and Mabel longed to be with her Aunt Nell, but it was impossible for her to leave Kennington. She was thankful that Daisy was there for her aunt, because Miss Kate Chalcott still had a few convalescents at Pinehurst and Alice seldom visited at Pear Tree Cottage. Mabel supposed that Alice would now have her eye on Pinehurst when Aunt Kate had gone to live with the widowed Nell. *Thank goodness it's got nothing to do with me*, thought Mabel wearily as she got on her bicycle for the daily round of visits.

But in this she was wrong. A letter arrived from Aunt Kate in which she again asked about her niece's future plans.

'We were all so dreadfully sorry about dear Captain

Drover,' wrote Miss Chalcott in her formal style. 'I have always known that you planned to run a children's refuge under the auspices of the Salvation Army and I wonder if you still wish to care for homeless children? My dear Mabel, it would give me great pleasure to offer you Pinehurst for this purpose. You have seen for yourself how well it accommodated victims of war and I feel that it should continue to be used for a worthwhile cause.'

Mabel's head whirled as the meaning of the words dawned upon her.

'Are yer all right, Mabel?' asked Ruby in concern. 'Not more bad news, is it?'

'No, Ruby, it's from Aunt Kate. She's offerin' me Pinehurst – me mother's old family home at Belhampton – to use as a children's home. I just can't take it in.'

Mabel had told nobody but Albert of the three thousand pounds left to her by her grandmother Court – Prudence Lawton – which was still lying untouched at the London and Provincial Bank in her name. Now it seemed that her way ahead had become wonderfully clear, for she could offer to buy Pinehurst from her aunt, and never mind what Alice and Gerald Westhouse might think, for she now realised that this was what she wanted above all else. There had been times when she'd pictured Pinehurst, that solid Victorian house built by her grandfather Chalcott, being filled with children enjoying a healthy country life, far from the deprivation of their backgrounds. She gave a smile of anticipation as she saw this picture about to come to life, and for the first time since the deaths of Harry and Albert new hope sprang up in her heart that she might soon see a lifelong dream fulfilled. The Lord had not deserted her and she would dedicate her whole life to this new venture!

447

It was Dr Henry Knowles who advised about her next step. Now retired and a semi-invalid, it was some weeks before he heard about Albert, and then went straight to Deacon's Walk and simply held out his arms to her. She went to him wordlessly, resting her head on his shoulder. When they sat down to talk, she told him about her legacy and how she intended to use it.

'Mabel, my dear, I can't think of anything better. I'm so pleased that old Mimi Court – that your grand-mother's money is to be used in this way. But tell me, how will you manage the day-to-day running of your home?'

When Mabel confessed that she had not much idea about administration, but hoped that her Aunt Chalcott would advise her, Knowles gave her the advice for which she was always to be grateful.

'Go to the Waifs and Strays Society Headquarters, Mabel, and put yourself in their hands. Tell them your circumstances and how you want to use your money. They're well experienced in this kind of thing and they have an excellent record of caring for children – think how they saved your friend Maud and her brother.' He leaned forward and gave her a penetrating look. 'But at present they're sadly overburdened and to have a privately owned property put at their disposal, together with a ready-made Matron with means of her own – oho, Mabel, they'll welcome you with open arms!'

Mabel beamed. 'Oh, *yes*, Dr Knowles, that's a won-derful idea. There was a time when I thought I might work with the Waifs and Strays and now I *shall*!'

'And remember that it will be *your* property, which will give you status and far more say in the way the place is run – I mean the actual care of the chil-dren, their mealtimes, bedtimes and so on. Administra-tive details like wages and catering costs will be taken over by the Society, but you'll be in charge, Mabel!'

'That's just what Albert said in his last letter!' she cried, her eyes shining. 'Dear Dr Knowles, ye've proved to be me best friend once again!' And on an impulse she flung her arms round his neck in a grateful hug . . . which of course made her think immediately of his son, for so long pushed to the back of her mind. And she had not even asked about the family. Rather awkwardly withdrawing from him, she set about making up for the omission.

'How's yer wife these days, Dr Knowles? An' young Mrs Knowles, how's she keepin'? An' little Lily, she must be walkin' by now.'

'Fifteen months,' he replied with a fond look. 'Though we don't see much of her, I'm afraid. My wife and I are rather a pair of crocks, and as for poor Phyllis, I really don't know, Mabel.' He sighed deeply and gave a little shrug. 'She probably needs to get away from her parents and stand on her own feet, run her own home, look after her child – but my son doesn't seem able to give her the sort of support she needs to make the first step. Very much under her mother's domination, I believe. Other people's marriages can be – um – one has to be so careful.'

He paused. Mabel noticed that he had never once mentioned Stephen by name and wondered if he and his son were on good terms. In fact, Henry Knowles had long realised how the land lay and checked himself from saying more.

'So, my dear, apply to the Society's Headquarters – only round the corner from you! – and with your references from Booth Street and Shadwell, you'll be a gift to the Waifs and Strays!'

*   *   *

Mabel's interview went as well as Knowles had predicted, and she wrote to her Aunt Kate and gave three months' notice to Lambeth Borough Council. A team of visitors from the Society was sent to inspect Pinehurst, which was duly pronounced as an ideal 'cottage home' for about ten children. Edward Rudolf, the founder of the Church of England Society for the Provision of Homes for Waifs and Strays, disliked large, regimented homes, and insisted on small family groups headed by a housemaster and Matron. Due to the enormous loss of manpower through the war, it was difficult to find suitable men to be 'masters', but Mabel had hatched her own plan regarding this problem: she intended to invite Norah McLoughlin to be her partner in the Pinehurst project, sharing the work they loved and for which they were both well qualified.

But tragic fate once again took a hand and struck at the Midway Babies' Home. The deadly influenza swept through the area around the Elephant and Castle, and both Sister Norah and Mrs Lovell were laid low with it. The Board of Guardians were at their wits' end and sent staff from Booth Street to try to deal with the crisis, but when four young children died within a week, the home was closed and the little inmates sent to wherever a place could be found, in homes, infirmaries, even workhouses. Sister Norah was taken to Booth Street where she recovered in Women's I, but Mrs Lovell developed pneumonia and did not survive.

The newspapers had a field day with the story, finding the Midway a target for their righteous indignation at 'Dickensian conditions in England today'. Photographs were published of the dark entrance passage, the stone-floored corridor, the nursery with its iron cots, the playroom with its high barred windows. It led to a vilification campaign against Olive Spearmann, widow of the 'war-profiteering Jew', a manufactured scandal that sold newspapers and diverted people's minds briefly from the growing sense of anticlimax in a drained and exhausted country to which servicemen were returning to look for employment.

Mabel dreaded that Norah would read a report of the Midway's fate, and when she received a scrawled message from Maud asking for news they arranged to meet and visit their friend, whom they found lying listlessly in her bed in at the end of the ward, though she quickly sat herself up when they appeared.

'Ah, Mabel – an' Maudie, darlin' – have ye heard that the Midway's been closed? An' poor Mrs Lovell an' the children all gone?'

'Ssh, Norah, dear, most o' the children've gone to other places, an' maybe it was time the Midway was closed, anyway,' Mabel said, trying to sound reassuring. 'Listen, I've got the most *amazin'* news –' And she went on to tell her friends about Pinehurst and the legacy.

'And I've got a wonderful idea, Norah. Come with me to Belhampton! There aren't enough men to be housemasters, so we can be two house Matrons, workin' partners, doin' the sort o' work we both love best – come on, what d'ye say?'

Maud, now looking quite elegant in a light-grey coat and hat, gave Norah an encouraging grin. 'That's right, gal, go ahead, you an' Mabel togevver'll make a first-rate team!'

Norah lay back on her pillows, a strangely resigned expression on her pale features. When she spoke her voice was weak but steady. 'No, Mabel, darlin', but thank ye a thousand times. I'm goin' back to bein' an Irishwoman agin, y'see. Mother Patrick wrote me from St Joseph's to ask me to help her wid the orphanage, the one I grew up in meself.'

Mabel could not hide her surprise and disappointment. 'Oh, Norah! Norah, *dear* – d'ye think yer could settle down over there in Cork after five years o' livin' in London?'

Norah reached out for her hand. 'Yes, Mabel, so I could. Wait now while I tell ye what I wrote back to Mother Patrick. When I lost him who was all the world to me, I knew I'd never love another man on this earth, so I must turn the love in me heart to Himself above. I'm goin' back to enter the convent an' take me vows to become a Sister o' Mercy an' serve Him for the rest o' me life.'

'*Norah!* Yer don't mean ye're goin' to be a *nun*?' gasped Mabel at this totally unexpected announcement. 'But yer can't – yer *can't* – turn yer back on the world like that!'

'I may be turnin' me back on the world, but I'll be spendin' me life wid children, just like yeself, Mabel,' replied the Irish girl seriously. 'An' one day, if God wills it, I'll take over from Mother Patrick an' serve God an' the motherless mites He gives me to care for. It's the way that I must take, Mabel, can't yer see? – an' Albert will be wid me, right up to me dyin' day.'

She closed her eyes, tired by this emotional speech. Mabel sat in stunned silence, unable to think of a response; she was utterly dismayed at the prospect of losing Norah in this way. It meant that she would have to tackle the Pinehurst project alone, without the help and support of her dearest friend.

But Maud Ling spoke up in unexpected agreement. 'I can see ye've made up yer mind, Norah, gal, an' I ain't all that surprised, to tell yer the trufe. Albert always said yer was like a little nun, didn't 'e, Mabel? An' 'e was right, Gawd love 'im.'

Norah gave her a grateful glance. 'An' what about

yeself, Maudie? Did ye get a job near to Teddy at – where was it, that film studio place?'

'Twickenham,' replied Maud with a little self-conscious smile. 'Yeah, not 'alf! An' I got meself a part in a film they're makin' dahn there – it's called *Downfall of a Nobleman*.'

'Go on, Maudie, have yer really?' Mabel, still dashed by Norah's news, looked up with interest. 'Are yer the heroine?'

'Nah! I'm 'er sister, the Lady Blanche, a right schemin' 'ussy. Lovely costumes we got, must've cost a fortune, but this Ralph Jupp who owns the studio reckons it'll be a big moneymaker – got 'is eye on the American market, Teddy says.'

Her eyes sparkled, and her two friends caught a glimpse of the old, smart, cheeky Maud they remembered from the days when all three had been in love and full of hope for the future.

Mabel was delighted. 'Good on yer, Maudie! I bet ye'll go on to be a big star one day an' make us proud o' yer.'

'Well, yer never know, do yer, gal?' Maudie gave a modest simper. 'Me bruvver says there's one fing abaht films, they can't 'ear Lady Blanche's cockney accent, can they?'

Young Mrs Westhouse stared incredulously at Miss Chalcott, scarcely able to believe what she was hearing. 'But Gerald and I can offer you the full market price, Aunt Kate – more if you want! How much can the Waifs and Strays scrape up?'

'It's nothing to do with the Waifs and Strays, Alice,' replied her aunt levelly. 'Pinehurst belongs to your sister Mabel and she is allowing the Society to use it as a children's home with herself in charge.'

453

Alice was so astonished that she stood with her mouth open, unable to frame a reply for several moments. 'You mean you've *given* it to her?' she said at last.

'That is not your concern, Alice, though I never made any promise to sell Pinehurst to you – or to leave it to you after I've gone. Mabel has proved herself to be far more deserving of it and she won't be using it for herself, but for children in need of a home.'

'It's your decision, Aunt Kate,' said Alice, trying to regain her dignity, but still unable to believe that she had lost her cherished dream to be mistress of Pinehurst. 'Though I must say I think you'll live to regret it. Imagine that lovely house – your childhood home – overrun by the sort of badly behaved brats that Mabel's always made such a fuss about, all sticky paws and dirty habits. This is a respectable neighbourhood and there'll be complaints, mark my words!'

'We managed well enough with war casualties and I'm sure that Mabel will be able to deal with any complaints – with my backing and support,' retorted Miss Chalcott, looking hard at her niece's flushed face. 'You and your husband should look for a smaller property, and if you'll take my advice, Alice, you'd do well to influence Gerald to cut down on his drinking and get back into his father's law practice. You can't live off the Westhouses for ever, you know.'

Pinehurst Cottage Home for Waifs and Strays was opened in May 1919, with Miss Mabel Court appointed as the Society's youngest Matron at twenty-five. A full-time cook was engaged, two resident assistants to help with the children, and two housemaids; extra daily help was employed, and between them they cooked and cleaned, washed and ironed. There was also Mr Yarrow, an ex-serviceman who came in daily to be handyman, boilerman and gardener. Six children between the ages of five and ten were introduced to their new home, to be joined by four more by the end of the month.

Mabel discovered very early on that looking after sick children in a large institution under supervision was one thing, but dealing alone with a mixed bunch of bewildered and insecure victims of circumstance was a very different kind of challenge. The children were defensive and suspicious, having been pushed from pillar to post in the course of their short lives, and now, faced with what appeared to be a palace and a smiling lady to welcome them and give them regular meals and a bed to sleep in, they were not necessarily ready to trust their luck. Habits of self-preservation died hard, food was grabbed and stored under beds, favourite toys were hidden rather than shared. At the local church school they met round-faced, rosy-cheeked children who stared at them and spoke in a funny way, as unfriendly as it was unfamiliar.

And day after day there were sheets hung out on the line and tight-lipped faces among the staff because of the bed-wetting that went on and on. Matron Court had to buy rubber sheets to prevent the mattresses from becoming permanently stained.

'Dirty little monkeys,' the maids would mutter, though Matron Court never said anything but just made sure that they went to the WC or used their chamber-pots before going to bed. Regular offenders were roused at ten o'clock to go again if they could.

Then there were the head-lice, previously unheard-of at the church school, or so the teachers said, though Matron Court told them without a trace of embarrassment that outbreaks were common in London schools, and that she herself had had lice as a child. Out came the toothcomb and sassafras oil, its lingering odour reminding her of those far-off days when her own mother had done the same for herself. And there were threadworms, for which Dr Forsyth, the local general practitioner, ordered special pills which gave them tummy-aches and led to accidents. 'Talk about a house o' smells,' grumbled the maids, hanging out more washing.

To Mabel these were mere practical problems which she took in her stride. Far worse were the behavioural difficulties which led to clashes with her staff and a couple of resignations. The hard-working assistants were not used to putting up with bad language, rudeness such as the sticking out of tongues and pulling faces when told to come and listen to a story being read. The naughty ones would far rather bounce up and down on the sofa or crawl underneath tables to do unspeakable things like *playing with themselves*, an activity that caused much shock and disgust among the well-meaning countrywomen. When one of the helpers dragged a boy to Matron's sitting-room with the awful accusation that he had been 'doing it again', Mabel simply told him to run along, and when he was out of earshot she reprimanded the indignant woman.

'Yer don't know what that child's been through, starved o' love and attention,' she said. 'The habit isn't criminal and it won't cause blindness, that's all nonsense, an' there's no need to make such a fuss about it.'

It was generally agreed that Matron Court had some very odd ideas and the assistants whispered among themselves that she was not firm enough with the little terrors. Nobody but herself was allowed to punish a child: all misdemeanours had to be reported to her and she dealt with them in her own way.

'I'm in the place of their mother,' she said firmly,

'and what they do is *my* responsibility and nobody else's.'

Which was why only the staff called her Matron. The children called her 'Mother' if they wished and the younger ones happily said 'Mummy' from the start. Others who remembered their own mothers could choose to call her 'Aunt Mabel' or 'Auntie', but there were objectors.

'*You* ain't me muvver!' roared a boy when she remonstrated with him for breaking a window. 'Nor yet me aunt, neiver – ye're just an ol' woman!'

'Very well, yer can call me Woman, and I'll call yer Boy,' she replied at once. 'Everybody else'll have names except us two.'

And as the weeks went by she gradually began to gain the trust of the children, even the most recalcitrant. Her path was a lonely one, for she felt that she should not make any particular friends among her staff; time and again she longed for Norah McLoughlin's understanding, someone who would have given her unconditional support. When her sister Daisy wanted to come to live at Pinehurst, Mabel regretfully told her that at fifteen she was too young to cope with difficult children all day long, so she came over at weekends and accompanied them all to church on Sundays; they walked two by two along the lane, with Mabel and Daisy bringing up the rear. Back at the house they all sat down to Sunday dinner, both staff and children, for Matron insisted that they should eat as a family. Cook would bring in the roasted joint – or the mutton stew or the fish pie, depending on what day it was – and Matron would serve everybody according to age and appetite.

On Sunday afternoons the Rector called with his son Cedric – poor Cedric, so handsome and clever, but on

457

crutches because of his lost leg – and Mabel sometimes talked with them about any problems she had
with boys, there being no housemaster. Mr Drummond
encouraged them to join the local Scout and Cub troops,
just as the girls joined the Guides and Brownies, proudly
parading in their uniforms. His wife did her duty by
inviting selected children to tea at the Rectory, two or
three at a time, and in the new post-war world the
Pinehurst boys and girls became an accepted part of
Belhampton life. As Mabel patiently pointed out to
Polly, a particularly defiant girl of seven, 'No matter
what yer do, no matter *how* badly yer behave, ye're
not goin' to be sent away again, d'ye hear me? D'ye
understand, Poll? This is yer *home* an' here yer stay, so
there's no need to go on testin' yer luck!' And having
made her point clear, she enfolded the unhappy child
in a hug.

Two letters arrived for Matron on a warm June morning
and she saved them to read after breakfast, when the
children had gone to school. She recognised the hand-
writing on both, one was from Ruby Swayne and the
other from Violet Stoke-Marriner. She opened Ruby's
first, and as she drank a second cup of tea she was
thankful to read that Herbert had been released after
completing three and a half years of his sentence, so was
now reunited with his wife and sons at Deacon's Walk,
and back to being a Captain in the Salvation Army.

'Your friend Mrs Hodges has married again,' the letter
went on, 'to Mr Clark, the Chairman of the Council.
He was a widower much older than her but they
seem happy and they say he thinks the world of the
three children. She runs a War Widows' Association to
raise funds for poor women bringing up families on
their own.'

Mabel smiled to herself, glad to hear of her friend's new-found domestic happiness and to know that her children had a good father.

But then came very different news about another wave of influenza, and Mabel's hand flew to her mouth as she read that it had claimed the lives of Dr Henry Knowles and his wife: they had died two months ago.

'Oh, Dr Knowles, dear Dr Knowles,' Mabel whispered, unable to take in that her good old friend had gone. So *this* was the reason she had not heard from him since Pinehurst had opened. To think she hadn't known about his death, hadn't sent a message of sympathy to his son, not that she would have done so anyway, that was something in the past, all over now. But dear Dr Henry Knowles! At least she knew how highly he would approve of the work she was doing now.

She picked up the other letter and sat reading as if turned to stone.

'I've thought very long and hard about sending you this letter, Mabel,' wrote Violet. 'I still don't know whether I'm doing the right thing . . .'

Mabel's fingers trembled as she held the single sheet of paper and read on.

Dr Stephen Knowles's wife died last week in this third wave of Spanish influenza that has taken so many lives. He has gone to Northampton and we suppose that his little daughter will now be brought up by her grandparents. It is particularly tragic that this should happen now that the war is over, and Dr Knowles also lost both his parents in May from the same cause. I thought I would let you know, Mabel, though it probably makes no difference to you now . . .

459

Mabel was still sitting at the table when the maid came in to clear away after breakfast.

'Be y'all right, Matron? 'Ee gone as white as a sheet,' remarked the girl.

'What? No, no, it's all right,' muttered Mabel. 'Is there another cup o' tea in the pot, Mary?'

'Tha's gone stale now, Matron, but I can soon make 'ee a fresh 'un.'

'No, don't bother, it's all right.' Mabel got up and hurried away to calm herself and collect her thoughts together. Violet was right, the news made no difference now: she had her new life here at Pinehurst, her responsibility to her children who called her Mother.

And she had a new child arriving today, an eight-year-old boy from London, and there was no time to sit around examining her feelings about something that was over and done with.

The boy pressed himself into his corner of the compartment and only spoke when the lady asked him a question. He had never been on a train before and it was going ever so fast, taking him to somewhere else. Through the window he could see all sorts of different scenes rushing by, stretches of green and sandy open spaces and tall pine trees, very different from the crowded streets he'd known all his life.

'You'll love it at Pinehurst,' the lady said brightly. 'You'll have other boys and girls to play with and a big garden. The Matron's called Miss Court and I've heard she's very nice.'

The boy curled himself up with his knees under his chin and his arms wrapped round his legs. He didn't want to meet other boys if they were like Rob and he hoped that Miss Court, whoever she was, wouldn't shout and holler like Ma Grigson who ladled out bowls

460

of soup and slices of bread every day to the four children boarded out with her. She lived in a narrow-fronted house with two nearly grown-up girls and Rob, who took the children to and from school and never lost an opportunity to make their lives a misery. The house had a small backyard, where a half-starved dog was tied up all day to warn off intruders, and the stink of the adjoining tannery hung over the whole neighbourhood. At night the boy slept in a small bed with an older lad who cried out in his sleep and wet the bed, for which they both got cuffed by Ma Grigson who in her turn was bawled at by a big red-faced man who turned up from time to time and threatened her, shoving his fist in her face while she shrank back and glowered helplessly.

But it was Rob whose constant tormenting had been the worst of all. He'd said, 'Ye're a little bastard, ain't yer,' and held him up by his ankles until the boy gasped out, 'Yeah.'

'Yeah what?'

'I'm a little bastard.'

That wasn't half as bad as the other thing, the thing he couldn't even bear to think about.

'Listen, bastard, I'll chuck yer out o' the winder if yer don't stay still an' shut yer gob.'

So he closed his eyes tightly, gritted his teeth and bunched his fists while Rob did that horrible rude thing to him. It hurt and made him feel as bad as Rob, and that's why he'd run away and hidden in alleys and doorways around Waterloo Station. Passers-by had thrown him their spare coppers, and he'd found a warm spot to sleep behind a chop-house until one night a policeman had picked him up and taken him to a place where they'd given him sweet tea and asked a lot of questions. He'd begged them not to send him back to Ma Grigson's, and they'd taken him to a house where

461

there were some other children and an office where he first heard the words, 'waifs and strays'. He wondered which *he* was, a waif or a stray. Then somebody had said 'Pinehurst' and now he was on a train with a lady he didn't know, heading for a destination he knew nothing about.

From his earliest recollections the boy had always been surrounded by lots of other children, more or less the same age as himself. They'd had to sit on potties and push down until they did poo-poos, and it had given him an aching, dragging feeling in his bottom that still hurt him down there sometimes, especially when Rob – ugh! he recoiled from the thought. When he'd left that first babies' place he'd been sent to a big, noisy, crowded building full of children of all ages, where he'd slept in a long dormitory with twenty other boys in two rows of narrow beds. He had made a few friends there, but when he was seven he'd been boarded out with Ma Grigson, along with two girls and the other boy. And that was where he had learned the meaning of fear.

But the boy had a secret. Deep in his heart he cherished a memory, a dream that had really happened and which he had never shared with anybody else. At some point near the end of his time at the babies' home he had been very ill with a dreadful pain in his ear: his whole head had buzzed and quivered and blazed with the agony of it, and he had screamed and screamed. One day he woke up and found himself in a big room where there were lots of old ladies lying in beds. The pain had been cured; in fact, he scarcely remembered now how bad it had been. What he *did* remember was that Somebody had looked after him then, Somebody warm and cuddly and safe, who had comforted him, hugged and kissed him and called him her good boy. She had coaxed and cajoled him to eat and drink, she had come to him when he cried, she had taught him the meaning of love. In his dreams she still returned to him, though when he woke up she was gone again. But he clung to her memory; he would never forget her.

The train drew up at a funny little station, and the lady picked up the bag with his few clothes in it and said they had arrived. Out in the station yard was a man with a trim little pony trap to take them up to the house. He said his name was Yarrow and smiled at the boy in a friendly way, saying that he looked as if he needed feeding up.

When the fine big house came into view, the boy felt very nervous, and when the lady rang the front doorbell he wanted to run away and hide from more strange faces.

But then the door was opened and a lady stood there smiling – and then she stared hard at him and put her hands up to her face.

'*Timmy!* Timmy Baxter,' she whispered and he gazed in unbelief as the distant, far-off memory stirred inside his head. Was she – could she possibly be –? She wore a white apron and a cap on her fair, wavy hair, just as he remembered. She had the same blue-grey eyes, the same tender mouth that had kissed him, the arms that had held him safe . . . yes, she was the very same one – his *Somebody* again!

And now she was going down on one knee, so that her face was close to his. 'Oh, Timmy, don't yer remember me? Yer Nurse Mabel? All that long time ago?'

The name found an echo in his long-ago dream. Mabel. Maby. Yes, that was her name.

His lady companion from the Waifs and Strays looked down at them both in astonishment. Never before had she seen a new child welcomed into a cottage home in this way; there were actually tears in Miss Court's eyes.

463

He put out a hand and touched Maby's shoulder. She was real and alive, this was no dream!

'Aren't yer goin' to say hello to me, Timmy?'

He found his voice at last and asked a question. 'Am I gonner stay 'ere wiv yer?'

'Yes, Timmy, ye've come to live here with me,' she told him, her eyes fixed on his.

'Wot, all the time?' He had to be sure. He couldn't yet believe that it was true.

'Yes, Timmy, me love, all the time. This is where ye're goin' to live from now on, don't yer understand? I'm goin' to be yer mummy.'

He held out his arms and she gathered him close to her. Timmy Baxter had come home.

Epilogue

'Blimey, there it goes agin! 'Oo is it this time?' asks Joe, standing on a chair to see who's ringing the doorbell.

'Yer not to say blimey, an' git dahn orf that chair or yer won't 'alf cop it,' Polly tells him.

''Ere, it's that Mrs West'ouse, collectin' 'er money,' he shouts, peering through the bay window. 'She ain't got the baby wiv 'er.'

'If it's any bus'ness o' yours, nosey!'

'Look out, 'ere comes Mum,' warns Tim Baxter. 'Git dahn!'

Joe hastily drops to the floor as Matron Court appears.

'Mum, can I answer the door?' pleads Polly. 'I can reach the 'andle.'

Matron stifles a sigh, shakes her head and goes to let her sister Alice into the entrance hall and through to her little sitting-room, which also serves as an office. She unlocks a drawer.

'Ye're lookin' much better since the baby, Alice,' she remarks, nodding her approval. 'I've got it ready for yer, here we are, in this envelope.'

'It's most generous of you, Mabel. Thank you.' Alice stows the money in the leather satchel she uses for collecting the monthly subscriptions, and writes *Pinehurst: £5 0s. 0d* under August 1920 in her accounts book.

'How're me nephew an' niece?' asks Mabel.

'Geoffrey's a little resentful of Geraldine, but I suppose that's only to be expected,' replies Mrs Westhouse, not quite meeting her sister's eyes. 'Her daddy thinks the world of her, of course, and it's just as well that we're in our own home now, or she'd be in danger of being thoroughly spoiled.'

'And Gerald?'

'Oh, he goes to the office on three days each week now and I've engaged an excellent nursemaid, so I'm able to do a little more work for the War Memorial Hospital Fund.'

Yes, thinks Mabel, it must be like escaping from prison to get away from the Westhouses at last – and to see Gerald returning to something like normality. Thank heaven for little Geraldine, now four months old and so obviously her father's child.

'I see the buildin's goin' up quite quickly,' she says aloud. 'It'll be such a boon to local people, not havin' to go to Winchester.'

Alice nods. 'Just think, twelve beds, an operating theatre and an X-ray machine! Alderman North is pressing for two more general practitioners in Belhampton, with up-to-date experience in surgery and anaesthetics.'

'Yes, Dr Forsyth's interviewin' for a partner, an' really we could do with a younger doctor for the children, anyway.'

'Don't worry, Mabel, I can assure you as a member of the Board of Governors that Alderman North is quite determined to convince the council,' says Mrs Westhouse, subtly emphasising her position in Belhampton, and Mabel sees a flicker of the old sparkle in the dark eyes, a hint of the superior airs she affected in the past. 'Anyway, how are you, Mabel? I'm sure that you work much too hard – oh, hello, Daisy, I didn't realise that you were here.'

'Yes, I come over every day in the summer holidays to help out,' explains Daisy Somerton, now a pretty girl of sixteen with Alice's dark-brown eyes and hair.

'The aunts keep hoping that you'll call on them with the babies.'

'They're next on my list this afternoon,' says Alice, but Daisy breaks in with her own exciting news. 'Lucy Drummond went to the pictures last night and what d'you think – Maud Ling is absolutely marvellous in *Downfall of a Nobleman* – she's the wicked Lady Blanche and ever so much better than the heroine, Lucy says, and all the men are swooning over her! She's got this white face and huge dark eyes that burn right into you when she looks out from the screen!'

'Maud Ling? You don't mean that girl that Alex Redfern was –'

'Oh, yes, we do, Alice!' Mabel's tired eyes light up with pride. 'Maudie's goin' to be a big star one day soon, an' ye'll be tellin' Geoffrey an' Geraldine that yer knew her as a child.'

'Good gracious!' Alice is clearly taken aback by the Ling girl's rise to fame. Gerald might want to see this film, she thinks. He's been so much easier to live with since the arrival of his darling daughter, for which Alice thanks her lucky stars – and to be free of her in-laws and Gerald's mother's accusing silences.

Young Daisy's bright face glances from one sister to the other. Alice at twenty-three has kept her looks, though her once slender waist has thickened considerably after two confinements. She gives the impression of a brave and beautiful woman who has come through difficult times with a war-scarred husband, to find a new niche for herself.

By contrast, Mabel at twenty-six looks at least thirty, stern-faced and straight-backed. She has a reputation for being firm with officials, strict with her staff but always gentle and loving towards the children in her care – her family, as she calls them. Privately Daisy is inclined to agree with Cook that 'Mum' is too soft sometimes, like when little Fanny has those awful tantrums, screaming and kicking out at everybody. Mabel calls them brainstorms and tries to hug Fanny out of them, even though she's had her hand bitten. Daisy wonders if a good hard smack might be more effective, but does not dream of saying so.

Daisy sometimes worries about Mabel who must feel dreadfully lonely for her lost fiancé and brother – and her friend Norah McLoughlin, once so close but now shut up in an Irish convent preparing to take her vows and become a Sister of Mercy. Mabel may not ever see her again. And heaven only knows where Maud will end up! Will she forget her old childhood friend in her brilliant new career as a film star? Yet Mabel never complains; in fact, she has told Daisy that God has been good to her and given her this family of children, these waifs and strays. 'They are my life now, Daisy,' she says.

Two days later the boys are playing leapfrog on the back lawn and Matron Court is sitting at her sewing, when Tim Baxter hurtles through the open french-casement door.

'Mum! Mum, can I go rabbitin' wiv Yarrow an' 'is dog down the bottom field? The farmer's goin' to shoot 'em all, so we might as well catch a few first – please, Mum!'

There is a ring at the doorbell and Matron rises to her feet, wearily putting aside her work-basket. 'Just a minute, Tim, dear, while I see who this is,' she says, and Tim climbs on a chair.

'Blimey, Mum, it's anuvver one! A little kid in a pink dress an' a bonnet, an' a man' wiv 'er, ever so tall an' old-lookin'.'

'What?' Mabel suddenly catches her breath and holds

the back of the chair. 'But I haven't heard anythin' from Headquarters about – another – child.'

Her voice sounds oddly jerky and Tim looks at her. 'Y'all right, Mum? Shall I fetch Miss Daisy to see 'em?' he asks, jumping down from the chair.

'No – no, I – I'll take a peep from the window,' she whispers, aware of her heart pounding and her mouth gone dry. She puts out her hand and flicks the edge of the curtain just for a moment.

It is enough. She sees. She knows. 'Timmy – oh, Tim, me dear little boy,' she says under her breath, and he is quite alarmed.

'Are yer *sure* y'all right, Mum?'

'Yes, yes – only come with me to the door, Tim.'

It has happened. The dream that has visited her time and time again in the lonely hours of the night is here and real. *He* has come back and brought his daughter with him. Words from the past echo in her head: *I don't want her to be brought up by grandparents.*

She takes a deep breath, holds Tim Baxter's hand – and opens the door.

'Mabel.' Oh, the look in his eyes. He is older, greyer, sadder – but he has not changed.

'Stephen. And this must be Lily.'

'Yes, Mabel, she's my Lily. Three next month.'

Another child at the door. Shall I pick her up? Mabel wonders to herself. Yes, I will. I *will*. I'll stoop down and lift her up in my arms. If she cries and turns away from me, I shall know it's not going to happen. But if she takes to me, I shall know that she's to stay. And her father.

'I've had an interview with Dr Forsyth today, Mabel,' he is saying. 'He has offered me a partnership and I've told him that I'll let him know by tomorrow.'

His blue eyes darken as they meet hers. Lily holds tightly to his hand.

'It all depends on you, Mabel,' he says, and waits in hope and fear for her answer.

She lets go of Tim's hand, bends down and lifts Lily Knowles in her arms. He lets go of the child's hand and she gazes solemnly at Mabel who straightens up and smiles at her.

'Hello, Lily.'

Two soft little arms go round Mabel's neck – oh, so familiar does it feel – and a pink cheek presses against her face. 'May – Maby.'

Tim Baxter looks up as if mesmerised, but Mabel's eyes close briefly in thanksgiving. She has her sign. *Yes!*

'She needs a mother, Mabel,' says Stephen.

'An' my children need a father,' she answers. 'Ye'd best come in, the pair o' yer. Come on in. There's room enough for yer both.'

If you enjoyed *A Child at the Door* why not try
Maggie Bennett's first novel . . .

A Child's Voice Calling

**The powerful story of a young girl's struggle to save
her family . . . and herself**

Young Mabel Court, child of her mother's hasty marriage to a spendthrift, becomes 'little mother' to her
brothers and sisters growing up in South London at
the start of the twentieth century.

With poverty never far from the door, the battle to stay
respectable is finally lost when the family breaks up in
tragic circumstances, and Mabel is thrown upon the
dubious mercy of her grandmother, the sinister Mimi
Court, who has her own dark secrets.

But faithful Harry Drover of the Salvation Army, in love
with Mabel, gets an opportunity to prove his devotion
when Mabel falls foul of the law and has to fight for her
own survival . . .

Read on for an extract . . .

Chapter One

'Come *along*, Albert, never mind about dilly-dallying with them Paddys,' Mabel called to her brother outside their school. 'It's my piano lesson today and Mum'll give it to me if I'm not home when Miss Lawton comes. Why're yer shuffling along like that? Oh, just look at yer bootlaces, ye'll trip and fall for sure – here, let me do 'em up!'

She stooped down at the kerbstone and quickly laced up his boots while he fidgeted, conscious of the grins of the Irish boys. '*I* ain't got no lesson,' he muttered.

'You mean you *have not got a lesson*,' Mabel corrected him, straightening herself up and taking him firmly by the hand.

'Ah, de poor liddle feller, see, he has to go wid his big sister!' jeered the tousle-haired boys forced to attend the London County Council School in Hallam Road for lack of affordable Catholic education.

'Shut yer faces, yer dirty Paddy-whacks, hope the boat sinks that brought yer over!' retorted Mabel, whose tongue could be versatile when required. Breaking into a half-run she dragged the protesting six-year-old through the streets. There was no time to stare up at the high windows of the Women's Rescue just off Lavender Hill with its iron gate through which the children could sometimes see the rescued women and girls sitting out of doors hemming sheets; today she had to hurry, for there would be trouble is she was not at home when Miss Lawton arrived on her bicycle.

There would be trouble anyway when her mother saw the white card she had been given to bring home. Better wait until the lesson was over and Miss Lawton had gone, not that the timid spinster would be likely to pass anything on to Grandmother.

Mabel enjoyed her piano lessons and the daily practice was no hardship either, except that there was rarely time for a full hour at the keyboard. At seven years old she already had her responsibilities in the house, especially in helping with the care of the younger children.

'There you are at last, Mabel, and about time too,' scolded their mother, standing at the door of number 12 Sorrel Street with four-year-old Alice and little Georgie who was not yet two. 'There's Miss Lawton just coming round the corner, so hurry up and get your music out. Oh, Albert, what a dirty face – here, let me wipe it – and your hands too. Just *look* at you, you little gypsy!' She dabbed vigorously at the squirming, sun-browned boy whose black hair and eyes proclaimed him Jack Court's living image. 'Georgie must go into the kitchen while Mabel's playing, otherwise he'll be into everything. Alice can sit and listen to the music if she's good and keeps quiet. Good afternoon, Miss Lawton,' Annie continued, raising her voice as the black-clad lady dismounted and leaned her bicycle against the low railing. 'Mabel's all ready for her lesson.'

Georgie gave a frustrated howl as his mother hoisted him up to carry him into the kitchen. Beneath her apron a fifth child was beginning to show, drawing on her reserves of strength, already drained by four children and a miscarriage.

The years had taken their toll of Anna-Maria Chalcott; there was now little trace of the headstrong girl who had become Annie Court. The once bright hair was pulled up into a knot on the top of her head from which stray tendrils hung and the blue eyes were surrounded by a network of fine lines, the result of a continual struggle to survive on an income that could never be guaranteed from one week to the next, though the overall trend was downwards.

Yet she smiled and her face lit up as Mabel's nimble fingers began to play a scale on the second-hand upright in the front room. She often said that her eldest daughter was her chief comfort, for the beautiful baby had become a sunny-tempered child whose grey-blue eyes were always bright with interest in the world around her. Her heart-shaped face, which reminded Annie of her own mother, was framed with abundant light-brown hair that hung down her back in shining waves. By contrast Alice was dark like her father and Albert, with the same strong white teeth, while Georgie was fair like Mabel. It was often remarked that the combination of Jack Court's swarthy looks and his wife's delicate fairness had produced some uncommonly fine-looking children.

While the music trickled through, interspersed with Miss Lawton's gentle directions, Annie got on with preparing supper. It was mutton stew this evening, ready to serve at any time. She never knew when to expect Jack who liked to have his meal on the table when he came in; otherwise it had to be something that could be quickly done in a pan, like rashers of bacon fried with onions and potatoes. Eggs were an expensive luxury, for there was no room to keep chickens in the backyards of Sorrel Street.

The piano lesson finished with quiet praise from Miss Lawton who proclaimed Mabel the best pupil in her grade. Annie smiled proudly and patted her daughter on the shoulder, which made Mabel all the more reluctant to produce the shameful white card from the newly appointed school nurse: for her lovely fair hair had been pronounced *verminous*.

Mabel could not ever remember seeing her mother so angry. 'How *dare* they! I've never heard of anything so disgraceful!' It was a relief to know that her indignation was directed against the school, and the nurse in particular, for labelling her daughter a dirty child with head lice, when in fact the school itself was so obviously the source of the infestation. 'I've a good mind to go and speak to that head teacher myself and tell her what I think,' declared Annie with a flash of her old spirit. 'Sassafras oil indeed, the sheer, barefaced *cheek* of it! Talk about adding insult to injury – your father will have something to say when he hears of it, I shouldn't wonder!'

But Jack Court had other matters on his mind when he got home just after seven. 'Haven't much time – got a couple o' blokes waiting at the Falcon, a dead cert running tomorrow at Goodwood,' he muttered, striding through to the kitchen and frowning at the sight and smell of the stew Annie was ladling out. 'Is that all yer can do for a man who's been workin' all the bloody day? Mabel, go down to the corner for a jug o' beer – here's tuppence, that'll do.'

'But she's just sitting down to her supper, Jack!' protested Annie.

'It won't take her five minutes there an' back, and there're still plenty o' kids playin' out, so why worry?'

'You know I don't like ours mixing with that rough lot. It lowers the whole neighbourhood, having children running around and yelling till all hours. And I don't like Mabel being seen going down to the public.'

Annie looked prepared to stand her ground, but he dismissed her with an impatient gesture. 'Run along,

Mabel, there's a good girl – for yer daddy.'

Mabel half rose, while glancing anxiously at her mother who threw down the ladle in a rare gesture of defiance. 'No! I'll go myself, rather than send Mabel to that place. You see to the supper, Mabel – there's some bread on the table to dip in the bowls.' And Annie put on her jacket, hat and gloves, for she refused to wear a shawl like some factory worker or laundress; she picked up an earthenware pint jug and marched out of the house.

Jack frowned, glancing round at their faces. Georgie had fallen asleep and Alice was busy with her spoon, but Mabel and Albert met his eyes accusingly.

'Poor ol' Mum,' said Albert with a most unchildlike scowl.

Jack Court shrugged, frowned and turned his attention to little Alice. 'Who's Daddy's best girl, then?' he asked, taking her upon his knee at the table and ruffling her dark head. Even at her tender age Alice was well aware that she was specially favoured by her father.

She smiled up at him artlessly. 'Poor ol' Daddy,' she said.

The ongoing battle against head lice became part of daily life. Mabel was by no means the only sufferer and several mothers had marched to the school to complain rather than to make excuses for the outbreak revealed by the nurse's inspection.

A toothcomb was bought, and after Mabel's hair was washed her mother pulled the comb through it strand by strand, searching out the offending black insects and their greyish 'eggs' or 'nits' that stuck to the hairs and would hatch out another generation if not removed. Oil of sassafras was rubbed in and a cotton cap worn overnight, followed by more hair-washing and combing until Annie was satisfied that Mabel was free of lice and nits; but how the girl's heart went out to the persistent offenders who had to sit in a separate group in class, threatened with the ultimate disgrace, a shorn head. The smell of sassafras continued to linger, forever associated in Mabel's mind with the school nurse's visits.

Sunday tea at 23 Macaulay Road was a time for clean pinafores and best behaviour. Jack's mother received her son's family with matriarchal formality, though she very seldom appeared at Sorrel Street. At fifty she had put on a little weight and now wore her hair curled like Queen Alexandra's, with a fringe.

Everybody had been warned not to breathe a word about the head lice.

Jack kissed his mother as soon as she opened the door, though Annie who was carrying Georgie kept him firmly between herself and her mother-in-law.

No sooner had Mabel, Albert and Alice crossed the threshold than their grandmother gave a suspicious sniff. 'My word, Annie, I hope that horrid smell isn't what I think it is, else yer neighbours'll draw their own conclusions.'

Annie sighed deeply and mumbled that there had been an outbreak at the school for which all the pupils had had to be treated. Mimi looked entirely unconvinced. She never lost an opportunity to criticise or contradict her daughter-in-law in front of Jack and the children, thereby implying that Annie was a poor manager.

When it became apparent that another child was expected, Mimi had rolled up her eyes as if unable to believe that such carelessness was possible. 'I'd've thought ye'd've had enough sense to wait a while after the last time, Annie – give yerself a chance to build up yer strength a bit.'

Annie had answered her with unusual sharpness: 'You'd better have a word with your son, then.'

'Oh, shame on yer, Annie, in front o' them innocent children! Whatever next?' had come the shocked response, followed by a very pointed change of subject.

They all trooped after her now into the living room, a veritable Aladdin's cave to the children, being stuffed with furniture, pictures, ornaments and bric-a-brac of all kinds. A dining table was covered with a purple velvet tasselled cloth over which a white lace-edged one was spread. There was a sideboard, a sofa, a piano and a glass-fronted cabinet crammed full of china and crystalware. A minefield of footstools and pouffes littered the floor space, which delighted the children, but for Annie the room was full of potential trippings-up and breakages; she was on constant tenterhooks for fear of a disaster.

'Well, then, Mabel, how're yer getting on at school?' asked Mimi Court condescendingly. 'Yer mother seems to think ye're uncommonly forward.'

'Miss Thomas asked me to stand up and read from my exercise book to the whole class,' answered Mabel promptly, catching her mother's eye and smiling.

'Did she indeed? And what was this masterpiece all about?'

'Well, there was this Salvation Army meeting, y'see, and these two men came out o' the public and they were shouting an' making fun o' the man who was speaking, see,' said Mabel eagerly, warming to her subject. 'Some o' the people laughed, but the band picked up their, er, oompahs or whatever they're called, and started to play this hymn, ever so loudly, "Onward Christian Soldiers" I think it was, an' so these two men had to shout louder – and then some other men came along an' told them to pack it in and clear off. "Shut yer great gob!" one of 'em said – "Stow it, Bill Wilkins, d'ye hear? Unless yer wants a clip round the –"'

'That's quite enough, thank yer very much,' interrupted her grandmother with a pained air. 'For a child o' your age, Mabel ye've got far too much to say, an' a most unfortunate way o' sayin' it.' She looked reproachfully at Annie as she spoke.

'*Most* unfortunate,' mimicked Albert in a squeaky voice just loud enough for his grandmother to hear. She turned sharply and was struck once again by his resemblance to Jack at that age. She would have loved to make a fuss of him and favour him with little treats like the new silver threepenny piece in her purse or a chunk of her home-made toffee; but the boy was quite ridiculously attached to his elder sister and he was now whispering something into Mabel's ear, holding up a not very clean hand to cover his mouth. Less than a year apart in age, they were as different in character as in looks, yet there had always been this special bond between them, which Mimi distrusted. As babies in the same pram, Albert had scowled while Mabel had smiled; as a toddling bundle of mischief he had crawled into every cupboard, pulled out drawers and pee'd into them, clutched at saucepans on the kitchen range and only escaped a scalding through Mabel's prompt grabbing hold of him. Yet he always responded to her smiles or frowns; she alone could persuade him out of his sulks, while he never failed to tease her into laughter when she was downcast. In Mimi Court's opinion, the pair had never learned their manners and she blamed Annie.

Mabel caught her mother's eye, adding to Mimi's irritation.

Alice saw her opportunity. 'Please, Grandmother, may I play with Humpty-Dumpty?' she begged in the sweet little good-girl voice she knew would contrast well with Albert's unsatisfactory behaviour.

'O' course yer may, yer dear little soul,' replied Mimi approvingly, taking down the painted wooden eggshell character from his shelf; he always landed the right way up, no matter how hard or how often he was pushed over. 'Grandmother likes good children who mind their manners – doesn't she, Georgie? Let yer little brother play with Humpty-Dumpty too, Alice – but Albert can keep his grubby hands orf. I can't understand why yer don't take that boy in hand, Annie.'

Albert assumed an air of bored indifference and murmured something about babies' rubbish, though Mabel burned with indignation and when tea was served she infuriatingly refused the fruit cake.

'Why, what's the matter with it, girl? Ye've always taken two slices before,' snapped her grandmother. 'If there's anything I can't abide it's a child who sulks.'

'Well, I'll leave you ladies to yer gossip,' said Jack who had seen a couple of old drinking pals going past the window. Ignoring the tightness of his wife's mouth he added, 'If I'm not back by five, ye'd better get the Clapham omnibus from outside the new hospital down the road.'

By which Annie knew that he would not be home till late.

Autumn came in with cold, damp weather, bringing the Court children their share of coughs and colds. Annie grew more tired and depressed as the months went by and much as she disliked keeping Mabel away from school, she made the coughs and sneezes an excuse for demanding her elder daughter's help on the dreaded washing days. Mondays were particularly miserable in wet weather when the sheets, towels and clothes hung draped over wooden 'maidens' in both kitchen and living room, keeping the air chill and moist. If the range fire was kept in all day it made the washing steam, causing the walls to stream with condensation. Even by getting up at six to light the copper to heat the water by seven and get the washing done by nine and mangled to flatness by ten, it would still not be properly dry until the next morning, sometimes not even then. With Mabel to mind Alice and Georgie, Annie was better able to get through a wet Monday, though she was exhausted by evening, and the coughs and running noses of the little ones sorely tried her nerves.

'You're my greatest comfort in the world, Mabel,' she murmured as her daughter brewed a pot of tea for them both. These words were reward enough for Mabel, though her mind was on Albert who was due home from school.

Annie stirred her tea and went on talking, or rather thinking aloud. 'If Jack doesn't come up with ten shillings by the end of the week, I don't know how I'm going to feed us all.'

Mabel was dismayed by the anxiety in her mother's face and voice. The use of Jack's name instead of 'dad' or 'your father' had the effect of distancing him while drawing her into sharing her mother's troubles. 'Don't worry, Mum, we'll manage,' she said reassuringly, though with no idea of what could be done if the money was not forthcoming. She knew from things she had heard at school that there were poor children who had not enough to eat, and went ragged and barefoot, foraging for whatever they could find by begging or petty thieving; but this was usually because one or other of their parents had become ill, or perhaps had even died. Mabel shuddered involuntarily at the very thought of losing her mother, the loving centre of her world. As long as she was there to kiss and comfort them all, the family was surely safe. And yet here was that same mother talking of poverty and not having food enough to go round.

They were drinking a second cup of tea when Albert arrived home from school, his trousers torn and his hair unkempt.

'Albert! We told you to stay with Lily Finch and her brother,' said Annie, horrified at his appearance.

He stuck out his bottom lip. 'She kept 'angin' about wiv daft girls, an' Jimmy went to play football,' he muttered in a surly tone.

'Have yer been in a fight?' demanded Mabel.

He shuffled his feet. 'Yeah, but I kicked 'em 'ard up the yer-know-what, an' they let me go.'

'Heavens, he talks like a guttersnipe,' groaned Annie.

'Why couldn't *you* take me, Mabel?' he asked reproachfully.

Mother and daughter exchanged a guilty look; the washing hung damply and depressingly around them.

'I'll go over and see Lily Finch about this,' said Mabel grimly.

'But we didn't pay her to take him, did we?' Annie reminded her.

'Yer won't 'alf cop it from Miss Thomas for stayin' away,' added Albert with a meaning look at his sister. 'She didn't 'alf go on about it, worser 'n last week.'

Annie put her head between her hands. 'You'll have to go to school next Monday, Mabel. It isn't right for you to fall behind with your lessons. I'll just have to get through it, that's all – other women have to manage.'

But the sight of her mother's weariness and knowing her worries about money had made a deep impression on Mabel, and she began to form a plan to earn some money and keep the family supplied with whatever cheap food she could find. Her small face hardened as she summoned up the necessary determination to carry it through.

First she needed a few pence to get started, and an idea came through seeing one of her classmates taking and fetching a neighbour's two young children to and from school every day. She had to take care of Albert, so why not another one or two? She began to look out for an opportunity to offer her services and a few days later she found one.

One of Albert's classmates and his five-year-old sister had been brought to school by a neighbour because their mother was about to give birth to a baby. On the way home Mabel called with Albert at their house in Darnel Street to find the household in chaos. The baby had been born but the mother was very poorly, so the neighbour who was preparing the tea said. Mabel's offer was accepted and it was arranged that she should call the next morning at half past eight to take the two children to school, returning them in the afternoon, for which she would be paid two pence per day. It meant that she and Albert would have to leave home a quarter of an hour earlier, arriving back that much later in the afternoon, and on this particular Tuesday Mabel was only just in time for her piano lesson; but after earning her first two pence on the Wednesday, she was ready to put the second part of her plan into action.

She had heard from some of the poorer children at school that their mothers or older brothers or sisters got up early and lined up outside certain shops which sold perishable goods cheaply before the official opening time. So on Thursday morning she quietly got up at six and hurried through the dark streets to the bakehouse on Wandsworth Road. The first batch of loaves was just being taken from the ovens, and one of Mabel's pennies bought two stale loaves from the previous day. She then crossed the street into Victoria Rise where a shabby queue of women and older children were standing outside the butcher's, waiting for him to take down the shutters. They were after the 'trimmings', the beef and mutton scraps that could be stewed with onions and potatoes to make a meal. Mabel took her place behind them and her other penny bought a bagful.

Of course this new regime had to be carefully presented to her mother and a few little white lies told; for example, that she had been specially asked by the family in Darnel Street to take the little boy and girl to and from school while their mother was recovering from the birth. As for the bread and meat, Mabel put them down on the table with such a flourish that Annie could not possibly object to the early shopping trip, though she shed a few tears in private at the thought of Mabel feeling so responsible for the whole family. The food was put to good use and if Annie half regretted burdening her little daughter by speaking her fears aloud, she was touched beyond measure by Mabel's response.

'Oh, Mabel, dear, to have a daughter like you makes up for everything,' she said as she hugged her close; but when the girl had gone to school, and Alice and Georgie were playing on the rag rug, she whispered to the empty air that Mabel deserved a better life than this. How different life would have been in the healthy country air of Belhampton . . . She remembered Eric's words on the train: '*I would have married you, Anna-Maria. I would have married you and called the child mine.*' Her beautiful, fair-haired daughter could have been Mabel Drummond.

Yet Annie Court could not imagine her life without Albert, Alice and Georgie, her children who were the reason why she carried on the day-to-day struggle to bring up her family respectably while living on the poverty line. They helped her to repress her memories of the past, that other life which was now never spoken of because of what had happened to her poor papa and the unforgiveness of her sisters.

Encouraged by her success at early morning shopping, Mabel next decided to try her luck at the Friday night stalls in Nine Elms Lane. Albert begged to come with her and so, with Thursday's and Friday's earnings in her pocket, and promising her mother that they would come straight home, they set off to walk over the railway bridge and along Battersea Park Road to the line-up of stalls and costers' barrows beneath the gas lamps in the late October dusk. A mist curled up from the river, which mixing with the pall of chimney smoke gave a greenish tinge to the lights. A barrel organ was playing on the corner of Tideway Walk, and a crowd of rough-looking children had gathered to listen and caper to the music while workers from Price's candles and Doulton's pottery had come over to spend their pay, rubbing shoulders with gasworkers, laundrywomen and clerks. Newsboys shouted the headlines and racing results, and flower girls eyed the better-dressed men strolling between the stalls.

Holding tightly to Albert's dragging hand, Mabel surveyed the busy scene, though with so many street sellers competing for trade she wished she had somebody to advise her on how best to spend her four pennies.

''Ad a good look, 'ave yer? I'll turn rahnd, so's yer can see me backside an' all.'

Mabel started, realising that she had been staring at the ragged girl who had just spoken. She was wrapped in a long, grimy shawl which she drew around herself and the baby she carried in her arms. Her features were sharp, her hair lanky and uncombed, and her toes stuck out of her worn shoes. She was about the same size and height as Mabel, though her face appeared older and in better circumstances she might have been quite pretty. Jostled by the crowd, the two girls found themselves standing next to each other and Mabel was unpleasantly conscious of the smell of the girl's unwashed clothing. 'I'm sorry,' she said awkwardly. 'I didn't mean to be rude.'

The girl nodded towards Albert. ''Im yer bruvver?'

'Yes – and is that *your* baby brother or sister?' asked Mabel, just to show that she too could ask questions of a stranger.

'Yeah, bruvver. Bleedin' 'eavy 'e is, too. Got any more at 'ome, 'ave yer?'

'A sister younger 'n me, and another brother. What about you?'

'We've 'ad two bruvvers an' a sister kick the bucket – only me 'n' Teddy left.'

Mabel was so horrified by this that she had no answer and the girl shrugged. 'Yer from rahnd 'ere, then?'

Mabel nodded. 'Are you?'

The girl gestured with her head. 'Over Vaux'all way.' She looked curiously at Mabel. 'Don't s'pose yer got a spare copper on yer?'

Mabel's fingers curled protectively round the coins in her pocket. 'Not to spare,' she said very definitely.

'What yer after, then – cheap grub? If I wasn't weighted dan wiv this 'un, I'd soon be under some o' them stalls, not 'alf I wouldn't! 'Ere, come an' 'ave a gander.'

She led Mabel to a greengrocer's barrow and advised buying one pennyworth of speckly apples and another of four squashy oranges, both items being sold off at half price; potatoes cost another three halfpence and then, moving on to the roast chestnut man's glowing brazier, Mabel spent her remaining halfpenny on as many as he would let her have. Turning to the girl she offered her a chestnut and a choice of an apple or orange.

'Cor, ye're a lidy – I'll 'ave the orange, ta! Orf 'ome now, are yer?'

'Yes, my mother'll be waiting for us. My father'll be home later tonight,' added Mabel, hoping that this week's business would have made him a decent profit and put him in a good mood.

The girl grimaced. 'So'll mine, drunk as a pig an' nasty wiv it. That's why Ma sends us out o' the way Friday nights.'

'Oh, how *awful* for yer!' exclaimed Mabel, who had absorbed much of her mother's horror of drunkenness, not without reason; sometimes Dad had to be helped to bed when he came home from the public, which was no joke for Mum, who always seemed to be tired these days. 'And when . . . when will yer be able to go home, then?'

'After 'e's 'ad a good knock arahnd an' passed out on the floor, most like. Then Ma'll go frough 'is pockets an' take what ain't bin taken orf 'im already.'

Mabel had heard terrible stories of men who beat their wives and ill-treated their children, but not at first hand. Not until now. 'Can't yer mother take you an' yer brother to go an' live somewhere else away from the man?' she asked.

'Cor! Couldn't we jus' grow wings an' fly, eh? Where to – the work'ouse? Fanks for the orange, anyway. What's yer name, 'case we meets up agin?'

'Mabel Court – and my brother Albert.'

'Maudie Ling – an' my bruvver Teddy.'

'Goodbye, Maudie – an' good luck when yer get home.'

And so began a friendship that was to outlast many changes in both their lives.

That evening ended on a high note for when Jack Court arrived home he was in a good humour and, as he himself said, quids in. Business had taken him to Epsom, where his natural flair had stood him in good stead. Having long discarded his hopes of a career in photo-portraiture, Mabel now gathered that he was considering going into books; there was a fortune just waiting to be picked up if he made his own book, or so he eagerly told them, kissing Annie and chucking Alice under the chin.

As often happened when he'd had a windfall, Jack was open-handed and had brought presents for them all. Annie had a new brooch shaped like a horseshoe, as well as an incredible *five pounds* towards house-keeping. Albert had new boots and Georgie a large red and white striped ball to bounce. Mabel gave a whoop of joy at receiving a family songbook with piano scores for each one, both simple and more elaborate accompaniments; and Alice had the best surprise of all, a doll's house with a front that lifted off to reveal an upstairs and a downstairs with two rooms on each floor, complete with beautiful tiny furniture and fittings.

They had fried fish for supper that Jack brought with him, and pork chops for dinner on Saturday. For afters they had a jam suet pudding that Mabel had helped her mother to make, which Jack said was the best he'd ever tasted.

As the young ones frolicked around and Albert thumped the roof of the precious doll's house – a thunderstorm, he said it was – the mother and daughter exchanged smiles.

'There, what did I tell yer, Mum? No need to worry about money – or anything.'

'Yes, dear, your daddy can be very kind when he's had a good day. But I'll never forget what you've done for me this week.'

If only Dad could always be as lucky! But Mabel was soon given an ugly reminder that his family did not necessarily share his good luck.

Only two weeks later, on a Friday night at the beginning of December, Mabel was awakened by the sound of stumbling steps and her mother's voice raised in protest above another sound – her father singing in the silly, tuneless way he had when drunk. Mabel's heart sank in dismay and she felt a shiver of fear. She'd seen how weary Mum was, being now big and unwieldly with the baby she was nearly due to have, and yet here she was struggling to get Dad up the stairs and into their room.

'She's my lady-love – she ish my love, my baby dove –' warbled Jack.

'Careful, Jack, for God's sake don't fall and send up both flying!' cried Annie, and Mabel jumped out of bed and ran to the top of the stairs, scared as she was.

'What's the matter, Mum? What's he doin'? Are yer all right?'

'Oh, Mabel, this is no job for a child – I can manage him, dear. Go back to bed and don't wake the others,' pleaded Annie, while Jack sang romantically: 'I know she likes me – I know she likes me, because she says sho—'

At the top stair he stumbled, and Annie shrieked.

'All right, Mum, I've got him – come on, Dad, this way,' ordered Mabel, taking hold of his arm with both hands and pulling with all her strength, though she was trembling with cold and a kind of horror at seeing her dad in this state. She knew that she had to brave and overcome her repulsion for Mum's sake, but her instinct was to get as far away from him as she could.

'Because she says sho – because she says sho – whoops!'

Together the heavily pregnant woman and the seven-year-old girl pulled and pushed the man through the door, whereupon he fell across the bed. Annie was out of breath and clutched at her bulge: Mabel stood barefoot in her nightgown, regarding him as she would a drunken man lying in the gutter. Her own *father*!

'She ish my lily of Laguna –'

'I'm not going to bother with undressing him, he can sleep in his clothes,' panted Annie. 'If we could just get his boots off to save the quilt – I'll hold his legs and you pull, Mabel, first this one – ah! Now the other. Good girl.'

'She ish my Lily and my rose!'

'He's had a good day on the course, but he was with that Dick Sammons and they've drunk the lot between them – and no doubt he's treated half a dozen others,' said Annie with a sigh.

The boots were slung into a corner and Mabel began trying to turn her father round on the bed so that he was lying in his usual place on the right side.

'Not yet, dear, there's something else he'll have to do first,' Annie sighed. 'Can you pull the chamber pot out from under the bed? Come on, Jack, you've got to have a wee-wee before you go to sleep.'

But Jack was too drunk to stand without support and Mabel had to hold the pot while Annie fished in his trousers and pulled out his male member, which immediately rose in her hand to a half-erection.

'For shame, Jack, it goes down, not up – here – I'll

hold it for you while you go. Hold the pot higher, Mabel, don't let him miss it. Careful, Jack – you can go now.'

And go he did, a streaming torrent that hit the chamber pot and splashed up in Mabel's face. Annie directed the flow as he tried to kiss her.

'Wheee-eee!' he giggled, gushing like a waterspout and swaying between wife and daughter. 'She ish my lily of Lagooonaaah – she ish my lily and my rose!'

Mabel forced herself to grip the sides of the pot until the stream had finally dribbled to a stop and Annie tucked the spout into his drawers, leaving his trousers unbuttoned. 'Your grandmother Court taught me that,' she said, her face white with fatigue. 'Always make a man pee out the drink before sleeping, she told me, or you'll have a flood before morning – but oh, Mabel, you little dear, what a sight for you to see!' And she burst into tears.

Mabel rushed to throw her arms round her mother. 'Poor Mum! Don't cry, Mummy, please – oh, I just *hate* him when he's like this, he's not like Daddy at all.'

Annie hastily wiped her eyes on her apron. 'Don't mind me, Mabel, your father gets very silly when he's drunk, but he's not a bad man like some. He's never deliberately hurt me. Not like poor Mrs Finch, Lily's mother – her husband's a brute when he's drunk, and hits out at her and the children. And I know for a fact that he's wet right through a feather mattress till it dripped on the floor beneath – ugh, just imagine it.' She shuddered, then smiled and patted Mabel's cheek. 'As your grandmother says, it's a man's world, Mabel. Now get back to bed, dear, or you'll catch cold.'

Mabel returned to the bed she shared with Alice, thankful that her little sister had not been woken up by the daddy she adored. But she lay awake for some time, thinking of her mother lying beside Dad with his sour-smelling breath and his heavy snoring. And how *rude* he had been, showing his great big *thing* like that, and laughing while he wee'd in front of her and Mum like some dirty boy who didn't know any better. Albert would never do a thing like that, even though he was often naughty in other ways. Before she finally fell asleep Mabel vowed that she would never get married; she simply couldn't understand why any woman would want to.

As Christmas approached Annie drooped, and the care of the younger children fell more and more on Mabel's shoulders; yet she still found time to escort children to and from school as the need arose, delivering them to their classrooms and fetching them as soon as the bell sounded for the end of lessons. Mothers recommended her for her watchfulness, the way she kept the children from straying, and they all liked and trusted her. For her part she enjoyed being with her charges and loved the little clinging hands in hers, the anxious eyes of five- and six-year-olds looking out for her – and the way their faces brightened when she appeared to collect them from their homes or their classrooms. Teachers would call out, 'Who's waiting for Mabel Court? Don't worry, she's on her way' – or, 'She's just seeing to a little boy who's lost his cap.'

'There's a children's nurse in the making,' she heard one of them say as she went off with her flock one afternoon as the light was failing.

'As long as she's not worn out before her time, like so many of those girls,' came the reply.

Mabel also became much more adept at spending her earnings to the best advantage, knowing exactly how much bread, tea, sugar, or offal could be had for her halfpennies and farthings, carefully counted out; she learned to bargain with street traders and when she managed to save a few coins she hoarded them for Christmas in a small canvas bag she kept under the mattress.

There was no time to linger at the Friday evening stalls, now darkened by December fogs, but Maudie still lugged Teddy there, coughing as she pulled the malodorous shawl more tightly around them both.

'What'll yer get for Christmas, Maudie?' asked Mabel as they shivered beside the chestnut man's welcome blaze.

'Chris'muss? Don't make me larf – the ol' man'll be canned the 'ole time, an' so'll me muvver an' all.'

'*What*?' Mabel thought she had not heard right. 'Did yer say yer *mother*'ll be drunk too?'

'Lor' bless yer, she puts up wiv 'im pissed every Friday, so she reckons it's 'er turn for once,' Maudie explained as if this were quite reasonable. 'Yeah, they'll bofe be rollin', same as last year. Glad when Chris'muss is over, I am.'

'Oh, Maudie – oh, *Maudie*, yer poor thing – and little Teddy too – oh!'

Mabel did not know what to say. Since she had begun to earn and spend a little money of her own, she had seen much more of the darker side of life, the daily drudgery endured by women and children, especially when the man of the house was brutalised by habitual drinking. She saw the burden it placed on families already short of the basic necessities of life.

But the thought of *mothers* getting drunk truly upset her, and her heart ached for her friend and the poor little baby brother, the only survivors of a family of five children. What had happened to the other three, what kind of lives had they had and how had they died? Mabel thought of how horrible it was when her own father had come home so drunk and she hardly dared think of what might have happened to the helpless little Ling children. She longed to be able to help Maudie and Teddy in some way, and other children in need of love and care, and the thought came to her that one day she *would* be a children's nurse as the teacher had said; but for the time being it seemed that there was nothing she could do, nothing she could give.

Only the fragile friendship of a child.

Annie had insisted that she didn't want Mimi to deliver her fifth child and had booked Mrs Lowe, one of two midwives who attended most of the women in their neighbourhood. A Mrs Bull two doors away had agreed to come in and look after the family while Annie was lying-in, and all the preparations had been made. Georgie was moved into the children's room to share Albert's bed next to Mabel's and Alice's, and the cot was made up ready beside Annie's bed for the new baby. Clean cotton rags, towels and newspaper were stored in an orange box, along with a cake of soap and baby clothes. A washing bowl and jug, a chamber pot and two buckets stood in readiness.

When the pains started on a blustery night five days before Christmas, Jack was away and the younger children in bed.

Annie gritted her teeth and pressed her palms into the small of her back where the pain was sharpest during contractions. It's strange, she thought, how you always forget how bad it is until the next time comes and then you remember. Whatever happened, she must not frighten the children; in a small house every sound carried. 'Mabel! You'd better call Mrs Bull and then go for Mrs Lowe. I don't think this one's going to be long.'

497

While Mabel went to call the midwife, Mrs Bull arrived and busied herself in the kitchen, relighting the range fire to heat water for the midwife's use and to brew tea.

Mabel came running in, her face red with the exertion and her hands cold from wearing no gloves. 'Mrs Lowe's out with somebody else, but Mrs Clements'll be comin' as soon as she can!'

Annie groaned. 'She'd better be quick, then – oh! Aah!' She bit the sheet and gripped the bedhead topped with its brass knobs.

'Go back to yer bed, Mabel, this ain't no sight for a little gal,' said Mrs Bull, but Mabel was reluctant to leave her mother's side. When they heard the knock at the door she ran down to let in Mrs Clements who was short and stout, and carried a black bag that matched the hat and coat which she removed and hung up in the narrow hallway.

Once in the bedroom, her sharp button eyes took in the situation at a glance. She opened her bag and took out the first requirement, a bottle and an enamel mug. 'Come on, Mrs Court, come on, dearie, 'ave a swig o' this to 'elp yer pain an' settle yer, like,' she said firmly, holding the mug to Annie's lips. ''Ere we go!'

Standing outside the door, Mabel listened wide-eyed as her mother was made to drink, choking and gagging on the potent liquid. 'It's gin, isn't it?' she gasped. 'Ugh, I never touch it.'

'Drink up, pet, it'll 'elp yer more than anyfin' else will. One more little drop an' yer won't care if it snows. Good gal!'

Mabel heard her mother moan and make a retching sound in her throat.

'Hey, don't go fetchin' it up again – take some big,

deep breaths in an' out, that'll 'elp keep it down – good gal!'

Annie hiccuped and moaned faintly as another contraction hardened her belly.

Mrs Bull came puffing up the stairs with a jug of hot water. 'I told yer to go back to y'bed, Mabel – this ain't no place for a little 'un.'

Mabel reluctantly returned to her roon and got in beside the sleeping Alice. Georgie snuffled and whimpered beside Albert, then cried out in sudden panic, 'Ma-ma!'

Mabel got out of bed and went to kneel beside her frightened little brother, enfolding him in her arms. 'All right, Georgie, it's all right, I'm here,' she whispered as he clung to her in bewilderment. 'Yer Mabel's here, an' ye'll see Mummy again in the mornin'.' Kneeling on the uncarpeted floor in the icy room, she stroked his forehead and soothed him until his breathing took on the soft and regular rhythm of sleep. Slowly she released her arms and tucked the covers around him. Albert and Alice had not woken. Stiff with cold, she got to her feet. A sound of women's voices could be heard in the other room, urgent but indistinct. Mabel stepped out on to the landing again and listened.

Mrs Clements seemed to be giving orders to the neighbour. ''Ave that bowl 'andy, Liza, and spread the towel down there, see? That's the way – and 'ere it comes, see, I told yer it'd push its own way out, di'n't I? And afore midnight, too!'

There followed some confused exclamations, panting and the smack of a hand on flesh.

'There we go – and it's a boy.'

'Is 'e all right? 'E ain't 'alf blue.'

'Fill that bowl wiv warm water to dip 'im in – quick, that gets 'em goin' as a rule.'

'Is 'e breathin'? 'E's ever so limp, just as if 'e was –'

'For Christ's sake, Liza Bull, shut yer trap an' do summat useful! Fill me a bowl o' water!' Mabel heard the note of panic beneath Mrs Clements's irritation and shivered in fear. Why didn't her mother say something? Was she – oh, please, our Father who art in heaven, let her not be dead . . . *Oh, Mummy, Mummy, don't leave me, don't leave us all on our own, Mummy, please! Please!*

'Look, 'e's givin' a few little grunts, an' 'is chest's goin' up an' down, thank Gawd,' muttered the midwife in relief. 'I'll jus' tie the cord off an' cut it, an' then 'e can go down in the cot.'

'Shall I make a pot o' tea?' asked the other woman.

'When I got the afterbirth out yer can. She won't want any, she's out for the count, but we can do wiv a cup – an' a drop o' summat in it, an' all.'

The door opened and Mrs Bull nearly collided full tilt into the child cowering behind it. 'Mabel! 'Ow many times 'ave I told yer to go back to bed? Ye'll catch yer death o' cold out here.'

Mrs Clements looked up. She was holding something like a big chunk of raw meat, which she let slide down into one of the buckets. Her florid features wore an expression of satisfaction. ''Is that the little gal who came for Mrs Lowe? All right, pet, yer can come in just for a minute and see yer little baby bruvver. Come on in, don't be frightened.'

Mabel stared into the room lit by an oil lamp on the chest of drawers. Her eyes went straight to the bed where her mother lay with flushed cheeks, her hair clinging to her forehead in damp wisps. Her mouth was open and she was snoring heavily. Mabel could have cried with thankfulness.

'Fast asleep, quite worn out, poor thing,' said Mrs

500

Clements. 'Look over 'ere, pet, see, in the cot, there 'e is, yer new baby brother.'

Mabel dragged her eyes away from her mother's unconscious form and turned to the cot, which had seemed so small for Georgie but now appeared huge for the tiny scrap of humanity lying wrapped in a towel and blanket. A little bluish-white face peeped out: he was making weak, gasping sounds as if every breath was an effort.

''Ad yer ma got a name for 'im?' asked the midwife.

'She said he'd be called Walter if he was a boy and Daisy if he was a girl,' faltered Mabel.

'Then Walter's 'is name.' The midwife nodded.

'Is he all right?' asked Mabel fearfully. 'I thought babies always cried when they're born.'

''E'll be all right after a bit, when 'e's 'ad a little sleep.'

Mabel glanced at Mrs Bull who did not seem so convinced that all was well with Walter. ''E's one o' them little angels, come down from 'eaven,' she said with a doubtful shake of her head. 'An' maybe 'e'll stay an' maybe 'e won't.'

''E'll perk up after a bit,' insisted Mrs Clements.

Mabel leaned over the cot. She knew that this baby was going to need lots of looking after, more than Albert or Alice or George. Their mother would need all the help that Mabel could give. 'Hello, little brother Walter,' she whispered. 'I'm yer sister Mabel and I'm going to take ever such good care o' yer.'

But Annie saw and heard nothing at all.

To find out more about Maggie Bennett and other fantastic Arrow authors why not read *The Inside Story* – our newsletter featuring all of our saga authors.

To join our mailing list to receive the newsletter and other information* write with your name and address to:

The Inside Story
The Marketing Department
Arrow Books
20 Vauxhall Bridge Road
London SW1V 2SA